THE

Matzah

Ball

JEAN MELTZER

THE Matzah Ball

▶ mira

ISBN-13: 978-0-7783-1213-0

The Matzah Ball

Mira
22 Adelaide St. West, 40th Floor
Toronto, Ontario M5H 4E3, Canada
BookClubbish.com

Printed in U.S.A.

For my *bashert*.

THE

Matzah

Ball

From: Lisa Brown <l.brown@cachingliteraryagency.com>
To: Rachel Rubenstein-Goldblatt <margotcross@northpole.com>

Sent: Thu, 9 December
Subject: Meeting Tomorrow at Romance House (!)

Hey, Rachel!

Just a quick heads-up that tomorrow's meeting at Romance
House will be all hands on deck. Editorial, Marketing, Publicity—
the whole team! Apparently, Chandra has something BIG in the
works and wants YOU to be a part of it! ($$$$$$$$) Make sure
you bring your best ideas and plenty of that Christmas spirit!

I'll see you in the lobby at ten!

Lisa

PS: Happy Hanukkah! (I think it starts this Monday, right?)

1

She just needed one more.

Rachel Rubenstein-Goldblatt stared at the collection of miniature Christmas figurines spread across her desk. She owned 236 of the smiling porcelain Santas from the world-famous Holiday Dreams Collection. When her best friend, Mickey, arrived, she would complete that collection with the addition of the coveted Margaritaville Santa.

Oh, the Margaritaville Santa. How she had dreamed of the day when that tiny porcelain Santa, in a Hawaiian shirt and wearing Ray-Ban sunglasses, would sit atop her prized collection.

Rachel had scoured eBay for the tiny limited-edition figurine, set up price alerts and left frantic (somewhat drunken) posts at three in the morning on collector blogs. Now, after six years, five months and seven days of hunting, the Margaritaville Santa would finally be hers.

The anxiety was killing her.

Rachel glanced out the window of her apartment. It was snowing outside. Gentle flakes fell down onto Broadway and made New York City feel magical. She was wondering when Mickey would actually get here when there was a knock at the door.

"Finally!" Rachel said. Excitement bubbled up inside her as she raced to the front door, throwing it open. And then, disappointment. Her mother stood in the threshold.

"I was in the neighborhood," she said, a perfectly innocent smile spread across her two round cheeks.

Her mother was *always* in the neighborhood.

It was one of the downsides of living on the Upper West Side while her mother, a top New York fertility specialist, worked out of Columbia Hospital just ten blocks away.

Rachel had to think quickly. She loved her mother, and was even willing to entertain her completely intrusive and unannounced visits, but the door to her home office was still open.

"Mickey's about to stop by," Rachel warned.

"I won't be but a minute," her mother said, lifting up a plastic bag from Ruby's Smoked Fish Shop as a peace offering. "I brought you some dinner."

Dr. Rubenstein pushed her way inside, letting her fingers graze the mezuzah on Rachel's doorpost before entering. Making her way straight to the refrigerator, she began unloading "dinner."

There was a large vat of chopped liver, two loaves of pumpernickel bread, three different types of rugalach. Dr. Rubenstein believed in feeding the people you love, and the love she had for her daughter was likely to end in heart disease.

"How are you feeling?" her mother inquired.

"Fine," Rachel said, using the opportunity to close her office door.

Dr. Rubenstein looked up from the refrigerator. Her eyes rolled from Rachel's hair, matted and clumped, down to her wrinkled pink pajamas.

She frowned. "You look pale."

"I *am* pale," Rachel reminded her.

"Rachel," her mother said pointedly, "you need to take your myalgic encephalomyelitis seriously."

Rachel rolled her eyes. Outside, the gentle snow was gathering into a full-blown storm.

Dr. Rubenstein was probably one of the few people who called Rachel's disease by its medical term, the name research scientists and experts preferred, describing the complex multisystem disease that affected her neurological, immune, autonomic and metabolic systems. Most everyone else in the world knew it by the simple and distasteful moniker chronic fatigue syndrome.

Which was, quite possibly, the most trivializing name for a disease in the entire world. The equivalent of calling Alzheimer's "Senior Moment Syndrome."

It did not begin to remotely describe the crushing fatigue, migraines, brain fog or weirdo pains that Rachel lived with daily. It certainly did not describe the 25 percent of patients who found themselves bed-bound or homebound—existing on feeding tubes, unable to leave dark rooms for years—or the 75 percent of patients who could no longer work full-time.

For now, however, Rachel was one of the lucky ones. She had managed to graduate college with a degree in creative writing and, over the last decade, build a career working from home.

"Ema," Rachel said, growing frustrated. "My body, my choice."

"But—"

"Change the topic."

Dr. Rubenstein pressed her lips together and swallowed the words on her tongue. It was not an easy feat for the woman. "And how's work?"

"Good." Rachel shrugged, returning to the couch. "Nothing that interesting to report."

"And the freelance work you're doing—" her mother craned

her neck to peep around her apartment "—it's keeping you busy?"

"Busy enough."

Dr. Rubenstein raised one eyebrow in her daughter's direction.

Rachel knew what her mother was *really* asking. *How can you afford a two-bedroom apartment on the Upper West Side simply by doing freelance editorial work?* But Dr. Rubenstein had learned an important halachic lesson from her husband, Rabbi Aaron Goldblatt, early on in their marriage; you don't ask questions you don't really want the answers to.

For all Rachel knew, her mother believed her to be a webcam girl. Or a high-class prostitute. Or the mistress of some dashingly handsome Arabian prince. All of which, Rachel was certain, would be preferable to what she actually did for a living.

"Ema," Rachel said, steering the conversation away from her career. "What is it you're really here for?"

"Why do you always think I have an ulterior motive, Rachel?"

"Because I know you."

"All right!" Dr. Rubenstein threw her hands up into the air. "You caught me. I do have an ulterior motive."

"Baruch Hashem."

"Now, it's nothing bad, I promise," her mother said, taking a seat on her couch. "I simply wanted to see if you were available for Shabbat dinner this Friday."

There it was. The real reason for her mother's visit. Shabbat at Rabbi Goldblatt's house was not just a weekly religious occurrence, it was a chance for Dr. Rubenstein to kidnap her daughter for twenty-five hours straight and force her to meet single Jewish men.

Over the years, there had been all sorts of horrible setups. There was the luxury auto dealer who used his sleeve as a napkin during dinner. The rabbinical student who spent an entire

Saturday afternoon debating aloud with *only* her father over what to do when an unkosher meatball falls into a pot of kosher meatballs.

And then, there was her favorite blind date setup of them all. Dovi, the Israeli mountain climber, who had traveled the world in his perfectly healthy and functioning body, before telling Rachel that he didn't think chronic fatigue syndrome was a *real* disease.

Chas v'chalilah.

Rachel had no intention of spending another Friday night, and Saturday afternoon, entertaining her mother's idea of a dreamboat. Especially not when that dreamboat had the word *Titanic* embroidered across the bottom of their knitted kippah.

"No," Rachel said.

"Rachel!" her mother pleaded. "Just hear me out."

"I'm too busy, Ema."

"But you haven't been home in ages!"

"You live on Long Island," Rachel shot back. "I see you and Daddy all the time."

Her mother could not argue with this factoid.

"Jacob Greenberg will be coming," her mother finally said.

Rachel nearly choked on her tongue. "What?"

"You remember Jacob Greenberg?"

The question sounded so innocent on the surface. *Jacob Greenberg.* How could Rachel forget the name? The duo had spent one summer together at Camp Ahava in the Berkshires before the seventh grade.

"Jacob Greenberg?" Rachel spit back. "The psychopath who spent an entire summer pulling my hair and pushing me into the lake?"

"I recall you two getting along quite well at one point."

"He set me up in front of everyone, Mom. He turned my first kiss into a giant Camp Ahava prank!"

"He was twelve!" Dr. Rubenstein was on her feet now.

"Twelve, Rachel. You can't hold a grown man accountable for something he did as a child. For heaven's sake… The boy hadn't even had his bar mitzvah."

Rachel could feel the red rising in her cheeks. A wellspring of complicated emotions rose up inside her. Hate and love. Confusion and excitement. Just hearing his name again after all these years brought Rachel smack-dab back to her adolescence. And sitting there beside all those terrible memories of him humiliating her were the good ones. Rachel couldn't help herself. She drifted back to that summer.

The way it felt to hold his hand in secret. The realization that there was more to their relationship than just dumb pranks and dead bugs left in siddurs. Jacob had gotten Rachel to open up. She had trusted him. Showed him a side of herself reserved for a select few. Aside from Mickey, she had never been so honest with anybody in her entire life.

Dr. Rubenstein dismissed her daughter's concerns with a small wave of the hand. "It was eighteen years ago. Don't you think you're being a tad ridiculous?"

"Me?" Rachel scoffed. "You're the one who's hosting my summer camp archenemy for Shabbat."

"He's in town from Paris for some big event he's throwing. What would you have me do—*not* invite him?"

"While you're at it, don't forget to invite Dana Shoshanski. She made me cry every day in third grade. In fact, let me get you a list of all the people who made fun of me for being *Rachel Rubenstein-Goldblatt* growing up. I want to make sure you don't miss anybody."

Her mother did not blink. "I'm sorry it was hard for you… being our daughter."

Just like that, her mother had twisted all those feelings back around on her.

Rachel bit back her words, looking up to the ceiling. She loved her parents more than anything in the world. They had been there for her at every stage of her life, doting and wonderful. Still, the Rubenstein-Goldblatt name came with pressures. They were pressures that, even as an adult, still managed to follow her.

A knock at the door drew their attention away.

"Let me get that for you," Dr. Rubenstein said sweetly, rising from the couch.

"Ho, ho, ho-oooooooh…" Mickey said, standing at the door, his smile fading into panic. He was holding a medium-sized red gift bag in the air. He glanced at Rachel, who signaled the immediate danger by running one finger across her throat. Quickly Mickey hid the bag behind his back.

"Dr. Rubenstein!" he said, his eyes wide. "I didn't expect to see you here."

"Not to worry, Mickey," Dr. Rubenstein said, adjusting her scarf. "I was just getting ready to leave." She turned back to her daughter one last time. "Just think about coming to dinner, okay? Daddy and I won't be around forever, and there may come a time in your life when you miss spending Shabbat at your parents' house."

Mickey waited for the door to shut firmly behind him and the elevator at the end of the hall to ding before turning to his best friend. "Whoa," he said. "That woman is a pro when it comes to Jewish guilt."

"Tell me about it," Rachel said, collapsing on the couch.

"So what did our fine *rebbetzin* want this evening?" Mickey asked, taking his boots and jacket off at the front door.

"You'll never believe it if I tell you."

To everyone that knew them, it seemed that Mickey and Rachel had been *bashert*, soul mates, since time immemorial, having met at Camp Ahava when they were eight years old.

Since Rachel couldn't be sure what drew the pair together, she assumed it had something to do with how other people at their camp had treated them. Mikael, the adopted son of a powerhouse lesbian couple from Manhattan, was Black. And Rachel, as everyone who met her cared to remind her, was the daughter of Rabbi Aaron Goldblatt. *The* Rabbi Aaron Goldblatt.

Whether they liked it or not, when Mickey and Rachel walked into a room, people noticed them. People watched them. This shared experience formed the basis of their comradery and, later, extended far beyond Jewish summer camp.

"She wanted to set me up with Jacob Greenberg," Rachel said.

Mickey finished pulling off his boots. "Jacob Greenberg? From Camp Ahava?"

"The one and only."

"Wow," Mickey said, coming over to sit beside Rachel. "That's a name I haven't heard in forever. Didn't he give you mono?"

Rachel squeezed her eyes shut. She did not want to think about that first kiss with Jacob Greenberg. "Can we seriously not talk about this right now? I've waited seven long years for this moment, Mickey...and just like some of the other most important moments of my life, Jacob Greenberg is ruining it."

"You're right," Mickey said, laying the red bag on the coffee table between them. "And I have just the thing to take your mind off He Who Shall Not Be Named."

This was it. The moment she had waited for. With eager fingers, Rachel reached into the bag, pulled out the tiny figurine and gently removed the plastic bubble wrapping that protected it.

It was even better than she had imagined.

Santa smiled back at her from atop a surfboard. His blue-and-white Hawaiian shirt sat partly unbuttoned while, in his right hand, he nursed a fruity drink decorated with a tiny green umbrella. It was that umbrella, in mint condition, that made the Margaritaville Santa so valuable.

"It's perfect," Rachel whispered.

Mickey shook his head. "You are a sick, sick woman."

"Let's put him with the rest!"

The two rushed, giggling and screaming, back to her office. Mickey threw open the door—he was the only person in the world who had ever seen inside—and gasped at the sight laid out before him. For it was mid-December, nearly Christmas, and Rachel Rubenstein-Goldblatt had clearly lost her damn mind.

"Girrrrrl," Mickey said, placing his hand on his heart. "Did you straight up rob a Christmas store?"

"I might have gone a little overboard this year."

"Ya think?"

Garlands draped across the ceiling and desk hutch. A silver tinsel tree, flickering with lights, nearly overtook a desktop computer. But perhaps most impressive of all was the tiny red-and-green choo-choo train, set up to circle the room, every hour, on the dot.

The place was filled to the brim with Christmas cheer. One could barely make out the rows of shelves just behind the decorations, which held an impressive array of Christmas-inspired romance novels. Or the posters above them—four now in total—advertising made-for-TV Christmas movies.

Rachel placed her coveted Margaritaville Santa in front of the work of fiction it had inspired. On the movie poster above her, a couple kissed as a sun set on a dreamy beach behind them. Santa, clad in a blue-and-white Hawaiian shirt and Ray-Ban sunglasses, smiled knowingly from a lifeguard chair.

"'Christmas in the Caribbean,'" Mickey read the words aloud. "'By bestselling author Margot Cross.'"

Margot Cross. Rachel had found the pen name rather clever when the idea was first suggested by her agent. But now, after nearly a decade, she found the moniker stifling. Margot Cross was like a bad Shabbat guest who had come invited and overstayed their welcome.

"Are you judging me?" Rachel asked.

"I'm not judging you," Mickey said, exasperated.

"Because you sound very judgy."

"Fine," Mickey admitted. "I'm judging you a little. But seriously, Rachel. You're the bestselling author of over twenty Christmas romance novels! You have four Christmas movies on television. And nobody in the world even knows about it. Not your readers, not your fans, not your parents! I mean, I'm all for keeping folks in the dark about one's personal life, but don't you think it's time to come out of the Christmas closet? Or in your case…the Christmas office?"

Silence permeated the room.

Rachel wanted to tell people the truth about what she did for a living, but *coming out* wasn't that easy. She couldn't just stand up on the bima, like Mickey had done at his bar mitzvah all those years prior, and tell everyone the truth.

"Fifth grade," Rachel finally said, aloud.

"What about fifth grade?"

"My mother caught me putting up a construction paper Christmas tree in my room. Do you know what she did, Mickey? Do you know how my sweet and loving *ema* responded to the sight of a green construction paper tree taped up to the wall? She tore the whole thing down. Ripped it to shreds. Pointed her finger in my face and said, '*We do not celebrate Christmas in this house.*' Just like that. No debate. No questions. What do you think my mother will do when she finds out I'm really Margot Cross, bestselling author of over twenty Christmas romances?"

Mickey considered her story. "That was twenty years ago, Rachel. You were just a little kid. Even my mothers would stomp into my public school every once in a while, and demand to know why we were singing 'O Holy Night.' Now, they couldn't care less what I'm singing. Things change."

"Things change for you," Rachel reminded him. "My father is still Rabbi Aaron Goldblatt."

Mickey grimaced. Even he couldn't find a bright side to that argument.

Rabbi Goldblatt wasn't some no-name low-level rabbi. He was a *macher*, a bigwig, in her community.

He served a synagogue of twelve hundred families on Long Island. He had written six books on Jewish law and frequently spoke on the synagogue lecture circuit. He was known for his brilliant *teshuvot*, Jewish legal responsa to questions, and set Jewish legal precedent for millions of Jews worldwide. Even beyond all these things, her name came with a legacy.

Her great-great-great grandfather, the honorable Rabbi Pinchas Goldblatt, had been a noted scholar back in Poland. Her great-uncle, famed philosopher Elliot Rubenstein, had helped establish a Jewish seminary in New York. Her great-great-grandmother, Eliza Goldblatt, worked alongside Mordechai Kaplan to create the first JCCs, or Jewish Community Centers. Even her older brother had followed in the family tradition, becoming a rabbi himself, taking a major pulpit out in Los Angeles after ordination.

Meanwhile, Rachel—sick and disabled, unmarried and childless—had leaned in fully to her betrayal. She had taken her secret, shameful love of Christmas and turned it into a successful career.

"I don't know," Mickey said, throwing his arms into the air. "You're nearly thirty years old. You're a full-fledged and independent adult. What are you gonna do? Hide who you are forever because it might blow back on your father, or destroy some ridiculous family legacy?"

"I've considered it."

"You deserve better than that, Rachel."

Rachel nodded. The problem was...so did her parents.

Congregants expected their rabbi to be beyond reproach. A person whose dedication to Jewish law and living moved them beyond human frailties. It was a pressure, unfortunately, that often extended out to the families. Rabbis—like their partners and their children—learned very quickly not to share vulnerabilities.

Rachel could still remember the way her mother warned her before every Shabbat and holiday service to be on her best behavior. *Don't fight with your brother. Don't fidget in the pews. Remember that people are watching.*

Eventually, Rachel internalized the message. She became constantly aware of what she said and how she presented herself to others. She stopped whispering secrets to friends. She stopped having fun. She never once, in her entire life, forgot the lesson handed down from her mother. People were watching. Your choices, and your actions, could affect the entire family.

Now Rachel spent far too much time envisioning the worst that could happen. Her father would lose his contract at his beloved synagogue and no longer be allowed to be an arbitrator of Jewish law. Her mother, who lived for hosting guests on Shabbat, would suddenly find herself shunned by their tight-knit Jewish community. Perhaps her parents would even go so far as to consider her dead. Tear their clothing in fits of grief before sitting shiva for her.

It had happened before. In the past. To other rebellious Jewish children.

The worst part of all, Rachel was certain, would be seeing the look of disappointment on her parents' faces. She loved them so much. She couldn't bear the thought of hurting them. She wanted to be a perfect daughter—a nice Jewish girl. Someone her family could *kvell* about and be proud of.

Suddenly, the room sprang to life. A thousand twinkling lights exploded around them, as an animatronic Santa sashayed back and forth. The train *chug-chug-chugged* around its track, dipping in and out of the tiny Christmas village displayed on floating shelves above her head, playing a happy mechanical tune. Mickey jumped at the sound, nearly knocking over one of her tiny Christmas trees, loaded down in cat ornaments, in the process.

He clutched his heart. "Jesus."

"Sorry," she said, pulling out the chair from her desk. "I have it set to go off every hour."

Standing upon it, she searched for the small power button located behind a row of Christmas garlands, shutting down the epic display. The music moaned to a standstill, the lights in her office returned to normal, and the train, the one she had so lovingly and painstakingly set up around her office, came to a stop right next to a writing award for Margot Cross.

"Every hour? How the hell do you sleep?"

"I can't hear it in my bedroom."

Rachel stepped down from the chair. She knew it was odd—the way she hoarded Christmas trinkets inside her secret office—but she found it comforting. She loved everything about Christmas. The music. The throw pillows. The decor. It brought her to this place of unapologetic joy, where nothing bad ever happened and everyone found their happy ending.

"I just love it so much. I can't help myself, Mickey. I've tried to quit a dozen times, write something else, find some other story filled with the same level of magic…but I always wind up going right back to Christmas."

"It's Christmas, Rachel. Not a drug addiction."

"It feels like a drug addiction."

"You know what your problem is?" Mickey snapped his fingers. "You've never experienced a real Christmas."

Rachel sighed dramatically. "I know."

While both of Mickey's mothers identified as Jewish, Sheryl, who Mickey referred to as Mom, had been raised Southern Baptist. But after Sheryl met Elana, Mickey's *ema*, during a drunken midnight run for munchies in the East Village, the duo—both law students—quickly realized they were heading toward a permanent partnership. Children came later, along with the decision by both women to build a home centered around Jewish values.

Mickey was Jewish. He lived with both feet as firmly in the Jewish community as Rachel. But unlike Rachel—whose family tree had not been shaken up once since the shtetls of Bialystock—Mickey had non-Jewish family. He had non-Jewish grandparents, cousins, aunts and uncles. And growing up together, when the winter holiday break came, Mickey often went to see them.

It used to make Rachel all types of jelly.

"I'm serious, Rachel," Mickey continued, rolling his eyes a little in her direction. "Your entire frame of reference for the holiday comes from Hallmark movies and aisle sixteen at Target. *It's not real.* Come to my aunt Vivian's house for the holidays. Watch Uncle Joe get drunk and say offensive things to my mothers. Trust me, you won't think it's so magical then."

Rachel fell into silence. Maybe Mickey was right. Maybe her entire life, wrapped up in red-and-green Christmas ribbon, was just another fiction. She was used to them, after all. She had been doling them out her whole life. But her best friend since forever was forgetting one thing.

"I don't want it to be real," Rachel said quietly.

Mickey blinked. "Rachel—"

"It's okay." She forced a smile, downplaying her sadness. She didn't talk about it much, but chronic illness, like her career writing Christmas romances, were two events that had developed together.

"No." Mickey took her hand. "I get it, okay? I didn't mean to stomp all over your Christmas safe-space. You're amazing, all right? This room is amazing! I totally get why you love Christmas."

"You do?"

"Yeah." Mickey smiled. "I mean…what do us super-Jewy types really get anyway? Apples and honey on Rosh Hashanah? Twenty-five hours of fasting on Yom Kippur? Sleeping outside in a cold-ass, roofless hut in the middle of October?"

Rachel laughed. "You've always hated Sukkot."

"With a passion! And don't even get me started on Hanukkah."

"Ugh," Rachel groaned. "Hanukkah."

"Frozen latkes, crappy dreidel games—"

"Plus, you always burn your fingers on the menorah."

"That holiday is a giant fire hazard," Mickey said, punctuating his next set of words with full snark. "Honestly, it's amazing half of New York doesn't burn down every Kislev."

Rachel warmed like a cup of hot cocoa on a cold winter day. It was just like Mickey to say the right thing, pulling her out of any sadness. He was one of a kind, truly. She would never take his love or devotion for granted.

"So yeah," Mickey said, pushing one brown curl out of her eyes. "When it comes to which holiday has the more festive spirit, I think every Jewish person on the planet would agree with you... Christmas wins."

Rachel threw her arms around him. "I love you."

"I love you, too," Mickey said, before adding, *"Rachel Rubenstein-Goldblatt."*

Later that evening, after Mickey had departed, Rachel couldn't sleep. Normally, she would assume her insomnia was the by-product of her chronic fatigue syndrome, what doctors often referred to as a disrupted sleep-wake cycle. This evening, however, Rachel knew that her tossing was the result of something far more insidious.

Jacob Greenberg was coming back to New York.

Rachel groaned beneath her covers. She couldn't get him out of her head. Lying in bed, memories of that terrible summer came flooding back to her. *Pushing her into the lake. Leaving a dead bug in her siddur. Scratching on the window above her bunk at midnight, pretending to be a serial killer.* All of which she could have probably forgiven, but he had taken the joke too far.

Rachel needed to relax. Rising from her bed, she knew just the thing that would help. Returning to the living room, she drew shut the curtains. The rest was ritual, a Christmas-themed pattern she had played out a million times since moving to her two-bedroom apartment on the Upper West Side. She headed to her office and powered on her Christmas monstrosity.

The room sprang back to life. The thousand twinkling lights turned on around her. The hum of an electronic jingle, the chugging *choo-choo* of her Christmas train finishing its happy path. Rachel leaned against the doorway, taking it all in. Her magic Christmas world, her safe and special place…her most dark and shameful secret.

Usually, it helped.

Rachel closed the door and returned to her bedroom. Heading to her closet, she stood on her tiptoe, pulling down a large flowered box.

Normally, as a kid, she had been obsessive about collaging. This box, which had traveled with her through most of college and into adulthood, contained the extras that hadn't made it into picture frames. It contained years' worth of photographs from Camp Ahava, letters long sent and forgotten, plus a hodgepodge of random friendship bracelets and other summer camp trinkets.

She took a deep breath and opened it. Surprisingly, the act didn't injure her. Sorting through photographs, she found herself smiling. The ones of her and Mickey, in third grade, tiny and adorable. She stopped on a picture of her with him, both of them wearing red bandannas, smiling toothless at the camera.

There were plenty from the girls' side of camp, too. Rachel burst out laughing at a random shot, blurry and unfocused, of bunk 7G. It was absolute filth. Wet towels hung from every railing. Hair dryers and curling irons, with their cords unwrapped, lay open and exposed on beds. She landed on a photo of Leah Abraham drinking out of her favorite pink water bottle. The one Rachel's father had specifically bought Rachel because it had her name painted in silver gemstones on the front.

Rachel had loved that damn water bottle.

She kept flipping through, each image bringing back with it a dozen memories. There really was nothing quite like Jewish summer camp. She saw the same familiar faces, year after year, summer after summer. At least, she had…until Jacob Greenberg arrived.

Jacob Greenberg burst into the Camp Ahava scene a total anomaly. He was Jewish, of course, but he didn't come from her Jewish world. He made fart noises during morning minyan. He purposefully mixed meat and dairy dishes during meals. He was a notorious prankster, a total bad boy, never once giving a damn about what anybody thought of him.

No wonder Rachel fell so hard for him.

She wasn't the only one. The *l'shon hara*, or gossip, that summer about Jacob was unrivaled. His mother was a French model. His father was some über-rich businessman. He lived in a seventeen-bedroom penthouse in New York, where he could order candy via delivery service, and even had a television in his bedroom. Most of which—Rachel now realized as an adult—was probably not true. None of that mattered to the seventh graders of Camp Ahava. Jacob Greenberg was all question marks and mystery. Everyone fell under his spell.

Rachel came to a photo of the boys of bunk 7B. Twenty-six gangly males stood in a half-moon circle outside their cabin. There was Mickey, Avi, Ben and Aaron. But in the middle of those familiar faces, poised like a king with his arms crossed, stood Jacob Greenberg. Grinning.

Ugh.

She was positive he was still grinning, laughing at her from *oh, so fabulous* Paris, the city he'd moved to with his mother after their one summer together at Camp Ahava. Her eyes wandered over to a stack of letters held together by a rubber band. She didn't have the heart to open them up.

But she remembered how relieved she'd felt to read his final letter. The way she and Mickey had celebrated, jumping up and down on her bed, squealing aloud in sheer delight. Jacob Greenberg was leaving New York—and the United States—*forever*. He would never be returning to Camp Ahava.

And yet, despite the shrieks of gratitude emanating from her tiny pink bedroom on Long Island, when Rachel found herself alone at night—when she thought about all that had transpired between them that summer—there was a part of her that was sad to hear he was leaving.

Jacob had been her first love, after all.

Rachel threw down the photo. It was such sentimental stupidity, and for what? Jacob probably didn't remember her, let alone recall the myriad ways he had broken her heart. But Rachel would always remember it. Always recall the way it felt to look up from her first kiss, and see the boys of bunk 7B hiding in the bushes with flashlights and cameras. Because Jacob Greenberg had turned her first kiss into a giant Camp Ahava prank.

He had never loved her. He had never cared about her, either.

Rachel closed up the box, returning it to the closet. Crawling back into bed, she decided that her mother was wrong. She was not being ridiculous. Jacob Greenberg had stolen something precious from her. Something important that she could never get back.

She had no intention of ever seeing that *shmuck* again.

2

Entering Charles de Gaulle Airport, Jacob Greenberg was too busy rifling through the front pocket of his carry-on to notice the wide-eyed and nervous whispers of the three young attendants standing at the counter. He didn't mean for his harried pace and downturned lips to come off as discourteous. But, as CEO of Greenberg Entertainment and a man who had built his multimillion-dollar business from the ground up, he had far more pressing issues on his mind.

"Bonjour," he said, pulling out his French passport.

"Good morning!" the attendant chirped, elbowing her friend to get to the computer terminal first. "How can I help you today?"

Jacob forced a smile. She had detected his American accent and immediately switched from French to English. He tried not to be insulted by this. After all, it was far too common an occurrence in his life to be offensive. Still, it drove him nuts. He had been living in Paris now for almost two decades, and at every turn he was reminded that he was an outsider.

"I'm heading to New York," he said.

"New York!" she chirped, sifting through papers. "Fabulous. Have you been before?"

Jacob shifted uneasily in his shiny black loafers. It was odd how a simple question asked by a stranger could make him want to turn on his heels and run. "I was born there," he said carefully. Cautiously. "My mother is...*was* French."

"You're American?" she asked, looking up from his French passport.

"I have dual citizenship," he said, hoping his clipped tone would put an end to her line of questioning. It worked.

Forty-five minutes later, he was comfortably settled in the waiting area of gate C-19.

Though *comfortable* was perhaps too strong a word.

Since arriving at the airport, he had been met with a growing sense of anxiety in his belly. He couldn't quite pinpoint where his nervousness stemmed from. Maybe it was the conversation at the ticket counter that reminded him of the broken home from which he came. Or maybe it was something far more immediate. He had never thrown an event like the Matzah Ball.

Pulling out his laptop and powering it on, he stared at his massive to-do list. The week of a major event was always the most trying. There were guests to please, suppliers to confirm, lighting and sound checks to accomplish. It would be all hands on deck for every person on staff and every local volunteer seeking a ticket.

But Jacob was used to the craziness of an event production schedule. As the mastermind behind such events as Launchella and Sunburn, he had made a fortune selling one-of-a-kind parties to wealthy millennials seeking out Instagram-worthy experiences. Now he was heading to New York to launch the first ever Matzah Ball Max. A high-end and formal event on the eighth night of Hanukkah, which promised ticket holders one thing: the Hanukkah event of the century.

"Jacob!" Shmuel was waving at him from the end of the terminal. "There you are."

Shmuel Applebaum was a squat man who stood, on loafers with risers, five feet and four inches tall. But what he lacked in height he made up for in pure, unadulterated energy. Storming down the busy terminal, tzitzit waving while he walked, he was holding three different plastic bags in addition to the blue backpack slung over his shoulder.

"You'll never believe it," Shmuel said, sitting down next to Jacob. "They're telling me I brought too much stuff!"

Jacob carefully regarded his friend and colleague. It was an almost eight-hour flight to New York, but Shmuel Applebaum had come prepared to survive the apocalypse. Bending over in his seat, his yeshiva-bocher belly spread out in rolls around the handrails, he began sifting through the plastic bags. Four sacks of baked goods, six bottles of water and a small roast chicken struggled to remain in their allotted sections.

"You know," Jacob said, raising on eyebrow in Shmuel's direction, "they feed us on this flight. Kosher food and everything."

Shmuel looked up from the mess. "You can never be too prepared, Jacob. The Talmud says, 'A person should be prepared to sell the beams of his house in order to put shoes on his feet.' These are my shoes, Jacob. A person needs shoes."

"Right."

"Let me use your laptop bag," Shmuel said.

"What?" Jacob snapped back. "No!"

"Come on," he said, reaching for it. "I know you. You'll be working the whole flight anyway. Plus, I don't want to have to check my baggage. You know how these airlines are. Total crooks. They'll lose your bag and charge you extra for it!"

There was no point in arguing with the man. Shmuel was like a gerbil on a wheel when he wanted something, incapable of stepping back or taking no for an answer.

That same singular drive coupled with a severe lack of social skills were what made Shmuel so damn good at his job. Shmuel could pull money from a rock. The man was amazing at fund-raising, gifted at getting people to say yes, savvy at marketing. Over the years, the duo had become more than just colleagues. They had become friends.

Jacob handed over his very expensive Briggs & Riley laptop bag and watched Shmuel turn it into a makeshift picnic basket for kosher baked goods.

"I spent four hundred dollars on that bag," Jacob said, cringing.

"It's a very nice bag," Shmuel said, oblivious. "Maybe not four hundred dollars nice...but very nice."

Shmuel finished his impossible task. With the hand precision of a two-year-old, he shoved the last of his baked goods into Jacob's bag before tugging on the zipper. The Briggs & Riley now stretched to maximum capacity, he sighed happily and slunk back into his seat.

"So nu?" he said, looking at Jacob. "What's up with you?"

"Nothing."

"Nothing," Shmuel repeated, elbowing him a little. "You're nervous."

"I'm not nervous."

"You're not *not* nervous."

Shmuel had pegged him. Jacob was, in fact, nervous. There were just so many unknowns for the young CEO. He was returning to New York City—and the Jewish community there—after a lifetime away. He was investing huge sums of money into throwing the Matzah Ball Max, an event unlike any he had done before. And there was this one other thing weighing on him. There was a chance, just a small chance that he would bump into Rachel Rubenstein-Goldblatt.

Her name alone caused a pendulum of emotions to swing inside him. One moment he was thrilled. The next he was terrified. He felt stupid for still thinking about her, confused over what had happened so many years ago, irritated that she could have done that to him.

But mainly, when he thought back to the summer of blooming adolescent love at Camp Ahava, he remembered her as the skinny girl with braces who was the shining light of his life in a year that was otherwise altogether completely dark.

Rachel Rubenstein-Goldblatt had saved him.

And then she had broken his heart.

"Don't be nervous," Shmuel said, pulling a bag of peanuts out of his side pocket, "I have everything on my end handled, all right? Kosher food...we got it. Ten-foot menorah...it's arriving on Sunday. All the Jewish aspects of the party are handled, okay? All you need to do now is get the *hechsher.*"

"Hechsher?" Jacob had not grown up as observant as Shmuel.

"The stamp of approval, you know?" Shmuel said, turning over a bag of peanuts to reveal a small OU sign printed on the back. "You need to get the blessing from Rabbi Aaron Goldblatt. Make sure our big Jewish music festival on the last night of Hanukkah is kosher."

The dietary laws of kashrut, or kosher, specified which foods could be eaten and which foods were prohibited. But while the laws of kashrut were usually limited to foods, the concept of things being kosher or not had seeped into every aspect of Jewish culture.

Despite the fact that there was no real halachic reason for a rabbi to be in attendance or light the final Hanukkah candles, Jacob felt that having the presence of Rabbi Aaron Goldblatt at their party would give their Matzah Ball a feeling of authenticity. He was a *macher*, after all, and one of the most respected Jewish thinkers of their generation.

"You're going to his house for Shabbat, right?" Shmuel asked.

"Yeah," Jacob said, feeling his stomach sink.

"I still don't know how you bamboozled that invitation."

Jacob shifted in his seat. "Me, either."

Jacob had never intended to be invited for Shabbat to the home of the world-famous Rabbi Aaron Goldblatt. In truth, when he had first rung their house from his office in Paris, he hadn't even expected anyone to remember him. His instinct was to simply keep things professional, to extend the invitation to Rabbi Goldblatt and his wife, Dr. Rubenstein, to light the final candles of the menorah at his Matzah Ball Max.

Much to his surprise, Dr. Rubenstein had picked up the phone. With great warmth, she exclaimed how delighted she was to hear from him. She spent the next twenty minutes chattering his ear off, plowing him with questions, before *insisting* he come stay with them for Shabbat.

What were his options, really? His ninety-one-year-old bubbe would not be returning from Thailand until Monday. He also didn't feel like spending Shabbat with Shmuel and his fifty-two cousins down in Brooklyn. Despite the difficulties involved—namely the very real possibility of running into her daughter—it had to be done.

"Actually," Jacob rubbed the back of his neck. "I dated the daughter once."

Shmuel stopped eating peanuts. "You dated the rabbi's daughter?"

"*Dating* is probably too strong a word," Jacob backtracked. "It was summer camp. Camp Ahava, actually, in the Berkshires. We were both twelve."

It took Shmuel a minute. He squinted, confused. "You went to Jewish summer camp?"

"For one summer." Jacob shifted again. "Before I moved to France with my mother."

Jacob could see Shmuel trying to work out this whole *meshugas* thing Jacob was telling him beneath his black skullcap. Finally he just gave up on the impossible endeavor. "Well," Shmuel said, popping another peanut into his mouth, "don't mess it up."

An announcement came over the loudspeaker. Flight 1668

to New York was ready to depart. Gathering up his stuff, Jacob shoved the memory of Rachel Rubenstein-Goldblatt down and away. She had been a blip on the radar screen of his life. Nothing more.

3

Rachel awoke to the sound of the alarm clock buzzing on the nightstand beside her bed. Turning beneath the covers, she blinked and took a careful accounting of how she was feeling. Would it be a good day or a bad day? She could never be certain.

Some mornings she woke up feeling well, only to find herself completely depleted two hours later. Sometimes it was the opposite. She would crash for days at a time, with no ability to do even the most menial tasks. Her disease was constant but fluid. It peaked and ebbed with only one discernable pattern. Everything she did, *everything*, from writing two pages to carrying the groceries one block to her apartment, came with a kickback.

It was her normal.

Dragging herself to the kitchen, she began her morning routine. Meds. Coffee. There always needed to be coffee. Just like she always set her meetings for late morning.

Showers were saved for special occasions because they required standing and holding your arms above your head while you rinsed shampoo out of your hair. All of which, though she couldn't completely understand how, seemed to require an extraordinary amount of effort. Otherwise, she preferred baths, where she could lie down.

When Rachel was finally dressed, when she stood in front of the mirror and checked herself one last time before departing, the irony of her life was apparent. She didn't look sick. If anything, she appeared the picture of polished charm and perfect health. Tight black skirt. White silk blouse. She would tie it all together with a smart red coat and designer bag.

This was an important meeting with her publisher, after all.

Rachel exited her apartment and hailed a cab. She knew the subway would be cheaper and faster, but she had to do a careful cost-benefits analysis to guard her energy. Like one of those video games she would sometimes play with Mickey, she ran the stats. *Showering: -10 damage. Cab: +15 strength. Sitting in a room for forty-five minutes and talking to a panel of editors: She would need an extra life.*

Rachel wasn't sure when this chronic illness calculator had first appeared in her brain, but it ran continuously in the background, as essential to her well-being as food and water.

Climbing into the cab, she tried not to think about it. Today was a good day. *Thanks be to Mickey.* He had saved her valuable energy points by picking up the Margaritaville Santa for her from the post office. As the driver pulled away, Rachel made a point to text her best friend.

Just wanted to say thank you again for last night.

Her phone buzzed to attention only seconds later:

Girl! Don't even worry about it! You know I got your back.

Rachel smiled. Slinking into the seat, she put the phone away. She wasn't worried. She knew that she never had to explain herself with Mickey. He simply took her at her word—forever and from the beginning—which was rare in a world where very few people understood chronic illness.

Still, she *felt* guilty. She wanted to be a better friend, to call more often, to show up when he threw parties. But Rachel was far too focused on simply surviving, and CFS was a disease that cast a wide net of suffering.

When the cab pulled up to the thirty-three-story tower of glass that was Romance House, Rachel entered the building to find her agent, Lisa Brown, waiting by the elevators. Her cell phone pinned between her ear and her neck, Lisa was too busy taking notes on a potential new contract to notice her arrival. Rachel tapped her gently on the shoulder, and Lisa jumped, surprised. "One second," Lisa said into her phone, then mouthed the words, *You look fabulous!*

Rachel warmed into a smile. Mission accomplished.

No one in Rachel's professional circle knew about her disease. Not her agent. Not her editors. She wasn't hiding it from them, obviously. It simply…had never come up in conversation. At least, that's what she told herself.

Besides, she reasoned, after ten years of working together it would be weird to tell her agent now. Like that show on MTV where people learn they've been catfished. The poor woman would suddenly have an image of her client that did not line up with the photo she'd been looking at all these years. What would happen then?

She needed her publishing contract. She needed her book deals. There was no nine-to-five job in Rachel's future. Her body simply was not reliable enough to function on a normal, full-time schedule.

Lisa finished her phone call and turned her attention to Rachel. "So," she said, with the fiery zeal of a linebacker during the Super Bowl, "are you ready?"

"I'm ready!" Rachel shot back.

"Let's do this thing, then!"

The sixteenth floor of Romance House was where the most important meetings were held. Coming off the elevator, the duo was greeted by Sasha, the intern, who quickly led them to the main conference room.

The chaperone wasn't necessary. Meetings with her publisher were a lot like synagogue services. They had a flow and pattern. There were the obligatory handshakes. The traditional offering of coffee. The pointing out of breakfast muffins and sandwiches before someone, inevitably, made a joke about going off their diet. It was all pleasantries and niceties doled out among four different editors, two marketing executives and Chandra Brouchard, Romance House CEO. Until finally, the group agreed to sit down around the conference table and get to work.

"So, Rachel." Chandra smiled at her from across the room. Her large gold ring, encrusted with diamonds and an emerald, glimmered. "We wanted to thank you again for taking the time to come in and meet with us today. As you know, your current contract is up...and we are all just so very curious about what you have planned next."

"Of course." Rachel smiled. "I'd be happy to share what I'm thinking."

Rachel had a zillion ideas and tore through them, curious which one would stick.

There was the Texas cowboy with secret triplet babies. The forsaken politician meeting the big-city reporter during a blizzard. The K-9 detective and the veterinarian thrown together after finding a litter of abandoned puppies. These were tried and true stories, all taking place over Christmas, with the hooks and twists her readers loved.

Her agent nodded and smiled. Her editors listened intently. And then, when she had exhausted almost every viable idea she had come up with for this meeting, she waited for a response.

Instead, there was silence.

It was weird. Normally, after a pitch session, there were wows and accolades. One year, Chandra Brouchard herself had risen from her chair to hug Rachel and declare her "Romance House's Most Valuable Player" in her idiosyncratic slow drawl.

Today there were no enthusiastic exclamations. No editors chiming in with notes. There was simply a strange and awkward quiet, and the bizarre way everyone at the table was casting furtive glances at one another.

"What is it?" Rachel asked.

Lisa inched closer. "We were thinking that maybe this year… you could try something different."

"Different?"

"Something that will feel really authentic," Chandra chimed in. "Something with…oh, I don't know, less Christmas?"

"*Less* Christmas?" Rachel laughed at the statement. "All I write is Christmas!"

More silence.

And then Chandra Brouchard came out with it.

"We want you to write a Hanukkah romance."

"*What?*" Rachel knocked over her cup of coffee. Lukewarm brown liquid splattered all over her white blouse. An editorial assistant rushed to offer her napkins, but Rachel was too shellshocked by her publisher's ambush to make sense of what was happening.

"You know," Chandra said, speaking with her hands, "a Hanukkah romance. Like one of your Christmas stories, but just, make it Jewish. You can do that, can't you?"

Now Rachel was the one left speechless.

Hanukkah was *not* Christmas.

"What's the problem?" Chandra asked.

"It's just—"

"You're Jewish, aren't you?"

"Yes."

"And isn't your father some sort of world-famous rabbi?"

Rachel did not want to talk about her father. "It's just," she stammered, "Hanukkah isn't magical."

"Of course it's magical!" Chandra bellowed, looking to her staff for confirmation. "There's the menorah. And that little top that spins. And those, what are they called again, *late-keeees*! Potato *late-keeees*. Surely, you can come up with something from there?"

Rachel could feel bubbles rising up in her chest. How could she explain it to this well-meaning and good-intentioned group of non-Jewish folks? There was a reason no one had ever written a Hanukkah romance before.

Jews didn't throw dreidel decorating parties. They didn't hold *late-keeee*-making competitions. You couldn't wrap a blue ribbon around a squirming Labrador puppy and leave it beneath the menorah for the children to find. Labrador puppies would get burned that way.

Indeed, if her publisher wanted a true and honest look at Hanukkah in the American Jewish community, it would be two nights' worth of semi-decent presents, followed by six nights' worth of school supplies.

"Look," Chandra said, suddenly getting serious. "I didn't want to bring this up, but the sales on your last three Christmas books...they haven't been that great. People don't want to read the same old thing anymore, Rachel. They want diversity! They want their experiences and world reflected. And Christmas is *sooooo* last year. It's time to spice things up! Bring in the Jews! Everybody loves the Jews."

"That's actually...famously not true."

"And think of the movie deals," Lisa interjected. "Netflix. Amazon."

"*Exactly!*" Chandra said, nodding like a bobblehead. "Now is the time. Everyone is just champing at the bit for a proper Hanukkah romance. I really think—if you value your relationship with us as your publisher—you will take this opportunity."

Rachel swallowed hard. "What are you trying to say?"

"I'm saying—" Chandra met her eyes directly "—that we will not be offering Margot Cross another contract for more Christmas romances this year. However, there is an opportunity for Rachel Rubenstein-Goldblatt to keep working with Romance House...providing she writes us a Hanukkah novel."

4

It was panic. Pure and unadulterated panic settled inside Rachel Rubenstein-Goldblatt as she raced from Romance House. Standing on a bustling New York street during lunchtime rush hour, she tried not to cry, but her Christmas snow globe world had just been rattled.

"Rachel!" Lisa was chasing after her. "Please, hold up a second."

Rachel spun around, fists balled up at her sides. She couldn't play nice anymore. She was mad. Furious. Tears welled up in her eyes. "You ambushed me, Lisa! You and Chandra—you completely ambushed me!"

"I just found out this morning, okay?" she said, out of breath. "I swear. Kaitlyn called me this morning and told me what they were thinking. I'm sorry I didn't give you some warning. I got caught up in a…a Twitter thing with another client."

"Twitter?"

"But," Lisa interrupted her, "I also didn't think it would be a problem for you. I mean, you've been wanting to retire Margot Cross for some time now, right? Well, here's your chance. I thought you'd be happy."

Rachel bit her lip. There was truth to what Lisa was saying even though it was a bitter pill to swallow. This wasn't just an opportunity to bury Margot Cross once and for all, but to potentially publish under her own name.

She could stop lying to her parents.

She could stop lying to…well, everyone.

Still, Christmas had been a red-and-green blanket she had wrapped herself up in for the last decade. It had protected her and kept her fighting, even on her very worst days. Beyond all these things, Rachel knew Christmas. She loved Christmas. She had none of those warm and fuzzy feelings she would need to switch gears like that.

"How am I supposed to write a book about Hanukkah?" Rachel asked, deflated.

"Well, what do you do for your Christmas books?" Lisa asked. "You draw inspiration from real life and make it magical. So do the same thing here. You live on the Upper West Side. You're connected to the Jewish community. Go around and see what people are doing. Go out and see how people are celebrating. You'll figure something out."

Rachel nodded. She could tell that the conversation was over. Lisa headed off to another client meeting, and Rachel—still in full freak-out mode—decided to use the afternoon to heed her agent's advice.

She began at the closest department store. Forcing herself to ignore the many aisles of Christmas trees and ornaments, she hunted down the Hanukkah section, which was one sad little shelf display. Unless she was planning to write a book about Christmas envy, she would have to keep looking.

Next, she headed to the JCC. After checking in at the front desk of the community center, she wandered the halls, a hyperventilating and panicky mess. She passed by kids on their way

home from swim lessons and old Jewish ladies doing group cal-
isthenics in the gym, before ripping ten different flyers about
Hanukkah off the noticeboard. She probably could have stayed
for another hour, but at the sight of her unbridled anxiety, a security guard asked her to leave.

Finally, she went to a popular rabbi at a large synagogue on
the Upper East Side. Sitting down in his office, she told him that
she was writing a book about Hanukkah and that she needed his
help. He told her that Hanukkah was a minor holiday, and that
if she really wanted to write a book about an important Jewish
holiday, she should try writing about Yom Kippur.

She felt as defeated as a Maccabee staring at one night's worth
of oil.

On the subway to the Upper West Side, the well of emotion
Rachel had been holding in throughout the day burst forth in
a flood of fully formed tears. Slinking into her seat, she bawled
uncontrollably, the smell of coffee from her stained shirt assaulting her nostrils. As if today hadn't been bad enough, she had
chosen to wear white.

At least, she told herself, she was alone in the subway car, the
indignity of today saved by this one small fact.

It was no use. Her search for inspiration had yielded nothing—there was no way she'd drum up enough excitement to be
able to do what Romance House wanted from her. She had no
idea how to survive without her publishing contract. She had
bills to pay, a two-bedroom apartment on the Upper West Side
to maintain. Plus, kosher food was really freaking expensive.
And beyond all these things, there was the never-ending fear
lingering alongside her life with chronic illness. How could she
survive, remain financially independent, if she couldn't work
from home, on her own schedule?

The panic she had pushed down began rising in her chest
once again.

She needed a miracle.

Closing her eyes, Rachel forced herself to calm down. Leaning her head against the window, she listened to the roar of scraping wheels and metal creaking beneath her. It was comforting in a way, the normalcy of it all. The whole of Manhattan passing by above her, blissfully unaware of her life falling apart in the subterranean depths below.

When Rachel opened her eyes, however, another surprise was waiting for her. A Haredi man was sitting in the seat across from her.

Rachel blinked a few times to make sure she was certain, then glanced down the train car to confirm that it was empty, as she remembered. But he was real. Quintessential black hat. Long gray beard and two curly peyot. A newspaper, *Jewish World News*, sitting on his lap.

He must have been a thousand years old, incapable of moving at high speeds or great distances, but he was suddenly there, inches away from her, feet almost touching, smiling warmly in her direction, with rosy red cheeks and twinkling brown eyes.

"Shabbat Shalom," he said.

"Shabbat Shalom," she replied.

He was still smiling as the subway car rolled to a stop.

"This is Rockefeller Center," the automated subway lady announced.

With great and heaving effort, the old man rose from his seat. Rachel would have offered to help, but she was acquainted with the lifestyle of the Ultra-Orthodox. Men and women, outside of marriage, were not supposed to touch. Instead, she kept her eyes on the ground and let him have his privacy.

The doors parted. The old man stepped out. In the process, his newspaper fell from beneath his arm. Realizing what had happened, Rachel raced to pick it up. "Sir!" she shouted, leaning out of the subway car. "Sir! You dropped your—"

But he was gone.

The old man had disappeared as quickly as he had arrived.

Sitting back down in her seat, she held the newspaper in her lap. Rachel was familiar with the publication. It had been a staple in her childhood home, delivered every Sunday, for most of her young life.

Maybe because she was still hopeful, or maybe because the old man's seemingly magical appearance inspired her, she opened the newspaper. Flipping through the pages, she skimmed the recent stories. It had all the typical stuff one might expect, a highlights reel of the Jewish community, and then something caught her eye in the Lifestyle section.

Sold-Out Matzah Ball Max Promises
to be Hanukkah Event of the Century

Rachel's hands began to shake. *Matzah Balls.* She knew right away they weren't talking about the round and fluffy dumplings found in chicken soup.

Rachel didn't know who had created the first Matzah Ball, which had existed for nearly forty years in America. Historically, they were large-scale parties, held in nightclubs on Christmas Eve, and served as a place for Jewish singles to gather when their non-Jewish friends were off celebrating Christmas.

Over the years, the concept of the Matzah Ball had expanded. They went from parties in clubs to social events sponsored by synagogues, to singles events hosted by dating apps such as J-Mate. They took on strange intonations of their original name, appearing with titles such as Latkepalooza and became more defined in their targeted audience. Some Matzah Balls were only for people over fifty. Some were for members of the LGBTQ+ community. Some were held before Christmas, or after Christmas, or on ski slopes in Aspen. But this Matzah Ball Max was different from previous varieties...

Because this Matzah Ball Max had a definitive Hanukkah twist.

Suddenly, the whole world began to make sense. A thunder started in her belly and worked its way up into her chest. *The Matzah Ball Max*. Yes, this was what she needed. This was the real and authentic Hanukkah experience that could provide much-needed inspiration for her book.

Too bad it was completely sold out.

Still, Rachel Rubenstein-Goldblatt was not the type to just throw in the *shmata*. She knew a lot of people in the Jewish world. She was Rabbi Aaron Goldblatt's daughter, after all. There was a chance, albeit a small one, that someone she knew would be able to get her a ticket.

Quickly she skimmed the article:

The whole world has been waiting with bated breath for the Matzah Ball Max to finally launch in New York City. Planned for the eighth night of Hanukkah, this high-end event is completely sold out. Organizers say that the response to their initiative has been overwhelming, and tickets are nearly impossible to come by at this late date. Jacob Greenberg, mastermind behind such events as Launchella and Sunburn, is the creator behind this first of…

The newspaper dropped from her hands. A small puff of air escaped her quivering lips as the rumbling in her belly twisted into nausea. Could it be? Could the only person in the entire world capable of getting her a ticket to the Matzah Ball be *Jacob Greenberg*?

The same Jacob Greenberg who had ruined her first kiss, and given her mono, and humiliated her in front of everyone at Camp Ahava? The same Jacob Greenberg who had returned to New York and was currently spending Shabbat at her parents' house on Long Island?

She hated Jacob Greenberg with a fiery passion.

But she needed that ticket. Her career was riding on it.

Glancing down at her watch, she noted the time. It was 3:15 on Friday afternoon. Candle lighting, and the start of Shabbat, which prohibited travel, began at 5:19. If she ran through the stations and didn't meet delays on the tracks, she would just make it home in time for Shabbat dinner.

No doubt her mother would be thrilled.

From: Rachel Rubenstein-Goldblatt <margotcross@northpole.com>
To: Lisa Brown <l.brown@cachingliteraryagency.com>

Sent: Fri, 10 December
Subject: Hanukkah Romance

Lisa,

Sorry for freaking out at you after the meeting today. I just didn't expect to be asked to write a HANUKKAH romance. ☹

I've been thinking about what you said, and you're right. *I can totally handle this!* I'm heading out to Long Island tonight to do some first-class Hanukkah research. Hopefully, it yields good results.

Wish me MAZEL!!!

Rachel

PS: I'll be at my parents' house for Shabbat so, you know… no phone.

5

The car service that brought Jacob from the airport to Rabbi Goldblatt's house arrived forty-five minutes before candle lighting.

Walking up to the house, Jacob took a centering breath. It was a modest house, made of white stone stucco, and sat within walking distance of Congregation Beth Or. Even as he approached, Jacob knew he was about to enter a Jewish home. The scent of kugel and chicken soup wafted through the air. Three little girls, in winter coats and long skirts, played on a swing set under the watchful eye of their father. And though it was still daylight, the sun less than an hour away from setting, the porch light had been left on for receiving visitors.

Shabbat was coming.

Jacob loved these aspects of Jewish life. There was a focus on tradition and family and doing the right thing, *tikkun olam*, in order to make the world a better place. All the things he had wanted as a child and never got.

"Jacob!" Dr. Rubenstein flung open the front door. "Shabbat Shalom!"

Without warning, she threw her arms around him, squeezing him tightly. He had not seen her for many years. Not since she had come to their apartment in Manhattan, armed with three different types of kugel, to visit his mother. But he remembered how kind Dr. Rubenstein had been. How she would sit at the kitchen table with his mother for hours, listening intently while she cried, head in her hands, a woman on the verge of losing everything.

"My, my..." Dr. Rubenstein stepped back. "You have certainly gotten handsome."

Jacob blushed. "I don't know about that."

She kept her hands on his arms, gentle and supportive. "And so tall! What are they feeding you in France?"

Jacob laughed. "I eat a lot of takeout, honestly."

"Must be the takeout then." She smiled kindly.

Indeed, their paths may have never crossed had it not been for that one fateful summer before seventh grade. After Rachel stood Jacob up at the Camp Ahava final dance, he had called her house repeatedly, demanding to speak to her. It was the nonstop and tearful badgering that led Dr. Rubenstein to finally demand to speak to his mother. The truth came out.

Although not a complicated story, it was one he avoided sharing with others. When Jacob was in the sixth grade, his mother fell ill. In the span of a week, she went from being his loving, devoted—and completely healthy—mother to a woman who could barely walk. Soon, the paralysis got worse. His mother struggled to form words. She struggled with incontinence. She spent two weeks in the hospital before the doctors diagnosed her with multiple sclerosis.

His father responded to this news by working more. He worked evenings and weekends before disappearing on "business trips," his mother's euphemism for shacking up with a woman named Peggy who lived downtown. Eventually, his father stopped coming home at all. He abandoned them, refusing to return phone calls or show up for visits like he promised.

Of course, Jacob wasn't completely alone. He had his bubbe—his father's mother—who thankfully lived in New York, and did her best to reason with her wayward son while simultaneously supporting her French daughter-in-law and American-born grandson. He had kind members of the Jewish community like Dr. Rubenstein, armed with her kugels and her warm heart. And then, his mother made the difficult decision to take Jacob and move back to her native France.

Not that she had any real choice in the matter. Even his bubbe agreed it was the right thing to do. His mother had family in France. She could speak the language. More important, she had access to nationalized health care in a system she could maneuver. Twelve-year-old Jacob couldn't rationalize the upheavals. He blamed his mother for getting sick. It was her fault his father had left. If she had only been stronger, he wouldn't be living in some foreign country where everyone pointed out his American accent.

He took all his anger out on his mom.

Now, as a man, he understood. It was not his mother who had failed him. It was her disease, and the medical establishment, and his father. His father who up and abandoned them the moment that things got rough. But Jacob didn't really understand the magnitude of his mistakes, or the time he lost with her in making them until his mother was diagnosed with stage four breast cancer two years ago. She died six months later.

Jacob would always carry the scars of his youth, but he could make peace with scars. No, what kept Jacob up at night, what compelled him to throw lavish events and donate a large portion of the proceeds to MS research, were his mistakes.

"Come now," Dr. Rubenstein said, waving for him to enter. "Come inside. Let's get you situated before Shabbat. Most of the guests will be arriving after services."

Jacob picked up his luggage, following her inside. He had never been in the Rubenstein-Goldblatt home before. Quickly, she ran him through a tour of the premises.

There was the entryway where a large *ketubah*, or marriage contract, was displayed. The kitchen, where sixteen different types of *parve* cookies were piled high. In the living room, a young woman, her head covered by a scarf, was rocking a baby while making conversation with two gray-haired old women wearing pants.

Jacob took in this picture of Jewish life and community. The Jewish art, a mixture of pastels and angles, decorating the walls. The books, both fiction and otherwise, spilling from every end table and shelving unit. But it was the Shabbat dinner table, so lovingly set with a large white tablecloth and two covered challot, *that* made his soul ache.

He so desperately wanted this for himself one day. A home that would welcome visitors. A life where his family came first. A community.

He wondered if one of the twenty-two metal folding chairs arranged around the table would belong to Rachel, but he didn't have the courage to ask aloud.

"You must be exhausted," Dr. Rubenstein said sympathetically.

"I'm used to bouncing around time zones."

"I heard," she said with a wide smile. "You're a big party planner now?"

"That's correct."

"Do you ever get tired of it?"

"What?"

"All the parties? All the noise? It must get disorienting, bouncing around like that. Doesn't leave much time for family." Her eyes wandered down to his left hand. "Or for dating. Are you dating anyone, Jacob?"

Jacob smiled politely. "No."

"Really?" She touched her heart. "I can't believe it. Someone as handsome and successful as you?"

Jacob cracked his jaw, unsure how to answer the question. "I guess I haven't found the right person yet."

"Well..." Dr. Rubenstein linked one arm inside his own. "Maybe we can change that this weekend, hmm? You know, there's a belief in the Jewish culture that every person in the world has a person they are destined to marry. Your *bashert*. A soul God cut and created, designated just for you. Isn't that the loveliest concept?"

"It's beautiful."

"I wonder who your *bashert* will be," she said sweetly, before stopping in front of a guest bedroom. "This is where you'll be staying for Shabbat. Towels are in the closet. Bathroom is to the right. Shabbat timers are in the top nightstand. No pressure to use them, of course. As I tell everyone who enters my home, you are our guest. You do whatever you're comfortable with in terms of observance, okay?"

"Thank you, Dr. Rubenstein."

"Wonderful," she said, turning to leave. "Then come into the kitchen after you're settled. I'll get you a little something to nosh on before services."

Dr. Rubenstein returned to the kitchen as Jacob sat down on the bed, smiling. It was nice to see that some people never changed.

His eyes drifted to the hallway. A few doors down, he could make out the pink walls of an adjacent bedroom. He wondered if it had once belonged to Rachel, then decided firmly that it must have. Who else would have pink walls in the Rubenstein-Goldblatt household? Rachel only had one other sibling, an older brother. Jacob could almost envision the girl he'd once known, with the hot pink shorts and high ponytail, racing through these hallways.

Where was she now?

Over the years, he had tried to find her. Hunted for her on Facebook, and searched for connections on LinkedIn. In a world where everyone had some social media account or profile, Rachel Rubenstein-Goldblatt was a ghost. There was no online imprint of her *anywhere*. It was odd. Even his ninety-one-year-old bubbe had an Instagram account. Though Jacob had no evidence to support it, he got the sense that Rachel avoided visibility on purpose. She had always been good at hiding.

Peeking down the hallway to make sure no one was coming, he headed toward her bedroom. Quietly he pushed open the door. An explosion of pink frill, juxtaposed with shelves stuffed full of books, met his entrance. He couldn't help himself. Glancing behind him and making sure the coast was clear, he stepped inside.

He started with the bookshelves. She must have had hundreds of novels, everything from literary masterpieces to commercial fiction, in both English and Hebrew. She was clearly a reader. But what surprised him most was the vast collection of philosophy books on the bottom two shelves. He ran his fingers over names he barely recognized: Maimonides, Kaplan, Sacks. He recognized Foucault, though.

The only thing that rivaled the number of books in her small bedroom were the photographs. Covering every free inch of wall space were self-made collages of family and friends. Jacob leaned in closer to inspect. There were so many of them—bar mitzvahs and trips to Israel, family vacations and summers at Camp Ahava—a lifetime of love.

Jacob swallowed hard. He had pictures of his life, too. They littered his Instagram and Facebook feeds, garnering thousands of likes. Beautiful women hanging off his shoulders. Buddies toasting their good fortune on the deck of fifty-foot yachts. Jacob knew countless celebrities. But if you asked him to name half the people in his photos, he wouldn't be able to. If you wondered aloud which of those rich and famous folks knew when his mother had died, he would shrug his shoulders and say it didn't matter.

Like most of Instagram, Jacob and his life were fake.

Returning to the kitchen, Jacob found Dr. Rubenstein stirring chicken soup.

"I was so very sorry to hear about your mother," she said.

"Thank you."

She shook her head sadly. "She was such a lovely woman."

Jacob nodded. Even though his mother had passed almost two years ago, he still found it hard to talk about the loss.

Dr. Rubenstein put down the spoon, wiping her hands on a kitchen towel. Perhaps her many years as a *rebbetzin* in a thriving Jewish community had made her doubly sensitive to the way a young man could shift in his loafers or avoid a question, because she broke into a wide smile and changed the topic.

"Do you like potato salad?" she asked, heading for the refrigerator.

"I love potato salad."

"I have three different kinds." She grinned. "One with dill!"

Dill was, apparently, all the rage in an American potato salad.

Dr. Rubenstein began piling up a plate. Jacob sat down to eat, grateful for the opportunity to avoid conversation.

It was his mother's loss that had brought Jacob back to his Jewish roots. Consumed by guilt and sadness over her death, he had decided to take up the ancient tradition of reciting the Mourner's Kaddish. Three times a day, for almost a year, he went to a synagogue in Paris to pray with a minyan. The Jewish community that had only peripherally been a part of his childhood showed up for him in full force.

Still, Jacob was by no means an expert on Jewish religious life. Even after a year of daily services, he struggled with anything beyond basic Hebrew. The unfortunate byproduct of his shoddy Hebrew school education in New York, which ended abruptly when he turned thirteen.

But Jacob valued his Jewish identity. He especially valued the Hanukkah traditions that had been passed down to him from his bubbe. When he thought back to his childhood, and to that one summer spent away from his crumbling home life at Camp Ahava in the Berkshires, he remembered it fondly.

Rabbi Aaron Goldblatt appeared from his study. Checking that his knitted kippah was firmly attached to his head, he began doing final checks. He set the timers on the lights. Turned off the cell phones. Powered down the computers. Shabbat was to be twenty-five hours without technology, without work, without interruption, and Rabbi Goldblatt took his religious obligations seriously.

Dr. Rubenstein responded to her husband's lead in this dance like an expert partner. Without saying a word, she was in movement, turning down the stove, turning on the hot plate, taking off her apron. Finally, she gathered up the guests from the living room and called in the kids from outside. It was time for candle lighting.

Affixing a small lace doily to the top of her head, Dr. Rubenstein struck a match. The three little girls peered over the kitchen counter, sticking their fingers in their mouths. It was beautiful, magical, the type of moment Jacob wanted to preserve in his memory forever…when the front door burst open.

"Wait!" came a shout. "I made it! I'm here!"

In the threshold, out of breath, hair all disheveled, stood Rachel.

6

Rachel stood at the entryway to her parents' house, surprise registering on her face in the form of two raised eyebrows. The six-foot-tall Semitic Adonis that stood in the kitchen had met her frantic arrival with an unwavering gaze.

It was impossible. Unimaginable, really. Jacob Greenberg was smoking hot.

Her lower lip dropped to the floor. Simultaneous feelings of desire and disgust rumbled up in her belly.

Oh, it was too much. The picture of him, perfect and ideal, standing in her family's kitchen. She knew she should look away, pop every one of those quickly rising bubbles, but she couldn't help herself. Her eyes landed on the tip of his smart loafers and began their journey up.

The slim cut of his pleated pants, expensive and dark. The way his white button-down shirt and pressed blue jacket highlighted the V shape of his waist.

It was like he had been crafted from clay, a supernatural being called down from the heavens, constructed with the distinct purpose of driving her wild.

She despised every centimeter of his stylish open collar and ridiculously good looks. She wanted to scoff aloud at his chiseled chin, the disturbingly sexy shape of his gorgeous and prominent nose; instead, her heart only beat faster. Gone was the little boy from Camp Ahava that Rachel remembered. Jacob Greenberg had morphed into a full-grown and totally kosher stud-muffin.

"Rachel!" Dr. Rubenstein said, heading toward the door. "What a lovely surprise."

"Sorry," she mumbled under her breath, removing her red coat in a frantic fumble of buttons. "Am I late?"

Her father looked at his watch. "Two minutes."

Rachel had long ago stopped being *shomer* Shabbat, or observant on the Sabbath. She watched movies, used electricity, traveled. But her father was *machmir*. Strict. He believed that the law given at Mount Sinai and expanded upon by the rabbis was the divine will of God. And you didn't mess around with the divine will of God.

Of course, some prohibitions were simple. They needed no explanation or expansion. The prohibition against lighting a fire on Shabbat, for instance. In order to prevent the Jews from mistakenly lighting a fire *after* Shabbat had started, the rabbis of yore created a rule. Jews were commanded to light their Shabbat candles at *exactly* eighteen minutes before sunset.

"Two minutes." Rachel sighed a tiny wisp of relief. "Great."

"Plenty of time." Dr. Rubenstein beamed, taking her coat.

Moments later, Rachel watched as her mother's eyes landed on the center of her blouse. Oh, Gawd. She had forgotten about her blouse.

"I should—" Rachel pointed down the hall with both thumbs. "I'm just gonna go change."

"One minute," her father informed her.

She waved her acknowledgment, racing off to her bedroom.

Throwing off her shirt, she pulled out a sleek blue sweater from the closet. Then, with only seconds left to spare, she took a few centering breaths.

It didn't matter that Jacob Greenberg was drop-dead gorgeous. Or that she had met him, after all these years, with coffee stains up and down her shirt. Whatever romance there was between her and Jacob Greenberg had ended abruptly at Camp Ahava.

She needed that Matzah Ball ticket. She needed to save her publishing contract. It was the only thing driving her now, and she kept that thought burned into the forefront of her mind as she returned to the kitchen for candle lighting.

Everyone was waiting for her.

Slinking past her father, she squeezed into the semicircle formed around the candlesticks. Her mother lit the candles, covered her eyes, and recited the blessing. A chorus of Shabbat Shalom, kisses and hugs, went around the room. Rachel did the rounds before, finally, landing in front of Jacob.

An awkward moment stretched between them. Normally, and even with a stranger, Rachel would lean in and give the man a welcoming kiss on the cheek. But something about kissing Jacob Greenberg, after everything that had happened between them years ago, didn't feel right.

"Rachel," Dr. Rubenstein said, intervening. "You remember Jacob Greenberg. I believe you both went to Camp Ahava together." Her mother was positively beaming.

"Hello," Jacob said warmly.

Rachel felt her mouth go dry. "Hey."

His smile was beautiful. Like a hero out of one of her romance novels, all dimples and charm. She could imagine waking up to that face every day for the rest of her life.

"Jacob is staying for all of Shabbat," her mother said, glancing at her daughter. "Isn't that wonderful, Rachel? You two will have plenty of time to catch up!"

Dr. Rubenstein flittered off, giving the uneasy couple a quiet moment alone before services.

"You're *shomer* Shabbat?" Rachel asked.

"Oh…" Jacob teetered back and forth on his black loafers. "Not really. I'm trying to be more observant…but, mainly, your mother insisted."

Of course she did.

Like everything in Judaism, Shabbat had an order. Friday night began with candle lighting, after which you left your candles burning in the kitchen or on the table and shuffled along to services.

Upon returning home, there were usually a few minutes of chitchat and getting settled, while the host and hostess prepared the final details of the meal.

Next, there were a series of blessings. *Shalom Alecheim* was sung to greet ministering angels. *Eishet Chayil* was recited as a song of gratitude by husbands to their wives. If there were families present, you included the blessing over children.

Afterward came Kiddush, or the blessing over the wine. Then hand washing, followed by another blessing, followed by *Hamotzi*, or the blessing over the bread. Only after all these things did you actually sit down and eat.

The meal concluded, *finally*, with the singing of festive songs, and *Birkat Hamazon*, or the blessing after the meal. It was at this point that anyone not being hosted for the evening was supposed to take the hint and leave.

If you were being hosted, however, it meant that you stayed for all twenty-five hours of Shabbat. Hosting was usually reserved for out-of-town guests, folks who didn't live close enough to walk to synagogue and thus could avoid one of the prohibitions of driving to shul.

Jacob would sleep down the hall, in her brother's old bedroom. He would wake up in the morning, eat breakfast in her family's kitchen and head to shul with her parents. He would spend the entire afternoon revolving in her general vicinity. Rachel tried to convince herself that this was a good thing.

Upon their return from Shabbat services that evening, Rachel found the house crammed full of people. Widowers with nowhere else to go. Young families with small children in tote. Rachel pushed her way through the crowd, ducking between bodies and avoiding getting pulled into conversations, in order to find her mother.

"Excuse me," she said, avoiding elbows. "Sorry."

When she was a small child, she had loved the busyness of the Jewish calendar. She especially loved the old people who would come to her house on Shabbat and fawn over her, smuggling tiny kosher candies in their pockets and playing tea—utilizing the *kli shlishi*, of course—with her for hours.

But as she got older, she began to resent the life her parents had built. She wanted freedom to explore the world for herself, the option to go to the mall with friends on Saturdays. *She wanted to try a cheeseburger.* Mainly, she grew tired of feeling like yet another employee of the synagogue. The rabbinic family came as a unit, after all.

Rachel found her mother in the kitchen, mismatched oven mitts on her hands, pulling a kugel out of the oven.

"Ema," Rachel said, grabbing a dish towel. "Let me help you."

"Absolutely not," Dr. Rubenstein yanked the kugel away. "Go sit down and rest."

"But—"

"Go sit down and rest!" she said, fixing her gaze on her daughter.

Rachel nodded. She knew what her mother was saying. Rachel had already done enough today. She had gotten dressed and fixed her hair. Taken the train out to her childhood home on Long Island. Plus, there had been that whole walk-to-shul thing and an hour's worth of standing up and sitting down during services. Now, there would be a drawn-out dinner with lots of conversation that could easily last for hours. Her mother didn't even know about the long day she'd had prior to coming out here.

Rachel found a quiet spot on one of the couches and collapsed into the soft cushions. Grateful for the respite, she took a careful accounting of how she was feeling. She was tired, but there was none of that bone-crushing fatigue that made some days unbearable. No doubt she would crash soon, though. One of the hallmarks of chronic fatigue syndrome was something called PEM, or post-exertional malaise.

PEM meant that within twenty-four to forty-eight hours of physical or mental exertion, the symptoms of her disease would get worse. For Rachel, this meant the fatigue would go from manageable to intolerable. Her body would explode in a barrage of weirdo flu-like symptoms. Sore throats. Low-grade fevers. Night sweats. Aching joints and migraines.

There was no way to know how long these crashes would last. It could be hours, days, weeks…or even years. The only way to avoid the flare-ups was through a very unscientific method of pacing oneself and rest.

The problem was, of course, that Rachel was *awful* at pacing herself or resting.

On good days, she pushed even harder. On bad days, she still pushed…usually making herself way worse in the process. She wanted what so many others had, what everyone standing around her parents Shabbat table seemed to take for granted. She wanted normalcy. She wanted a career and a family and the ability to walk around a museum for two hours without her body punishing her for it.

But Rachel couldn't allow herself to think about the future. It was too scary and gray, too terribly overwhelming. She had learned to survive by just focusing on the day. Focusing all her energy on one task, one goal, and pouring everything she had into it.

Rachel scanned the living room. Most of the guests were from her father's synagogue. They were people she had grown up with. Folks she had sat beside in the pews while she played with toys as a toddler. They were as intimate as any family.

There was Tillie Stein, a widower who split her time between New York and Florida. There was Shana Eisenberg, a girl she had gone to Jewish day school with who now taught math at that same school, and was happily married with three little girls of her own.

There was Maxwell Cohen, a familiar figure in the Rubenstein-Goldblatt home, as he was the current president of the synagogue. He spent his time before dinner huddled in a tightly formed circle, trying to convince members that it was time to remodel the synagogue.

The only interloper among them was Jacob Greenberg. It was impossible to ignore him. At six feet tall, he stood out among the crowd of shrunken Jewish grandmothers that surrounded him. All of whom, with their gray hair and brightly colored jewelry, oohed and aahed over Jacob as if he were a freshly cooked brisket straight out of the oven.

"Oh, Jacob...it must be so exciting living in Paris!"

"Are you really the creator of the Matzah Ball Max?"

"But you're so tall!"

"You know, Jacob... I have a daughter in Boca."

It was over-the-top, honestly. Their fawning. Their sycophantic smiles and slithering. Rachel tried not to vomit.

Alas, the tractate on Jewish Mating & Dating in New York was clear. If a successful, good-looking and single Jewish man arrived to your Shabbat dinner, then every Jewish mother in a ten-mile radius was *muad* to find him. Jewish mothers and goring ox shared many similarities that way. (*Long Island Talmud*, The First Date 23b–24a.)

Rachel found herself in a conundrum. She needed to talk to Jacob, to convince him to give her a ticket to his sold-out

Matzah Ball. But with every Jewish mother in the room vying for his attention, she had no idea how to pull him away. She needed an expert.

Rachel's eyes drifted over to her mother, now floating through the living room, passing out tiny blue prayer books. In the gladiator ring of Jewish mating and dating in New York, no one could hold a shield against the carefully timed swings of Dr. Rubenstein.

"Ema," Rachel whispered, calling her over.

"Everything okay, darling?" Dr. Rubenstein asked.

"I need your help with something."

"My help?"

"I need you to make sure I get seated next to Jacob Greenberg at dinner."

Dr. Rubenstein beamed. "I told you to give the man a second chance."

"I'll give him eight chances." Rachel smirked. Dr. Rubenstein floated off, and her father appeared, holding a Kiddush cup.

Everyone took their cue, quieting down and gathering around him in a circle. The many blessings and songs were sung. The many hands were washed. The gold-and-white cloth covering the two braided challot was pulled away. Rabbi Aaron Goldblatt said the *Hamotzi*, the blessing over the bread, and finally, it was time to eat.

The room made a mad dash for the best seats. Everyone wanted to be at the head of the table, near Rabbi Goldblatt, where they could listen to his brilliant musing on Jewish law, life and community.

As for Jacob, Rachel knew exactly where her mother would seat them. Right in the center of the table, near the half-drunk bottle of red wine and soon-to-be destroyed challot, where Dr. Rubenstein could keep an eye on their conversation.

"Oh, Jacob," Dr. Rubenstein called out, waving the young man over. "Why don't you sit right here, hmm?" She pulled out a chair, then quickly elbowed through the crowd of old ladies to find the spot right across from Jacob. "And, Rachel, darling, why don't you sit over here, right across from Jacob. That way, you two will have a chance to catch up after all these years."

Rachel slid down in the seat across from Jacob and offered him a nervous smile. Jacob settled into his seat, confident and poised, before gracefully laying his napkin across one knee. An awkward silence fell between them.

"You look good, Rachel."

"Thank you," she said quickly, looking up from her lap. "You, too."

Jacob nodded.

Rachel nodded.

More awkward silence followed.

"So," he said, tapping his fingers on the white tablecloth. "What have you been up to all these years?"

"I'm a writer."

"A writer?" he asked curiously.

"Well, writing and editing," she explained. "I went to college for it. Nothing that interesting."

"Anything I would know?"

"Probably not," Rachel said, downplaying her career. "It's mainly freelance stuff."

"Like articles?"

"Kind of."

"Books?"

"No," Rachel lied. "Definitely not books."

"Do you work for a specific company?"

"Sometimes."

"I'm sorry," Jacob said, shaking his head. "I'm still not entirely sure what you do for a living."

"I told you already," Rachel said, growing frustrated. "It's no big deal."

His smile faded, injury spreading across his face. Rachel was screwing this up. Royally.

Granted, her lack of social aptitude wasn't entirely her fault. She had spent most of her life as the rabbi's daughter, living in the fishbowl, constantly under scrutiny. Her adult life had only followed this trajectory.

But, unlike everyone else at the table, Rachel couldn't talk about her career. And the other major part of her life was also off the table—she especially couldn't talk about her daily struggles with chronic illness. It wasn't just that people didn't want to talk about something depressing around a dinner table. It was her illness, specifically. That stupid name, *chronic fatigue syndrome*, which compounded her suffering with a side order of shame.

It suggested that Rachel was a malingerer, that her disease was not serious and therefore did not have serious consequences. It implied that her daily struggles were nothing more than a state of being *tired*, something easily fixed with a long nap and a strong cup of coffee. None of which was true, of course. ME/CFS had determined the course of Rachel's life since she had first fallen ill at eighteen. It had robbed her of every aspect of normalcy, and it hurt like hell to have someone casually question the reality of her lived experience.

"I'm sorry," Jacob said. "I didn't mean to pry."

"You're not." Rachel looked away from him. "I just…it's Shabbat. I don't want to talk about work on Shabbat."

"Okay," Jacob said, agreeing solemnly. "Well, do you have any pets?"

"No."

"A plant?"

Rachel shrugged. "I killed a bonsai tree once."

"Hmm." He frowned.

"What?"

"You just don't strike me as a murderer."

In spite of herself, Rachel laughed.

Jacob met her eyes across the table. They were the same eyes she remembered. Kind and gentle. Except now, they had a crinkle at the edges that highlighted his age. Rachel couldn't help herself. Her mind wandered back to the summer they'd spent together.

It wasn't all bad.

She thought back to the first time he'd pushed her into the lake. She had been so angry at him. She tried so hard to be good, after all—and Jacob's attack had felt totally unnecessary and completely unwarranted. She remembered lying on the bottom bunk of her bed, listening to Leah Abraham snoring, dreaming up every form of his demise.

His act demanded swift retaliation.

Two nights later, while everyone in Camp Ahava was sleeping, Rachel snuck out. She slunk through bushes and darkness, going beyond the lake that separated the boys' and girls' cabins, making her way toward 7B. After pushing the screen door open, she found Jacob's sneakers. And then, with hands shaking and heart racing, she dumped two tubes full of toothpaste into his shoes.

Dropping the evidence of her crime in the garbage outside the door, Rachel took off. The wind whipping at her cheeks, her brown hair coming loose in messy strands around her high ponytail. For the first time in her life, no one was watching. The humid air that often accompanied her summers at Camp Ahava no longer felt stifling.

She was free.

Over the next two weeks, Rachel had given in to her newly discovered dark side. If Jacob stole her towel after morning swim, she replaced his shampoo with ketchup. When her favorite pink water bottle went missing, she stole his underwear, leaving it to wave like a flag outside the front door of girls bunk 7G. With each salacious act he pursued, she upped the ante. Until one day, during movie night, the same boy who had pushed her into the lake...reached over and took her hand.

And she let him.

The irony being, of course, that continuing the prank war had been her idea.

No one could know about their secret love. It wasn't just that the whole world had a certain expectation of her, it was the fear of garnering a reputation. Everyone knew which girls snuck out to meet which boys. In her tight-knit Jewish community—where you saw the same familiar faces throughout summer camp, college, graduate school and life—your reputation could follow you into adulthood. She, especially, didn't want her parents to find out.

The pranks had been a front for their hand-holding and sneaking off together. A way to leave messages, via ketchup and toothpaste, that no one would ever suspect.

The only person who ever found out was Mickey. But only because he knew Rachel, and confronted her about *all the time* she was spending with *stupid* Jacob Greenberg instead of him.

Jacob gave her freedom. He never judged her for her choices, never asked her to be someone else. He allowed her to escape from the protective, somewhat suffocating bubble that came with being the daughter of Rabbi Aaron Goldblatt. When Jacob was around, Rachel felt brave.

It was hard to believe, falling into his warm brown eyes now, how wrong she had been about him. That was the problem with their game. At some point, Rachel stopped playing...and Jacob never did.

She had to remember that about him. Hold the thought in her mind, as much as she needed that Matzah Ball ticket. He was a prankster. He had tricked her into falling in love, turned her first kiss into a giant Camp Ahava prank. He was not someone who could be trusted.

"So what about you?" Rachel asked.

"Me?"

"Do you have any pets?"

"I have a cat. *Paree.*"

Rachel stopped eating. "You named your cat Paris?"

"What's wrong with Paris?"

"I don't know." Rachel shrugged. "Just seems a little on the nose."

Jacob laughed, a real and hearty laugh that made his whole face turn red. "Actually," he said, his voice softer, "my mother named him."

Rachel didn't understand. "You let your mom name your cat?"

"No, I…" Jacob stammered, getting flustered. "I inherited the cat. From her. After she died."

"Oh." Rachel bit her lower lip. *Foot meet mouth.*

She had heard about Jacob's mother through the Jewish grapevine, and Dr. Rubenstein, who had mentioned it once in passing, after her name wound up in the *Yizkor Book of Remembrance* on Yom Kippur. Other than that, and a little *l'shon hara*, or gossip, over Shabbat dinners with friends from Camp Ahava, she didn't know anything about his life. Jacob had left New York City the way he had arrived to Camp Ahava that summer, a complete and total mystery.

But Rachel wasn't heartless. Even though he was her summer camp archenemy, and she was only talking to the man in order to snag a ticket to his Matzah Ball, she still felt sympathy for him. As overinvolved as her own mother could be, Rachel couldn't imagine life without her. Losing her mom would be like tearing her heart from her chest.

"I'm sorry," Rachel said genuinely.

Jacob swallowed hard. "Thank you."

As dinner progressed, Rachel kept her eyes and ears peeled for an opportunity to ask about that ticket. But, between the gefilte fish and chicken soup, she couldn't get a word in edgewise. The handsome and successful entrepreneur, newly returned home from France, was the most popular person in the room.

"So, Jacob," Maxwell Cohen said, smiling from the end of the table. "Let me ask you a question. How does a young man like yourself—a man who seems smart, and capable, and who's clearly got a good thing going—go from throwing events like Launchella and Sunburn...to hosting a Matzah Ball?"

"Well," Jacob said, commanding the room, "it's quite a long story. But about two years ago, I was partaking in the great Jewish tradition of eating Chinese food on Christmas."

The room chuckled in acknowledgment before falling quiet once again beneath his sway.

Rachel panned over the faces of the guests. It was amazing how Jacob could do that. Command everyone with his presence. Like he was Moses himself, dragging the children of Israel around a desert for forty years, telling everyone they were heading for the Promised Land, when they were actually freaking lost. Rachel couldn't help but be both annoyed, and impressed.

"Normally," Jacob continued, "I would be eating it with my mother, but that year, unfortunately...it was just me and a carton of chicken lo mein. Anyway, I was thinking about how for Jews, Christmas can feel kind of lonely. All your non-Jewish friends off celebrating with their families. Everyone else participating in this great tradition. I began to wonder if there was a way I could resolve this. Could I put on an event of some kind, huge and grand, but also totally Jewish?"

He let a long and dramatic pause float through the air.

"Bam," Jacob said, smacking the table, sending everybody's wineglass shaking. "I got the idea. I wanted to throw a Matzah Ball. Not just any Matzah Ball, either—but the biggest and most high-end Matzah Ball the world had ever seen. The Matzah Ball Max. A Jewish music festival to rival the likes of any party I had created previously. I called up my partner right then and there and told him what I was thinking."

"And your partner thought this was a good idea?" Dr. Rubenstein asked.

Jacob shook his head. "My partner thought I was crazy!" The room erupted in laughter. "Remember, we had made most of our money hosting high-end parties on islands with yachts, designed to attract influencers. This was something…well, something completely different. Everybody tried to talk me out of it, honestly. But it was my company, and ultimately, my choice. I wanted to throw my name behind it."

"And the response…" Rabbi Goldblatt perked up at the end of the table. "The response to this initiative has been good?"

"Better than good," Jacob said. "Outstanding, in fact. We opened ticket sales almost a year ago, and we sold out in under twenty minutes. People are coming in from all over the world to attend. Celebrities. Journalists. Political leaders. Providing everything goes according to plan, it should be the hottest Hanukkah event of the century."

"And there really are no more tickets left?" Maxwell asked.

"Unfortunately, no," Jacob explained. "We have quotas for these types of events. Number limits we can't exceed without risking the health and safety of our attendees. At this late stage of the game, all the tickets we could give out have either been sold or are on reserve. I'm afraid the most I can do for anyone now is put them on a waiting list."

"How long is the waiting list?" Rachel asked.

"About three thousand people."

"Three thousand people!" Rachel could feel her heart sinking inside her chest. This was not good news, at all.

Still, she was not the type to give up on a dream. Gathering her courage, she decided to make her move.

"But what if someone really needed a ticket?" she asked, trying not to sound completely desperate. "Surely, as the creator, you must be able to pull some strings?"

"Well, it's funny you should mention that, Rachel," Jacob

said, rising to his feet. "Because I do have two tickets, stashed away, for some very special people. If I could have everyone's attention for a few moments..."

Rachel squinted, confused. People normally didn't make speeches at Shabbat dinner, but Jacob Greenberg was all confidence. Moving to the center of the room, Jacob picked up his glass of red wine and lifted it into the air.

"First off," Jacob said, commanding his audience, "I want to thank Dr. Rubenstein and Rabbi Goldblatt for hosting me this Shabbat. As most of you probably know by now, I've been away from New York for some time, and my friends here are few. To that effect, this is certainly much nicer, and far more familiar, than eating cold kosher food alone somewhere..."

Dr. Rubenstein smiled. "It's our pleasure, Jacob."

"Thank you," Jacob said. "I hope that should you ever have cause to visit Paris, I can extend the same invitation to you."

"We would like that very much," Rabbi Goldblatt said.

Jacob nodded. "I also need to ask for your forgiveness. You see, when I contacted you both last week, I wasn't just looking for one of your famed Shabbat dinners or inspirational morning sermons. Believe it or not, I came here with an ulterior motive..."

"Jacob!" Dr. Rubenstein jested. "How scandalous."

"Rabbi Goldblatt, Dr. Rubenstein," Jacob said, lifting his wineglass higher. "I think everyone can agree that when it comes to contributions to the Jewish community, no one holds a candle to you. Whether through good deeds, charitable works, or brilliant sermons, you two have consistently modeled your values for others. For this reason, it is both my honor and my pleasure to offer you the last two tickets to the Matzah Ball, and ask if you would light the candles and say the final blessing on the eighth night."

Rabbi Goldblatt rose to shake Jacob's hand. Dr. Rubenstein squeezed her way past the metal folding chairs, embracing the young entrepreneur in a warm hug. The whole room sparked with energy and excitement, except for Rachel. Rachel stared down at her half-eaten bowl of chicken soup and suddenly felt nauseated.

Her life, like her publishing contract, was over.

7

With the final recitation of *Birkat Hamazon,* the blessing over the meal, the last of the guests trickled from the living room and returned home. With an early morning ahead of him at shul, Rabbi Goldblatt said good-night and retired to his bedroom.

Jacob remained in the dining room, helping Dr. Rubenstein put away dishes. Wearing a smock, Rachel stood quietly in the kitchen, rinsing plates mindlessly, and stared out a window. It was hard to believe she was the same little girl who had broken his heart.

The last time he had seen Rachel was when they were twelve years old. It was down by the lake, long after lights-out, when the only people up were the kitchen staff, blasting the radio while they finished cleaning dishes. "Crazy in Love" by Beyoncé drifting over the water.

Back then, she was a skinny girl in braces. An adolescent nowhere near womanhood, with a penchant for hot pink shorts and high ponytails. He had a picture of the two of them embedded in his mind from that night. The way she looked, spitting cherry bubblegum into her hand, telling him she was ready. The cheesy way he tried to be suave, pointing out stars and constellations in an effort to wrap an arm around her, pulling her close.

God, he was nervous back then. He felt the same way now. On edge. Antsy. A thousand tiny bubbles floating up from his feet into his chest.

Rachel Rubenstein-Goldblatt was no longer skinny. The sneakers and banged-up knees he remembered had been replaced by voluminous curves and impractical shoes. But the eyes were the same. Brown, with little flecks of gold inside, like they were holding some secret treasure. He would recognize those eyes anywhere.

"Here you go," Jacob said, handing her a plate.

Wordlessly, she took it from him.

What had happened between them at dinner? Jacob couldn't be certain, though he knew something had shifted inside her. Her face was a mask. Her demeanor stone. She had shut herself down, stopped engaging.

He so desperately wanted to talk to her. To use the quiet that had finally appeared in the Rubenstein-Goldblatt household, to catch up with her again after all these years, maybe even ask her about what the hell happened between them...but she looked tired. Lovely, of course, but even without arriving to Shabbat dinner with stains on her blouse, it was clear she'd had a rough day.

And yet here she was tending to other people's needs rather than her own.

It was so much like the Rachel Rubenstein-Goldblatt he remembered from summer camp. The way she always worried about others, offering up her water bottle when some camper forgot to trudge along with their own. The way she sacrificed herself constantly—choosing to stay behind after morning minyan, picking up siddurs—instead of racing off to breakfast with everyone else. She was so incredibly thoughtful. And sensitive.

And good. And then—the thought sparked his imagination once again—she also had this side that was so perfectly naughty.

She didn't show it to most people. But it was there. Like those flecks of gold in her eyes, and the hints of red in her brown hair. If you looked at her long enough, cared enough to really notice, she would show you the truth of who she was.

In the meantime, however, he just wanted to make her life easier. She was still his first love, after all. Even if she did completely break his heart, stomp all over his trust, and compound the abandonment of his father with her cruel and unrelenting silence, he owed her something. Grabbing an apron off a hook on the wall and putting it on, he moved to rectify the situation.

"Let me do that," Jacob said.

Rachel returned from wherever she was. "What?"

"You look tired." Jacob smiled gently before attempting to make a joke. "And I look amazing in an apron."

She didn't even crack a smile. "I'm fine."

Rachel continued washing dishes. Jacob chewed on his lower lip, his frustration with her growing. There she went again, shutting him down. It was disconcerting, really, the way she completely ignored him. How she gazed out the window, not even blinking, like he wasn't standing centimeters away from her. It didn't make any sense. But he couldn't shake the feeling that she was completely and totally pissed off at him about something.

"Um, Rachel…" Jacob said carefully. "Is everything okay?"

"Fine."

"Because if I've done something to upset you—"

She tossed a dish into the drying rack, letting it clatter.

Jacob cracked his jaw. Rachel was, obviously, not fine.

In truth, her attitude was beginning to bug him. It wasn't just the way she was treating him, like he had no more value in this world than a piece of gum stuck to the bottom of her shoe. It was her silence. Jacob hated being ignored like that. It reminded him of his father.

Anyway, her open hostility toward him made no sense. If anyone had a right to be angry about what had happened at Camp Ahava, to still hold grudges after all these years, it was him. Rachel was the one who had stood him up at final dance, after all.

"Ema," Rachel said, finishing the last plate. "Is there anything else you need me to do?"

"No, honey. You get some sleep."

Rachel took off her apron. Kissing her mother good-night, she headed for her bedroom.

Watching the door shut behind her, Jacob recognized the same crumpling feeling he had felt standing alone on a dance floor, a bouquet of wildflowers in his hand. The painful realization that Rachel—his first love, his first kiss—had abandoned him. It hurt almost as much as the unanswered phone calls and letters that had followed.

It was terrible to be abandoned by the people you loved. Even worse when it happened repeatedly. Maybe there was something broken inside Jacob. Some great flaw that Rachel and his father had seen, which Dr. Rubenstein, in all her warmth and kindness, thankfully didn't.

"Everyone seems to have disappeared on us," Jacob said.

Dr. Rubenstein glanced up from the stack of *benchers* she was organizing. "Don't take it personally. Aaron simply has to be up early in the morning for shul. But we've had a wonderful time with you this evening, and we're both so honored to be able to attend your Matzah Ball."

"You make a good team."

Dr. Rubenstein grinned. "Don't we?"

Before this evening, he had never met the famous Rabbi Goldblatt. But it struck Jacob how different Dr. Rubenstein was from her husband. She could sashay around a room, a sweet potato kugel in one hand and a bottle of kosher wine in the other, treating every guest like an honored visitor. Her friendliness was contagious.

Rabbi Aaron Goldblatt was the opposite. A scholarly type, known for his uplifting sermons. He was far more comfortable with hours spent locked in his study than offering someone a hug. It blew Jacob's mind that two people, so clearly opposite from one another, could ever make a marriage work. But they did. They complemented each other perfectly, two halves of one heart, designated by the heavens. *Bashert*.

Jacob wanted what they had one day.

"And Rachel?" Jacob asked nervously.

"What about Rachel?" Dr. Rubenstein asked curiously.

Jacob rubbed the back of his neck. "She barely talked to me at dinner."

Dr. Rubenstein sighed heavily. "Rachel has always been more like her father, I'm afraid. But don't judge her too harshly. She has a good heart, and good intentions, even when *terribly* misguided. We should have given her…more room to grow."

Jacob noted a tinge of regret in her voice. "You seem like perfect parents to me."

"Oh, Jacob," Dr. Rubenstein said, cupping his cheek with her hand. "No one is perfect. Least of all me."

Dr. Rubenstein gave Jacob one last hug before departing. Jacob remained in the kitchen, back pressed up against the sink. Even though it was nearing midnight and the entire house had scurried off to bed, he dreaded returning to the guest room Dr. Rubenstein had arranged for him. He could blame jet lag, but Jacob was used to shuffling between time zones. In reality, he was searching for something to do.

Suddenly, the Shabbat timer on the living room and kitchen lights switched off and Jacob was plunged into darkness. With no other options left, he retired to the guest room.

Sitting down on the bed, Jacob reached for his carry-on bag and pulled out his phone. He had an instinct to text Shmuel, to let him know that things had progressed smoothly. Rabbi Goldblatt had agreed to recite the blessing and light the eighth candle at the Matzah Ball. Their one-of-a-kind Hanukkah party would now have the blessing of a world-famous rabbi. It was good news, all around.

On second thought Jacob decided against it. Shmuel took the laws of Shabbat seriously. Unless the Moshiach himself was arriving with trumpets blaring, he would not want to be bothered. Even then, it was iffy.

Besides, Jacob was trying to be more observant. You weren't supposed to use your phone on Shabbat. You weren't supposed to watch TV or touch the light switch. All of these things—though Jacob couldn't exactly explain how—were considered work. The silence that could fall over a house during a Shabbat was magical. The problem was, Jacob hated the quiet.

It had been that way ever since he was a child. At least when there was noise—his father storming out of the house, his mother crying herself to sleep—he could convince himself that his tiny little world in New York City would remain the same. Nobody was pulling him out of school or moving him across the Atlantic.

When it was quiet, when his bubbe closed the door to his bedroom and had long talks into the night with his mom about *facing reality*, that's when things went bad. For Jacob, like many children of divorce, a quiet night always meant terrible news in the morning.

Was it any wonder then that he had filled up his life with parties?

Noise. Busyness. Activity. That's how Jacob handled his emotions. Over the years, this form of self-prescribed therapy had worked for him. He kept his schedule full, never slowing down, existing in a firestorm of activity. Then his mother died, and he was staring at a life where every second was filled and none of it had meaning.

The things he missed now, he'd never expected to miss. He missed the cards she sent on his birthday. He missed the way her voice sounded on late-night phone calls—she could never remember what time zone he was in. He missed sitting in her room, the sound of her ventilator moving up and down, on their final days together. And though he could barely remember a time when she was healthy, when she was normal, she was still his mom.

He would not have traded her for all the healthy moms in the world.

Jacob lay down on the bed and tried to breathe through his discomfort. At least in Paris he could go for a walk. Drown himself in the lights and noise of Paris. In the Rubenstein-Goldblatt household, he was stuck. There was nowhere to escape the silence. He needed something to distract him.

He decided to freshen up. It had been a long flight from Paris. Plus, he could smell the chicken soup and kugel from dinner embedded in his skin. Heading into the hallway, he found the linen closet. Next to it, the door to Rachel's room was closed.

He wondered what she was doing in there. He even thought about knocking, seeing if she was still up. Like with Shmuel, he quickly realized it was a terrible idea. Rachel was clearly uninterested in him. Plus, it was creepy, standing outside her room listening for breathing. Quickly he moved away from the door.

Finding the bathroom, Jacob began getting undressed. Much like her old bedroom, this bathroom clearly remained Rachel's domain. A dozen different types of moisturizers and scented soaps lined the sink.

It was interesting. Many parents reclaimed their children's rooms and the extra space in the house the moment their adult children flew the nest. Rachel's family was the opposite. It was still *her* room from childhood. *Her* bathroom. Even though they clearly needed the space for out-of-town visitors, their beloved daughter always took first dibs.

He wondered what it would be like having parents who so clearly wanted you to come visit. Everything designed as an open invitation to come home.

Jacob leaned into the moisturizers and carefully pulled one out from among the mess. Bringing it to his nose, he tried to find her scent. Apple and buttercream, with tiny hints of honey. It reminded him of Rosh Hashanah. He went to put it back, focusing his attention on a green bottle with aloe, when the door to the bathroom came flying open.

Moisturizer bottles went crashing to the floor.

"Oh, my Gawd!" Rachel said, covering her eyes with one hand. "What are you doing?"

"Showering," Jacob said.

"On Shabbat?"

He was confused. "Am I not supposed to shower on Shabbat?"

"I mean, you *can*. It's a thing with the water heater, but…can you put on a shirt or something?"

Jacob obeyed, reaching for his sweater to throw it back on. But the sound of Rachel screaming, combined with the crashing of two dozen moisturizer bottles, must have jolted the house awake. Seconds later, the door at the end of the hall creaked open.

"Oh, no," Rachel said, and pushed him inside the bathroom.

Jacob fell back onto the toilet seat. "What the—"

"Sheket," she said, and put one finger to her mouth.

Jacob had no idea what was going on. The woman who had barely spoken to him at dinner had suddenly morphed into someone else entirely. With both hands pressed up against his naked chest, Rachel used her foot to close the door and flipped off the light switch.

"Are you out of your mind?" Jacob asked.

"I don't want my mother knowing about this," Rachel whispered.

"About what?" he asked, still totally confused.

"This!" she said, whispering through the blackness. "You know what a honey badger is?"

"Yes."

"Well, if you make any noise, I will shove a honey badger down your throat."

Rachel stared at the door and listened for footsteps. Dr. Rubenstein was at the door, hovering, like a helicopter on police patrol. Through the pitch-black darkness, he listened to Rachel breathe. *In and out. In and out.* Jacob couldn't help thinking about their first kiss.

The footsteps diminished down the hallway. With silence once again falling over the household, Rachel released Jacob from her grip, flipping the light back on.

Jacob was flabbergasted. "You—you touched the light?"

"So?" Rachel squinted in his direction. "What are you, the Shabbat police?"

"I just didn't expect that."

"Yeah, well," Rachel said, rolling her eyes, "I live to subvert your expectations."

Jacob took a careful accounting of the woman standing across from him. The fierceness in her demeanor did not match the pink footie pajamas she was wearing. He couldn't help wondering if she had a secret identical twin stashed in an attic somewhere, someone they only let out at night.

"I need to talk to you," she said, crossing her arms against her chest. "It's important."

"Considering you have me trapped, half-naked, in the bathroom, I'm all ears."

Rachel huffed out the words. "I need a ticket to the Matzah Ball."

"*What?*" Jacob laughed. "You can't be serious."

"Jacob!" She stomped her foot on the fuzzy pink mat. "I'm serious, I need a freaking ticket to your Matzah Ball."

Jacob was floored into silence. She *was* serious. Who was Rachel Rubenstein-Goldblatt? The thought tumbled inside him like laundry.

"Tell me why," he demanded.

"What?" she said, stepping back.

"Tell me why you need a ticket to the Matzah Ball so badly?"

He could see her thinking, processing his request. "My parents are old," she said finally. "And *very* frail. I need to go to the Matzah Ball to help them, to make sure they don't trip, or hurt themselves."

"Really?" he deadpanned.

"New York can be *very* dangerous for the elderly. Last time my father was there he almost got mugged, by a gang…from the circus."

"Your father," he repeated carefully, "almost got mugged by a gang from the circus?"

"My parents don't really like to talk about it."

"Seriously, Rachel—"

"All right," she snapped back at him. "Fine. I'll tell you the truth." He was waiting with bated breath. "I can't tell you, okay?"

"You are unbelievable," Jacob said, rising to leave.

"Jacob! Please." She grabbed his hand, forcing him to stay. "I need a ticket. I know it doesn't make sense. I know I sound completely bonkers. But my entire life is on the line right now, and you're the only person who can help. If I ever meant anything to you at all…help me get a ticket to the Matzah Ball."

Jacob felt his stomach dip. The feel of her hand, the memory of those hazy Shabbat afternoons together came flooding back to him. He had loved her once—in that innocent, first-love sort of way—the feeling overtaking him completely. He floated back to their first kiss, and then standing on the dance floor alone.

A dual instinct rose up inside of him. He had a Matzah Ball to organize. He didn't have time for love or romance. Plus, Rachel Rubenstein-Goldblatt had already broken his heart once. But staring into those familiar brown eyes, a thought arose from deep within him. A lesson, learned from his mother, sitting there upon his heart. Life was too short to waste a second chance.

"I can't give you a ticket," Jacob said gently. Honestly. "Like I explained at dinner, we're completely sold out. As much as I would like to help you, we have limits on numbers, for health and fire codes, for a reason. Letting people in at the last minute could get us into trouble, and could endanger people. All that being said, I do have another option for you. We reserve tickets for volunteers. If you'd be willing to help us out over the next week, we have a space open for one more volunteer."

"A volunteer?"

"You give me eight days of your time." Jacob met her eyes directly. "You volunteer for the Matzah Ball, and, providing you do a good job, you can have a ticket."

8

Rachel tiptoed back to her bedroom. Quiet as a church mouse, she shut the door behind her, leaning her head against the wood paneling. Despite the victory, she did not feel triumphant. Her anxiety was spiraling, reaching endemic proportions.

Eight days with Jacob Greenberg. Eight days volunteering full-time with chronic fatigue syndrome.

There weren't enough drugs in the world to get her through this.

Closing her eyes, she balled up her fists at her side. There it was again. That chronic illness calculator in her brain. Today had been a good day. Rachel had sprinted through New York, commuted to Long Island, attended Shabbat dinner. She actually didn't feel completely terrible. But it had been a good day precisely because she had conserved three days' worth of energy—thanks be to Mickey—before today by remaining in her home and resting. She would not have that luxury volunteering in setting up the Matzah Ball.

Crawling back into bed, she was determined to focus on the

positive. She had a ticket to the Matzah Ball. Better yet, she had eight full days of Hanukkah research and inspiration ahead of her. She would figure out the rest.

Rachel heard the water turn on in the bathroom. Jacob was showering. In the same shower she still used when she stayed over at her parents' house.

Oh, how she wished her parents' house was bigger. If only her mother had seen fit to buy a house with three full bathrooms thirty-five years ago. But property was expensive on Long Island, and her *ema* had fallen in love with the expansive dining room, close to the synagogue, where she could spend the rest of her natural life welcoming visitors.

Now Rachel suffered. Groaning aloud, she dug her head beneath the pillow. The water *pinged* and *dinged* in the distance, hitting tiles, hitting skin, stoking her already overactive imagination.

The last thing Rachel wanted to do was think about sexy Jacob—naked and wet—rubbing *her* soap all over *his* junk. She couldn't help herself. Her mind wandered. The memory of his naked chest, those perfect pectoral muscles flexing beneath her hands, arose in her imagination. The possibility of them going further, kissing one more time...

She stopped herself right there.

She needed something to take her mind off the obvious. Rachel reached for her purse.

Not wanting to arouse suspicion, she refrained from turning on the light, using her hands to guide her journey. Feeling through her bag, she pushed her fingers past a wallet, notebook and compact before finally finding her cell phone. *Jackpot.* She pulled the pink covers all the way above her head.

Beneath the safety of her sheets, she breathed deeply. She felt like the worst daughter in the world. It would have been bad enough disrespecting her parents and their belief by using her phone on Shabbat. Worse, though, she was going to use her phone on Shabbat…to watch Christmas movies.

Alas, this was the problem with addiction.

Rachel was powerless when it came to Santa.

She had asked her father about it once. After she had signed her first contract with Romance House. She had come home, fully expecting to sit her parents and brother, who was also a rabbi, down and tell them the truth.

Then, during Shabbat dinner, Rachel had made a mistake. She asked her father about the halacha, or Jewish religious law, surrounding someone like Irving Berlin, the Jewish composer who wrote Christmas music. Her brilliant rabbinic father, as he was wont to do, went on a whole long diatribe.

Judaism had survived thousands of years thanks to an almost obsessive rejection of assimilation. Rachel's version of Judaism, the kind she had been raised with, allowed her to exist somewhere in the middle. She was Jewish *and* American.

But there was always this fear lingering in the background of that straddling. It was a fear that became especially palpable after the Holocaust. That Judaism, and the survival of the Jewish people, was on a slippery slope. That the continuity of their faith and their peoplehood could be lost as simply as the placement of Christmas garland upon a mantel.

Was it a fair fear? Rachel had no idea. She lived in a Jewish world, with Jewish friends, in a tight-knit Jewish community. It was still enough of an anxiety for her parents that Christmas books—like Christmas songs, Christmas movies and even Hanukkah decor that mimicked Christmas styling—were forbidden in her house growing up.

Powering on her phone, Rachel found her Hallmark Movie app. Opening it up, her guilt floated away. All her Christmas darlings were there. She melted into one of her favorites. A movie about a retired pianist sent to educate the daughter of a grumpy prince.

She loved this story specifically because it was just so darn unrealistic. The grumpy prince, mourning the death of his first wife. The snarky daughter who brings them all together during a Christmas Ball. She adored it all. The angels, disguised as friends, pushing you toward your destiny. The Christmas prince starting out as your enemy before he sweeps you off your feet.

Rachel wanted a prince. She wanted somebody to appear out of nowhere and make her believe in happy endings. She dreamed of a perfect little snow globe world where she was never sick, and even if she was, someone else would do the laundry.

It seemed so simple, really.

The shower at the end of the hall turned off. Rachel hit Pause on her movie, listening for footsteps. How ironic, she thought, that she had first developed her love of Christmas after that disastrous summer with Jacob.

The details of what happened were insignificant compared to where they eventually led, but Rachel had returned home from camp that summer a jumble of confused tween feelings.

Her mother, using her background as a reproductive endocrinologist, had tried to help. Bought her countless books with titles like *What's Happening to my Body* and *It's Totally Normal.* Pulled out two giant felt genitalia puppets, digging her hand inside, giving them disturbing character voices in order to expand on every aspect of human sexuality with her developing daughter. While all those books—*and puppet shows*—could explain the physical changes of puberty and adolescence, none made sense of her developing heart.

She needed someone to talk to her about love. She needed to understand how she could go from a good and dutiful rabbi's daughter to launching underwear up a flagpole. But lying in bed that night—sneaking Christmas movies—Rachel understood. It all came from the same instinct, really.

Jacob Greenberg, with his outrageous antics and complete disregard for camp rules, had seen the truth inside her. She was not a nice Jewish girl. She was not the dutiful rabbi's daughter. Indeed, sometimes it felt like all Rachel really wanted to do was kick down every fence around the Torah that her family had built.

Jacob was merely the outlet.

And Rachel liked it.

She liked filling his shampoo bottle with ketchup. She liked stealing his underwear, letting it wave like a flag, the way all the girls in bunk 7G screeched aloud at the sight. She adored the feeling of being naughty, laying her sweatshirt on her lap during movie nights, letting Jacob sneak his hand beneath the material. The feeling of his hand, sweaty fingers searching to find her, before wrapping his fingers around her own.

She wanted to be even naughtier with him.

When Jacob had asked her to meet him one night in secret down by the lake, Rachel had gone. Like the biblical story of Dina, Rachel "went out." And then, like all the biblical women before her, hell-bent on leaving the security of their tribal tents in an unabashed act of self-determination, Rachel was promptly punished.

Returning home to Long Island, she had every reason in the world to hate him. And yet, she thought about Jacob constantly. The memory of him overtook her, often causing her to break down in hysterics even though her devotion to him made no logical sense. If this was love—if this spinning, hurtful thing was all she had to look forward to in the future—she was planning on remaining celibate.

Finally, in early November, Rachel was well enough to go to her local library. She had always been an avid reader, and nearing thirteen years old, she was quickly outgrowing the children's section.

Walking inside, she saw a circular table. It was loaded down with books beautifully displayed on a tablecloth of red. Above those books, on a giant white poster board, decorated with evergreen trees and floating Santa heads, were the words: *Fall in love this Christmas.*

Rachel remembered the feeling as she walked toward the table. Her heart racing, she picked up one of the books. It was the image on the cover that drew her in. A man in a knit hat held a smiling woman in a red sweater close. Snowflakes fell down around them, a dreamy camp-like setting in the background, as they angled their lips together.

It was so obvious from the body language that they were about to kiss. But, unlike Rachel, the woman on the cover didn't look like she was going to be spending the next eight weeks bawling her eyes out.

Rachel needed to know more. Glancing around her, that naughty feeling she had discovered with Jacob appeared again. She made sure that there were no congregants lurking about. And then, knowing full well that she was doing something her mother would not approve of, she checked that book out.

She devoured it in one night.

Before long, she was reading every Christmas romance she could find. She was watching the Hallmark movies alongside her novels, all in secret. And then, while a freshman in college, in the middle of her first semester studying writing, Rachel fell ill.

In the span of a few weeks, she went from a straight-A student at the top of her class, to sleeping twenty hours a day. She had night sweats and swollen lymph nodes, massive weight loss and sore throats. She returned home to Long Island, and began the lengthy process of medical evaluations and testing. Eventually the doctors diagnosed her with chronic fatigue syndrome.

Rachel was far too sick at the beginning of her disease to think about the future, or writing, or Christmas. She simply slept. She slept for months, a regular sleeping beauty, only waking up for doctors' appointments. But by summer, the fog she existed in began to fade. She could get out of bed, go for a walk, write.

Though she would never return to pre-illness levels of wellness, she could have some version of normal.

It was in the hazy ending of that summer that she made two important decisions about her life.

The first was to keep her diagnosis a secret. Not because she was ashamed—she knew her illness was real—but because she had suddenly been handed a diagnosis that did not, at all, reflect her experience. Names were important. They came with histories and legacies. This name would not be doing her any favors in the future.

Her second decision, related to the first, focused on simple practicalities.

Although dreams don't die just because your body fails you, Rachel understood the limits of her own physicality. She felt the limitations on her time, especially. There just wasn't enough energy in her life to do everything she wanted. And so, that evening, in the quiet of her childhood bedroom, she confronted her new normal. She wrote down the three things she wanted for her future—a writing career, a partner, children—and crossed off two.

For the next three years, Rachel went to college part-time, using her summers to pick up the extra credits, never telling anyone the truth about her disease. She gave up on dating and Shabbat dinners with friends, spending her weeknights and free time in bed, saving up energy for the week. She funneled any good days she had, all her extra energy, into her writing.

Rachel spent most of college desperately trying to write a book that would sell. She had all sorts of close calls and false starts, including an agent who had dumped her via text message. But mainly, and no matter how many manuscripts Rachel pumped out, publishing was a giant disappointment.

One day in her senior year, feeling just awful about everything, she found herself watching a Christmas movie. It was like the clouds opened up and Santa himself came down from the heavens to bless this new endeavor with yuletide inspiration. She sold her first book to Romance House six months later.

It was an easy jump. Christmas filled a void and turned her painful daily struggles into a tolerable reality. No one was ever sick in her Christmas romances. No one was ever heartbroken by the antics of a childhood sociopath. Indeed, no one was even Jewish. She didn't have to be Rachel Rubenstein-Goldblatt in her novels. Christmas provided the ultimate escape.

Rachel heard Jacob return to his bedroom. Sighing heavily, she glanced over to the clock sitting on her nightstand. It was late. She shut off her movie. Like always, her happy ending would have to wait.

9

That night, Jacob dreamed. He dreamed of a desert. Of a great pit he had fallen into and couldn't escape. He dreamed of tigers, twelve in total, all with faces like the investors from his Matzah Ball. He dreamed of his mother. Her voice in the distance, calling his name. The dreams themselves weren't unusual. Jacob had long been plagued by nightmares. But now, they were turning biblical.

Jacob awoke to the sound of dishes clanging in the kitchen. Blinking open his eyes, he shook off the nightmares. He wasn't sure if it was the jet lag or the creaky queen-size bed beneath him, but he had not slept well. Despite the ease with which Dr. Rubenstein had welcomed him into her home, he felt unsettled.

He sat up on the corner of his bed, rubbing out the tension from his forehead. He recalled the events of last night. Rachel tackling him, half-naked, in the bathroom, begging for a ticket. He couldn't believe he had agreed to let her volunteer for his Matzah Ball. She certainly didn't deserve his help; yet, after all this time, Rachel still managed to throw him off his game.

Rising from the bed, he pulled out a smart blue blazer from his suitcase, pairing it with a cashmere sweater and pleated pants. Taking one last look at himself in the mirror above the bureau, he adjusted his collar. Fixed his hair so that his auburn curls fell away from his eyes. He was a good-looking man, which, paired with a thriving multimillion-dollar business, meant he never had much trouble with women.

Except when it came to Rachel.

Jacob shook the thought away. Heading for the kitchen, he found Dr. Rubenstein, still in a house robe, setting out plates for breakfast.

"Jacob," she said, rushing over to give him a hug. "Shabbat Shalom."

Jacob couldn't help himself. He fell into her embrace. It had been so long since he had been hugged—since he felt the genuine arms of a mother wrapping around him—he didn't realize how much he missed it.

"Shabbat Shalom," Jacob said warmly.

"Would you like a little breakfast?" she asked, hands still on his arms.

"I'm okay."

"Come now," she said. "You're a growing boy. You should eat a little something. We won't be eating again till Kiddush."

Kiddush was, literally, three hours away. But not wanting to be rude, Jacob took a seat. God forbid you left a Jewish household hungry. There was no greater sin. In return, Dr. Rubenstein began spinning, shifting from refrigerator to drawer to pantry. She loaded up the table, a veritable buffet of fruits, cookies and jam.

"Is there anything I can help you with?" Jacob asked.

"I'm fine, dear." Dr. Rubenstein glanced back from the pantry. "Please. Start eating!"

Jacob hesitated. "You don't want me to wait for you?"

"No, I had a little nosh before you woke up."

Jacob stared at the table full of food. "And Rachel?"

Dr. Rubenstein came to a full and complete stop. It should not have been a difficult question. The woman had put out enough food to feed a small army.

"Rachel?" she asked, her voice rising an octave.

"I'm assuming she'll be joining us for breakfast before services?"

Dr. Rubenstein turned bright red. "Oh, no," she said, twisting toward the sink. "It's just…well, Rachel doesn't usually do Shabbat services on Saturday morning. We'll probably see her later, either at Kiddush…or this evening at Havdalah."

He was surprised to hear this. Jacob would have thought that a rabbi's daughter would be gung ho about attending Shabbat services. It was strange that someone raised in an observant home would choose to sleep in. Jacob reasoned it away as yet another mystery regarding Rachel.

"Oh," Dr. Rubenstein said, touching her forehead. "I almost forgot."

Heading to a counter, she stood on tiptoe, pulling down a pink box wrapped up in white twine.

"I got these for you," she said, sliding down in the seat next to him. "They're kosher! You know that fabulous little bakery in Brooklyn? The one that's been in the same family for five generations? Well, I had them make that special."

Jacob was touched. Pulling the pink box closer, he opened it up. Inside were a dozen fresh croissants.

"Dr. Rubenstein," Jacob said, shaking his head. "You didn't need to do this."

She waved away his concern. "I figured it would be nice for you to have a little taste of home."

Home. The word fell from her lips and landed like a sledgehammer in his gut. Jacob stared down at the croissants. France had not felt like home in some time. It wasn't just the anti-Semitism rising both in Paris and around the world. It was the death of his mother. Since losing her, his world had been turned upside down. Still, the gesture was so kind, so sweet, it broke through his carefully constructed walls.

"This is too much, Dr. Rubenstein."

"You know, in Judaism, they say that every person has their mitzvah. One good deed they do, above all others. For some, it's keeping kosher. For some, it's visiting the sick. This is mine, Jacob. I like Shabbat. I like having visitors." She smiled, leaning into him. "And I especially like you."

Jacob believed her.

"Now," she said, rising from the table. "I'm going to go get dressed for services. You hurry up and eat breakfast. After that, we'll walk over together."

Jacob watched Dr. Rubenstein flitter off. The house returned to that uncomfortable quiet he so desperately hated. At least the sun was shining. The light streamed through the curtains in the kitchen, casting colors across the table of food that Dr. Rubenstein had so lovingly set out for him.

Shmuel had once remarked that when you marry a Jewish woman, you marry their family. Jacob had never really understood the sentiment before. Picking up a croissant, he smiled at the thought. Dr. Rubenstein would make a good mother-in-law to somebody. She would welcome them into her home with open arms and way too much food.

Alas, given his trajectory with her daughter, it was unlikely to be him.

Looking back on it now, he could see what a troubled kid he had been. He'd pulled pranks, often at the expense of others. He was out of control, demanding attention, begging for someone to take notice. But, he reasoned, his bad behavior hadn't been *entirely* his fault.

His mother had been sick, prone to not only physical problems like incontinence and falls but also the depression that often accompanied a chronic and life-altering disease. His father—the same man who used to take him to Mets games and once even bought him a retired mascot costume in the shape of a baseball—had stopped coming home entirely.

He was a broken kid...from a broken family.

In his darkest days, he'd even thought about killing himself.

Jacob had never even considered going to camp until one day, during Hebrew school, they were handing out brochures. For most everyone in his class, Camp Ahava was akin to eight straight weeks of punishment. The place where the super-Jewy kids went, where they forced you to pray three times a day, and you sat around doing nothing for all of Shabbat. Nobody from his surroundings went to such religious camps.

Jacob had taken one look at that brochure—with its focus on community, its beautifully manicured lawns and happy smiling faces—and begged his mother to let him go. He pleaded and cried, pouring out his life savings of twenty-six dollars and thirty-seven cents onto her bed before finally calling his bubbe. Eventually, they all agreed that Camp Ahava would be a good break for everyone involved.

Jacob understood his parents were using that summer to finalize their divorce. He didn't know that, four months later, he would be moving to Paris. Arriving at Camp Ahava that summer, his bag stuffed full of swim trunks and itching powder, Jacob found his escape. He burst onto the scene, making friends and falling in love.

He couldn't help himself. His mind wandered back to the first time he saw Rachel.

It was during opening ceremonies in the outdoor arena down by the lake, and their counselors were performing a skit onstage. Everyone was whooping and hollering, making a racket, except for this one girl sitting directly across from him. Her frizzy brown hair in a high ponytail. Her hands folded politely in her lap. She was barely smiling.

Even at twelve years old, it struck him as odd. Who comes to summer camp and acts so austere?

Later he would learn from his newfound friends exactly who she was. Rachel Rubenstein-Goldblatt was the daughter of *the* Rabbi Aaron Goldblatt. He had no idea who that was—nor did he have any interest in discussing fathers with the boys of bunk 7B—but in great and excitable detail they warned him off her.

Rachel was nice and all—the type of camper always willing to share her water bottle with you—and also *completely* boring. She picked up siddurs after services. She always went to bed *exactly* at lights-out. Plus, everybody knew, since it was written in the Talmud: if you touched Rabbi Goldblatt's daughter during summer camp, you would get struck by lightning.

It seemed there were good and logical reasons to avoid the skinny girl with the high ponytail. But Jacob saw something in Rachel the others did not. He recognized in her quiet, almost self-imposed solitude from others at camp an almost kindred spirit. They were both hiding. They just had different ways of doing it.

Rachel used silence.

And Jacob—like always, he reasoned—used noise.

Perhaps pushing her into the lake was not his finest moment, but it had worked. The Rachel that emerged from the waters was all colorful dichotomy. Fireworks exploding up in the sky on the Fourth of July. He adored the mischievous little smile she shot him during services. He thought her pranks were brilliant. He liked her so much, in fact, that he came to adore the smell of ketchup in his hair, and the feeling of toothpaste in his sneakers.

She was like one of those fireflies they sometimes caught together in secret down by the lake. A little spark of brilliance, a wild and underestimated creature, zipping by in the night.

He needed her light that summer.

Jacob never told Rachel—or anyone at Camp Ahava, for that

matter—the truth about his home life. But Rachel seemed to have a sixth sense about everything he was going through.

When Jacob had nightmares about his mother, he awoke to find toothpaste in his sneakers. When mail day came, and everyone else got letters from their fathers, Jacob would return to his bunk to take a shower, and find ketchup in his shampoo. She was still that good-natured and thoughtful girl that all the boys in bunk 7B had described—she was also terrifically fun. Most nights, he went to bed with his cheeks aching from laughter. And when Jacob felt alone in the world, Rachel laid her sweatshirt on her lap and let him take her hand.

He would always and forever cherish the memory of their first kiss.

He was twelve years old, in the throes of first love, and he was certain that their love was *really real*. And then, for no reason he could ever understand, she disappeared from his life. Ghosted him completely, refusing to take his phone calls or answer any of his letters, after standing him up at the Camp Ahava final dance.

It broke his goddamn heart.

And yet, despite the myriad ways she had abandoned him, Jacob wasn't angry at Rachel. Indeed, it was the opposite. He felt quite keenly that he owed her something, that he had a debt of the most valuable kind to repay. Because that summer, Rachel had saved his life.

Dr. Rubenstein returned to the kitchen, fully dressed for Shabbat services.

"Is everything okay?" she asked.

Jacob cleared his throat. "Fine. I was just thinking about the last time I was in New York."

"It's been a long time, *nachon*?"

He nodded. In all his travels around the world, in all his visits to meccas for mega events, Jacob had purposefully avoided returning to the city where his father still resided.

Then, for no reason in particular, Dr. Rubenstein hugged him. He accepted it, fully.

Whatever questions still lingered inside him—whatever demons still needed to be confronted—would have to be saved for another time. For, unlike Rachel, Jacob had grown up in a world where there were both gods and monsters, and he was determined more than ever to remain on the side of good.

10

Rachel craned one ear toward the door, listening for voices rising up from the kitchen or footsteps tromping up and down the hallway. But her first impression was correct. Jacob and her parents had left the building.

She threw off her covers. Taking deep breaths, she mustered the energy to sit up. She did not feel good. Her head was groggy. Her arms and legs felt like they had been loaded down with weights, and for some strange reason her left kneecap was swollen. If it hadn't been for Jacob Greenberg, she would have stayed in bed.

Alas, the thought of leaving Jacob alone with her parents made her nervous. She didn't want him spilling the beans about what had happened last night in the bathroom. Or worse, talking about her volunteering for the Matzah Ball. It could raise all sorts of problematic questions. She had no choice. She needed to push through.

Heading to the kitchen, Rachel rummaged in a pantry. She pulled out a sugar-free Red Bull and chugged it down. Then, rifling through the medicine drawer in the bathroom, she added a caffeine pill. The combination probably would have sent most folks pinging off the walls, but caffeine barely made a dent in Rachel's fatigue.

She would have stopped there, but she knew her body. So she loaded up on painkillers, a mixture of Advil and Tylenol, in order to ward off any migraines or joint pain that might arise in the next three hours. Finally, because she had taken all medicine on an empty stomach, she finished off her breakfast by grabbing a croissant from a pink box on the counter.

Back in her bedroom, she pulled on a blue dress and black microfiber stockings.

There were times Rachel couldn't believe she didn't just drop dead from all the crap she loaded into her body. This was one of the great ironies of her life with chronic illness.

Marathon runners keeled over from heart attacks at the age of thirty-three. Healthy young executives, with their entire lives ahead of them, were suddenly diagnosed with stage four cancer. Rachel was *just* chronically ill. She was exhausted every freaking day in varying degrees of disabling intensity. Thus, she was certain—absolutely positive—that she was going to live forever.

Baruch Hashem.

She did one final check in the mirror. Her hair was a disaster. Her curls, having been slept on, now frizzed and angled out in several different directions.

Rachel didn't want to upset her parents by using a curling iron on Shabbat so she settled on the next best thing—a black headband with a large blue flower that her great-aunt Sylvia had given her for her thirteenth birthday. It was, quite possibly, the ugliest damn headband in the entire world, but it would have to do.

Rachel arrived to synagogue right in the middle of Torah reading. Sneaking into her father's office, she grabbed her tallit bag from a top shelf and headed toward the main sanctuary.

She was met by Paul, the usher, who scooted right over in his electric wheelchair the minute he saw her.

"Shabbat Shalom," Rachel said warmly.

"Shabbat… Shalom," the words came slow and stilted. "How are you…this morning?"

"I'm good," Rachel chirped back. "And you?"

"Good. Same…seat…as always?"

"That would be perfect."

"Follow…me."

Rachel obeyed, following after Paul as he zipped her toward the back row.

Paul was a fixture in her father's synagogue. He was so proud of his electric wheelchair. So proud of his job, ushering attendees to their seats on Shabbat morning. In truth, the job was unnecessary. Even for a popular synagogue on Long Island, there were plenty of open seats. But Rachel understood why Paul showed up every single Saturday morning to volunteer his services. Everyone needed to feel valuable.

"Here…you…go," Paul said, using one finger to point out an aisle.

"Thank you, Paul."

He left, and Rachel took a seat.

She always took the very last pew in her father's synagogue. Most people assumed it was because she had a tendency to mosey in late. In reality, and like Paul zipping around shul behind her, Rachel stayed in the back because of her disability.

Rachel loved synagogue. Stepping through the doors of the main sanctuary, hearing the ancient words of Hebrew and Aramaic, felt like an extension of home. She didn't want to be late or miss shul as often as she did. But, for Rachel, the issue was far more complicated than simply being a lapsed Jew or wishing to sleep in.

She found synagogue exhausting. It wasn't just getting up early and getting dressed, but all the things that came with attendance. It was the music and singing, which even on a good day felt like someone crashing symbols against her ears. All the Shabbat Shalom hugs and catch-up conversations, things she loved once but could no longer tolerate.

The part that kept her at home, however, came in the form of two simple words—*please rise*—often uttered by the rabbi or the cantor. The tradition of rising to your feet whenever the ark was opened, the constant up and down, left her in a wave of dizzy spells.

The back pew allowed her to simply sit through services. Away from peering eyes, she could exist in quiet tandem with her disease, free from scorn or judgment. Without some old lady whispering loudly to her husband, *"Look how rude the rabbi's daughter is…"*

It had happened. More than once. Because unlike Paul, in his wheelchair, Rachel's disability was invisible.

After finishing her prayers, Rachel took a seat. Her eyes scanned the front pews and landed on Jacob. He was sitting in the front row, alone. Her mom had abandoned him. Rachel watched him, her curiosity growing. It was interesting, really. Jacob hadn't been particularly religious at Camp Ahava. Watching him now, though, his shoulders squared, his face angled up to the eternal flame, she got the sense that he was considering something prescient.

There were things Rachel knew about Jacob's life. She had learned it from his letters after summer camp, and later via her mother and the Camp Ahava rumor mill. She knew that he had moved to Paris with his French mother while his American father remained in New York. She remembered hearing that his parents had been involved in a particularly nasty divorce. Looking at Jacob now, thinking back on their youth together, she couldn't help viewing their past through a different lens.

It must have been hard for him.

She chewed on her lower lip, debating her options. Chronic

illness had softened her to the potential unseen pain in others. She considered the small, almost infinitesimal possibility that her mother was right. She was being unfair. At the very least, she could attempt to be cordial to the man.

She glanced down at her watch. Services were almost over. She could handle this.

"Hey," Rachel said, and slid down in the seat next to Jacob.

Jacob twisted in his seat, surprised. "Hey! You're here."

Rachel squinted. "Where else would I be?"

"Your mom said you normally don't come to Saturday morning services."

"Oh." She uncrossed her arms. "Yeah. Normally, I don't."

"Well..." Jacob smiled, red flushing his cheeks. "I'm happy you're here."

The moment shifted, like the Hatzi Kaddish, the prayer for transitions, floating between them. Their knees, by accident, bumped together and remained touching. Some spark, some happy memory from that faraway summer, floated its way into her heart.

Rachel swallowed hard. "Me, too."

Jacob was surprised to see her. Surprised at the strange feeling creeping up in his chest, a mixture of nerves and excitement. She looked adorable. A smile spread out across his face, wild and wide, as he took in the full picture of Rachel.

The ridiculous headband she was wearing, black velvet with a giant blue tulle flower at the top. The large tallit that draped across her shoulders, swinging down to the top of her knees. It was the oddest juxtaposition, the playfulness of the headband against the seriousness of the prayer shawl. It was so quintessential Rachel. Complicated and quirky.

"I like your tallit," he said. "Is that... Rachel?"

"Miriam," she said, pulling out the edges to display the pattern. An abstract female shape with a tambourine danced across blue waves, while several other women followed her. "Rachel is the one who…married Jacob."

Jacob smiled. "It's beautiful."

"Thanks."

An old lady leaned in to shush them. Like two kids caught in some crime, they shared a simple and guilty giggle together before returning to listening to the Torah reader.

Forty minutes later, services were over. The entire congregation streamed into the adjoining banquet hall for Kiddush luncheon.

Jacob joined them, following after Rachel. Laid out in the center, in buffet style, were all the typical Ashkenazi favorites. Bagels—onion, plain and sesame—rested on platters decorated in flowers. Cream cheese and salads sat in bowls with giant spoons. It all looked delicious, but everyone, from the smallest mobile toddler to the old woman with the walker, was making their way over to the three platters of lox.

"Wow," Rachel said, gazing over the spread. "Someone really splurged on Kiddush today."

Jacob shifted in his loafers. He decided not to mention that he was the person who'd sponsored Kiddush today.

Suddenly, a voice called out to the crowd. Rabbi Goldblatt was waving his daughter over. "Rachel," he shouted, holding a silver Kiddush cup in his hand. "Do us all the honor, please?"

Rachel groaned. "Excuse me."

Jacob watched as she took her place, front and center. The entire congregation gathered round as she lifted the cup into the air. She didn't even need a book. The Hebrew words, the ancient hymn, fell from her tongue as simply as "Happy Birthday." It would take Jacob weeks or months to learn the same prayer, and probably years to deliver it with such confidence.

Rachel finished Kiddush. Her father, in one of those sweet and unconscious moments, briefly touched the back of her head before allowing her to depart. It was such a small yet sweeping gesture. The kind of thing a father would do to his small child. Not a grown woman.

But in Judaism—as Shmuel often made a point to remind him—you weren't really considered an adult unless you were married. It didn't matter if you ran a multimillion-dollar business or owned several homes. There was something about committing to another person, starting a home and a family, that separated the boys from men, the girls from women.

Rachel returned to her position at Jacob's side.

"You're really good at that," he said.

She laughed. "Years of practice."

"It, uh…" He stumbled on the words. "It reminded me of Camp Ahava."

Her face was a mask, unmoving. She twisted to grab two plates. "I think it's time to get something to eat."

Jacob didn't know what he'd said wrong. Rachel was suddenly flying through the buffet line, loading up heaping mounds of food. Jacob followed after her, trying to keep up. She headed toward a table where a man in a wheelchair was sitting. Jacob recognized him as the usher who had brought him and Dr. Rubenstein to their seats earlier that morning.

"Paul," Rachel said, sliding down between the two men. "This is Jacob. Jacob, Paul."

"Hello," Jacob said, offering his hand.

Paul lifted his hand into the air, his plastic fork held like a chopstick between two paralyzed fingers. "Hel…lo."

"You need any help, Paul?" Rachel asked casually.

"I'm fine," he said, and dug his fork into the food. "You look…beautiful today."

"Oh, Paul." Rachel touched her heart. "You are my favorite flirt."

Paul grinned from ear to ear. "You, too… Rachel."

It was interesting watching Rachel interact with Paul. Except for last night in the bathroom, she was rather stuffy with

Jacob. She seemed guarded and on edge constantly. With Paul, Rachel relaxed. Practically floated.

Paul stopped flirting with Rachel long enough to turn his attention to Jacob.

"What kind of…car do you drive, Jacob?" he asked.

Jacob was surprised by the question. "Car?"

Rachel explained. "Paul's favorite topic is cars."

"Ah," Jacob said, taking his cue. "Well, actually… I don't have a car."

Paul was shocked. "No car?"

"I don't need one." He shrugged happily. "I live in Paris."

Paul pointed to Rachel. "Like you…in Manhattan."

"Yep," Rachel said, nodding her head. "We're both city dwellers."

For as much difficulty as Paul had speaking due to his disease, it didn't stop him. He spent the next forty-five minutes regaling Jacob and Rachel with the intricate details of the Parisian metro system. How he knew so much about European mass transportation was anybody's guess. Jacob—quite politely—held his own. He happily answered questions, going into great detail about the streets, the parking spaces and the maps. Paul was delighted, and Rachel… Well, he looked over at one point to find her chin folded into the palm of her hand, watching them intently.

After some time an aide appeared to take Paul home, and Jacob finally found himself alone with Rachel.

"You were good with him," Rachel said quietly.

Jacob returned the compliment. "He was good with me."

Rachel smiled. It was warm and genuine. Jacob couldn't help smiling along with her. He watched her eyes drift over to the exit. Outside the main sanctuary, Paul was being loaded up into an accessibility transport.

"A lot of people don't see Paul," she said thoughtfully. "Because of his disability, and because sometimes he can be sort of quirky and obsessive in his interests. But you know what the Midrash says? God only works through broken vessels."

Jacob swallowed. A lump of something hard and uncomfortable worked its way down from the center of his throat. "Midrash? Is that some type of Jewish philosophy?"

"Kind of." She shrugged. "It's more like biblical commentary. But, if you think about it, brokenness is all over the bible. Moses has a speech impediment. God requests a half-shekel, and not a full shekel, from all the Israelites. Even the world was created from something unformed and void. God could have just as easily said, *I create this universe from nothing.* But he didn't. So, you know…there's probably a lesson in that."

Jacob blinked. She was so smart. Rachel pushed him into conversations that were challenging, a rarity for a man more accustomed to screaming over music than having in-depth discussions with a woman at a table.

"Anyway," Rachel said, staring down at her lap. "I don't want to bore you."

"You're not boring me. I find it fascinating." He found *her* fascinating. "So what's the point of it?"

"What?"

"Brokenness?"

"Well…" Rachel considered the question, "I'm gonna do something super-Jewy here, and throw the question back at you. Why do *you* think God prefers broken things?"

"Maybe it means… God loves us no matter what?"

She cocked her head. "That's a very Christian way of looking at a Jewish God."

"I suppose that makes sense," Jacob shrugged simply. "I did go to Catholic school."

"Wait." Rachel squinted. "You went to *Catholic school*?"

"Three years," he explained. "Grades ten through twelve."

He could see the question lingering on her face. How the heck does a nice Jewish boy, someone who went to Camp Ahava for one summer, wind up in Catholic school?

"Your parents were okay with that?" Rachel asked.

"My mom was doing her best."

"What about your dad?"

"My dad didn't really have much say," Jacob said honestly. Quickly he moved the topic away from his father. "But my bubbe, when she found out… She had a total conniption."

"Well," Rachel said, and nodded her head, "who can argue with bubbes?"

Jacob laughed. "Exactly."

He was careful not to reveal any more of the story than that. He didn't want Rachel to know the truth about him. Suffice to say, after his father abandoned him, and his mother had no choice but to move them both back to France, Jacob struggled. The same problems he had brought with him to Camp Ahava that summer followed him into his teen years. In Paris, he became a full-fledged disaster.

Looking back on it now, he could see how his anger was an extension of his grief. He would talk back to his mother, get in trouble at school, miss dinner, *like his father*. He recalled standing on their balcony, lighting up cigarettes in front of her, a habit she absolutely despised. He caused his mother every possible form of grief he could manage, daring her to stop loving him, wanting her to prove this thing he already knew about himself.

Getting kicked out of school was just another way to hurt her. He went through four schools, in fact, before landing at the only place left in Paris willing to take him. A Catholic school.

"Was it weird?" Rachel asked, playing with a curl of her hair.

"It was odd at first," Jacob admitted, before adding, "but the priests were pretty nice…and they actually wound up helping me through some stuff. Plus, I learned all about catechism, so it wasn't a total loss."

"I don't even know what that is."

"It's the doctrines of the Catholic faith."

"Like their Talmud?"

"I don't think so? Though, I don't really know enough about the Talmud to compare."

Rachel shook her head. "I can't even imagine going to Catholic school. Were there crosses everywhere?"

"Quite a few."

"Did they hit you with rulers?"

"Only when I really deserved it."

She gasped.

"I'm kidding." Jacob couldn't help laughing. "It was pretty normal, aside from the fact that it was Catholic. And, like I said, the priests helped me through some stuff. One priest, in particular, Father Sebastian, was actually the person who got me interested in music."

It was Father Sebastian who had taught Jacob that there could be healthier outlets for his anger. After school, and during breaks between classes, he educated Jacob on styles beyond pop, introducing him to opera, heavy metal and jazz. Music quickly became an escape, a way to make sense of his confusing feelings, and later, as an adult, he turned that passion into a business.

"Wow," Rachel said. He could see the writer in her thinking it through, putting herself in his size-twelve loafers. "I've never been to Catholic school," Rachel said simply.

"Shocker."

"But I'll tell you a secret…" She fiddled with a string coming off the tablecloth. "I have watched a Christmas movie."

Jacob leaned in, whispering, "Was it any good?"

Rachel exploded with laughter. Full-blown hysterics, covering her mouth, gasping for air. Jacob couldn't help himself. Just the sight of her in such a state of sheer delight filled his heart with joy. She didn't laugh enough, he realized. He liked being the reason she smiled.

"You know," Rachel said, leaning in, "I used to think the whole world was Jewish."

"You're kidding me."

"Jewish family. Jewish school. Jewish summer camp. Jewish friends. I even played on Jewish sports teams." Her eyes landed on her parents. "Nobody did it on purpose, of course. There just wasn't any space left for the rest of the world."

He noted a certain sadness in her voice. "Well, Rachel," he said, reaching across the table to take her hands. "I fear being the one to break this to you...but the whole world is not Jewish."

She laughed again. Whatever sadness was inside her dissipated.

And that's when he realized they were holding hands. Sparks flew through his body at the feeling of her warm skin against his own. He had forgotten how warm she could feel, an instinct rising inside of him to hold on to her forever. Her eyes floated from their hands over to the tables where congregants were gathered. Quickly she sat up in her seat and pulled away.

"I'm sorry," Jacob said. "I didn't mean to overstep any boundaries."

"It's okay." She shook off his words nervously. "You didn't. It's just...people are watching."

"You're not allowed to hold hands with a boy at thirty?"

She shifted in her seat. "It's more complicated than that."

He remembered this about Rachel at Camp Ahava, too. She was always so worried about what other people thought. She had made him promise, up and down and every way to morning minyan, to keep their relationship a secret. He had started their prank war, of course, by pushing her into the lake. But it was her idea to keep the facade going even when they started to like each other.

Jacob had done his best to honor her wishes, but it was hard. He liked her more than anything in the world. He wanted to shout it from the treetops surrounding their camp. He wanted everyone in bunk 7B to know about it, too. Still, he did his best to safeguard her privacy.

"So what happens now?" Jacob asked.

"Now," Rachel said, sitting back up. "We go back to the house, my mother tries to feed you again, and then we all head back to our rooms for a Shabbat nap. After which we wake up, do Havdalah…and my mother sends you back to New York with more food than you could possibly ever eat."

"There seems to be a theme here."

"Eating." Rachel nodded. "Eating is the theme."

"And then…" He felt the need to confirm this thing with her. "I'll see you on Monday morning?"

"Yeah." She smiled gently. "I guess so."

Damn. If they weren't in the middle of shul, with half the congregants nosily watching, he might have leaned in and kissed her.

"Listen, Jacob," Rachel said, edging in closer. "I was wondering if I could maybe ask you a favor."

"Another one?" He liked where this was going.

She rolled those perfect brown eyes. "I know. Just hear me out, okay? I know it sounds weird, I know it makes no sense, at all…but if the topic happens to come up with my parents, please don't mention that I'm volunteering for your Matzah Ball."

Jacob sat back in his seat, totally confused. "Why?"

"I just think it'll be better if it's a surprise. You know, like they show up to the party, and bam. There I am. Think about how happy that will make them."

Jacob felt his heart sink inside his chest. What the hell just happened? One minute, he was talking to Rachel—deep and purposeful and honest—and then, in the blink of an eye, the woman from the bathroom had reappeared.

"Rachel, nobody hides *volunteering* for a *Jewish event* from their parents."

"I know. But please, Jacob—I need you to do this for me."

She was touching him, clutching his knee, sending shivers

up and down his thighs. He wanted to deny her—tell her that she could take their deal and shove it—but he also didn't want her to pull her hand away.

"On one condition," he said.

"Anything."

"Tell me the truth." He pinned his gaze on those tempting pink lips. "Tell me the real reason you so desperately want a ticket to my Matzah Ball."

She let go of his knee, sitting up in her seat. "Wha—I mean, why?"

"Because this is all very dramatic for a Hanukkah party, Rachel. And frankly, I'm beginning to get worried. Are you using my party to deal drugs? Are you wanted by the mob? Blink twice if you're in trouble."

She did not blink twice. Instead, her eyelids went wide and she looked up at the ceiling. It might not have been obvious to others, but he saw through it. He could tell when she was weaving up a tale inside her mind, planning out her next lie.

"Look," she said finally, "just because I'm a top-secret spy for the Israel Defense Forces, and I don't want you to blow my cover to my parents…"

He raised an eyebrow in her direction. "A spy, huh?"

"A trained assassin," she whispered. "Mossad."

"In a flower headband?"

Rachel leaned in dramatically. "I've killed seventy-six men with this headband."

It took Jacob a few seconds, but he laughed. He shook his head, annoyed with himself. He knew she was joking, but something about Rachel felt dangerous. Like allowing her into his life, with her inconsistencies and lies, would lead to something worse.

And yet, he couldn't refuse her. This was Rachel Rubenstein-Goldblatt. His first love. His first kiss. The girl who had saved his life. He owed her something. Most of all, though—and as was his nature—he wanted to help her.

"Okay, Rachel," he said, throwing his hands up. "You win."

The Jewish Goodbye at Rachel's house took forty-five long minutes to complete. There were all the traditional aspects of delay—the many thanks and gratitude, the promises to do it again and see each other soon—before Dr. Rubenstein offered up *one last hug* for the ten-thousandth time. Eventually, Jacob got out the front door.

"Well," Dr. Rubenstein said, shutting the door behind him. "He is just lovely."

"Ema…" Rachel knew where this was heading.

"What?" Dr. Rubenstein said defensively. "Such a lovely *neshama*, such a warm and gentle soul…he will just make a wonderful husband to someone."

Rachel rolled her eyes. She knew what her mother was doing. Putting ideas into her head. Trying to butter her up, like that box of croissants she sent home with Jacob.

It wasn't her mother's fault, entirely. After the Holocaust, in which so many Jewish families were murdered or displaced, Dr. Rubenstein saw it as her personal mission to help repopulate the world with Jewish babies. Now, as a top reproductive endocrinologist in New York City, she looked at her daughter the way she looked at all her patients coming to her after years of unexplained infertility and failed IVF treatments. A wealth of potential, of happiness and mazel, locked up inside a willful womb.

Rachel was an easy target.

Dr. Rubenstein bent down to fiddle with snow boots by the front door. "And it was so nice of Jacob to sponsor Kiddush today."

"Wait," Rachel said. "Jacob sponsored Kiddush?"

"Hmm," she said, all innocence, as if dropping the news by

accident. "Made a large and extremely generous donation to the synagogue before he arrived. He didn't mention it?"

"No."

"Ah." She stood up from her fiddling, mission accomplished. "Well, my mistake. I thought he would have said something, considering how much time you two spent together at Kiddush...and the way he kept looking at you."

Rachel blinked. "Looking at me?"

"Oh, Rachel." Her mother laughed a little. "Even your father noticed."

11

Rachel collapsed into a seat on the Long Island Rail Road. Her bag in her lap, she breathed a heavy sigh of relief as she made the return trip back to Manhattan. Shabbat was over. She had her ticket to the Matzah Ball. She was going to save her publishing contract.

She stared out the window at the dark night. The only thing she could see beyond the lamps and the tracks were the Christmas lights flickering on homes in the distance.

They were so beautiful. You could tell a lot about a family by the way they decorated their home for the holidays. If the lights were pristine and white, lined up in perfect little stripes and lines. Or a hodgepodge of color, thrown up hastily around trees and bushes. Neat or messy, they all made her feel warm.

Odd, really, because that was also how she'd felt with Jacob today.

Gazing out the window, Rachel couldn't help thinking about what her mother had insinuated a few hours earlier. Had Jacob really been looking at her during Shabbat? Were the feelings she had experienced, those sparks of something like attraction and excitement, reciprocated? It seemed impossible. Especially since this was Jacob Greenberg.

But Rachel had seen a side of Jacob during Shabbat she did not expect. He was charming and sweet. He enjoyed complex thoughts and conversations. But the moment that had really thrown her—the moment that made her think this man may have true romantic potential—was when he'd interacted with Paul.

Men came with all sorts of qualities. Some had broad shoulders, large wallets or a decent sense of comedic timing. But when she thought about walking down the aisle, when she thought about standing beneath the *huppah*, getting ready to make someone the center of her world—she knew she would only marry a *mensch*. A good person.

A commotion at the end of the train car drew her attention. A young couple had stepped into the car. They were clearly tipsy, it being Saturday evening in New York. She gathered that they were dating, as they seemed quite friendly, hanging all over each other, whispering. She watched them from the corner of her eye.

The young man turned to her.

"Excuse me, ma'am?" he asked.

Was she old enough to be a ma'am? Rachel didn't think so, but when she looked around the train car, it was empty. The young man had, indeed, been talking to her.

"Yes?" Rachel said politely.

He pulled out his phone from his pocket. "I was wondering if you wouldn't mind taking a picture of us."

The woman held up her left hand and squealed. "We just got engaged!"

"Oh." Rachel stood up, smiling at the news. "Mazel tov!"

"We're going home to tell my parents!" she screamed.

They were a bubble of excitement. Practically bouncing out of their winter boots, their whole lives about to begin. No wonder they were so wrapped up in each other. They were in love, and seeing two people in love was always magical.

"Smile big!" Rachel said as she stood up and took their picture. "Maybe one more? Just to be certain."

"Thank you so much," they said genuinely as she handed them back the phone.

Rachel returned to her seat. Staring back at her Christmas lights, a ball of sadness landed in her belly. She was familiar with that ball, the never-ending circle of grief, the constant losses that came with chronic illness. Rachel wanted to fall in love. She wanted to get married, find her person.

But who would love her with CFS?

And what nice Jewish boy would want to be with a Christmas romance novelist?

Not that she hadn't tried. Rachel had J-swiped right on love plenty of times. Dated someone, only to reveal one small piece of her truth and be very promptly dumped. At nearly thirty years old, and still very much single, Rachel had learned her lesson. Romance was meant for characters in her Christmas novels. Love belonged to healthy blonde chicks with below-average BMIs.

Rachel was none of these things.

But didn't everyone deserve a happy ending?

The train approached Manhattan. The feeling of sadness bubbling up in her belly began to overtake her. She texted Mickey: You around?

He did not text back. Strange. But she reasoned it was Saturday night. He was either working, throwing some Jewish event as part of his job as Director of Social Engagement at B'nei Shalom or on a date. Either way, she would catch up with him tomorrow.

She put her phone away and settled back in her seat. The strangling feeling had worked its way into her chest. She wasn't ready to go home. She wasn't ready to collapse into bed and stare at the ceiling for the next four hours. She needed to make herself feel better. Now.

The train rolled into Penn Station. Grabbing her bag, she made her way out onto 34th Street. For Rachel, this was the epicenter of Christmas in New York. The place where Santa rolled into town every Thanksgiving, waving from his sleigh. Her heart soared as she found herself gazing into the store windows, a never-ending menagerie of Christmas displays.

Tiny dancing elves wearing mittens. Singing carolers, their mouths pointed toward the sky. Perfume and lingerie wrapped up in red ribbon, the suggestion of romance, the promise of love on a snowy Christmas morning, two hearts meeting beneath the tree.

Her eyes landed on a smart beige cardigan in a window display. It had cording down the side and a full collar turned up at the neck. She couldn't help thinking it would look good on Jacob. But, just as quickly as the fantasy had come, it faded. Rachel didn't have anyone to buy sweaters for. She would be alone on the holidays, like always.

Across the way lay the ice-skating rink at Rockefeller Center. Oh, it was magical. The giant evergreen tree lit up between the skyscrapers. The skaters, floating playfully across the ice below. She could smell toasted marshmallows and hot chocolate, fried dough and cinnamon. She walked to a booth where a skinny kid in a blue monogrammed shirt was working.

"I'm here to see Santa," she said, slamming fifty bucks on the table.

"How many people?" he asked, unimpressed.

"Just one."

He took her money and handed her a ticket. "Merry Christmas."

Rachel could hardly contain her excitement as she waited in line. She knew it was ridiculous. A grown woman—without children in tow—waiting to get a photograph with Santa.

But she reasoned away her strange holiday tradition with some certifiable logic. Santa had always been there for her when she needed him. Besides, who would ever know about her taking a quick little trip to a fake North Pole?

"Oh, God," Santa moaned the moment he saw her. "You again?"

"Listen." Rachel sat down on his lap before he could escape. "I'm sorry to bother you again, but I really need your advice."

"Lady," Santa said, not at all jolly, "I told you a thousand times—I'm not a therapist."

"I know," Rachel said, frowning and serious. "But I paid fifty bucks and waited in line for forty-five minutes, so here we are."

Santa grumbled. "You need help."

She wrapped her arms around his neck. "That's exactly why I'm here."

Santa sighed. But Rachel understood what this was between them. She had seen it countless times in both her Christmas novels *and* movies. The grumpiness was just a front. Santa obviously loved her.

"Look," she said simply, "here's my problem. There's this guy, Jacob…and I think I like him. The problem is…*geneivat da'at.*"

"What."

"I'm stealing his mind," she explained succinctly. "I'm making him think I'm someone I'm not. It's totally what he did to me at Camp Ahava, which I guess is only fair…and also, totally dishonest. And maybe I wouldn't care, Santa, because of what happened between us. But grown-up Jacob, he's so handsome. He's so kind. You should have seen him with Paul. He's not anything like that terrible little boy I remember. But can you really trust someone who was your summer camp arch enemy?"

"I have no idea what you're talking about."

"I know," Rachel said. "I also realize you're not real…but this is helpful."

"Wonderful."

"I don't know." Rachel tossed the idea around in her mind. "Maybe I should give him a chance."

"Sounds like a plan to me." Santa tried to push her off his lap.

Rachel refused to budge. "The thing is, giving him a chance means I'd have to be honest. About everything. And being honest could hurt my parents. I mean, I asked my dad about it once. I was like, 'Dad. What's the halacha around someone like Irving Berlin?' You know, the Jewish guy who wrote all those famous Christmas songs? And my dad went on this whole long shpiel about the Talmud and the *Shulchan Aruch*, and whether or not a Jewish person can sell a cross at the market. And basically, what I got from that conversation is, it's a solid no."

"Look, lady—"

"Rachel."

"Rachel," he said, exasperated. "Can you do me a favor?"

"Anything, Santa."

"Can you maybe boil this all down to one or two things that you want for Christmas?" He nodded at his wife, Mrs. Claus, waiting impatiently with a camera. "We're running a little long here."

Rachel sighed, thinking over his question. "I guess what I really want for Christmas this year…is a happy ending. I've been writing them for so long for other people, cheering everyone else along the way. But I think, for once, I'd like the world, and the universe, to work out for me. I'd like a happy ending of my very own."

"Is that it?" Santa asked.

"Yes," she said firmly. "That's it."

"Great," Santa said, and angled Rachel's chin toward Mrs. Claus. "Then smile big for the camera."

12

Jacob found the key the superintendent had left for him outside and entered his bubbe's dusty apartment on the Upper East Side, dropping his luggage just inside the door. The blinds drawn down over the windows, a plastic sheet covering the green couch—it had been eighteen years since he last stayed with his grandmother in Manhattan, and the apartment remained unchanged.

Jacob pulled up the blinds and opened the windows, letting the sounds of Second Avenue come rushing inside. Light streamed through the apartment.

By New York standards, it was a large apartment. Six rooms that stretched across the seventh floor of a mid-rise building at 65th and Second had been in his family for generations. Stuffed to the brim with bits and ends, fabrics and artifacts from his father's side of the family. A collection of *chanukiyot* littered the tiny ledge of the windowsill and spread across every surface in the living room into the hall.

It was tradition in his family, with his grandmother, to spend

Hanukkah together. They had done it for years, first here in New York, then in Paris…and then, wherever their adventures took them.

But for many years Jacob had spent every Hanukkah in this apartment. It seemed only right that, upon returning to New York, he should return to the place that had brought him so many fond memories.

He smiled, remembering sufganiyot, powdered jelly doughnuts, piled high on the table. The way the flames of the menorah looked, a menagerie of gold and blue, flickering through the window.

Though Jacob knew there were far more important holidays in the Jewish calendar, Hanukkah was still his favorite.

He lifted up his favorite menorah, an antique. The silver had tarnished after years of oxidation, but the imperfections only heightened its beauty. Eight slender branches decorated in tiny swirling flowers wove upward while two lions stood guard on the sides.

A dove in the center, wings spread, ready to fly, served as the *shamash*.

Every menorah in his bubbe's collection had a story. The one he was holding came from Eastern Europe in the early nineteenth century—a time of pogroms, before the Holocaust, but it symbolized all that was important to the Jewish people. Faith. Courage. Continuity. Jacob often wondered about the families who had lit these very same candles before theirs.

"*Yankele?* Is that you?"

A wide smile crossed Jacob's face. Putting the menorah down, he swung around to greet his ninety-one-year-old grandmother.

In so many ways, Toby Greenberg was your traditional Jewish bubbe. She believed in attending synagogue on the high holidays. She overfed everyone who came into her home, and considered it a *shanda*, a sin, for a guest to leave your house hungry. And she wanted her only grandson to marry a nice Jewish girl.

But, in every other way, Toby Greenberg was an exception. She had survived the Holocaust, hiding her identity while snaking her way from her native Germany through Europe until the end of the war. She had marched for civil rights in Alabama, and hurled her heels into trash cans during the feminist movement of the seventies.

Toby would never claim courage. But when she lost her husband at sixty-four, she didn't just curl up into a ball and wait to die. She met the next stage of her life with all the zeal of a woman who had spent her youth fighting for the things and people she believed in.

"Oh, look at you," Toby said happily before licking her thumb to wipe a bit of invisible *shmutz* off Jacob's face. "So tall. So handsome! I think you grew three inches since the last time I saw you."

"I'm afraid I have remained steadfastly at six feet."

"Ah," she sighed. "I must have shrunk then."

Toby entered her apartment, breathing deeply, her black puffy winter coat standing in stark contrast to the white parachute pants she was wearing. Jacob's eyes trailed down to the wooden slippers, embroidered with gold and pink thread, she was wearing. They were completely inappropriate for winter in New York.

"How was Thailand?" Jacob asked.

"Thailand?" she asked, confused.

"Last time we talked you were in Thailand."

"Oh!" Toby said, thinking back. "You're right. But then I heard about this fabulous little restaurant in Kolkata, with the most amazing fish curry…so I decided to go to India."

"You went to India—" Jacob blinked "—for a meal?"

"Well, India, El Salvador…and then Peru. I just flew in from Lima, in fact."

Bubbe dug her hand into a large black purse and pulled out a phone covered in blue and white crystals.

"You see," she said, angling the phone toward Jacob, swiping through photographs. "Thailand, India…oh wait, I forgot I did a detour to Malaysia. They were having a Dragon Boat Festival. Oh, *Yankele*…you should have seen it! It was just amazing. The colors! The people!"

Jacob watched her world tour unfold before him. There was a photo of Toby in Thailand, riding an elaborately decorated elephant. Another in India, where she performed the perfect vriksasana in front of the Taj Mahal. There was even a photo of her at a bar, surrounded by men nearly half her age, sipping a green fizzy drink the size of her head. Toby was ninety-one going on twenty-two.

Finally she landed on a photo of herself in Peru. Standing on a beach outside Lima, her short gray hair wet and sandy as she angled a surfboard against her hip.

"Bubbe, you went *surfing*?"

"What?" Toby said, pounding her chest triumphantly. "You think an old lady like me can't go surfing?" Jumping into a squat, she rode an invisible wave. "I will have you know that I was wiping the ocean floor with twenty-year-olds."

"I have no doubt," Jacob said gently. "I just worry about you, is all."

"*Yankele*," Toby said, rising to meet his eyes. "The very best part of surfing is wiping out."

Jacob laughed, pushing away his concern. He worried about his grandmother more than she realized. It wasn't just her age and that, though she was loath to admit it, she was slowing down. His bubbe was his last real connection to family. His mother had died. His father and he weren't on speaking terms. He didn't have any siblings. If anything happened to Toby, he would be alone in the world. The thought kept him awake at night.

Jacob would never dream of stifling her spirit. She resembled that silver bird on top of his favorite menorah. To attempt to cage her under the guise of safety would only be a death sentence.

Toby Greenberg would live free and fearless until the day God Himself decided to take her, and even then, Jacob was certain she would put up a fight.

"Come," Bubbe said, squeezing her grandson one more time. "Let's get settled in, then order some Chinese food, and you can tell me all about this fabulous Matzah Ball!"

Four hours later, Toby had ordered enough food for a small synagogue Kiddush. Pulling cartons of General Tso's chicken, vegetable chow mein, spring rolls and more from a dozen plastic bags, she set up a smorgasbord across the dining room table. The food had come from Peng's Famous House just four blocks away. Though years had passed and the management had changed, it was a pleasant reminder of his childhood Hanukkah traditions.

Jacob sat down at the table, grabbing a plate and a spring roll. The taste of the fried wrapper oozing oil made his tastes buds zing, recalling all those happy memories shared with his grandmother. It reminded him of the way he'd felt when he first saw Rachel.

"So," Toby said, piling up a plate of her own. "Who is she?"

Jacob put his spring roll down. "How did you know?"

"I'm your grandmother," she said with a wry smile. "That gives me superpowers."

Jacob felt his heart warm. His relationship with his bubbe was special even if he wasn't sure how to describe his feelings for Rachel. There were too many question marks, too many secrets and mistakes made between them. And yet, he felt drawn to her, his longing for those fun days of summer together going against his better judgment.

"Do you remember Rachel Rubenstein-Goldblatt?" Jacob asked.

"From Camp Ahava?"

Jacob nodded. "She was at Shabbat dinner this weekend."

"Oh, my." Concern stretched across her face.

Jacob told her everything. He described meeting her at dinner, the strange way she shut down during Shabbat dinner, only to tackle him in the bathroom and ask for a ticket to the Matzah Ball. He told her about the shelves full of philosophy books, the easy way she could quote Midrash and lead an entire congregation in prayer. Toby took it all in, listening intently before finally offering up her own version of events.

"So, you like this girl?"

"I don't know," Jacob said, exasperated. "The problem is, she's so secretive. You can see her thinking before she talks. Then, when no one else is around, she shows you this other side of herself. She's funny, and brilliant, and totally quirky, and I think I kind of like that. And that side of her when she's not pretending…that side is dynamite."

"So you *do* have feelings for this girl."

"Maybe," Jacob admitted. "But I didn't come to New York to fall in love."

It was the truth. Jacob had never intended to run into Rachel Rubenstein-Goldblatt over Shabbat. He'd certainly never expected to hand her a volunteer position and have to spend the next eight days working beside her. He couldn't believe he had been so easily swayed by those beautiful brown eyes. Everything felt on the line for Jacob now. Not just his heart, which had already suffered so much loss, but his business.

The Matzah Ball Max was unlike any event he had previously done. It had a different clientele, a different feel, a different audience. If Jacob messed up any one of those factors, it could bankrupt him. And yet, what he risked by falling in love was so much more than financial.

He thought back to an old Yiddish saying, *"Love is nice, but tastes better with bread."*

Toby raised an eyebrow in his direction. "You're worried about money?"

"I'm worried about everything."

Jacob didn't have the gall to bring up his father. The man had abandoned them both, after all. The topic of conversation was always painful for his bubbe.

"Jacob," Toby said seriously, "if you like this girl—"

"The same girl who broke my heart?" Jacob interrupted her. "The same girl who stood me up at the final dance of Camp Ahava? Who left me standing in the center of a dance floor with a bouquet of wildflowers in my hands, totally heartbroken? I called her every day for weeks, bubbe! I sent her letters filled with scented stickers and poop jokes! And I never once heard back from her."

"She was twelve, Jacob."

Jacob stared down at the thorn-sized scar that lived at the tip of his finger. He had received it sneaking off into the woods that surrounded Camp Ahava, in an effort to pick her out the perfect wildflowers. He was even going to ask her to be his *permanent and full-time* girlfriend at the Camp Ahava final dance. Then Rachel had stood him up.

"Jacob—" Toby rubbed out her own headache now "—what is it you want from this woman?"

"Aside from showing up and actually keeping her promises?"

Toby smirked. "Aside from that."

He thought about it. "I want her to be honest with me."

"You want her to be real with you?"

"Yes," Jacob said, "if only to figure out my own feelings."

"Well, then!" Toby clapped both hands together. "That's easy enough. Take her out for drinks! Get her to open up. I bet you could certainly woo a young lady with your knowledge of French wines."

"I'm afraid all my social time is over," Jacob said seriously. "Once Monday rolls around, it will be nonstop work on the Matzah Ball."

"Okay, then," she said, not letting her grandson off that easily, "take her out to lunch. Surely, you have to eat over the next eight days?"

"Barely," Jacob said, pushing his plate away. "I'm hosting our investors *and* Silvers. My schedule is jam-packed with activity. Plus, I don't think it would make much of a difference. I mean, I spent all of Shabbat with her, and the most she told me about herself was that she once watched a Christmas movie. Honestly, bubbe… I don't think I've ever met anyone so guarded. Maybe she really is a spy. I should just tell her our deal is off."

He picked up his phone, then just as quickly stopped himself. There was that dual instinct again, that feeling of uncertainty bubbling up inside his chest. She made him feel unsteady. Like the whole earth was wobbly and he couldn't find his balance. He didn't like feeling that way. It reminded him of sitting by the phone waiting for his father to call.

"I don't know what to do," he said honestly.

Toby rubbed the bottom of her chin. "Listen. She's not the first Jewish woman in the world to spend too much time obsessing over nothing. Find some way to loosen her up, challenge her to come out of her shell. At the very least, you'll have fun with each other! And that's really the best part of dating."

"We're not dating."

"You know what I mean, *Yankele!*" She slapped him playfully on the arm. "You could use a little fun, too. Don't be so serious about everything. Just enjoy your time with her. You're leaving for France right after the Matzah Ball, right?"

"The next morning, actually."

"Well, then," Toby said, raising one eyebrow in warning. "This may be your only chance."

From: Rachel Rubenstein-Goldblatt <margotcross@northpole.com>
To: Lisa Brown <l.brown@cachingliteraryagency.com>

Sent: Sun, 12 December
Subject: Matzah-Ballin'(!)

Lisa,

Great news! I'm back in the city now after visiting my parents on Long Island, but think I found the perfect platform (and person!) to garner some much-needed Hanukkah inspiration for my new book! It's still percolating...but I'm starting here:

MatzahBallMax.com

AND YES! YOUR GIRL SNAGGED A TICKET!

Let me know what you think!
Rachel

13

"Rachel! Girl, are you alive?"

Rachel awoke to the sound of Mickey pounding with full force on the front door of her apartment. Scrambling from bed, she reached for her alarm clock, noting the time. It was one thirty. She had been hoping to use Sunday, the day before her first day volunteering for the Matzah Ball, to recoup some energy.

Alas, her best friend did not seem to get the memo.

"Rachel!" The screaming increased in volume. "I will take this door off the hinges!"

Rachel opened the door. "I'm alive."

"*Thank Gawd,*" he gasped, throwing his arms around her in a tight embrace. "Where have you been? I've been trying to reach you all morning."

Rachel patted Mickey on the back. Granted, Rachel had a ton of health issues, but Mickey could be a tad melodramatic. Still, he loved her with an unrivaled ferocity. He protected her and showed up even when nobody else did.

Mickey pushed his way inside, two plastic bags in his hand. He raised one eyebrow at the pile of clothes scattered haphazardly all over the couch. Then his eyes gravitated to a photograph of Rachel and Santa on her coffee table.

He picked up the picture. "On another bender?"

Rachel snatched it from his hand. "It's cheaper than therapy, Mickey."

"I pray for you, Rachel." Mickey bowed his head solemnly. "I include you in my *misheberach* for the ill every Saturday."

"Well," Rachel said, heading for her office, "I should hope so."

She placed the photo of her and Santa safely beneath her computer monitor. There was nothing quite like waking up to Christmas. It was almost better than coffee. After taking one deep breath full of cinnamon brooms and pine needles, she returned to her living room. Mickey had moved her clothes aside and made himself comfortable on the couch.

"Here." He shoved one of the plastic bags in her direction. "I brought you lunch."

She peered into the bag. "Why is everyone always trying to feed me?"

"Because we're Jewish," Mickey explained succinctly. "And that's what we do. We feed the people we love. Now go on... It's chicken soup."

"Kosher?"

"Duh."

"Aw," she said. "You splurged on meat for me."

"Well, obviously," Mickey exclaimed. He reached into his own bag and pulled out a plastic container filled to the brim with imitation crab salad. "I couldn't reach you all morning! I figured if my best friend since forever is dead, I could eat your soup."

"Your love has no limits."

"I know, right?" he said. "I'm not staying long, so don't worry."

Rachel shifted uncomfortably in her spot. "I'm fine, Mickey."

"It's nearly two o'clock." He eyed her. "And you're still in pajamas."

"Work wear," she corrected him. "This is my work clothing."

"Chronically fabulous."

"But enough about me and my amazing fashion sense," Rachel said, pointing a plastic spoon at his head. "Obviously, if you are here on Sunday with chicken soup, something happened. So, my dearest friend, where were you last night?"

Mickey smirked. "I had an extremely hot date."

Rachel gasped. "Jewish?"

He shook his head. "Acrobat."

Rachel burst into hysterics. Leave it to Mickey to find a non-Jewish acrobat to date. "Your mothers will be thrilled."

"You think you have it bad?" Mickey rolled his eyes to the heavens. "They're already planning the wedding for this weekend, and the baby shower for next month."

Rachel laughed again. Knowing Sheryl and Elana, there was a good chance he wasn't joking. Rachel didn't know two people in the world that put a higher value on the word *love*.

Indeed, and growing up together, it was one of the things that Rachel always loved about visiting Mickey in the city. Over Shabbat dinners, Sheryl and Elana would tell the most amazing stories about their meeting, and falling in love, as law students in Manhattan.

Rachel always loved their stories. She especially loved the sweet way they looked at each other while telling them, the light of the Shabbat candles illuminating their smiling faces. Maybe she had been destined to become a romance writer. But looking back on it now—her eyes drifting over to the open door of her Christmas office—she couldn't help intuiting something deeper. Mickey came from a committed Jewish home. It was bound up in all the same rules and traditions as her own. And yet, something about their Judaism always felt freer.

Rachel teased her best friend. "So our promise to grow old together is officially off?"

"You will be my one and only until the day I die."

"Or until you meet an acrobat."

"Exactly."

Rachel continued eating while Mickey filled her in on the juicy details. The acrobat had a name, Stefan, and he was in town with a circus visiting from Russia. It was all quintessential Mickey, who would tell you without any shame that he had already dated every Jewish gay man in Manhattan and therefore had no choice but to outsource.

"By the way," Mickey said, pointing his plastic fork in her direction. "Where were *you* this weekend? I tried calling you like ten zillion times to tell you about my spinner."

"I had my phone off."

"Wait." Mickey blinked. "Does that mean…"

"Yep, I went to my parents' house."

"No."

"Jacob Greenberg was there."

"No!"

"We spent *all* Shabbat together."

"No!"

Rachel told him everything, starting with the ultimatum from her publisher and working her way forward. He listened, eyes wide, occasionally rolling them, before she finally rounded out the story with her visit to Santa last night. Mickey swallowed hard, taking it all in and shaking his head in pure disbelief. He set the plastic container of food down on the coffee table.

"Rachel," he said gently, "you know I love you, so don't take this the wrong way…but how are you going to volunteer anywhere, for a week, with chronic fatigue syndrome?"

Rachel considered the question. "Cocaine?"

"Jesus."

Rachel sighed. "I don't think He can help, either."

She was waiting for Mickey to laugh, to cut her some slack considering her situation. But Mickey was far too concerned about her health to play along with her reindeer games.

"You need to tell Jacob about your disease," Mickey said.

"No."

"You need to at least explain to him what you can and can't do."

"Absolutely not."

"Rachel!" Mickey was practically on his feet now. "It's not good for you."

"And what?" Rachel said, growing frustrated. "Have him think of me as some sort of charity case? Have him pity me because my world is so much smaller than his? I have fought my whole life for some semblance of normal, Mickey. I am not *invalid*!"

He met her intensity. "You psycho, nobody thinks you're invalid, okay? That's your own *meshugas*, your own junk you're projecting on everybody else. You need to start owning who you are, girl! Because who you are is fabulous."

Rachel stared down at what remained of the chicken soup that was growing cold. Chronic fatigue syndrome had robbed her of so much. It would have swallowed her whole had it not been for her books. She couldn't lose her publishing contract. Like Paul scooting around in his electric wheelchair every Saturday, it gave her purpose.

Mickey sat back down on the couch. "I'm sorry."

"It's fine," she said, and meant it. "I need your honesty in my life."

"I just worry about you is all. I don't want you to get sick again, like how you were…"

"I know."

There were only a handful of people who had seen Rachel on her darkest days, both when she had first fallen ill and in the aftermath of crashes that followed. Mickey was one of them.

He had loved her through it. He had come over to her parents' house and lain beside her in bed, stroking her hair when she was too tired to speak or move. He read up on her disease, learned all about spoon theory and energy envelopes, called doctors at Stanford and Harvard. He never once said she was faking, which was a common refrain from people who didn't understand the disease. And on the darkest days of her life, he whispered in her ear to hold on. He promised her that things would get better—and they did.

Chronic fatigue syndrome was a spectrum disease. It varied in intensity and ran the gamut from mildly disabling to making you bedridden. Rachel knew she existed on that spectrum somewhere between moderate and severe. If she took care of herself—if she focused on her health and carefully managed the way she expended energy—she could have some quality of life. She could work from home, take walks, even travel.

The minute she veered off track, the minute she pushed beyond what her body was physically capable of, she crashed. And the crashes sucked. They could turn the simplest acts—opening a can of soup or crawling to the bathroom—into an impossibility.

"I love you," Rachel said, squeezing his hand.

"I love you, too," Mickey said, changing the topic. "At least, tell me this much—how does he look?"

Rachel grinned, mischievous. "He's gorgeous."

Mickey groaned.

"Drop-dead, in fact. He could probably model if he wasn't a super-successful businessman."

"No!"

She nodded sadly. "Also, incredibly stylish. I'm not sure if it's because he's French, or rich, but he basically oozes charm."

"You're killing me," he balked. "Is he still a jerk?"

"Alas," she said, "I dread telling you this, but he is positively decent."

Mickey shook his head. "Well, if you don't want him, I'll take him."

Rachel agreed wholeheartedly. "To tell you the truth, I can't find one logical reason to continue hating him. Except for the fact that he's perfect, which is slightly annoying. But it would be wrong to hold perfection against someone."

"So what are you trying to say?"

"Chronic fatigue syndrome aside, there is a part of me that wants to volunteer for this Matzah Ball. I'm kind of looking forward to seeing him again, spending more time with him. Is that weird?"

It took Mickey a moment. "Oh, my Gawd, you're gonna be another successful Camp Ahava match!"

"Please…"

"I'm serious, Rachel!" He couldn't stop himself from devolving into hysterics. "They're gonna put you in one of their newsletters. 'Jacob Greenberg and Rachel Rubenstein-Goldblatt, world-famous summer camp archenemies, are getting married.'"

"Okay." Rachel rolled her eyes. "I get it. Super funny."

"Oh, this wedding is gonna be *huge*."

"Look, I'm just saying maybe it won't be the worst eight days of my life. Obviously, I'm not aiming for anything more than a friendship here. Jacob lives in Paris. I live in New York. He throws parties for a living. I'm a sick chick who never leaves home. Plus, he thinks I'm a nice Jewish girl. He has no idea what I *actually* do for a living. But, at the very least, I can say it now with full confidence. I am, officially, calling a truce with Jacob Greenberg."

"Well, then—" Mickey lifted his plastic carton up into the air, as if offering it up as a toast "—to your truce with Jacob Greenberg. May you both live happily ever after, and wind up in a Camp Ahava newsletter."

14

Jacob knew the Jewish Day of Rest was long over because his phone was ringing off the charger. Hunched like a Hanukkah hobgoblin at the child-sized desk in his grandmother's apartment, he navigated between three spreadsheets, two laptops, five waiting text messages and one hundred forty-seven unread emails.

"Yeah," Jacob said, speaking on the phone to a member of his team. "I know. Well, tell him he's not getting paid then. Yeah, I don't care. He needs to work with you. And if he has a problem with that, fire him. You have my full authority, okay?"

Jacob hung up. Cracking his neck, he tried to work out the pain that had settled in the center of his left shoulder blade.

Normally, this was his favorite part of producing a high-end and large-scale music festival. The chaos of it all. Phones ringing off the hook. Text messages, one after the other, coming in from Shmuel. He loved the feeling of teetering on the edge of near-catastrophe before racing in to stomp out any impending fires.

He loved not having to think.

He had a gift for it, really. Throwing parties. His music festivals were highly organized and well managed. He had a talent for thinking ahead, a natural ability with numbers and a gift for preempting disaster. It was one of the reasons his investors trusted him. His ideas were often outlandish, he pushed past the boundary of what others thought was possible, but Jacob always managed to turn a profit.

At least, he had…until now.

Nobody thought the Matzah Ball was a good idea. Indeed, it had taken months of meetings, sometimes outright begging, by both Shmuel and Jacob, before any of their normal backers would go along with the idea. The only reason they had—the only reason they agreed to cough up the exorbitant amounts of cash it would take to put on this *meshuganah* Jewish party—was because *Jacob Greenberg* was throwing it. He had never let them down before.

It was a trust that was tentative, at best.

Jacob stood up to grab another document from his bag, inadvertently knocking over an airplane-shaped lamp in the process. It went crashing to the floor, taking several pages of work with it. Jacob sighed, staring down at the mess. He tried not to take it personally but the way it plummeted, nose first, felt like some Hanukkah harbinger of doom.

It was a mistake. Everything about this—the Matzah Ball, returning to New York, reconnecting with Rachel—was a terrible and awful mistake.

Jacob bent down and began cleaning up the pieces. He should have just stayed at the Presidential Suite at the Four Seasons. In a hotel, he would have had a king-size bed, room service, a proper desk. But he had reasoned that staying with his grandmother would give them more time together. Force him away from his workaholic ways, allowing him to come home for meals and candle lighting.

He never expected it to be this hard.

It wasn't just the twin-size bed, totally inappropriate for a six-foot man. It was the room itself. His father had grown up in this apartment. Spent his youth and adolescence sleeping in the very same bed. And when Jacob was old enough to visit his bubbe for long stretches of time over breaks and Hanukkah, the room had inevitably been passed down to him. Now, it was like a relic of the past, a time capsule he couldn't escape.

It suffocated him. The clutter his bubbe collected only heightened the bad memories. The collection of airplanes, modeling kits and art supplies. The baseball paraphernalia, posters and autographed balls. Photos of Jacob and his father at various games, arms wrapped around each other, smiling—before his mother fell ill. He looked up to see that goddamn baseball mascot costume, the one his father had bought him at some sports auction, sitting in a chair by the wall.

It had been grinning at him all damn night.

He had an urge to throw it in the trash. To treat it the way his father had treated him, as though he were worthless and expendable.

Jacob's phone buzzed to attention. Grateful for the distraction, he picked it up. "So nu?" Shmuel asked. "How'd it go?"

Jacob could tell from the sound of cars and voices chattering that he was on the street somewhere. "Good," Jacob said, turning away from the costume. "We're on with Rabbi Goldblatt."

"Excellent!" Shmuel said. "That's great news. And the bubbe?"

"Bubbe is good, too." Jacob stepped out into the hallway. "She's actually out now…catching up with some friends."

"Baruch Hashem!"

"Are you heading over to the Four Seasons now?"

"Just about to hop on the subway," Shmuel explained. "Can I expect to see you there?"

"I was already there this morning. Everything should be good to go. You can start doling out payments. Listen…" He rubbed the back of his neck. "There's something I wanted to let you know about for tomorrow. There's going to be a last-minute addition."

"An addition?"

"To the volunteers. Her name is—"

The phone went dead. Jacob tried to call Shmuel back, but it was no use. He must have lost service in the tunnels.

Jacob put his phone away. The feeling of being unsettled, standing on the precipice of danger, rose up inside him again. He needed a drink.

In the kitchen, he opened the fridge. It was nearly empty. Nothing except leftover Chinese food and beer. He wasn't surprised by the beer. His grandmother was German by birth, after all. But, probably because of his mother, he had never quite developed an appreciation for it. He put on a pot of tea, instead.

Leaning against the counter, he waited for the kettle to boil. His eyes wandered to the scar on his finger, and his mind went with it, floating over to Rachel. He would be seeing her tomorrow, spending eight days beside her as she volunteered for the Matzah Ball. He thought back to the advice of his grandmother. *Have fun with each other.*

How exactly was Jacob going to manage that? They weren't children anymore. They weren't in summer camp. He couldn't just sneak over to her bunk at midnight and scratch on her screen door, pretending to be a serial killer. He needed something funny, but appropriate. He wanted Rachel to play along.

The kettle whistled. Jacob took it off the stove and began rummaging through the cabinets for a box of tea. That's when it happened. A full-fledged Hanukkah miracle. His eyes wandered over to three boxes of matzah sitting untouched and unopened on one of the shelves.

Toby always kept a stockpile of matzah in her apartment. Not just because, like most Jewish homes, there was always some left over from Passover. But also because, like most folks of her generation, Toby had seen her fair share of war and tragedy, and matzah was the perfect food for duress.

Matzah was like the Jewish people this way. Hardy and resilient. It could be kept for years, hidden away in a pantry, pulled out during times of economic uncertainty or as a prescriptive for indigestion. Matzah was always there for you in an emergency.

It gave Jacob an idea.

Grabbing the boxes, he raced back to his bedroom. The idea seemed to come fully formed into his mind's eye. He dug through plastic containers full of arts and crafts supplies, hunting down a glue gun. He pulled out scraps of fabric, paint jars and glitter, lining them all up on the blue carpet. Then, as if readying himself for the final showdown in a great war, he turned to that grinning baseball costume.

Forty-five minutes later, he heard his bubbe entering through the front door.

"Yankele!" she called out. "I'm sorry I'm late, but I wanted to stop at the store and—" Toby appeared in the bedroom doorway. A scream escaped her lips as she stepped back, clutching her heart, almost dropping her plastic bags full of baking supplies. "What in God's name is that?"

Jacob looked up from his masterpiece. "It's for Rachel."

"Rachel?" Toby squinted. "I don't understand."

Jacob put down his paintbrush, completely serious. "You said to have fun…"

Toby was clearly horrified. "I meant flirt with her, *Yankele!* Get into a snowball fight, flick water at each other—"

"Bubbe," Jacob said, grabbing the glue gun. "I know what I'm doing."

Toby pursed her lips together, teetering at the edge of the doorway. Perhaps she was debating saying something, thinking about whether or not to point out the giant demon Jacob had just excised, the emotional baggage covered in matzah, laid out all over his floor.

Alas, Toby knew her grandson. Once Jacob got an idea in his head, once he landed on something, it was very hard for him to let it go. Sighing heavily, she turned, leaving him to finish his art project in peace.

"Okay," she said, shaking her head. "I hope you know what you're doing."

From: Lisa Brown <l.brown@cachingliteraryagency.com>
To: Rachel Rubenstein-Goldblatt <margotcross@northpole.com>

Sent: Mon, 13 December
Subject: RE: Matzah-Ballin'(!)

Rachel,

I just got off the phone with Chandra Brouchard at Romance House. She had NO IDEA that Jews throw Hanukkah parties?!? Say wha...?!?

Chandra is just CHAMPING AT THE BIT to get this Matzah-Ball inspired manuscript on their holiday production schedule! Do you think you could get her a synopsis and the first three chapters by the end of this week? I told her you would...

Talk soon!
Lisa

PS: OMG. Saw a picture of the organizer. Please tell me that's your person...

15

The Four Seasons in Manhattan touted itself as a luxury land-mark on billionaire's row. Stepping into the opulent lobby, Rachel thought that the marketing team for the hotel had been conservative in its description.

Granite columns decorated in swaths of gold and red stretched three stories high. A bellman in white gloves greeted her at the entrance. It all evoked wealth and prestige and fabulousness on every conceivable level. Rachel couldn't help feeling out of place in her off-brand black jeggings and three-year-old sneakers.

"Ma'am," the bellman said, chasing after her. "One moment, please."

Rachel clutched her purse to her chest. "I'm supposed to be here."

"Of course." He smiled, kindly. "I was just wondering if I could help you find something."

"Oh." Rachel relaxed. "I'm volunteering for the Matzah Ball."

"Right this way," he said.

Rachel traversed a maze of back hallways and conference

rooms. Passing by men in yellow vests holding extension cords and stylish assistants chattering on their phones, they came to the large room that was the epicenter of the Matzah Ball.

Everywhere Rachel looked, there was movement. A group of volunteers wearing Matzah Ball T-shirts popped locks and set up tables. Electricians stood on ladders stringing lights and calling each other on their walkie-talkies. It was all super-impressive. Rachel couldn't believe how many people were there.

The bellman pointed to a plastic folding table set up in the middle of the room where a squat man in a black velvet kippah was sitting with a clipboard. A queue of at least ten people were waiting to speak with him.

"You can check in with Shmuel Applebaum over there," the bellman said.

"Thanks," Rachel said, and got in line.

She couldn't help keeping an eye out for Jacob. She was nervous. Maybe it was all the stimulants, Red Bull and coffee she had guzzled this morning, but she was also fully out of her comfort zone.

For one, she couldn't speak French, and a lot of Jacob's colleagues were extremely French. She listened to them move between languages, wondering what they were saying. But more so than that—more than their sophisticated boots paired with fashionable jeans and black turtlenecks—she wasn't used to this. These people were strangers.

Jacob appeared from a back door, surrounded by a group of women, dressed in smart suits and clutching designer bags, as he gave them a tour of the premises.

Rachel swooned at the sight of him. There were men who walked, and men who strutted. Jacob Greenberg strutted. Even wearing a stupid ugly Hanukkah sweater, he oozed deliciousness like a jelly doughnut. It seemed unreasonable for any one person to be that pretty, but Jacob had clearly won the Ashkenazi genetic lottery.

Rachel stood on tiptoe and tried to wave to him. She knew she'd caught his eye—that Jacob had seen her standing in the volunteer line—but he didn't acknowledge her with so much as a nod.

It was strange. Rachel thought they had shared something over Shabbat, but now she felt abandoned. Watching him with what appeared to be the season-seven cast of *Real Housewives*, she was irked. Is this what his life was like? Traveling the world, throwing parties, a bevy of beautiful women hanging off his every word?

Rachel swallowed the rankled feeling bubbling up inside her. She just needed that Matzah Ball ticket.

She repeated this fact like a mantra inside her mind. It didn't matter about Jacob Greenberg. It didn't matter who he talked to or what women swooned in his presence. She would get through this week and write that stupid Hanukkah book for Chandra. *Chag* freaking *sameach*.

"Next!" Shmuel called to Rachel from his table.

"Good morning," Rachel quipped, putting her best face forward. "I'm here to—"

"Who are you?" he said, interrupting her. "What do you need?"

Rachel was taken aback. She was used to people being abrupt in New York, but this little man was downright rude.

"I'm Rachel," she said.

"Rachel, Rivka, Rachel-la," he said, scanning the sheet. "I don't have you on my list."

"It's okay," Jacob said, finally coming over. "She's with me. Last-minute addition."

"Last-minute addition?" Shmuel raised one eyebrow at Jacob. "We don't have room for—"

Rachel watched the men's conversation devolve into whispers. She tried to listen in, but they had switched to French. She couldn't believe it. They were talking about her, in front of her, in a language she did not understand. Unbelievable.

"I know, I know," Jacob said in English, "but this is Rabbi Goldblatt's daughter…"

Rachel felt a blood vessel in her brain pop. It was bad enough that she was tired and that Jacob didn't seem to care enough about her to even put her on the stupid volunteer list, but she despised being introduced to anyone as Rabbi Goldblatt's daughter.

"It's *Rachel*," she snapped.

Shmuel looked up from his huddle. "What?"

"Just Rachel." She glanced between the two men. "I'm my own person, you know."

Both men fell silent. Almost immediately, Rachel regretted the outburst. It was ridiculous to get this upset over an introduction. Regardless, there was something about people whispering secrets about her that stoked her anxieties.

"Okay," Shmuel said, scribbling her name at the bottom of his clipboard. "*Just Rachel*, you can follow Jacob."

Jacob led her through another maze of hallways. She could feel the tension pulsing through her body. He was acting weird. Maybe she was acting weird, too. It suddenly struck her, in some place that was deep and hurtful—Shabbat Jacob was totally different than work Jacob.

She didn't like this version of him. There was something about his energy, the way he bounced in his sneakers beside her, that felt off. Or maybe it just reminded her of the Jacob Greenberg she'd known at Camp Ahava.

"How are you today?" Jacob asked.

"Fine," she said succinctly.

"I was thinking about what you said the other day."

"What I said?"

"About being a writer," he explained. "About working for someone or other, doing freelance or something…"

"Oh," she said, remembering their conversation at dinner. "Right."

"We're very lucky to have someone with your background."

Rachel forced a smile. They were standing at the end of the hallway near what looked to be some sort of utility closet.

She assumed Jacob was going to ask her to write something, start a blog or begin proofreading marketing materials. Perhaps he had even set up a computer in that tiny closet. Rachel breathed a secret sigh of relief. Writing would give her the perfect excuse to remain seated for most of the week.

"You clearly know how to touch people," Jacob said, his voice booming through the halls. "So I thought to myself, how can I best utilize Rachel Rubenstein-Goldblatt this week? How can I make use of her many skills and talents? And then, I knew. I just knew."

Jacob opened the closet door. Rifling through coats and cleaning supplies, he struggled to pull out something large and round, hidden beneath a disposable dust cover. After several minutes of fighting, Jacob yanked it from the closet and tore the white covering away.

What Rachel saw beneath it was nothing short of an epic monstrosity.

A giant swollen ball of foam and compressed air, decorated by a wide and creepy smile, met her horror-stricken eyes. It had blue arms and red legs in tiny sneakers that dangled like deformed stubs at the bottoms and sides. But what made her want to shriek aloud in horror were the tiny pieces of real matzah, covered in purple paint and gold glitter, that someone had hot-glued all over the front.

"What sweet nightmare is this?"

"This," Jacob said, holding it up, "is a matzah ball costume."

"It's awful."

"You think?" Jacob said, tilting his head sideways. "I rather like it."

Rachel crossed her arms against her chest. "So, what...?" she asked, unamused. "You want me to get it dry-cleaned or something?"

"Actually," he said, pushing it in her direction, "I want you to wear it."

Rachel nearly choked on her tongue. *"What."*

Jacob beamed proudly. "I want you to be our very own *Lokshen Liaison!*"

"You want me to be a Noodle Liaison?"

"Oh, Rachel," Jacob said, frowning dramatically. "This position is so much more than being an egg noodle swimming around in a delicious bowl of chicken soup. You're the matzah ball. You're the centerpiece, the celebration of our round and hearty identity, amplifying Ashkenazi culture for all who cross your path. Everybody loves a matzah ball."

This was not happening. Rachel half expected a camera crew to jump out of the closet and tell her that she was being punked. But when she looked back at Jacob, he was still holding that leviathan of a costume, his face drop-dead serious.

"I can't wear that thing!" Rachel spit back.

"Why ever not?"

"Because..." she stammered. "It's three times bigger than me!"

"I assure you it's very lightweight."

"I have a skin allergy," she lied. "I'll break out into hives."

"It's made with all-natural and organic ingredients." He took a piece of matzah off the costume and happily ate it to show her it was safe. "You see," he said, as crumbs of purple paint and gold glitter fell to the floor. "Everything we used is nontoxic and completely hypoallergenic. That will likely come in handy tomorrow."

"Tomorrow?" Rachel whispered. "What happens tomorrow?"

Jacob beamed. "Telling you would ruin the fun of the surprise! You want to have fun, don't you?"

This was too much. He was too much. Her heart pounded as she struggled to find some way out of this disaster.

"Give me another position," Rachel begged.

"There isn't another position."

"I can't do it, Jacob!"

"Rachel," he said, getting serious. "We had a deal. Now, if you're not happy with the position available, I understand. Not everyone has the zest and pep needed to be a proper matzah ball. But, if that is the case, I'm afraid I'm going to have to ask you to leave."

"Leave?" she spit back. "Well, what about my ticket?"

"Unfortunately," he said, pursing his lips together, "I'd have to give your ticket to someone else. You understand. Limited numbers. It would go to someone…well, someone who keeps their promises."

Rachel stared into the dead eyes of the matzah ball costume. She had come this far in her journey. She couldn't sprint away now. Swallowing her pride, she reached one unsteady hand forward. Taking the hanger from Jacob, the weight of her new reality assaulted her nostrils, smelling like boxed matzah on Passover.

16

Jacob was thinking about the summer of pranks and fun that had blossomed into love, when Rachel emerged from the restroom at the Four Seasons.

The matzah ball costume was even better than he had envisioned. Swallowing his laughter, he forced himself to remain professional.

"Wow," he said, digging his hands into his pockets. "You look amazing."

She narrowed her eyes at him. "Thanks."

"Do you mind if I get a picture of you?" Jacob asked.

"I'm not really into social—"

He pulled out his phone and snapped a picture. "Look how cute you are," he said, showing her the photo.

A small puff of exasperated air escaped her lips. She looked up to the heavens, shaking her head a little. Jacob cocked his head, confused. Why wasn't she laughing?

The matzah ball costume—such a simple idea, a fun little prank to loosen her up—was now the delineation point between two very different people. Rachel, who hid so many secrets about herself; and Jacob, who never cared what other people thought of him.

But Jacob never had the luxury of caring. His early experiences in life had taught him that people were unreliable. Your mother could fall ill. Your father could abandon you. Like many children from broken homes, he learned to rely on himself.

Jacob didn't see a problem with the costume. He didn't see it as cruel or mean—he simply saw it as a game, and the more Jacob played that game, the better he felt.

"Okay, then," Jacob said, stepping aside to let her pass. "Let me show you where you'll be working today."

Waddling slowly behind him, Rachel left a trail of matzah crumbs as she went, and forced his staff to press their backs up against the corridor wall to allow her to pass.

Rachel turned bright red. "Do you really think this is a good idea?"

"I can't think of a better one."

They came to the main lobby. Beside the large Christmas tree decorated in blues and whites, his staff was already hard at work. Three women, all dressed stylishly in matching blue sweaters and black skirts, were setting up laptops and cameras. Jacob pointed to a long table lined with large silver gift totes.

"This is where you'll be working," he said.

"Great."

"As you know—" Jacob made it a point to be over-the-top in his delivery "—our main event will be held on the eighth night of Hanukkah. But while most of the staff is busy setting up the main event room, and as is typical with these types of large-scale productions, we also have the option of silver passes for a select few guests."

"Silver passes?"

"Silver passes offer guests special and exclusive access to events leading up to the big event. For those who elected to buy silver tickets, it will be eight days of nonstop and Jewy-themed fun, leading up to the Matzah Ball. There will be chocolate spa treatments, spinning classes by candlelight, a twenty-four-hour aromatherapy bar where you can craft your very own Hanukkah-themed essential oils."

"Well, who doesn't love essential oils!" Rachel met his enthusiasm.

"Exactly, Rachel!" Jacob said, ignoring her obvious snark. "Now, as our very own Lokshen Liaison, you will be in charge of greeting our silver-level guests. You will answer questions, escort them to their rooms, show them to their Hanukkah-copters."

"Hanukkah-*what*?"

"Eight fabulous helicopters painted gold and silver to look like flames! Just imagine them, flying over the Manhattan skyline."

"I'm imagining something."

"Now," Jacob continued. "You will make sure our Silvers are bubbling over with excitement, every single second of every single day that they are here. You will bring pep! You will bring energy! But first—" he picked up an elegantly designed schedule on silver paper "—you will make sure every single one of our silver guests gets a schedule."

She shrugged. "Sounds simple enough."

"Whenever one of our silver guests arrives, Maddie over there—" he waved to a woman with stylish short hair "—will check them in, get them all set up with our app. After which, you will personally be in charge of—wait for it, wait for it—giving them a gift bag and one of these schedules."

Rachel reached for the materials. "Got it."

"A schedule," he said, putting it in the bag, "in the bag."

"I got it, Jacob."

"Not outside the bag," he said, driving the point home. "But inside...*inside* the bag."

"Jesus Christ!" she finally snapped. "I'm not a moron, Jacob."

"Would you feel better if we practiced it?"

She was going to kill him. He could see it in her eyes.

Jacob pulled back, though only a little. "Look, it's just a matzah ball costume, okay? Don't be so intense about everything. We're here to have fun, all right? I promise you. You're gonna love being our Lokshen Liaison."

He was waiting for her to say something. Give him another round of that relentless snark. But she was off, deep in thought, staring at the spot where she would be spending the next eight hours greeting visitors. She seemed upset. Worried in a way that was different than he expected. He considered pressing her on it, when his phone buzzed to attention.

Shmuel had sent him a text message: You're late.

It was followed only seconds later by three more text messages in rapid succession:

?!?!?!?!?!?!?!?!?!

sjadhlsadjhsdalkfhslk

ARE YOU TRYING TO KILL ME, JACOB!?!?!?!?

"I have to go," he said, putting his phone on Silent.

"But—"

"I'll check in on you later, okay?" He turned and ran up the large set of stairs in the center of the lobby. "Oh, and, Rachel—" he beamed from the middle step "—don't forget to smile."

Jacob was certain Rachel was not smiling when he left her.

Then again, neither was Shmuel when he found him.

Shmuel met Jacob's frenzied arrival to the second floor with a disapproving cock of his head and two arms squared on the tzitzit at his hips. Though Jacob was technically Shmuel's boss in the company—the two men deciding years ago to share a sixty-forty split of profits in Greenberg Entertainment—he had always treated him like a partner.

It was a relationship that had developed over ten years, though, at first, Jacob had been hesitant to the idea of sharing his business with any type of partner. Greenberg Entertainment was his baby, after all. He had started it in college dorm rooms before expanding it out into empty storefronts and warehouses on the edges of Paris. As much as he liked Shmuel—as much as he knew that his contacts throughout Europe could expand his music festival empire—he was never going to be dependent on another person again.

Shmuel prayed on it and—perhaps, intuiting that there was something deeper going on for Jacob—eventually agreed. It wasn't always easy, of course.

Jacob could be forceful in his opinions, stubborn and obstinate. There were times in the first few years of their relationship where Shmuel had lost his cool with his *employer*, storming out of some meeting. But eventually, Jacob came to see Shmuel as a trusted ally and friend, and Shmuel came to see Jacob as the same.

"Sorry about that," Jacob said, running his fingers through his hair. "I got distracted."

"Distracted?" Shmuel said, throwing the word back at him. "We got a room full of billionaire investors waiting on you— billionaire investors who hate to be kept waiting, I might add— and you're playing with a matzah ball?"

"I'm not—" Jacob stopped. He wanted to defend himself against the accusation, but Shmuel was right. Jacob *was* playing around with a matzah ball. "It's complicated," he confessed.

"Clearly."

Jacob shook the thought of Rachel away. "How are things going?"

"Now," Shmuel said, nodding toward the conference room, "I've opened a bottle of our most expensive champagne, and not one single person is drinking it. You tell me how you think it's going?"

"I'll handle it."

"You better. You're the one they like, after all."

Jacob tore off his ugly Hanukkah sweater, smoothing out any wrinkles from the front of his button-down shirt as Shmuel handed him a smart wool jacket. Looking sharp, he made his way to the glass-enclosed conference room on the second floor.

"Good morning," he said, entering the conference room. "My apologies for keeping everybody waiting. As you can all imagine, we're very busy this morning."

In one terrifying and unified swivel, all the investors turned to face him. The finely coiffed hair and pressed-on smiles of his audience could almost be mistaken for pleasure. But make no mistake, everyone in this room was here on business. Jacob turned on the charm while Shmuel kept a careful watch from the door.

Jacob had twelve primary investors. Not all of them were physically present. Jacob took a careful accounting of his audience. Three had been conferenced in by phone. Two had sent executives from their own companies as representatives. One had sent their assistant.

His eyes trailed down to the name tag the young man was wearing. Brandon. With a splatter of freckles across his nose and a youthful face, he looked like a Brandon.

Jacob knew he could handle most investors or their stand-ins—it was easy enough to assuage fears with a few glasses of champagne and some expensive one-of-a-kind presents. But Morty Schweitzer, tech mogul and venture capitalist extraordinaire, would be his toughest challenge. Morty had flown in from his private bunker in Grenada to take this meeting himself.

"Let's get down to it," Morty said now, slamming his fist down on the conference room table. "I have a lunch appointment at noon, and we're already running behind schedule."

Jacob smiled politely. "Of course," he said, before pointing at a laptop and projector set up at the front of the room. "If you would all direct your attention to me, I'd be happy to go over the most pressing details."

It would take nearly an hour for Jacob to run over all the particulars. There were the obvious things he had to cover—costs associated, third-party affiliates, the contracts with suppliers. Jacob had a gift for making money, and he ran through the pages of his books with the ease of a man naturally inclined to making budgets.

As for his well-intentioned audience, nobody in the room really cared about the minuscule details. His investors had not become billionaires by micromanaging every single cell in their Excel spreadsheets.

All his stakeholders were really concerned about was their ROI. They wanted to make sure that the Matzah Ball Max would make more money than they had originally invested. It was a guarantee that, unlike with previous events, Jacob could not completely offer.

He finished his presentation and waited for the firing squad to return to their upright positions at the table.

"Have there been any requests for refunds?" Taylor asked.

"Not one," Jacob confirmed.

"Good," she said, tapping notes into her phone.

"Though everyone knows we don't make money from ticket sales," Morty interjected. "I want to know about social media, Jacob. I want to know if you're driving traffic to the website, and how many advertisers are begging for a piece of my Matzah Ball on Instagram. I want to go to bed at night cuddling my third-party data. But you know what I see when I look at my phone? Zip! Zilch! Nada! Where are my hashtags, Jacob? *Where's my Jewish Kendell Jenner that gets me trending on Twitter?*"

The room grew quiet. All eyes fell on Jacob.

He squared his shoulders confidently. "I can assure you we have everything in place to make this Matzah Ball a huge success. Once the actual event begins, once content starts being uploaded and downloaded from our apps and websites, you'll get the traffic you're looking for."

Brandon perked up from behind his laptop. "And if you're wrong?"

"I've never been wrong about an event before."

Morty considered this argument carefully, rubbing his chin. The Matzah Ball was gaining traction in the Jewish world. That was important, but for Greenberg Entertainment, the party itself was almost irrelevant. It was the images and video clips, pictures of influencers wearing bikinis while sunbathing on rocks that had brought in the bulk of his company's profits on previous events. It was all the uploads and downloads, shared links and mutual likes, and sponsorships and royalties that had sent their revenue into the millions.

Launchella and Sunburn had made Jacob a fortune. But those were large-scale events, held in the middle of deserts and on private islands with celebrities anyone would recognize attending. It was easy to garner interest and drive traffic utilizing these methods.

The Matzah Ball Max was different. It was going to be held indoors and had a smaller audience. It was created around Hanukkah, and designed to feature Jewish artists and performances. Plus, it was a high-end, formal affair. Instead of dreadlocks and portable toilets, there would be personal assistants and evening gowns.

Jacob knew he could throw a great party. But in order to fulfill his investors' demands for that all-too-important ROI, the Matzah Ball needed to have mass-market appeal. Its images and videos, like the story of the people who attended, would need to be shared by news organizations and social media influencers from outside the Jewish world. It needed to cross over.

Grace grimaced, concerned. "And what about...that thing?"

"What thing?"

"That ridiculous matzah ball mascot I passed in the lobby,"

she said. "Last I checked, that's not exactly the upscale feeling you promised us for this event."

Grace was right. The costume was not at all indicative of the high-end and formal affair that Jacob had promised investors. Something about Rachel made Jacob skirt common sense.

"That's mainly for the children of our Silvers," Jacob lied. "Our VIP guests who opted to spend a full week in New York before the main event."

"*Kids?*" Brandon asked. "Why are there kids at our Matzah Ball?"

"It's winter vacation." Jacob thought on his feet. "Kids are off from school. We figured we could do a little something for them. Provide some babysitting. Give the parents a break. Especially since not all our activities this week are particularly child friendly. If the kids are happy, the parents are happy, right?"

The room broke into murmurs and huddles. It was a good excuse. Jacob knew it.

And Shmuel was there to seal the deal.

"Plus," Shmuel interjected, "think of the memes!"

Morty perked up. "Memes?"

"Who loves social media more than a teenager, right?" Shmuel pulled out his phone. Scrolling through, he opened the Matzah Ball event app. There, on the very first page, available for download, was the image of Rachel's giant matzah ball bottom, squeezing itself uncomfortably through a doorway. Beneath the photo, in big block letters, were the words *NAILED IT.*

"Eh?" Shmuel said, pointing to his phone. "Funny, right?"

The room broke into hysterics. Everyone was thrilled.

Yes, the atrocious matzah ball in the front lobby would serve its purpose. To make money. Whether or not that had been Jacob's original intention was irrelevant. His investors were happy. Jacob could now return his attention to what mattered—making the event a success.

With his stakeholders' concerns muted for the time being,

Jacob raised a final toast to their success. "To Hanukkah," Jacob said, lifting his glass high into the air. "And to a healthy return on all our investments."

17

The epitome of miserable, Rachel stood in the lobby handing out schedules and tote bags to ungrateful Silvers. She couldn't be sure how many hours had passed since Jacob had assigned her this role as a Lokshen Liaison. All she knew was that he had lied. The matzah ball costume was not lightweight. Her feet were killing her, and to make matters worse, it was nearly impossible to put schedules into tote bags *when you didn't have arms*.

"Excuse me," Rachel said, chasing down a woman with three children in tow. "You forgot your schedule."

It was clear that Rachel's mere presence as a matzah ball offended the primly dressed woman. With one hand over her heart, she fixed Rachel with a look of sheer horror. Rachel tried not to take it personally. Yes, she was sweaty. Yes, she smelled like the meat counter at the 2nd Avenue Deli. But she was here to do a job.

"It's important that you and the children have a schedule," she explained, smiling down at the three kids. "You don't want to miss your Hanukkah-copter."

"I thought this was all on the app?"

"It is," Rachel said, trying not to show her frustration. "But our CEO wants to make sure that all participants also get a physical copy, just in case."

The woman was annoyed. Nobody liked paper in the modern age. Still, Rachel was determined, refusing to back down from her position, and the woman finally acquiesced. Snapping the paper from her hands, the young mother and her children headed for the elevator. Rachel watched as the paper flittered out of the tote bag and onto the floor unnoticed. *Great.*

Rachel watched the elevator doors close behind them, feeling like the biggest idiot ever. It was pointless. Nobody was listening to her. The stupid costume, like this ridiculous task, was a giant waste of time. She got the distinct impression that Jacob was messing with her, setting her up for failure. She just didn't understand why.

Rachel returned to her position by the front entrance. Gawd, she was tired. The only thing that seemed to keep her going was an adrenaline-filled fury.

The sound of laughter drew her from her thoughts. She glanced over to the welcoming table to find Maddie and team giggling hysterically. They were staring at something on her phone, passing it back and forth between them.

Rachel couldn't help but be curious. "What is it?" she asked.

Maddie held up the phone for her to see. The fury turned into blind rage.

Jacob Greenberg had turned her into a meme.

Her cheeks flushed red. Tears formed in the corners of her eyes. It seemed that every smile directed her way was at her expense. Rachel couldn't take it anymore. Tearing off the hood of her costume and sucking back those tears, she waddled—as fast as she could, anyway—to the nearest exit.

"Where are you going?" Maddie called out to her.

"To lunch!"

Rachel wasn't hungry. She simply needed space. A place away from her *adoring fans* and the relentless sound of laughter that followed her. She found that quiet solitude through a side door of the Four Seasons. Exiting into an alley, she slumped beside a trash receptacle, ignoring the discarded cigarette butts piled up around her feet.

Alone now, Rachel pulled the top of her costume down, stretched her arms, cracked her neck. At last she could breathe. The crisp winter air felt refreshing against her skin. She wanted to tell Jacob that he could take his stupid matzah ball costume and choke on it. But she needed that ticket. She still didn't have an idea for a Hanukkah romance that would win over the very persnickety Chandra Brouchard.

The tears began again.

"Excuse me?" A voice sounded at the end of the alley. Rachel glanced up to see a little old lady holding an aluminum container in her hands. A black leather pocketbook nearly half her size was slung over her shoulder. "Are you okay?"

"I'm fine," Rachel said, blinking back tears.

"You don't seem fine," she said, and came over anyway.

The old woman took a seat on the step beside her. Placing her giant purse to her side, she held the aluminum container safely on her lap.

"Are you here for the Matzah Ball?" the old woman asked.

"No." Rachel smirked. "I'm here for the bankruptcy conference."

The old woman grinned, pointing one spindly finger in her direction. "You have an excellent sense of humor."

"Not really. I'm a volunteer. Are you here for the Matzah Ball?"

"Me?" The old woman pointed to herself. "Oh, no. I'm just here to visit my grandson. He invited me to a party tonight, and I thought I would bring him some lunch."

"That's awfully nice of you."

"We don't get to see each other that often. I travel quite a bit, and he's always working. I have to figure out ways to spend time with him." The old woman opened the lid to her aluminum tin and angled the contents toward Rachel. "Are you hungry? I always bring extra."

Rachel stared down to find a tray filled with what appeared to be spring rolls.

"Oh." Rachel hesitated. "That's so nice of you, but I really shouldn't."

"You're on a diet? They're vegetarian!"

Rachel laughed before explaining, "I'm kosher...well, kind of. It's a long story."

There were different levels of kashrut, or kosher laws, observed among Jews. Rachel had grown up in a home where every item, other than produce, needed a *hechsher*, or kosher certification. But as an adult, independent of her parents, her own observance fluctuated as frequently as the weather. She never went so far as to eat pork or shellfish. But many days, she would eat vegetarian items cooked in nonkosher restaurants and kitchens.

"Hmm." The old woman stared down at her spring rolls. "You know, it's a tradition to eat fried foods on Hanukkah. To remind us of the miracle of the oil...and how it lasted eight nights, when the Maccabees only had enough oil for one. I rather like that, don't you?"

Rachel nodded. "It's a nice tradition."

"I don't know about you," she said, leaning in with a mischievous twinkle in her eye, "but I think it's important to maintain traditions. You sure you don't want one? You look like you could use a little nosh."

The kind woman wasn't wrong. Rachel was starving. She glanced down the alleyway to make sure no one was watching before reaching inside and taking one. The taste of cabbage and carrots fried in a crunchy wrapper brought all her feelings to the surface. She burst into tears.

"It's tough to be a matzah ball," the old woman said.

Rachel sobbed. "Jacob Greenberg is the worst person ever."

The woman raised an eyebrow in Rachel's direction. "Jacob Greenberg?"

"My summer camp archenemy," Rachel explained.

"Ah." She nodded. "Those can be problematic."

"He's just…" Rachel shook her head, confused. "He's mean to me for no reason."

She didn't understand. The Jacob she had met at Shabbat was so kind. She thought about the way he helped her mother after Shabbat dinner, donated money to the synagogue without mentioning it. She especially couldn't help but recall the way he had interacted with Paul. She couldn't reconcile Shabbat Jacob with the man who seemed hell-bent now on humiliating her.

"Maybe he has a reason?" the old woman offered up.

"Yeah," Rachel scoffed. "He's a monster."

"Maybe he secretly likes you?"

"Ha!" Rachel laughed aloud. "More like he secretly enjoys torturing me! This is his thing, you know? He sets me up. Makes me like him. Makes me fall for him! Then stomps all over my heart just for laughs."

The old woman raised a curious eyebrow in Rachel's direction. "So you *do* like him?"

"Of course not," Rachel said, defending herself. "Jacob Greenberg means *absolutely* nothing to me. He could choke on a latke for all I care."

"Oh, my…" The old woman chewed on a spring roll.

"You know what we call it in Jewish law?" Rachel asked. "When you misrepresent yourself like that?"

"No."

"*Geneivat da'at,*" Rachel said, tapping her temple. "It means 'stealing the mind.' And it's like…one of the worst things you can do. But that's what Jacob does *every time* to me. And you know what—" she grabbed another spring roll, stuffing it in her mouth "—shame on me! I should have seen it. I should have known better. I deserve to be a matzah ball."

Rachel finished off the last of her spring roll. The feelings stirring inside her went beyond blind fury. She was hurt. Jacob's reappearance in her life had made her dream of happy endings, a chance to be honest, a chance to feel brave again with him by her side. The fact that he had robbed her of that chance—or worse, never even considered it to begin with—stung.

"I should just quit," Rachel said hopelessly.

"Don't quit. It might seem hard now, but something good always comes from our most difficult challenges. That's how we make meaning, really. That's how we find light during the darkest of times. Besides, you don't strike me as a quitter."

Rachel nodded. She was like a dog with a bone when she settled her heart on something. She was not one to walk away from a challenge. Indeed, this singular and driven focus had secured her first book contract. Despite countless rejections, she had hunkered down, learned what she needed to, kicking open the door of Romance House. She would need that same singular drive to save her career now.

The old woman reached into her pocketbook and pulled out a plastic bag filled to the brim with sufganiyot.

"Do you like doughnuts?" she asked.

Rachel's mouth went slack in amazement. "You had all those in your purse?"

"We all carry more than we should." She shook the bag of doughnuts in her direction. "A little nosh on something sweet always makes me feel better."

Rachel shrugged. "Why not?"

The old woman dipped into her bag and pulled out two jelly doughnuts, one for each of them. It was still warm as Rachel sank her teeth into the doughy fried goodness. Powdered sugar fell all over her costume and hands. The woman was right. Rachel began to feel better.

"I'm sorry," Rachel said, wiping her hands. "I didn't even get a chance to introduce myself. I'm Rachel."

"Toby." She offered her hand. "It's nice to meet you."

Her kindness was enough to get Rachel through the rest of her day.

The afternoon floated by in a miserable drum of Silvers and their stupid freaking schedules. Rachel tried to push through—tried not to let Jacob Greenberg know that he had gotten to her—but all she could think about was going home. By the time five o'clock rolled around, Rachel took the liberty.

Heading to the bathroom, she removed her costume. Dragging it out of the stall behind her, she caught a reflection of herself in the line of mirrors about the sink. The fluorescent overhead lighting was not doing her any favors.

Suddenly the door opened. Maddie, the young woman in charge of directly overseeing volunteers, appeared beside her. Pulling out a bright red lipstick, she fixed her makeup in the mirror beside Rachel.

She compared herself to the woman. Her short pixie cut and strong chin made the woman striking. Rachel couldn't help but wonder about her relationship with Jacob. It seemed impossible that the two had not dated at some point.

"You want to borrow?" Maddie asked, holding the lipstick out to her.

"Oh." Rachel was surprised at the offer to share makeup with a woman she had just met. "That's very nice of you, but I'm good. Not really my color."

Maddie shrugged, put her lipstick away and began focusing on eyeliner.

Not that Rachel was jealous. She just realized how positively ridiculous it was for her to think that someone like Jacob—someone whose life was filled with fabulous people and non-stop parties—would ever be interested in her.

"Well," Rachel sighed, before heading for the door. "I guess I should get going. I'll see you tomorrow?"

"Wait—" Maddie squinted in her direction, surprised. "You're not staying for the party?"

"What party?"

"The Hanukkah party," she exclaimed. "Everybody is staying for it. Jacob didn't mention it to you?"

"No."

"Ah," she said. "Well, Jacob is bringing in dinner for everybody on staff. Drinks, too. I believe they are going to light first night Hanukkah candles, as well. He always does some sort of party for staff on the first setup night of his events. To say thank you for all our hard work, and to get everybody ready for the days ahead."

"The days ahead?" Rachel asked curiously.

"Yes," Maddie exclaimed, checking herself in the mirror one last time. "Today was easy, of course. First day. Set up. Welcome the early guests. But everything just gets more difficult from this point on. It will likely be a giant and exhausting mess...until it is not. That's always how it is with Jacob's events."

Maddie's words sent dread to the bottom of her stomach. It seemed impossible that her days could get any worse. Then again, Jacob had promised her a surprise tomorrow.

"Yeah," Rachel said, annoyed at him, and this whole terrible experience. "I think I'm going to skip out on this one."

"If Jacob should ask where you are?"

"Trust me," Rachel said adamantly, "he won't."

Rachel splurged on a cab home. It was a poor economic choice given the state of her career, but she couldn't bear the thought of expending any more energy on a subway. It seemed impossible, the idea of waiting on a platform for fifteen minutes. Or, worse, having to stand for the entire twenty-minute ride to her apartment. Besides, she would need all the energy she could muster to work on her proposal for Chandra Brouchard at Romance House tonight.

Landing back at her apartment, Rachel changed into her pajamas and went into her office. Taking a seat at the desk, she stared at the blinking cursor on Microsoft Word. She didn't know where to begin writing her Hanukkah romance. She had thought that volunteering for the Matzah Ball Max would leave her inspired; instead, all she felt was exhausted.

Her eyes wandered over to the photo of her sitting on Santa's lap. She sighed, picking it up, remembering what a great night it had been. She had been filled with hope and promise, her heart bubbling over with excitement after meeting Shabbat Jacob... and then Matzah Ball Jacob arrived.

The thought gave her an idea.

Waking up her computer, she typed the title of her new manuscript: THE HANUKKAH GRINCH.

Just seeing the words there in black and white made her feel better. A smile appeared on her face as she suddenly realized Toby was correct. She was going to make something good out of this dark situation.

Rachel had survived one day as a Lokshen Liaison. She had smiled through every repetitive, stupid and ridiculous task Jacob had asked of her. Now she was going to get her revenge.

Full of motivation, she began writing her book, an inspired version of Jacob serving as the terrible antagonist. Her story wouldn't be nice. Her prose wouldn't be complimentary. But she would make certain it was enough to secure her a contract from Chandra Brouchard at Romance House. As she pounded out pages, the moon lay visible over Manhattan, her unlit menorah sitting watch from the windowsill.

18

It was the first night of Hanukkah and Jacob was prepared for
a celebration. Standing in the main ballroom, he oversaw the
delivery of six different styles of food, including kosher Chinese
food, Italian food, and French-style charcuterie boards filled
with cheese and meats.

But glancing around the room—at his bubbe placing two colorful candles into a tiny menorah in the center of the room, and
his staff gathering around the makeshift buffet to pour themselves drinks—he realized someone was missing.

Jacob waved over Shmuel. "Mind taking over for me?"

"Mind?" Shmuel joked, waving away his concern. "I was
born to oversee food."

Jacob tapped his friend good-naturedly on the back and
headed for the front lobby, searching for Rachel. Surprised to
find it empty, he walked back through the twisting maze of
hallways that existed around the ballroom. He looked in the
bathroom, then finally saw Maddie sprinting by.

"Hey," Jacob said, catching her attention. "Have you seen Rachel?"

"Who?"

"The matzah ball," he reminded her.

"Oh, right. She went home already."

"Home?" Jacob couldn't believe it. "What about the party? First night candle lighting? She didn't want to stay for any of it?"

Maddie shrugged. "She didn't seem interested."

Jacob stood in the hallway feeling his heart sink. He knew it was ridiculous, getting upset about her leaving without telling him, but it felt like he was being stood up all over again.

Shaking off those feelings, he returned to the main ballroom. It was better this way, he reminded himself. Better that Rachel simply prove what he knew about her all along. She wasn't reliable. Better he learn this about her, finally put a stop to his ridiculous feelings, than get crushed later on.

"Oh, Jacob," Toby greeted him. "Everything looks delicious!"

"I'm so glad, Bubbe."

"This will be the best Hanukkah we've ever spent together."

"I hope so. Excuse me," Jacob called out. "If everybody could please join me in the main ballroom for the first night of Hanukkah, I have a few words I would like to share."

He took his place, center stage, next to the small menorah. Shmuel and the rest of his staff gathered around in a circle, holding drinks in their hands. Looking over the many familiar faces, Jacob suddenly felt the full warmth of the holiday season.

"First off," he said genuinely, "I want to thank everybody for all the hard work you've done until now, and the hard work you're going to do over the next seven days leading up to our Matzah Ball Max."

There were a few knowing chuckles, and grumbles, from his audience. Jacob continued, "I also appreciate how so many jumped in with full enthusiasm for our event. Even though we've never held an event like this before, you believed in the idea as much as I did. But, more important, you're here. You've shown up for me, again and again, and I want you to know I see you."

There were eager nods and a round of applause before he went on. "Now Hanukkah is full of traditions. For those of you who aren't Jewish, you've learned about these traditions in preparation for the event. You've read up on the miracle of the oil, the tradition of eating fried foods and playing a game called dreidel. And you have maybe also heard of a very important tradition, which is the giving of *gelt*, or money."

Jacob beamed like a regular Hanukkah Harry. "So, if you happen to find a little more *gelt* in your bank account this holiday season…it's not a mistake. It's just my way of saying thank you. Thank you for taking the time. Thank you for being here. I appreciate you."

Shrieks of delight went up from the crowd.

"Now, I make it a point not to talk about…my family—" Jacob stumbled a bit on the words before regrouping "—but I want to introduce you all to someone very important to me. Someone who taught me the *true* meaning of Hanukkah. Really the reason why we are all here today. My amazing, wise and beautiful bubbe, Toby."

The crowd applauded as Toby stepped forward. She blushed, waving away their accolades. "My grandson is too charming."

A few people laughed. Shmuel loudest of all.

"Bubbe," Jacob said, handing her a matchbook, "would you do us the honor of saying a few words about the holiday, and lighting the very first candle of Hanukkah?"

Toby began to explain Hanukkah. She described how it commemorated the rededication of the Second Temple in Jerusalem by the Maccabees and celebrated the miracle of the oil. "The Maccabees came to that temple, and discovered they only had enough oil for one night," she said. "But lo and behold, a miracle. That oil lasted for eight nights!"

Jacob smiled watching her describe how to use a *shamash*, a helper candle, to light all the other candles, how you were supposed to place your *chanukiyah*—the proper term for the item most frequently referred to as a *menorah*—in a window or public place so that the miracle could be publicized, so that the light would spread from house to house.

"My journey of Hanukkah," Toby said simply, "has spanned ninety-one years. I have celebrated this holiday in Germany, France, New York and Paris, all over the world with my grandson, during good times and bad times alike."

She quieted, a small sadness sitting there at the tip of her throat.

"But what I always explained to Jacob is that these candles are a metaphor. They remind us that we always have a choice. We can be someone who snuffs out another person's candle and, in the process, makes the world a darker place. Or we can be the type of person who spreads light. Better to be the *shamash*—one candle that lights all the others and brightens an otherwise dark world."

A few thoughtful sighs went up from the crowd. His bubbe lit the match, and, with everyone standing around together, they said the blessing for the first night of Hanukkah.

Shouts of "Happy Hanukkah" exploded from the room. Shmuel burst out into a playful song, humming *Maoz Tzur* as he sashayed his way over to the kosher Chinese food. All seemed right in the world and, especially, with Jacob's Matzah Ball.

An hour later, most of Jacob's staff had finished their food and had begun leaving for home. With the room finally quiet—and Shmuel off handling the delivery of their ten-foot menorah—Jacob found a quiet moment to spend with his grandmother.

Unfortunately, she couldn't stay any longer. It was late, and having been at the Four Seasons since the early afternoon, even Toby Greenberg was tired.

Jacob escorted his bubbe to the front exit. Linking one arm

inside her own, he wanted to make sure she didn't stumble. "I hope you had a good time tonight. I know my Hanukkah party was probably pretty tame compared to all the adventures of your travels."

"Oh, *Yankele*," Toby exclaimed, smacking him playfully, "I had a wonderful time tonight. You have no idea how much I enjoyed meeting your colleagues and getting to spend time with you."

"Me, too."

"And you really can't come home?" She turned to him, all sweetness. "I made my famous rugalach this morning. Chocolate and strawberry and apricot...your favorite. You sure you don't have time to share a little nosh and go back to work later?"

"I'm afraid I need to do some paperwork this evening."

"Ah," she said sadly. "Well, I guess I understand."

Jacob moved to hail a cab. *"Yankele,"* she said, before he could complete the task. "There is something I want to talk to you about."

Jacob frowned. He did not like her serious tone. "Is everything all right? You're not feeling ill, are you?"

"No, no," she said cautiously. "I'm perfectly fine. I just wanted to talk to you about Rachel."

"Rachel?" Jacob didn't understand. "What about Rachel?"

"What are you doing?"

Jacob squinted. He had no idea what his grandmother was implying. "I don't understand."

"You don't see a pattern here?"

"A pattern?"

"With your father..."

Jacob shook his head, confused. The last person Jacob wanted to think about right now was his father. He glanced down the snowy avenue, searching for a cab, suddenly eager to get rid of his beloved bubbe. Thankfully, a harried voice interrupted their chat. Shmuel came running down the steps of the Four Seasons, waving a set of papers in his hand.

"Jacob!" Shmuel said, bright red and out of breath. "Come quick—it's a disaster."

"Excuse me a minute, Bubbe," Jacob said, before turning to his friend. "What is a disaster?"

Shmuel grimaced, but refused to answer. "It's better you come see."

"I'm sorry," Jacob said, turning back to his bubbe. "I need to go deal with this."

A few minutes later, Toby was safely in a taxi on her way to her apartment and Jacob was following Shmuel up the steps of the Four Seasons. He held on to his black kippah, all anxious excitement, to keep it from blowing off in the winter winds.

"You'll never believe it," Shmuel said, shaking his head. "We're in serious trouble. I don't know how this happened! I said to Moishe, 'Moishe, make sure everything is lined up! Perfect!' We don't have time for any big problems…"

Shmuel was rambling, but Jacob was determined to keep his cool. All events had problems. Whatever it was, he was certain they could handle it. They came to a hallway. Twenty brown packing boxes, each the size of Jacob's head, were piled up in stacks along the wall. Jacob didn't understand. "What is all this?"

"This," Shmuel said, with dramatic flair, "this is our ten-foot menorah!"

"Excuse me?"

"The shining beacon of our Jewish identity," Shmuel said anxiously. "The centerpiece of our Matzah Ball! The thing that Rabbi Aaron Goldblatt is going to light with his wife, Dr. Rubenstein, to give our Matzah Ball Max the air of authenticity—"

"Yeah, okay. I get it. Why is it in boxes?"

Shmuel grimaced. "I forgot to, maybe…have it assembled?"

"That's a question?"

Shmuel looked through his paperwork, flipping pages. "Apparently not."

Jacob closed his eyes, breathing through his frustration. There were things Shmuel was very good at—raising money, for instance, or organizing volunteers. Jacob would never, in a million years, regret sharing a sixty-forty split with the man. Alas, ordering a specially designed ten-foot acrylic-and-silver menorah from an artisan community in Israel, and making sure it would be assembled upon delivery, was not one of his many talents.

"Are you mad?" Shmuel frowned. "Don't be mad, Jacob."

"Next steps," Jacob said quickly. "Let's just…focus on next steps."

Jacob did not like to get angry. It reminded him too much of his youth, the easy way he'd exploded at his mother. Now, as an adult, he guarded his temper with the cool control of a man raising the temperature on a thermostat. He would not lose control. He would solve the problem.

"Right," Shmuel said optimistically, lifting one finger in the air. "Next steps!" He considered the question before turning to Jacob. "What are our next steps, Jacob?"

"Does it come with instructions?"

"I don't know. I've only opened two of the boxes."

It was going to be a long night.

Jacob rubbed out a quickly developing headache from the center of his forehead.

"Here's the plan," he said, thinking quickly. "I'll start opening boxes, looking for instructions and taking everything into the main ballroom. You find someone who knows how to assemble a ten-foot menorah."

"Right," Shmuel said, clearly relieved that Jacob was not angry. "And don't you worry about a thing, Jacob, I'll get this fixed. I'll call everyone I know in Brooklyn if I have to. I'll call all of Kiryas Joel! You just leave it to me."

Shmuel raced off to make his phone calls, and Jacob got to

work. But, after opening the first box and staring at a million different unlabeled bolts and brackets, he couldn't help feeling he should never have come back to New York.

From: Rachel Rubenstein-Goldblatt <margotcross@northpole.com>
To: Lisa Brown <l.brown@cachingliteraryagency.com>

Sent: Tue, 14 December
Subject: The Hanukkah Grinch–Proposal

Lisa,

Please find attached my synopsis and the first three chapters
for *The Hanukkah Grinch*.

Let me know what you all think!!! As soon as possible would
be great—I'm eager to move on from the research phase.

Rachel

19

Rachel awoke to a hazy winter sun stretching through the windows. On the street below her apartment, a delivery driver was blasting Christmas music. Normally the cheery holiday tune would bring a smile to her face. But today she couldn't even muster the energy to hum along. Her CFS was flaring.

Rachel groaned at the realization. It was only the second day of volunteering, and already her body was failing her. All-encompassing fatigue stretched over her body. She knew she should stay in bed. Rest. But she couldn't bear the thought of losing her Matzah Ball ticket.

Dragging herself out of bed, she was determined to push through. She threw on a pair of sweats and pulled her unkempt hair into a ponytail. She hated how she looked with her hair up, the way the style accentuated her large nose and weak chin. But Rachel was far too exhausted to focus on vanity this morning.

She just needed to survive seven more days. Seven more days loaded down with coffee, popping medically prescribed stimulants, finding chairs, cutting precious energy corners. Then, she would be free of this nightmare.

Inside the Four Seasons, Rachel no longer had to ask for directions. She knew the way. Winding through the maze of hallways and back rooms, she returned to the closet that kept the matzah ball costume. The thought of wearing the smelly monstrosity for another ten hours was almost too much to bear, but she forced herself to march forward, pulling it on over her clothes.

The room was a flurry of activity. Men stood on ladders, wires and lights draping down to the floor. Women raced back and forth, barking orders into Bluetooth devices fashionably situated in their ears. Rachel scanned the room, looking for her archenemy. Instead, her eyes landed on a ten-foot menorah being set up by a team of three in the center of the room. Rachel watched as they worked to affix the *shamash*, the tallest branch, with the help of a small ladder.

It was an impressive sight. Even halfway complete, Rachel could see the effect Jacob was going for. From a clear base, three silver branches rose up halfway to the ceiling.

"Do you like it?" Jacob asked.

Rachel turned to find him standing behind her. He was all pep. Even first thing in the morning he bounced on the toes of his loafers. Rachel turned back to the menorah. "It's lovely," she admitted. "Is that glass?"

"Acrylic," he said. "It's actually more durable than glass and weighs fifty percent less. Once the menorah is finished, we'll set it up on the stage. But it should give the appearance that the flames are—"

"Floating," she finished the thought for him.

"Exactly."

"It's beautiful. Honestly, Jacob, it's very clever...and very you."

Jacob didn't say anything. Instead, his eyes narrowed in on her face before edging upward to the high ponytail she was

JEAN MELTZER

wearing. Rachel bit back a tiny sigh. She knew she was a total mess this morning.

Jacob swallowed. "You look—"

"Yeah, I know," she said, cutting him off.

"—nice."

Rachel could feel her heart skip a beat. Did he really just compliment her? It seemed impossible.

"I didn't shower," she said, not meaning to be so forthright.

Jacob smiled, a quick uptick of the lip. Seeing his enjoyment at her words cooled her embarrassment. Besides, her hair was nothing compared to the getup, and even that was just a matzah ball costume. It wasn't the worst thing in the world to ever happen to her.

Jacob clapped his hands together. "I hope you brought your pep this morning!"

Rachel lied. "Always!"

"Great," Jacob said, waving her to follow him down a hallway. "Because we have a very special assignment for you today."

Jacob led her past the giant menorah, behind the curtain and up a long accessibility ramp, where they came to a closed door located just behind the main ballroom.

He pointed with both thumbs at the door. "I want you to understand that the people in this room, they are silver-level guests. It's very important they are happy. If they want food, you get them food. If they want entertainment, you provide them with entertainment. Your job—and the only thing I am expecting of you—is to make them happy. Is that understood?"

"Of course."

"Because being a Lokshen Liaison—" Jacob blew all the air out of his chest "—is a super important role here. It's a role only a bright, capable and un-showered person like you could fulfill. So what do you say? Do you have the pep needed to entertain our most important guests?"

"Absolutely!"

184

"I can't hear you." He cupped his ear.

"Open the damn door, Jacob!"

Jacob obliged, throwing open the door. Rachel's mouth went slack at the image. The tiny prison of a room was crammed full with children, ranging from the ages of eight to thirteen.

Rachel shut the door. "What are they doing here?"

"Most of our Silvers are in upstate New York today, attending our Power of Miracles Retreat. While they're off setting their Hanukkah intentions, we figured we could do a little something special for the kids. What is more special than spending a day with our very own Lokshen Liaison?"

"No."

"But, Rachel," Jacob said, "you're the perfect person for this."

"Are you out of your mind, Jacob?" she shot back. "I don't have any experience with children."

Rachel turned, attempting to flee. Unfortunately, it was all for naught. She couldn't get very far in the large and uncomfortable costume. Jacob easily caught up to her and blocked her exit on the ramp, attempting to reason with her.

"Wait, wait, wait. You're telling me you were never a camp counselor at Camp Ahava?"

Rachel flustered. "Of course I was."

"And in all your years growing up at Congregation Beth Or, you never helped out with a Hebrew school class or taught a Tot Shabbat?" Jacob had clearly come prepared for the argument.

"Sure," she said, throwing her arms up in the air.

"So what is the problem?" Narrowing his focus on her, he waited for an answer. She sighed, looking back at the closed door waiting for her.

The truth of the matter was that Rachel loved children. She loved their carefree spirits, sticky fingers and brutal honesty. Since being diagnosed with CFS, however, she simply didn't have energy for them. Even when she visited her brother in Los

Angeles, she could only spend a few hours visiting her nieces and nephews before crashing completely.

Rachel feared that little ones, like falling in love and getting married, would never fill the pages of her story. Not that she was going to explain her rationale for avoiding children to Jacob. He was *a normal*. A healthy person. It was impossible for somebody like him to understand.

Still, she knew in her *kishkas* how to make the best of a bad situation. She had plenty of reasons to force a smile and push through this terrible and no-good task. Lifting the bottom of her foam skirt, Rachel stomped toward the door to meet Jacob's challenge.

20

These…these were not children. These were monsters. Horrible, amped-up little people covered in powdered sugar, chocolate and gelatin.

Rachel stood in the center of the room, hands shielding her face, attempting to ward off an attack of Silly String from a group of tweens hiding behind an overturned table.

"That's enough!" Rachel shouted, pulling Silly String from her hair. "I'm serious! I'm going to call all your parents."

It was no use. The young VIP guests of the Matzah Ball had no intention of listening to her. No matter what Rachel offered them in terms of entertainment—games, songs, pizza—they rolled their eyes and openly expressed their disgust. Now, in an effort to entertain themselves, the children had devolved into their true forms.

Rachel spun in her spot, her painfully obtrusive costume a major hindrance as she attempted to gain control of the situation. A group of middle-school girls jumped up and down on a sofa, snapping inappropriate selfies. An eight-year-old boy, his back turned to her, pulled down his pants and urinated into a potted plant. All of it would have been terrible but bearable had it not been for the three middle-grade boys crouching down behind an overturned table.

She knew those boys were going to be trouble.

Red, Freckles and Pharaoh. Those weren't their names, but after three hours with the vile and repulsive creatures, that's what Rachel preferred to call them. Red, because of the color of his hair. Freckles, because of the matzah-like pattern of dots splashed across his nose, and Pharaoh. Pharaoh was the worst.

It wasn't just that he was the quietest kid of this dystopian bad-boy trilogy. Pharaoh had a tendency to smile sweetly to your face, make you think he was going to bring Red and Freckles over to your side, before ducking behind your matzah ball costume and kicking you straight in the butt. Pharaoh was destined to live a long and happy life...in prison.

"Come on," Rachel said, attempting to wave them away from their game of Silly String. "Come out from behind the table. You know the Four Seasons people aren't going to appreciate you turning their furniture into a fort."

Red launched a jelly doughnut at her head. Rachel attempted to duck, but the heinous costume prevented the movement. The doughnut landed with powerful force at the center of her chest, splattering red jam all over her heart.

"Hey, look!" Freckles said, shooting up from behind the table. "We murdered the matzah ball!"

The room broke into unrivaled shouts and cheers. The middle-school girls balled up their fists, throwing them high into the air. The eight-year-old pissing into the potted plant turned on the heels of his designer sneakers and stuck his pointer finger into his mouth. They were like a pack of wolves, wild and unfettered, suddenly called together by one great and victorious howl.

Rachel needed to get control of the situation, and quick.

"All right!" she said, attempting to calm them all down. "You win, okay? You had your fun! Now, can you all please do me a favor and take a seat—"

"Kill the matzah ball!" Red shouted.

"Yeah!" Freckles joined in. "Murder her!"

But it was Pharaoh—leader of them all, destroyer of nations— that began the solemn chant. *Kill...the...matzah...ball. Kill... the...matzah...ball.* Rachel could feel terror rising in her chest. The children began to circle, eyes wide with excitement, eager to tear apart her Crayola-flavored flesh. She made an executive decision to leave.

Backing up toward the exit, hands outstretched, she attempted to appeal to their sense of humanity. "Listen," she pleaded, opening the door to leave. "I just need to step out for a minute, but I'll be right back. You all like ice cream, right? How about I order you all a dozen banana splits?"

Rachel came to a full and complete stop.

She was stuck in the threshold.

This was not happening. Her heart began to pound. Her head was suddenly on a swivel. There had to be some other way out. Perhaps a window, or a human-sized air duct, the kind that only existed in poorly written action movies. But when she searched the tiny room, she found she had nowhere to run. She was affixed to the door like some grotesque Hanukkah mezuzah.

"We can talk about this," Rachel said. "Let's come to some sort of agreement."

Granted, getting stuck in doors at the Four Seasons had become a common problem for Rachel since being tasked with wearing the matzah ball costume. But what had previously been a frustration had now morphed into life or death. The children were getting closer, and the eight-year-old with the incontinence problem was fiddling with the string on his pants.

There were many terrible fates that could befall a person. But today was not the day that Rachel Rubenstein-Goldblatt would get urinated on.

Gathering up her energy, she sank down into a squat inside her costume. The action would need to be purposeful, intense, if she wanted to dislodge herself from the door. She made a plan in her mind. She would leap like a track-and-field athlete, going up as high up possible, before throwing all her weight backward and through the doorway. It should work. If her one semester of college-level physics had taught her anything, it was that an object in motion tended to stay in motion.

Rachel jumped. With all the power she could muster, she launched herself up and back, popping out of the door frame. A rush of cool air brushed across her smiling cheeks. She was free from the fettered chains of Pharaoh. She was floating backward, eager to escape the wild horde of children still chanting for her death.

But she had made a mistake.

In her careful calculations regarding extrication, she had not accounted for landing. Any feeling of victory was short-lived. A new dread suddenly overtook her. With her movement limited, Rachel fell back and landed on her foam side.

No one was at fault for what happened next. It was simply physics, the will of the world, like nature bringing rain showers on an otherwise pleasant day. The rotundness of the foam costume met the soft downward slope of the accessibility ramp.

All at once, Rachel was spinning. Like a rolling pin, only her head and feet exposed, she went hurtling down the ramp, screaming the entire time. She was aware of feet jumping out of her way. She was aware of the terror. But she had no way to stop. No way to pull her arms from that hideous costume, dig her knees into the carpeting and anchor herself to the ground. She flew into the main event room, crashing into the newly completed ten-foot menorah like a bowling ball hitting a strike.

The lightweight acrylic base fell over. An explosion of silver bars, bolts and brackets landed around her. Rachel was in shock. She heard gasps from the crowd of onlookers and felt worried hands attempting to pull her from the rubble. Breathing a sigh of relief that she was still alive, she wiggled all her extremities. Thankfully, nothing was broken, and no part of the menorah had landed on her. The same rotund form that had set her propelling down the ramp had also shielded her from injury.

Jacob pushed through the crowd. "Are you okay?"

She was still lying flat on the ground, the reality of the situation not completely sinking in.

"Don't move," Jacob said, kneeling down to take her hand. "You're bleeding. Just stay still. We're calling an ambulance."

Was she bleeding? Rachel blinked, taking stock of her body, checking for cuts and bruises. Her eyes landed on the large red stain in the center of her chest. Her heart jumped at the sight. This was it. The end. Her grand finale. Death by ten-foot menorah while wearing a matzah ball costume.

Jacob edged closer, squeezing her hand tighter. He smelled good. Clean. Like soap instead of cologne. She marveled how a person who could provide such comfort could also be the source of her abuse. Gawd, how she hated him.

"It's jam," Rachel coughed out.

"What?"

"It's jam, you *shmuck*!"

Rolling away from him, she hoisted herself up. It was not an easy task. The costume made her movements jerky and spasmodic. She looked like a doll on strings, balancing haphazardly, trying to find her footing. But she was determined to maintain some amount of pride.

Arching back her shoulders, she found her equilibrium. Taking a deep and centering breath, she shook the shock from her body. Volunteers stood by, hands covering their mouths. Her eyes landed on Jacob. He was talking, muttering about how she needed to sit down. His words sent her into a blind fury.

She was done. Done with this man. Done with his stupid Matzah Ball and his impossible-to-get tickets. There was only so much one person was capable of taking.

"Rachel," Jacob said, hands outstretched. "Let me help you."

"No," she said, picking up one of the branches of the menorah and holding it out like a weapon. "Don't you touch me! Don't you dare come near me, Jacob Greenberg."

Jacob came to a stop in the center of the room. All eyes were upon them now.

"You…" Rachel seethed. "You think you're so funny? You think I don't have better things to do with my time than wear this stupid, stinky and ridiculous costume around for laughs? Are you happy now? Nearly getting me killed?"

"I didn't think—"

"Shut up," she shouted back at him.

Jacob obeyed, snapping his perfect lips shut. But his sudden acquiescence to her demands did little to calm the storm raging in her belly. In one fell swoop, Rachel tore off the costume. With heaving effort, she brought it over her head, letting it slump on the ground in a deflated heap of foam. Her audience gasped in horror.

Then, just for good measure, she stomped on it a dozen times. Beat it mercilessly with the menorah branch until she was fully out of breath, purple paint and matzah crumbs splattering all over the floor. But even with that terrible costume laid to rest for all eternity, Rachel was not done. Pushing her half-undone ponytail out of her eyes, she met her tormentor's eyes directly.

"You know, Jacob," she said, "people change. They grow up, and they learn, and they become kinder and better people. But you…you haven't changed at all. You're still that horrible little boy I met at Camp Ahava years ago. And you might have fooled all these people. You might have made them believe you're fabulous, with your good looks and your tons of money, but I know who you are. And you aren't worth it."

Rachel tossed the menorah branch down to the ground and headed for the exit.

"Where are you going?" Jacob called out to her.

"I quit!"

Outside the Four Seasons, Rachel did not waste a second pulling out her phone. Her hands shaky, she dialed Mickey. He picked up on the first ring.

"Hey, beautiful," he said, cheery as ever.

She could barely form the words before the tears started. "Jacob," she hiccupped, "and his stupid costume...and then, I crashed into a Menorah...and almost died!"

"I'll be right over."

Mickey hung up the phone. Rachel stood on the street corner and hailed the first cab she could find. She needed to get home. She needed to see her best friend since forever. Mickey would make it all better. He would come over, open a bottle of wine and let her collapse in his arms.

She would save all her tears for him. Sob into his chest and reveal every sordid detail of her last two days as a Lokshen Liaison. It didn't matter that her life was a mess. It didn't matter that there were no happy endings in her future. She still had her best friend. Not even Jacob Greenberg could take that away from her.

27

Jacob felt terrible. Sitting in a makeshift office in the Four Seasons, he buried himself in paperwork, pretending to go over Excel spreadsheets. Though it was well past dinnertime, and most of his staff had left for the day, he did not want to return to his bubbe's apartment on the Upper East Side. He couldn't stop thinking about Rachel.

Picking up his cell phone, he tried to call her again. It went right to voice mail.

Jacob wasn't surprised. He had called Rachel every hour on the dot to apologize. Just like he had texted her three different times, checking to make sure she was okay. His efforts were for naught. Rachel was ignoring him.

Pushing the paperwork away, he stood up. Stretching through his anxiety, he took three deep and centering breaths, her words echoing in his ears. He hadn't changed. He was still that horrible little boy she had met at Camp Ahava. He wasn't worth it.

Although he didn't want to believe her, Jacob often wondered if there was some flaw deep inside him that made him unlovable to others.

He shook the thought away. He was not the type of man to sit around feeling sorry for himself. The costume had been a joke. Just some lighthearted fun to break down her walls. It wasn't his fault Rachel was so damn serious about everything.

Besides, it was better for everybody that the thing just end before it ever had a chance to start.

Glancing down at his cell phone, he put the ringer on Silent and buried it deep in his pocket. It was time to sit shiva for Rachel Rubenstein-Goldblatt. In his mind, he covered all the mirrors and ate a hard-boiled egg. Then, just as he had done after his own mother's death, he settled on getting back to work. The first thing Jacob needed to tackle tonight was the broken menorah. Leaving the makeshift office, he headed to the main ballroom.

Shmuel was on his phone, arguing vehemently with someone. "Moishe, whatever it costs, we're willing to pay!"

Jacob could tell by the sound of his colleague's pleading, it was not good news. The team of Judaica experts Shmuel had found were no longer available. Jacob and Shmuel would have to fix the broken menorah on their own.

"So the President of the United States is more important than your cousin?" Shmuel said, laying the guilt on thick. "He's not even Jewish! Well, fine. But remember this at Yom Kippur, Moishe...when you're saying your *al hets* and asking for forgiveness—" Shmuel looked up from his phone. "He hung up on me."

Jacob was not surprised. "Is there someone else we can call?"

"Someone who has experience putting together giant menorahs? No."

Jacob sighed. "Then I guess we're on our own."

Jacob scanned the room. Tables were uncovered, many the wrong size. The lighting was hanging half-constructed from the curtains, wires still dangerously exposed. But it was the state of the ten-foot menorah—the shining centerpiece of his party—in pieces all over the dance floor that caused a twinge of anxiety to form at the bottom of his belly.

"I can handle this," he said, stepping over brackets and metal shards.

Branches were bent out of shape. The *shamash* had been sliced through at the tip, rendering it unusable. His specially designed and crafted *chanukiyah*, imported straight from Israel, had been circumcised...and turned into a candelabra.

"You wanted a Matzah Ball," Shmuel grumbled. "You wanted a matzah ball costume!"

"And I've never let you down before." Jacob interrupted him before he could really get going. "Have I?"

Shmuel huffed unhappily, crossing his arms against his chest. Alas, even Shmuel could not argue this point. Jacob Greenberg was wholly and forever reliable. In all their years working together, in all their sleepless nights over one of his ridiculous gambles, Jacob had never let Shmuel or any of their investors down. Greenberg Entertainment always turned a profit.

"Look," Jacob said, "why don't you head home for the night? Get some sleep. Let me handle the broken menorah, okay? But don't stress out about it, Shmuel!" He slapped his friend on the shoulder. "This is what always happens at our events! It's always madness and chaos...until it's not. We'll get it fixed, and everything will work out fine, okay? You'll see."

Shmuel hesitated, but eventually acquiesced. "I hope you're right, Jacob. For both our sakes, I hope you can pull this one off."

Alone, Jacob took stock of his situation. Shmuel was right, of course. His Matzah Ball Max was falling apart, but devolving into hysterics about it wasn't going to help anyone. He sat on the floor and focused on getting to work.

The menorah needed to be fixed. While he could borrow a smaller menorah from some Hebrew school or Jewish old-age home, it would not have the same effect as his ten-foot floating *chanukiyah*. He knew it would look amazing in video clips and photographs. His influencers, especially, would love the images, posting them once a year as a shout-out during the holidays, a consistent stream of royalties. Hanukkah would be the gift that would keep giving.

He began organizing the pieces into carefully arranged piles. Brackets. Branches. Bolts. Acrylic. And then, one final pile for the broken pieces. There were a lot of broken pieces.

Jacob sighed, glancing down at his watch. It was late. He would have to revisit this in the morning.

Gathering up his bags, he headed for the door. He was nearly halfway down the block, heading for the closest subway, when he heard someone call, "Jacob Greenberg?"

He turned around and found a tall gentleman with dark skin wearing a smart gray peacoat. A stylish multicolored scarf was tied in a loose knot around his neck. Jacob couldn't place him, but he felt familiar.

"I'm sorry," Jacob said, narrowing his focus. "Do I know you?"

"Mickey Goldman, from Camp Ahava."

Jacob warmed into a smile. It was so obviously Mickey Goldman. They had been bunk mates back during that fateful summer, though he had the faintest memory that the guy didn't like him.

Still, Camp Ahava had happened a long time ago. Jacob was just excited to see another familiar face from that summer.

"Mickey Goldman," Jacob said, moving to shake his hand. "How have you—"

Mickey interrupted him. "I'm Rachel's best friend."

"Oh." Jacob dropped the smile. "Is she okay?"

"She's fine," Mickey snapped back. "No thanks to you! I mean, seriously, dude? What is your problem? You think we don't have enough *shmucks* in New York City? You need to fly in from Paris and add one more?"

"I didn't mean anything by it—"

"Oh, you meant something by it!" Mickey pointed his finger directly in his face.

Whether it was intended as a threat or not, Jacob wasn't certain. Mickey had gone from awkward adolescent to full-grown man. He was taller than Jacob now. He could certainly hold his own in a fight.

Although Jacob really wasn't interested in fisticuffs on the streets of Manhattan, the thought crossed his mind that Rachel was lucky. She was lucky to have her family. She was lucky to have Mickey. The whole world showed up for her and fought for her.

"Look," Jacob said, pushing past Mickey. "I appreciate you coming out here. Really, I do. I'm also glad to hear that Rachel is doing okay. Believe it or not, I've been trying to reach her all evening. But if you don't mind, I have an early morning. I need to be getting home."

Jacob was halfway down the street when Mickey called out to him again. "She's sick."

Jacob froze. The words felt like an anchor tied around his heart. "Sick, how?"

"She wouldn't—" Mickey stammered, looking away. "It's not my place to tell her secrets."

"No!" Jacob stormed back over. "That's not good enough."

Jacob had a desperate urge to grab Mickey by the arms and shake him violently, but stopped himself. He knew from delicate business negotiations with investors that you won more flies with glue traps.

"You came here for a reason, didn't you?" Jacob shouted, the accusation falling from his lips. "You have something to tell me, so tell me. Sick, how? Is she dying?"

"Not exactly—"

"Cancer?"

"No."

"Heart disease?"

"Jesus, Jacob!" Mickey was growing flustered. "She'll kill me if I tell you."

Then Jacob knew. He knew because Mickey hesitated. He knew, because while people wore ribbons for cancer or marched for heart disease, they hid chronic illness.

"All I can tell you," Mickey explained, "is that she gets tired. She gets *really* tired. Like, 'not able to leave the house for days and weeks on end' tired. Honestly, she should have never agreed to volunteer for your stupid Matzah Ball, she's just so freaking—"

Jacob finished his thought. "Stubborn?"

"Yeah."

Jacob nodded. He had seen that side of Rachel himself.

He wished she'd told him. If he'd known, he would have worked within her limitations. He certainly wouldn't have asked her to wear a matzah ball costume and remain on her feet all day in order to garner a ticket. Rachel was right. He was a giant *shmuck*.

"Mickey," Jacob said, animated by a newfound determination. "I need a favor from you."

Mickey frowned. "What type of favor?"

"I need to know where Rachel lives."

Mickey crossed his arms. "How about when hell freezes over, and Satan hands out free Popsicles?"

"Please," Jacob begged. "I promise, I won't stay long. I just want to—" He stopped himself. What did he want from Rachel? He wasn't certain. He just knew that tonight, on the second night of Hanukkah, he needed to be with her. "I want to make things right."

"And I'm supposed to believe that you've suddenly found your inner *mensch*?"

"You can believe what you want," Jacob said. "But if you don't give me her address, I'll have no choice but to call Dr. Rubenstein. I'm sure her mother would be thrilled to tell me where she lives."

"You wouldn't dare."

"I'm a desperate man, Mickey."

Mickey puffed hot air from his nostrils. "Fine," he said, throwing his hands up. "You win. I'll give you her address. But I swear to Gawd, Jacob, if you hurt her, if you do one single thing to mess with her, I will get you blacklisted from every synagogue in Manhattan. You will never find high holiday tickets again."

Jacob smiled, offering his hand. "It's a deal."

22

An hour later, Jacob landed on the Upper West Side. Standing on the corner of Broadway and 84th Street, he was surprised by the impressive-looking high-rise that met his arrival. Though he was still not entirely sure what she did for a living, Rachel was clearly doing well for herself.

Secrets. The woman had so many secrets.

Bypassing the doorman with a quick dip of the shoulders, Jacob snuck into the elevator and headed upstairs.

He could understand why Rachel had hid her disease from him. He had learned from his own mother that there could be financial, as well as emotional, implications after revealing a chronic illness.

It still didn't explain why she needed a Matzah Ball ticket so badly. After all, she had agreed to do almost anything for it—wear a stupid costume, put up with him, risk her health. The fact struck him as doubly suspicious. Whatever Rachel was hiding from the world, she did so with tremendous effort.

The elevator dinged. Jacob exited on the fourth floor. Even

without the address or the gold number nailed above the peephole he would know Rachel's apartment belonged to her. He ran his fingers over the mezuzah she had chosen. It was colorful and quirky, a quilt of confusing patterns and angles, and very much Rachel.

Taking a deep breath, he moved to ring her buzzer, when it suddenly struck Jacob that this was a poor idea. It was after eleven. Rachel was probably sleeping. Plus, Mickey had mentioned that she was often tired. He turned, planning to go home, and then he heard the familiar refrain of a theme song blasting from a television. Jacob gathered his courage and knocked.

The television went mute. His heart raced. From his spot in the hallway, he could make out the sound of someone shuffling to the door. "Rachel," he said through the door. "It's Jacob. Can I talk to you for a second?" No response. Jacob tried again. "Please. I promise I won't take up more than five minutes of your time."

Rachel opened the door. Leaning her head against her hand, she was no longer the polished presentation of charm she staged for the world. Her hair was a mess. Her pajamas were mismatched. All the forced smiles and chirpy witticisms had been dropped. Jacob could feel the breath leaving his chest. She was beautiful. Imperfect. Real.

She didn't need makeup. She didn't need designer bags or formfitting black skirts to highlight everything that made her special. He thought back to that girl he'd met at Camp Ahava, who loved potato-sack races and lying on the grass during hazy Shabbat afternoons. Oh, what he would give to be holding her hand once more.

His heart swung wildly at the realization. The music in his mind returned. Somewhere "Crazy in Love" by Beyoncé played on repeat in the background. He could almost feel the braces back on his teeth. The way their first kiss clashed and clanged

202

together, making sparks in the night. She tasted like Bamba and bubblegum back then. Did she still taste that way?

Jacob snapped back to reality. "Your friend came to see me this evening."

"My friend?" Rachel blinked. "Mickey." She bit her lower lip.

His mind swirled. He had so many things he wanted to say to her, so many questions he needed to ask her, and he felt incapable of pulling out the words. Instead, he peered past her into her apartment.

The place was a mess. Laundry littered the floor in tiny heaps and piles. Her coffee table was peppered with medicine bottles. A half-eaten carton of Chinese food sat unattended on the window counter. It reminded him of his mother, on her bad days, when she was in too much pain to clean.

"You should have told me you were sick."

Her mouth fell open. "Freaking Mickey."

"Don't be mad at him," Jacob said, trying to assuage the situation. "He obviously cares about you, a lot. I just wish you would have told me. Maybe then—"

Rachel cut him off. "Then what? You would have treated me with respect? You would have treated me like a decent human being? What do you think, Jacob? You think I didn't realize, from the beginning, that your stupid matzah ball costume was just a way to humiliate me?"

"It wasn't to humiliate you," Jacob said honestly. How could he explain it? He found her impossible. Confusing. Beautiful. She was like that mezuzah on her doorpost, a beautifully crafted case guarding a secret scroll inside. "I wanted you to be honest."

"*Honest?*" Rachel scoffed. "I am completely honest!"

"Then why didn't you tell me about your disease?" Jacob snapped back at her. "Or why you really wanted a ticket to my Matzah Ball? Or what you actually do for a living? 'Cause not for nothing, Rachel, this is a really nice apartment for someone who lives in New York."

"Fine!" She threw up her arms. "You want to talk about honest, Jacob? Let's get honest! You put me in a ridiculous matzah ball costume! You turned me into a freaking meme. How in the world is humiliating me, and nearly getting me killed, supposed to make me want to be honest with you?"

"Because it worked at Camp Ahava."

"What? What are you talking about?"

"Come on," he said, frustrated. "Don't pretend like you don't remember that summer! All the games we played together. All the pranks we would pull. And beneath the prank war, we were friends, Rachel. We were real with each other, and you—"

"No." She stepped up to him. "We were *never* friends."

"You're right," he said, leaning into her, close enough for a second kiss. "We were *never* friends. We were so much more than just friends, Rachel...and you broke my goddamn heart."

Her face went white. She stepped back. "What?"

Jacob rolled his eyes toward the ceiling. "Now you're gonna pretend like you didn't know?"

"Know what?" she snapped. "That you never know when a joke is over?"

"I needed you," he said honestly. "I needed you at a time in my life when I had no one. And I get it, okay? You were just a little kid yourself, and it wasn't your job or responsibility. But you could have just picked up the phone, Rachel. You could have just said goodbye to me. You don't realize how much a goodbye is worth, until you never get one."

Confusion stretched across her face. All Jacob wanted was for Rachel to open up, tell him the truth, but his brash attempt at resolving their situation shut her down further. Rachel looked away, pressing her lips together. It was pointless. There was nothing left to save between them.

"Look," he said, digging into his pocket to pull out a small white envelope. "I didn't come here to lecture you or dredge up old memories. All I wanted to say is that our deal is off. You can have a ticket to the Matzah Ball, and you don't have to do anything else, either."

"You really think I want to go to your stupid Matzah Ball now?"

"Then don't go," he said, still holding the envelope out to her. "It's your choice, okay? If you feel up to it, great. I'd love to see you. If not, sell it online, or give it to a friend. But take the ticket, Rachel. You earned it. Consider it my apology for being a total jerk for the last two days."

Her eyes wandered down to the small white envelope he was holding, before snapping it from his hands. Jacob had accomplished what he had come here to do. Digging his hands into his pockets, he prepared to leave.

"Jacob," Rachel called out as he stepped into the elevator. "You want to know the real reason I'm not honest with you?"

"Yeah."

She said it simply. "Because you've shown me who you are."

The elevator doors closed. Jacob could feel her words stinging his chest the entire ride down to the ground floor.

23

Jacob had a strong suspicion that he would not be sleeping that evening. He considered going to a bar and drowning his thoughts in red wine and charcuterie. But not wanting to worry his bubbe, he returned to her apartment on the Upper East Side.

Stepping inside, he glanced down at his watch. It was past midnight. Jacob had been so distracted by Rachel he hadn't yet lit the menorah for the second night of Hanukkah. Heading over to his bubbe's collection, he ran his fingers over each piece of Judaica before landing on a favorite from his childhood. Eight tiny baseball players in various positions of play lifted up their respective branches.

His father had given it to him.

He placed it on the counter. After finding a box of candles and matches, he lit it, saying the blessing. Four tiny flames flickered in the reflection of the windowpane. Then Jacob stepped back and caught an image of himself inside that glass. He did not see a confident thirty-year-old man in the glass across from him.

He saw a boy. A red-haired and pudgy-faced boy, still mourning the loss of his father.

A noise from one of the bedrooms drew his attention away. Jacob looked up to find his bubbe coming down the hallway, pulling at the straps of her dressing gown.

"Yankele," Toby said, eyes wide with surprise. "Is everything okay?"

"It's a long story."

"Well, then," Toby said, giving his hand a little squeeze before moving to the kitchen, "this would be the perfect time for a little nosh."

Jacob followed her, taking a seat at the table as she put the kettle on. She set down a plate full of rugalach, and Jacob took a bite. The taste brought about memories of his youth.

"Do you think I'm a bad person?" he asked.

"What?" Toby sat down beside him. "What nonsense is this? Of course you're not a bad person."

Jacob shifted in his seat uncomfortably. He was a grown man now, free to make his own choices, yet there were days when it felt like he couldn't escape his past. It followed him like a legacy. A tradition, passed down by his father, like the baseball menorah sitting lit on the counter.

"The way I treated Mom," Jacob said, shaking his head.

"You were a child, Jacob."

"I should have known better," he said. "She was sick, and she needed me, and—"

"Listen to me," Toby interrupted, taking his hand. "Your mother loved you. She loved you more than anything in the world, and you were a great son."

His mother's death, unexpected and quick, had rattled Jacob to his very core. It had forced him to look back on his youth. It made him confront the lonely life he had built up around him. The way he used work to avoid having relationships with people. Though their relationship had improved in adulthood, he had not made his mother a priority.

There were so many things he could have done differently, so many chances to pick up the phone, or simply meet her for dinner. He would give anything to hug her one last time.

After her death—in the solitude of his apartment and during synagogue services—he would spend hours with her in his head, apologizing for his mistakes, wondering if she forgave him. When that didn't work, he funneled large sums of money from Greenberg Entertainment into MS charities and research. He did everything possible to be someone different from his father. But nothing resolved the wound inside him. The final message, left by his dad, lying there upon his heart. He was bad. He didn't deserve to be loved.

"I spent my whole adult life trying to be different than him, trying to be better than him—and I'm exactly the same, Bubbe. I'm just like Dad."

"You are nothing like your father."

"No," he said, refuting her. "You don't understand." He could barely form the words. "She's sick, Bubbe."

"Who's sick?"

"Rachel," he said, shaking his head. "She has a chronic illness."

Toby was quiet for a long time. "I'm sorry to hear that."

"And instead of being kind and compassionate, and taking care of her… I treated her just like Dad treated Mom. Just like *I* treated Mom."

The teakettle whistled. Toby rose from her seat and set about making a pot of chamomile for both of them. "Did you know she was sick?"

"Of course not."

"And if you knew she was sick, would you have done things different?"

Jacob thought seriously about the question. "I don't know."

It would have been easy for him to brush off his behavior, claim that if had he known about Rachel's illness, things would be different. But Jacob was tired of lying to himself.

"I put her in a matzah ball costume, Bubbe," he said finally. "I told myself it would be funny, that it would get her to loosen up, have fun, and lead her to be more honest. I nearly killed the poor woman in the process! And the whole time I was thinking everything was going great, thinking everything was fine between us…"

"She wasn't in on the joke."

"No."

Toby returned to the table, laying two cups of tea down between them. "So," she said, taking the seat beside Jacob. "We come to the heart of the matter."

"The heart of the matter?"

"*Yankele.*" His grandmother leaned into him. "Why did you come back to New York?"

"To throw a Matzah Ball," he said, surprised at the question. "You know that."

"No," she said, pushing him. "Think about it. *Why did you come back to New York?* When you first decided you were going to throw this Matzah Ball Max, where were you?"

Jacob stared into his cup. It was not a difficult question. The memory of that week would forever be etched into his brain. Jacob had first gotten the idea to throw a Matzah Ball two days before his mother died.

He thought back to that snowy Christmas Eve. Coming home exhausted from yet another day sitting at her bedside. He knew she was going to die. The hospice nurses, the doctors, had all warned him. Even Paree, her cat, was on edge. He recalled precisely the feeling as he had sat in the quiet of his apartment, eating a carton of cold Chinese food. He was a man without a family, a son alone in the world.

The idea for the Matzah Ball Max had struck him that night.

"It was the week Mom died," Jacob said.

"Hmm," Toby said, considering the statement. "You decided to throw a Matzah Ball on the week your mother died?"

"So?"

"You could have thrown the party anywhere in the world— Los Angeles, Tel Aviv, even Paris—but you chose to come back to New York. You chose to come back to Manhattan, a place you haven't visited in over eighteen years."

"I have contacts in New York. It made sense."

"You ask Rabbi Aaron Goldblatt, the father of your first love, to light the eighth candle at your party. You don't just ask him, *Yankele*, you physically go to his house for Shabbat dinner. You go to a place where Rachel Rubenstein-Goldblatt might be, and when you *finally* reconnect with the girl who broke your heart, and things are going good between you, you put her in a matzah ball costume. Made from the costume your father, who abandoned you, gave you all those years before."

Jacob felt his heart sink. "Oh."

"I'm not a therapist, *Yankele*. I'm only your bubbe. But it may all be related."

Jacob could feel his head swirling. His bubbe was right. He hadn't been able to see it, but when she laid it all out on the table before him, his actions seemed so clear.

All of the things he had done, the choices he had made, were never really about throwing a Matzah Ball. What Jacob had wanted to do was confront the people, and the places, that had shaped him. To prove, perhaps naively, that he had conquered the experiences of his youth.

"I'm an idiot," Jacob said, shaking his head.

Toby touched his wrist gently. "You made a mistake."

"She'll never forgive me."

"You don't know that."

"Bubbe—" he met her eyes directly "—I nearly killed the poor woman."

Toby smiled, leaning into her grandson. "On the bright side, things can only go up from here."

Jacob laughed. Leave it to his bubbe to find the silver lining to every cloud. He tapped on the edge of his teacup, debating his next steps.

Abandonment. The word was so heinous and ugly. It couldn't even begin to capture the pain it left behind. But Jacob knew what his issues were. He could pinpoint them, name them—he just didn't know how to stop them. It was like he was a hamster, bound up in a wheel, forever running in the same endless cycle.

He wanted love but didn't feel worthy of it. And so, even though he liked her, when Rachel showed him the smallest iota of interest he did what so many adult children from broken families do—he protected himself by pushing her away. As a kid he'd pushed her into the lake, and as an adult he rolled her straight into a ten-foot menorah.

"So what do I do?" he asked seriously. "How do I fix this?"

Toby rose from the table, putting her cup in the sink and scraping the last of her cookie crumbs into the garbage disposal. "Do you know what the difference is between you and your father?"

Jacob scoffed. "Are we different?"

She ignored him, turning around at the sink. "Your father is afraid of confronting his mistakes. He runs away from them, thinking he can avoid them, and instead the problem gets bigger. The problem grows up. And do you know what the saddest part about all that is, *Yankele*?"

Jacob shook his head.

"You would have forgiven him."

She let the statement linger in the air between them.

"You tried doing everything wrong," Toby said, that twinkle returning to her eye. "Okay! It was a disaster! So now, try doing everything right. See what happens."

"And if Rachel still hates me?"

"You mean—" Toby returned to the table "—if she still rejects you? If you wind up getting your heart broken all over again…being abandoned on a dance floor, like you were when you were twelve?"

"Yes."

"Look at me."

He looked at her.

"The trick is to know," she said, leaning forward and pressing her hand against his heart, "what's in the present…and what's in the past. You came to New York to confront these things. So confront them already! No more games. No more hiding. Confront them."

Toby retired back to bed. Jacob found himself alone in the kitchen once more.

Finishing his cup of tea, he considered his grandmother's advice against the events of the day. He had nearly killed Rachel. Destroyed a ten-foot, custom-designed menorah. Been yelled at, more than once, by two different people from Camp Ahava. His return to New York had been a failure on every conceivable level. He had no idea where to begin making amends with Rachel. And then, tapping on the edge of the tiny teacup, he noticed the smallest fragment of a scar. A tiny crack running down the porcelain side.

A broken vessel.

Chronic illness was not a moral failing, though some people had treated his mother like she was guilty of a crime. *If only she would exercise more. Eat better. She just needs to think positively, change her inner dialogue, meditate.* Just like someone always had a friend who had been cured by seeing this one doctor. Everyone was always so quick to offer advice. Nobody just came over and did the laundry.

It gave Jacob an idea.

And this time—he was at least 50 percent certain—it was a decent one.

From: Lisa Brown <l.brown@cachingliteraryagency.com>
To: Rachel Rubenstein-Goldblatt <margotcross@northpole.com>

Sent: Wed, 15 December
Subject: RE: The Hanukkah Grinch—Proposal

Rachel,

I couldn't resist sharing your DELICIOUS pages for *The Hanukkah Grinch* with Chandra! Not surprisingly, everyone at Romance House POSITIVELY LIT UP LIKE A MENORAH for this story!!! I've never laughed so hard!

Chandra is thinking this could be turned into a series!!! ($$$$$$$$$$$$$$$$$) That's more than a few years of work, girlfriend!

Are you available to come into a meeting next week to talk? I'm hearing rumblings of a seven-book deal...

Lisa

24

Rachel awoke with only a hazy memory of the previous night's events. She recalled Mickey coming over, having a glass of red wine, followed by six hours of *Golden Girls* reruns. Then suddenly the clouds around her brain lifted. She remembered Jacob arriving in the middle of the night.

Springing up straight in her bed, she panicked. Glancing over to her nightstand, she fumbled for the white envelope she had snatched from his hands. Opening it up, she stared down at the peace offering Jacob had left her. Inside was one silver ticket for the Matzah Ball.

Suspicion rose up inside her. Given everything she knew about the man, she assumed this ticket was probably another one of his pranks. She could imagine the scene now. She would arrive at the Matzah Ball decked out to the nines, only to discover that her ticket did not work. Maybe Jacob would even have her arrested.

She would not be made a fool of again. Tossing the ticket

back on her nightstand, Rachel was determined to repress the memory of Jacob Greenberg forever.

She pulled up the covers above her head and blinked through the fatigue stretching across her body. She didn't have the energy to worry about Jacob. She was beyond exhausted. Every inch of her skin hurt and felt inflamed. Her brain felt foggy and her throat ached.

Feeling the damp spot beneath her body, she knew she had experienced night sweats. She wanted to grab a towel and place it beneath her body, but she was just too tired. So she lay there shivering, waiting to fall back to sleep.

She was having a bad day.

How long would it last? Rachel had no way of knowing. Chronic fatigue syndrome was the Great Decider.

It had decided her career, where she traveled on vacation, with whom she could be intimate. It had influenced her relationships, stolen away friendships and forced her to live in constant uncertainty, robbing her of any practical ability to plan for the future. It had deprived her of normal. The privilege of having a choice. Yet, despite all these things, Rachel Rubenstein-Goldblatt was a fighter.

She so desperately wanted to push through it. If she could, she would head to her office and write. Add another ten thousand words to her manuscript, *The Hanukkah Grinch*. She knew the likelihood of that happening was zilch. Her brain was far too muddied to be coherent.

Still, she would settle for breakfast.

Rachel wanted nothing more than a cup of hot soup. It would calm her scratchy throat and fill up her starving belly. But the idea of standing at the stove, heating up a can for five minutes, felt monumental in effort. Her body was done. There was nothing to do but lie prone, waiting for the bad day to pass.

She drifted into that strange reality between sleep and waking, grateful for the respite, until she heard a knock at the door.

Rachel sat up in bed, forcing herself awake. Who the hell would be bothering her at this time of the morning? It was midweek in Manhattan. Almost every healthy person she knew would be at work. She grumbled at the idea of Jacob returning to her door asking for his ticket back.

Whoever was at the door, however, was certainly determined. The knocking and buzzing continued. Rachel forced herself out of bed, threw on a robe and peeked through the peephole.

A woman was standing in her hall.

Rachel did not recognize her. She was also getting seriously annoyed with her doormen. What was the point of paying exorbitant co-op fees if they let any solicitor or summer camp archenemy up to her apartment without warning?

She threw open the door. "Listen, I appreciate your efforts here, but I'm not interested in—"

"Good morning, Rachel!" The woman beamed, speaking with a slight French accent. "My name is Martha McBride. How are you today?"

Rachel blinked. She knew her name. It threw her for a loop.

She took a careful accounting of the small woman standing before her. She was wearing a modern black dress, chic and fashionable, lined with tiny white ruffles around the neck. It gave her a look of authority, which paired rather nicely with her wire-rimmed glasses. Still, Rachel had no idea why this woman was standing in her hall.

"I'm fine," she said, confused. "Is there something I can help you with?"

"Actually, my dear—" Martha pushed her way past Rachel and into her apartment "—it's what I'm here to help you with."

Rachel normally wouldn't let strange and chirpy women just waltz into her apartment. However, feeling foggy this morning, she was moving about two seconds slower than the rest of the universe. By the time she even realized what had happened, it was too late. Martha McBride was standing in her living room, tapping notes into a slim black tablet.

"I don't want you to worry about the mess," Martha said, moving around the room like some freakazoid, come-to-life version of Mary Poppins. "I have a cleaning team set to arrive in the next hour. But you, my dear, you need to rest. Can you sleep while I have a cleaning team here or should I send them away until after breakfast with your private chef?"

"I'm sorry," Rachel said, certain she was dreaming. "Who are you again?"

"I'm Martha McBride," she chirped, once again offering her hand. "And I am here to make your life easier."

Rachel laughed. "My life couldn't possibly be made easier."

"You would be surprised," Martha corrected her. "Money has a way of being the great equalizer in all things. Fortunately for us both, your benefactor has lots of money. Money he is most eager to spend on you, and my services to you."

"You're a nurse?"

"Oh, no," she said. "Not a nurse. I'm an executive assistant. One of the finest money can buy, in fact. Jacob Greenberg sent me."

Rachel could feel the ire rising in her belly. Returning to the door, she kindly motioned to the hallway. "Get out."

"I'm afraid that won't be possible, dear."

"Then I'll call the police."

"And tell them what?" She raised a trim eyebrow in Rachel's direction. "Some woman is standing in your living room, offering to clean your house and do your laundry? I think the police have better things to do with their time, no?"

"Fine." Rachel squared her shoulders, defiant. "Then you're fired. I appreciate you coming all the way out here, but your services are no longer required. Please go back to whatever chimney or Hulu series you crawled out of…"

"Alas, I was not hired by you. So, technically, you can't fire me. But I would be happy to remain out of your way, as much as possible, so you can rest. I am here, after all, to meet your every whim and desire."

Stalemate.

Martha McBride dug the heels of her sensible orthopedic shoes into Rachel's overpriced area rug. The woman was not going anywhere. Perhaps on another day, in another lifetime, Rachel would have had the *chutzpah* to throw Martha out. But the truth was, on this day, and in this lifetime, Rachel was just too tired.

She didn't have the energy to fight Mary Poppins. She didn't have the wherewithal to call Jacob, form a cohesive argument and tell him to shove off. All she wanted to do was crawl back into bed. Yet, despite the fact she despised Jacob, and didn't trust his intentions, she needed the help.

"Can you heat up soup?" Rachel asked, exasperated.

"My dear," Martha said, taking her arm and leading her back to the bedroom, "as I've already told you, I can do anything."

25

The glass high-rise downtown looked as imposing as it felt. Jacob sat on a bench outside, in a memorial park just across the street, watching the lunch crowd move past him. It felt surreal, being back here.

His phone buzzed to attention in his pocket. Pulling it out, he saw it was a text message from Martha.

All done. She's resting.

Thank you for letting me know.

Quite a bit of spirit on that one, though.

All spirit, actually.

Your mother would have liked her.

Jacob smiled at her words. Martha was right. Rachel had a

ferocity of spirit, and a willingness to put Jacob in his place, that his own mother would have appreciated. He texted Martha back:

I appreciate you flying out last minute.

I appreciate you sending a private jet. ☺

Jacob laughed, before adding one final text:

Please make sure she has everything she needs.
I don't care about the cost.

Of course.

Satisfied, he powered down his phone. With Rachel provided for, it was time for him to confront his father. Jacob rose from the bench, made his way across midday traffic and walked inside.

Greenberg Associates lay on the thirty-fifth floor of the stark and beautiful high-rise. Jacob rode the elevator up, counting each floor, before the doors finally parted and he entered the lobby.

It was everything you would expect from a successful law firm in Manhattan. Modern art decorated the walls alongside sculptures in weird shapes and angles. Still, for all its fancy and opulent artwork, the place was cold. Sterile. Except for the floor-to-window ceilings offering a God's-eye view of the world, his father's law firm was devoid of human personality.

Jacob moved to the front desk, where a woman in a tight beige sweater, her brown hair neatly pinned back into a bun, looked up from her computer.

"May I help you?" she asked.

"I'm here to see Richard Greenberg."

"Do you have an appointment?"

"I'm his son."

"Oh."

Jacob wasn't surprised by the shock that registered in clear splotches of red across the woman's cheeks. He could only imagine what his father told people about his life, if anyone even knew he had a nearly thirty-year-old son living in France, one he had abandoned as a child. Or if he did tell them…he wondered how his dad would spin it.

"It's Jacob," he said, "Marilyn's son. Just in case, you know… he needs help remembering who I am."

God, it felt good. It gave Jacob a strange sort of pleasure to finally be able to speak his truth aloud, without shame or embarrassment, after all these years.

The secretary cleared her throat. "One moment, please."

He watched her disappear down a back hallway. Jacob waited, tapping his fingers against the counter. Moments later, she reappeared, all smiles and good tidings, a perfect example of prim and proper professionalism.

"You know what," she said sweetly, apologetically. "Mr. Greenberg is extremely busy today. He was wondering if you wouldn't mind coming back tomorrow."

Jacob forced a smile. "I'll wait."

"But—"

Jacob took a seat in the lobby. Unless his father had a parachute stored under his desk, they were doing this thing today.

Jacob spent the next three hours waiting to see his father. At one point, he pulled out his phone and attempted to distract himself with work. He answered questions via text message and shot emails off to Shmuel and Maddie. Occasionally, his eyes drifted over to the abstract art in front of him. Copper angles and floating spheres, jagged edges without color. It was so cold and unfeeling, very much like his father.

Finally Richard Greenberg appeared. He came bursting out of his office, racing down the hallway, all smiles and energy.

"Jacob!" Richard said, shaking his hand. "Well, what a nice surprise."

It was all so very friendly. "Dad."

"Why don't we go into my office?"

Jacob followed him down the hall and into a large corner office with a city view. In the shelves around his desk were law books and awards, photographs and diplomas, and of course, a whole collection of baseball paraphernalia.

"Can I, uh—" his father twisted around at the door "—get you something to drink?"

"Hmm?" Jacob said, picking up one of the baseballs to inspect it.

It had an autograph, a name he didn't recognize. But he imagined, based on the way it was displayed on a clear plastic shelf with overhead lighting, that it was expensive. Something worthwhile and important. A thing worth keeping. Jacob put the baseball down.

"Coffee," his dad asked, ignoring the fact that he was touching his stuff. "Or maybe something a little stronger?"

"Water is fine," Jacob said.

His father disappeared down another hall.

Jacob breathed a sigh of relief. He was grateful for the quiet. He needed a few solitary moments to gather his thoughts.

Jacob had barely recognized his father when he'd approached him in the lobby. The image in his memory was of a young man. A superhero with black hair and huge arms who could toss you around the room, just for fun, while wrestling.

It had been nearly two decades since Jacob had last seen his father, and this man—this old man with white hair and a receding hairline—was a stranger. It struck Jacob that if he had passed Richard Greenberg on a street or sat beside him on the subway he wouldn't have recognized him.

His father returned with a bottle of water. Jacob took a seat in front of his desk. His dad, still chipper, pulled a drawer open, revealing a bottle of scotch and two crystal glasses.

"You don't mind, do you?"

"No."

"I figure this calls for a bit of a celebration?" He took the seat in front of Jacob, pouring two glasses.

He pushed one in Jacob's direction, but he didn't want it. He didn't feel like celebrating his trauma from twenty years ago with a stranger. He took it anyway, tapping on the glass.

"God," his father said, and rubbed the front of his face with one hand. "I can't believe it's you. How old are you now? Twenty?"

"Thirty."

"Thirty," his father repeated. "Wow. You still live in France?" Jacob nodded. "Paris."

"You like it there?"

"It's fine."

"And…" His father tapped on his glass with one finger, attempting to make conversation. "This is your first time back in New York?"

"Yes."

"Well…" His father took a drink. "I'm glad you decided to come and see me. It's been too long, right?"

Jacob's eyes wandered over to a photo on the desk. In a smart silver frame, a smiling woman in a field, long blond hair blowing in the wind, wrapped her arms around three equally angelic-looking children. He wondered who these people were or if they just came with the frame.

"You got remarried?" Jacob asked.

He put the drink down. "Oh, yeah. That's Sheila."

"Sheila?" Jacob scanned his memory. "What happened to Peggy?"

"Peggy?"

"The woman you were staying with when Mom got sick?"

His father shrugged. "Didn't work out."

Jacob didn't want to know, exactly—but he had to ask. "Are they yours?"

"Who?"

"The kids," Jacob said, nodding toward the photograph. "In the picture. Are they yours?"

"Oh." His dad looked over. "No. They're from her first marriage."

Jacob breathed. "Do I have any other siblings?"

His father put down his drink, insulted. "Of course not."

Jacob couldn't help being riled at his father's offense to a simple question. He had the right to know if he had brothers and sisters. He had the right to know if he had any *family*. But of course, selfish and narcissistic Richard was focused only on one person in the room. Himself.

"I called you," Jacob said. "After Mom died."

"Yes," his father said. "I know."

"You never called me back."

"What is it you want, Jacob? You need money?"

"No, I don't need *money*."

"Then what?" his father said, growing agitated. "Why are you here after all these years?"

"I want to know why you left."

His father hesitated, rose from his seat and poured himself another drink. "You think it was all me?" his father grumbled. "You think I'm the bad guy here, and your dear sweet departed mother was the saint? I spent a whole year trying to get you back!"

"A whole year?" Jacob scoffed.

"You were too young to remember what your mother was like," he said, returning to his desk. "She was depressed, Jacob. She wasn't right in the head! And she was determined to go back to France. What was I supposed to do, huh? She was sick, and stubborn, and Paris was a million miles—"

"She always put you on the card."

"What?"

"Mom," Jacob said. "Every birthday card…up until the year she died. She would put your name on the card. *Love, Mom and*

Dad. I used to get so annoyed at her. *Why do you do that? Why do you put him on the card? I haven't talked to him in years. I know Dad isn't sending me birthday cards.*"

His father squinted. "I don't understand."

"I didn't, either," Jacob admitted. "Even after she died, I sat with it, I wondered...why did she do that? Used to drive me nuts. But now, coming here, I understand. She loved me. She loved me so much...she let me keep the fantasy of you."

"What are you talking about?"

"She never talked ill of you," Jacob said in sudden realization. "Not once, actually. Not ever. Maybe she should have. Maybe I would have been less angry at her had she simply told me the truth about who you were. But you were my hero. You were the dad who took me to baseball games and bought me a mascot costume in the shape of a baseball, and she wanted me to have that dad. So she put your name on the card."

"That's not fair."

"Fair?" Jacob spit out the words. "You left her...you left *us*... because she was *sick*."

"I didn't—"

"Because you thought she had nothing left to offer, right? Because it's hard watching someone you love suffer. Well, guess what, Dad—it was hard for me, too. It was awful, watching Mom go through her very worst days."

His father sat, listening, not moving. Perhaps even the very best of lawyers knew when they had no defense left.

"But Mom..." Jacob said, his heart aching over every word. "Mom had this enormous capacity for love. She had this ability to be there for people, in a way that you will *never* understand. She lit up every room she was well enough to enter, and you, Dad... You think you got away, you think you escaped it...but you're the one who missed out."

Jacob rose to leave, finally and forever, but not before lob-

225

bing one last attack. It was the least he could do, after all, for his beloved bubbe.

"And call your goddamn mother."

Jacob exploded onto Fifth Avenue just as the sun was setting. The cold air nipped at his cheeks, forcing him to pull his jacket taut against the chill. And yet, despite the brisk weather, he felt warm. In his mind, he saw himself standing at his mother's graveside, tossing dirt onto her coffin, tucking her in gently for one final sleep.

He walked until he reached the East River. He walked until the monsters that had followed him his entire life were simply no more. For Jacob had wrestled with his father and, in the light of morning, had emerged changed.

From: Rachel Rubenstein-Goldblatt <margotcross@northpole.com>
To: Lisa Brown <l.brown@cachingliteraryagency.com>

Sent: Thu, 16 December
Subject: RE: The Hanukkah Grinch–Proposal

LISA!!!

This is such great news about turning *The Hanukkah Grinch* into a series!!! You seriously made my week! (And believe me—it's been an AWFUL one!) Tell Chandra I have more than enough material to fill LOTS and LOTS of books!

Yay!
Rachel

PS: Can we schedule the meeting for two weeks from now? I've come down with a terrible flu. (Cough, cough)

26

It was another *glamorous* day in bed. Another day stuck in her apartment, staring at four walls. It didn't matter that Rachel had been sick for close to twelve years. Even foggy and exhausted, the boredom that came alongside her disease was astounding.

She thought about facing her computer, getting some writing work down on *The Hanukkah Grinch*, but she was far too ill to be sitting up or putting together cohesive sentences. She considered her alternatives, glancing over to the side of her bedroom where a laptop rested. It was almost Christmas. Rachel had two books releasing. This was normally when Margot Cross would go online and connect with her fans. But even social media could set her back when she had crashed.

She was in that delicate place between better and bad. She could push through, which would likely lead to worse days and more lost time. The only way to get out of her flare was to stop completely. Deal with the boredom of staring at the walls. Put a mask over her eyes and plugs in her ears, cutting out any light and noise stimulation.

She lay back in her bed and tried to force herself to rest. Listened to the sound of footsteps creaking around in the apartment above her.

What day was it even? She reached into her nightstand and pulled out her Jewish calendar, which strung all the Gregorian dates against the Jewish lunar calendar. It was Thursday, December 16. The fourth night of Hanukkah was this evening.

Rachel shook her head, frustrated by her body. She couldn't believe she had only made it two freaking days volunteering for Jacob's Matzah Ball. It seemed impossible she could be this sick. Then, throwing the calendar back into her nightstand, she decided it wasn't completely her fault.

It was a combination of events. The physicality of Jacob's Matzah Ball chores, coupled with the mental exertion required to write her Hanukkah Grinch proposal. Plus, there was all that stress. It was an exhausting combination that had sent her postexertional malaise into a full-blown crash.

A light knock on the door drew her attention away.

"One moment," Rachel called out.

She sat up, smoothed out the wrinkles in her sheets, and attempted to push down her wild and frizzy curls. Chronic illness was an intimate state. Though Rachel could not deny that Martha was helpful...she wanted the woman out of her house.

"Okay," Rachel said. "Come in."

Martha appeared at her door with a tray. "Good morning, Rachel!" She swooped in, laying the tray down on the bed beside her. "I hope you don't mind that I've arranged for a light breakfast for you this morning."

Rachel stared down at the tray. It was not a light breakfast. Scrambled eggs sat beside freshly sliced avocado and fruit salad. And on the side, as if she wanted to provide the option for less healthy alternatives, were three silver-dollar-sized pancakes and two chocolate crepes.

"I didn't want to wake you to ask what you wanted," Martha

explained. "So I just had the chef make everything I like. Not to worry, of course. Everything is kosher. He used all the right plates and cooking utensils, too."

"This is too much, Martha."

"Nonsense," she said, returning to her bedside, delicately fluffing each and every one of her pillows.

Rachel suppressed the instinct to swat her away like a fly. The truth was she needed the help. Martha and her nonstop doting allowed Rachel to rest her body completely. It gave her the chance to recover, the opportunity to be fully cared for while never lifting a finger. It would likely get her out of bed sooner rather than later. She just hated the fact that it came from Jacob.

She couldn't believe that the same man who had nearly killed her was now her benefactor. He had thought of everything. A kosher chef to make meals. Delivery men to pick up prescriptions. Her laundry even arrived to her bedroom—pressed, ironed and folded. It was the dream, the fantasy she'd always wanted, delivered via Martha McBride, aka Martha Poppins. His perfectly wonderful gift—so generous and thoughtful—caused all types of confusing feelings to rise up inside of her.

"Now," Martha said, pulling out a napkin and attaching it to the top button of her collared pajamas. "While you are eating breakfast, I'd like to give this place a good scrub down. The reason I bring this up, of course, is because of that one room."

"Which room?"

"The locked room. The room that makes a weird little jingle sound every hour, on the hour. I would like permission for my team to clean that room."

"Ohhh," Rachel said. "That room."

Martha waited for acknowledgment, and permission, to enter the secret Christmas office. Instead, Rachel simply dug into her scrambled eggs.

"I will remind you," Martha said, refusing to retreat, "that everyone who enters this apartment, including me, has signed nondisclosure agreements. Your privacy will be safeguarded."

"And yet—" Rachel dropped her fork "—you work for Jacob."

"Beyond the fact that the NDA was his idea, and I have nothing to gain from—"

"Wait," Rachel interrupted her. "The NDA was Jacob's idea?"

"He mentioned you were very private and he wanted that privacy protected."

"Ugh." Rachel groaned, closing her eyes.

It was just like stupid Jacob Greenberg—her stupid summer camp archenemy who put her in a stupid matzah ball costume—to be so freaking thoughtful about everything. She didn't know whether to be grateful or throw up.

"You seem upset by this news," Martha said.

"It's complicated," Rachel sighed. "How much longer are you here for?"

"Until Jacob sends me home."

"Fabulous."

Rachel didn't mean to come off like an ungrateful snob. Martha was doing an amazing job. She was like a chronic illness fairy, showing up at just the right moment, making everything better. It was simply that every time she looked at Martha Poppins, she saw Jacob Greenberg.

The front door buzzer drew both their attention.

"I'll get that," Martha said.

Rachel picked up her fork, fully prepared to finish her eggs and stop thinking about Jacob, when she heard it. *French.* Lots and lots of French. There could only be one person standing at the door talking to Martha in French.

Rachel groaned again.

The man was obsessed with her.

She threw her fork down, her anger returning. Jacob had nearly killed her, after all. Worse than that, he had played with her emotions. Gotten her interested in him over Shabbat only to stomp all over her heart.

On the other hand, he had gone out of his way to make things right. He had apologized, sent her Martha Poppins, given her a ticket to the Matzah Ball. She didn't understand his ups and downs, but just hearing his voice at the door softened her heart to him once again. Even though it went against all her better instincts, she found herself rising from bed, heading to the front door.

"Martha," Rachel said, interrupting them, "it's okay. I can take this."

Martha stepped out of the way. Jacob was standing in the hallway. An awkward moment stretched between the three of them.

Gawd, the boy was hot. It seemed impossible, but he must have gone up about three degrees' worth of hotness since the last time she saw him. She loved his button-down shirt, the way his pants hugged his muscular thighs, the incredible way his black leather belt highlighted his V shape.

He was looking at her, too. *Up and down.* Almost immediately, all her insecurities about being ill and looking like a banshee on a bad day surfaced. She felt gross next to this man, the picture of good health and virility. But whatever... What Jacob didn't know was that sick girls did *everything* better on their backs.

"You know what," Martha said, grabbing her coat and scarf, "I was just heading out to pick up some more cleaning supplies. Rachel, do you need anything while I'm gone?"

"No," she said. "I'm fine."

"Very well," Martha said, heading for the elevator. "I'll be back in a bit then."

Rachel leaned against the doorpost.

He rubbed the back of his neck. "Can I come in?"

"No."

"Fair enough. How are you feeling?"

"Jacob." Rachel closed her eyes. "What are you doing here?" She was far too tired to deal with his games today.

"Right," he said, getting down to it. "I was wondering if you wanted to go out?"

"Excuse me?"

"The thing is—you won't believe this, but I have never been to the Empire State Building."

"Well," Rachel said, raising both eyebrows, "you should totally get on that."

"No—" He was turning bright red. "What I meant is… I would like to go with you to the Empire State Building."

She had to replay his words in her mind several times. "Are you insane?"

"Not that I know of. I might have some issues, though."

"Some?"

"What did you tell me again?" He bounced in his loafers. "God only works through broken vessels."

She scoffed aloud. "Don't you quote my own Midrash at me."

"Sorry."

Secretly, she was surprised he remembered that. Shocked, in fact, that those words had made such an impression on his heart. Rachel didn't know whether to love him, or hate him, or both. The only thing she knew for certain was that she wasn't going anywhere today.

"I'm sorry, Jacob," she said, and moved to close the door. "I can't."

"Why not?"

"I don't feel well, and frankly, I don't really trust you."

"Okay, so, I knew you would say that." Jacob held up one finger, body angled toward the service elevator. "Which is why… Just give me a second, okay? Please don't shut the door."

"Jacob—"

"Just…please," he said, disappearing down the hall, "one more minute!"

Rachel watched him struggle with something heavy and metallic at the end of the hall. She listened to him grunt and moan as he pulled it from the service elevator and wheeled something covered in a white blanket down the hall.

"If that's a dead body—"

"Just wait," he said, trying not to test her patience. "You're gonna love this."

He returned to her front door. Then, after a dramatic pause, he pulled off the white blanket like a magician.

"Ta-da!" he said, with full jazz hands.

"What the hell is that?"

"It's a wheelchair," he said triumphantly.

"I see that. What the hell is all over it?"

"Oh," he said, looking down at it. "I bedazzled it."

Jacob spun it around, pride beaming over his face. It must have taken hours to complete. Pink and silver gemstones littered the back and sides. Stars, hearts and diamond shapes encrusted the wheels and handles. But perhaps most impressive of all was the eighties-looking word highlighted in giant pink, neon green and silver puffy paint on the back of the chair: RACHEL.

"You spent all night bedazzling a wheelchair?" she asked.

"Not all night. Maybe a few hours. It that strange?"

"Nooo, totally normal."

"I really wanted it to be special."

"Your art projects are getting out of control, Jacob."

He grabbed the handle and pushed the chair forward. "Come on. Your chariot awaits."

Rachel sighed, staring down at the chair. The thing was… it was sweet. It was thoughtful. She had never before had anybody bedazzle a wheelchair for her.

It was like something out of one of her Christmas movies, if everybody in the cast was Jewish and the heroine had a disability. The problem was…this wasn't a movie. And Rachel—well, Rachel just wasn't ready.

She wasn't "out" about her disease. She wasn't out about... anything. Sitting in a wheelchair meant accepting you were disabled and dealing with awkward stares from healthy people.

Most of all, and because she had a disease with a name like *chronic fatigue syndrome*, there was always a fear tucked away inside of her that someone would look at her and say she was doing this for attention. That she really wasn't *that* sick. And so, though a wheelchair would certainly make her more mobile and give her a higher quality of life, she often chose to stay home.

"You don't really care at all, do you?" she said.

"What?"

"What people think of you?"

He shrugged. "Why would I care?"

It was like he existed on a planet Rachel had never visited.

There was a part of her that wondered what it would be like to date someone like Jacob. As if confidence and self-assurance could be spread like a cold. Rachel could use a heaping dose of whatever Jacob had—the inner strength that allowed him to move through the world not caring about what other people thought.

Rachel wasn't like Jacob. She didn't know how to be herself around others. She didn't know how to live authentically. It was a skill she had completely missed, a grade she had skipped over completely, after years of playing the role of the dutiful rabbi's daughter.

"My mom didn't like them, either."

Rachel squinted. "What?"

"Wheelchairs," he said.

"Your mom was disabled?"

She was surprised to hear this. In all her years of receiving Camp Ahava news and gossip, it had never been mentioned.

Jacob nodded. "MS."

Suddenly it all made sense. "So that's what this is about?"

"What?"

"Your poor dead mother was chronically ill." She couldn't believe she had been so stupid.

It took Jacob a minute. "Rachel—"

"No," she said, holding up a hand to stop him, "I get it now. You're gonna pity-date the sick chick, right?"

"I think you're misunderstanding me."

"Because my life is so much smaller than yours, right?"

"I didn't say that."

"Because who in the world would ever want to date someone like me?" She threw her hands up in the air. "I'm just doomed to stay single—"

"Rachel!" he shouted, interrupting her melancholy diatribe. "I don't pity you, okay? Not to be rude here, but you're way too much of a hard-ass to pity."

"Then why are you here?" she snapped back at him.

"I told you," he said, pushing the chair in her direction. "I've never been to the Empire State Building before. I thought it would be fun to go together."

She fell into his eyes. They were warm. Soft. He seemed genuine. But there was all this other crap wrapped up around him. Her crap, really. Even if she could push through her fears and anxieties, tell this man the truth about her life, it wouldn't matter. Because in this moment—in the here and now, with Jacob standing at her door, offering her a ride on a bedazzled wheelchair—Rachel was just too sick.

"I'm sorry, Jacob," she said. "I need to rest."

Rachel shut the door on Jacob. She shut the door, like always, on the possibility of love. And then—for no reason she could pinpoint, no reason in particular—she burst into tears. A deep wail escaped her lips as she crawled back into bed.

Chronic illness was the Great Decider.

And it had decided for her, once again.

From: Lisa Brown <l.brown@cachingliteraryagency.com>
To: Rachel Rubenstein-Goldblatt <margotcross@northpole.com>

Sent: Fri, 17 December
Subject: CONTRACT COMING!!!

Rachel!

GREAT NEWS! I just got off the phone with Chandra at Romance House and she is just SPINNING LIKE A DREIDEL after reading your pages!!! She'd like to contract Hanukkah Grinch ASAP...and work out the details for the next SIX BOOKS after our meeting in two weeks!

Are you cool with that? If so, I will review and then send over the contract today!

CONGRATS, GIRLIE!!!!
Lisa

27

On her third morning of bedrest, Rachel awoke feeling better. The fatigue had lifted from her eyelids. The night sweats had stopped. She could sit up in her bed and a chair without feeling she was going to straight-up die. With her energy returning to suitable levels, she texted Mickey:

Do you have time to talk? I need your advice.

Be there in twenty.

Twenty minutes later, as promised, Mickey arrived at her front door. Martha reacted to the appearance of an unexpected visitor with all the finesse of the French armed forces.

"And you are?" she sneered, blocking the entrance with her body.

"It's okay," Rachel said, jumping out of bed. "I invited him over."

Martha gave Rachel the side-eye. "Are you sure you're up for that?"

"I'm fine," she said honestly.

Rachel pulled Mickey into her bedroom, shutting the door behind them.

"Okay," Mickey said, tossing his bag down on the ground. "Who the heck is that?"

"That—" Rachel flopped down onto her bed "—is Miss Martha McBride, aka Martha Poppins, Executive Assistant to the Stars."

"Um," Mickey said, clearly confused, "but what is she doing in your living room?"

Rachel filled Mickey in on all the juicy details. She described how Jacob had come over, apologized and given her a ticket to the Matzah Ball. She described the way she had dramatically said au revoir, thinking they were well and truly done with each other, before morning arrived. At which point, Jacob had transformed from grinch to *mensch*, sending over a team of eager elves, and impressing her with his interest in arts and crafts.

"Hold up," Mickey said, stopping the story halfway through. "He sent you a Martha, a private chef, a cleaning crew…humored your obsessive need for privacy by making everyone sign NDA agreements…"

"Yes," Rachel admitted. "He did all those things."

"And then when all that didn't work—" he shook his head at the thought "—he bedazzled a wheelchair for you."

"He did."

"And we're still mad at him because—"

"He almost killed me."

"Well, technically," Mickey said, placing one finger on the center of his chin, "all he did was put you in the costume. The small children were actually the people who almost killed you."

"I don't know what to do."

"What do you mean?" he said, flabbergasted. "Call him up! Tell him to bring that damn bedazzled wheelchair back here, and go out with the man!"

"Absolutely not."

"Why?"

"Because this is obviously just another one of his pranks!" she said. "I can see it now! Us at the top of the Empire State Building. Me in the bedazzled wheelchair thinking this is all a wonderful and romantic start to our new beginning, and then *bam*! He pushes me off the ledge."

Mickey cocked his head sideways. "You have an amazing imagination, you know that?"

"He can't be trusted, Mickey. He's evil."

Mickey rubbed his temple. "Have you ever thought that maybe the guy actually likes you?"

Rachel scoffed. "Come on."

"I'm serious."

"He put me in a matzah ball costume!"

"So he's an idiot," Mickey said. "We've known since seventh grade that he was an idiot!"

"Mickey!" Rachel spun around, catching sight of herself in the mirror above the dresser. She looked all types of a mess. "Jacob Greenberg throws parties for a living. He's fabulous and gorgeous and rich. He could have his choice of beautiful—and healthy—French women."

"So *that's* what this is about."

"I didn't make it two days, Mickey! I couldn't even volunteer for one of his events for two days before collapsing completely. What kind of man is going to want a woman who spends half of her life in bed?"

Mickey shook his head. "Why do you do that?"

"What?"

"Constantly put yourself down. Constantly act like you don't have the same value as other people?"

"Because it's the truth."

"No," he shot back at her, clapping three times in her face to make sure she was paying attention. "It's not, Rachel! You're brilliant. You're quirky, and weird, and fun. You're one of the most loyal and loving people I have ever met. And even if you never sold another book in your life, even if you spent the rest of your days *in bed* watching Christmas movies…you would still be all those things. Being sick doesn't cancel out all the other amazing stuff about you, okay? You are not *invalid!*"

Rachel swallowed hard. She knew Mickey was right. She had been sabotaging herself rather fantastically for years when it came to love. It wasn't just that she couldn't imagine any man loving her enough to throw his lot in beside her, it was that chronic illness removed all her costumes.

It brought her to her darkest places, boiled her down to her most essential self. Some days, even she didn't want to spend time with that person. Loving someone required you to share vulnerabilities. It was a skill set she had never developed.

"How do you do it?" Rachel asked softly.

"What?"

"Be so brave about everything?"

"You know," Mickey said, after a few thoughtful seconds, "when my moms first got together, not everybody was happy about it. Dumbass Uncle Joe, especially, had to make a whole *thing* about it with my grandma Cindy…and for a really long time, on both sides of the fam, it seemed like people would never support them. And do you know what my mothers did in the wake of all that backlash over their love, when everyone was trying to tear them apart? They said, 'Screw 'em.'"

Rachel laughed. "Screw 'em?"

"Yeah." Mickey shrugged. "And that's what they told me, right before I came out at my bar mitzvah. My Mom looked me straight in the eye and said, 'Mikael, the world is filled with angry and miserable people. Those people are never going to be happy for you. So you go out there and you live your truth. *You be the person the universe asked you to be.* And anyone who doesn't celebrate you for it, anyone who doesn't love you through it, screw 'em. Because we love you. Just the way you are.'"

"Your moms are the best."

"I know." Mickey leaned across the bedspread, meeting her eyes with firm resolution. "And now, I'm passing that advice on to you. You're a good person, Rachel. You think about everyone, all the time. But you gotta learn to say *screw 'em*. Someone says your disease isn't real? *Screw 'em*. Someone says you're a bad Jew and a disappointment to the Goldblatt family name? *Screw 'em*. Someone hates your Christmas romance novel, or Hanukkah novel, or robot-octopus erotica—"

"Wait, what?"

"Just something I've been reading lately," Mickey explained, waving away her question. "The point is...*screw 'em*! For God's sake, Rachel, you're nearly thirty years old. Live your damn life already."

Rachel smiled. It was just like Mickey to bring her out of a daze. Then it struck her how similar Jacob and Mickey were. They both walked through the world, unapologetic about their existence. They both gave very little power to what other people thought of them. Maybe Rachel could take the hint and finally learn to do the same.

"I love you," she said.

"I love you, too."

Rachel sucked back a tiny tear before quickly changing the topic. There were more pressing romantic issues to discuss, after all. "But enough about me. I want to hear how everything is going with your acrobat."

Mickey frowned. "I'm afraid my brief torrid love affair with Stefan has ended."

"Oh, no!" Rachel gasped. "What happened?"

"I wish I could tell you he went out in a bedazzled wheelchair of glory..."

"Ha ha."

"Alas, it wasn't anything even remotely exciting. We just realized we weren't right for each other. I mean...he's always in the air, spinning around on hoops and things. Whereas I am firmly, and without a doubt, attached to the ground. Plus, you know how much I love challah. Stefan has been paleo for three years."

Rachel shook her head. "Bastard."

"We're going to stay friends. But breaking it off was the right call."

She reached across the bed, squeezing her best friend's hand. Though Mickey would never say it aloud, she knew he was disappointed. Like Rachel, he had been through his fair share of romantic breakups. Often, living and dating in Manhattan felt like an exercise in futility. Still, anyone would be lucky to have him. "You'll find the right one, Mickey."

"Maybe."

"I know it. You deserve all the happiness in the world." Rachel hugged him. Breathing him in, she felt safe. She could trust Mickey with anything. "So our promise to grow old together is officially back on?"

He wiped away a tear. "Girl, I've already started looking at property in the Hamptons."

They were both laughing when a knock at the door interrupted the bittersweet moment. Martha stuck her head inside.

"May I interrupt?" she asked.

"Of course," Rachel said.

"A package just arrived for you."

"Oh, great." Rachel turned to Mickey to explain. "It's probably the contract from my publisher. They're supposed to be sending it over."

"That is such good news," Mickey said.

"I know," Rachel said, before turning back to Martha. "You can just bring it to my bedroom."

"I don't think it's a contract, dear."

Rachel glanced askew at Mickey. Moments later, Martha reappeared, holding a large box in both hands. Wrapped in silver paper and tied up in the most elegant blue bow, it was easily the most beautiful Hanukkah present Rachel had ever seen.

"Mr. Greenberg sent it over," Martha said, laying the present down on the bed between them.

"You're kidding me," Rachel said.

"Not in the least," Martha said, before departing once again.

The gift sat untouched between them for several moments. Finally Mickey tapped her on the shoulder. "Well, go on," he squealed. "Open it! You know how much I love presents from summer camp archenemies!"

Rachel took a deep breath, pulling the box onto her lap. It was heavier than she expected. She couldn't help but wonder what sort of gift could be lurking inside. With trembling fingers, she tugged at the ribbon and wrapping. Then she gasped. Inside was the most beautiful blue-and-silver ball gown she had ever seen.

"He didn't," Rachel said aloud.

"Oh, he most certainly did," Mickey said.

She pulled the dress out, holding it up to her body. The gown was stunning. Strapless, with a built-in corset, flaring into a mermaid bottom. It would highlight all her best features. Her thick hips. The ample bosom she'd inherited from her grand-mother. Her waist, disproportionate to the rest of her curves.

A card fell out from beneath the folds. Bending down to pick it up, Rachel read the words before understanding their full meaning.

I'm sorry for not being more sensitive to your needs. If you feel up to it, please consider being my date for the Matzah Ball. I'd love to see you there.

"What does it say?" Mickey asked.

"He wants me to be his date for the Matzah Ball."

Rachel's face flushed with anxiety. She couldn't deny that

Jacob's gifts, thoughtful and generous, were raising all sorts of questions inside of her.

"There's something on the back of the card," Mickey said.

Rachel turned the note over to find a postscript scribbled in tiny blue letters.

PS: Please don't stand me up this time.

"Stand him up?" Rachel put down the card. "What is he talking about?"

Mickey shrugged.

"He probably got me confused with someone else."

And yet the dress she was holding in her hands seemed made for her. In spite of all her lies, Jacob had seen her completely. He had found her best parts, dressing them up in soft sweeps of silk and satin.

She could almost imagine herself at the Matzah Ball, dancing with Jacob. The way the silver and blue sequins would shimmer and shine beneath the lights. She was so used to hiding, being invisible, but this dress was designed to make Rachel visible. How could Jacob know that she was dying to be seen?

"You know," Rachel said, collapsing back onto her bed. "He said something strange when he came to my door the other night. He said… I broke his heart."

Mickey squinted. "I don't understand."

"To tell you the truth," she mused thoughtfully, "I didn't, either. But he kept going on about it. How he really needed me and I wasn't there for him, and how badly I hurt him…and well, it just didn't sound like someone who had turned my first kiss into a giant prank for all the boys of bunk 7B. Did you know his mom was sick?"

"No."

"MS."

"Oh, wow." Mickey started to chew on his fingers. "Do you think that's why they moved back to France?"

"I don't know," Rachel said. "Maybe. I remember hearing his parents got divorced."

"I remember hearing that, too."

"I was kind of glad when he didn't come back the next summer."

"Yeah," Mickey said quietly. "Me, too. I was pissed he gave you mono."

"Jacob didn't give me mono."

Mickey stopped. "What?"

Rachel sighed. "Leah Abraham."

"You kissed Leah Abraham?"

"No," she said. "The girl was always drinking out of my water bottle. I told her a thousand times to stop, but she never listened to me. She got mono that summer, too."

"Oh, crap."

"I just blamed it on Jacob," she said. "I don't know why. I guess...it just gave me more reason to hate him. Plus, you hated him, too. It was fun hating him together."

Mickey bit his lower lip. "Yeah."

"Truthfully, Mickey... I really liked Jacob Greenberg. I thought we had something real. I couldn't bear the thought of seeing him again. The very next morning I called my parents from the camp office, crying my eyes out, begging them to come take me home. You know what my parents are like. Hearing me blubbering like an idiot on the phone, they drove up that same day and took me home. I just wanted to forget about him. I guess I wanted everyone else at Camp Ahava to forget about him, too."

"Rachel..." Mickey went back to chewing on his fingers. "I have something to confess then, too."

"Okay."

"I was kind of...jealous of you and Jacob."

"Jealous?"

"Please don't hate me," Mickey said quickly. "I was twelve! I'll be the first to admit I didn't handle it great. But you were my best friend, Rachel! It had been me and you since third grade. And then one day Jacob Greenberg showed up to camp, and suddenly you weren't my best friend anymore."

"What are you trying to say, Mickey?"

"I might have…exaggerated some of what actually happened in our bunk that summer."

"Exaggerated how?"

"Look," Mickey said. "Jacob Greenberg was a giant jerk and a total prankster! Everybody at Camp Ahava would agree. And he did talk about you, Rachel…all the time. It was so annoyingly obvious that you two had something going on. But as far as I know, he never actually admitted it to anybody."

"I don't understand," Rachel said. "If Jacob didn't set me up, then how did people know we were going to be at the lake together that evening of our first kiss? I mean, all the boys from bunk 7B were hiding in the bushes with flashlights and cameras…"

"Because you told me—" Mickey cowered inside his palms "—and I told everyone else."

"What?"

"I was mad at you, Rachel! You were my best friend, and then you ditched me completely. I never meant to hurt you, though. I know it sounds horrible, but I just wanted my best friend back. Do you hate me?"

"Of course I don't hate you."

"You promise?"

She took his hand. "I could never hate you. I just don't understand why you didn't tell me sooner."

Mickey sighed. "I didn't know how. You were sick with mono, and crying all the time, and I hated myself for being the cause of all that. And then, the months passed…and the years… and Jacob Greenberg never came back to Camp Ahava. He never came back to New York City. You'd moved on. There was no reason to talk about it. *He was gone.* Au revoir, *off to France.* Honestly, I had forgotten about everything until you mentioned he was coming to Shabbat dinner."

"Wow."

"Yeah."

She shook her head. "So all these years I've hated Jacob Greenberg, blamed him for turning my first kiss into a giant summer camp prank, believed he never even cared about me...and none of that was true."

"No."

"Well." Rachel stood up, putting the gown back into the box. "I appreciate you telling me the truth after all these years, but it still doesn't change the fact he put me in a matzah ball costume."

"What are you doing?"

"Sending the dress back."

"Rachel." Mickey stopped her. "I love you to death, so listen to me when I tell you this—reconsider."

Rachel laughed. "Reconsider!"

"Let me finish," he said. "I'm not twelve years old anymore. I want you to be happy. I want you to find your person, because you deserve that."

"Mickey—"

"If you want to hate Jacob for the costume, fine. I get it. But the man has apologized profusely, sent you a Martha, bedazzled a wheelchair and bought you the most beautiful ball gown I have ever seen in an effort to make it up to you. All I'm saying is, before you give up forever on being a Mazel Board story in the Camp Ahava newsletter, consider the possibility that we *both* may have been wrong about Jacob Greenberg. Maybe he's actually a decent guy?"

Rachel huffed. "I'll think about it."

"Good," Mickey said, embracing her. "Because I love you more than anything in the world, and I am ready to fully and completely give you away."

★ ★ ★

Later that night—after Mickey had departed and Rachel had rested some more—she awoke from a deep slumber to find her apartment empty. Sitting up in bed, she listened for Martha shuffling about in the living room. The house was quiet. Martha Poppins had opened her umbrella and flown away for the evening.

She was feeling better but still unsettled. Mickey's revelation had left her as confused as ever.

Even if Jacob was the kindest and most honorable man, how could she be honest with him?

Knowing there was only one thing in the world that would help, she escaped to her office. Two-hundred-and-thirty-seven smiling porcelain Santas greeted her arrival. She breathed in the smell of pine cones and cinnamon before her eyes landed on the photograph of her with Santa. Picking it up, she drew the image closer.

"So where is it?" she asked Santa in the quiet of her Christmas office. "Where is my happy ending?"

Rachel put the photo back. After all, it wasn't Santa's fault that she was a sick chick, a Christmas romance novelist and a dreadful liar. Her fictions piled up on top of each other like snowflakes during a winter storm, creating blizzard conditions. Her parents didn't know about her career. Her colleagues didn't know about her health. Jacob Greenberg didn't know about any of it. Her reindeer games had managed to isolate her from everybody but Mickey.

Rachel needed to take her mind off her quickly devolving life. After pulling out her phone, she opened up the Hallmark app and returned to her movie, *The Christmas Prince and the Pianist*. It was right at her favorite part. The moment where the two characters realize that in spite of their differences, in spite of their misunderstandings, they may actually like each other.

They may actually be perfect for each other. Their opposite natures, when combined, made them both more whole.

She couldn't help but think about Jacob.

Leaving her Christmas movie, she made her way back to her bedroom. Standing on tiptoe, she pulled down the flowered box that held her hodgepodge of photographs, trinkets and letters from childhood. Pushing past photographs, she found the stack of letters held together by a rubber band.

She pulled one out and opened it up:

Dear Rachel,
How are you? I am fine. Why are you not answering my phone calls? I miss you. My mom says we are moving to France. Please say goodbye.
Love,
Jacob.

PS: I almost put shaving cream in this letter, but decided not to. JUST KIDDING. Hope you like the joke.

She lifted the letter to her nose.

Yep. Smelled like shaving cream.

What was she doing? *What was he doing to her?* She shook her head, annoyed with herself. But Rachel knew what this was. She had written about it a thousand times in her romance novels. There were some people in this world who seemed destined to wrap themselves up in your story.

She put the letter down. It was funny how stories could change. Not just the ones you told yourself, but the ones told about other people.

Rachel didn't need to volunteer for the Matzah Ball anymore. She had her Hanukkah romance. She had her book deal. She could easily avoid Jacob for the rest of her natural life. But there was something about him, some feeling lurking there like the smell of shaving cream.

She thought back to their shared Shabbat. Jacob hadn't blinked when she mentioned watching a Christmas movie. He didn't care that she was chronically ill. He wore ugly Hanukkah sweaters and commanded every room he walked into with confidence and swagger. *He bedazzled a goddamn wheelchair for her.*

It was like the man had no frontal lobe controlling his impulses. Like his mother hadn't stood at the door before Shabbat services, reminding him to be on his best behavior because everyone was watching. Jacob didn't give a damn about what other people thought. He was someone who easily and readily said *screw 'em.* She needed his *chutzpah* in her life.

She wasn't ready to say goodbye.

Gently placing the letter back inside the box, she made a firm and final decision. She was going back to help with the Matzah Ball.

From: Rachel Rubenstein-Goldblatt <margotcross@northpole.com>
To: Lisa Brown <l.brown@cachingliteraryagency.com>

Sent: Sat, 18 December
Subject: RE: CONTRACT COMING!!!

Lisa!

I got the contract from the courier yesterday evening. Sorry for not letting you know sooner. It's just things are SUPER busy for me right now...

BUT I will look it over ASAP and send it back as soon as it is signed.

Thank you so much for everything!!!
Rachel

28

It was all hands on deck inside the Four Seasons. Jacob paced, one hand anxiously pressing through his hair, the other tapping off items on his tablet as they arrived. Tonight they would be lighting candle six of Hanukkah. If everything went according to plan—and, indeed, everything needed to go according to plan—the Matzah Ball would finally start coming together.

The tables would be set up, decorated with smart blue coverings and expensive silver-and-gold centerpieces. The concrete columns and marble walls would be made unrecognizable, covered with expensive silk drapes and thousands of fairy lights. The stage would be set, ready to accommodate the most famous Jewish musicians and artists.

Jacob had a vision. An idea as wild and imaginative as any event he had ever held. He just needed to make sure it all came together.

"Four thousand pieces of chocolate *gelt*," a volunteer said, appearing at his side.

Jacob looked up from his tablet. "Just put them over there

with the rest." The volunteer nodded. Jacob tapped off the item on the screen, then got on his earpiece to Maddie. "How are we doing with those potatoes?"

"Fine," Maddie said, speaking into his ear. "Unloading them now. Careful!"

Jacob felt momentary relief until his eyes landed on the ten-foot menorah, in the process of still being set up in the middle of the main ballroom. It was a disaster. Despite finally finding instructions, and almost everyone on his staff taking a stab at it, no one could get the damn thing up and working again.

Twisted branches and a broken *shamash* were piled up in a corner of the room. The acrylic base, so thoughtfully designed to give the appearance of floating candles, now stood abandoned on the stage. Three branches of silver jutted out waywardly from the top. Jacob was reminded of a pitchfork, a tool of the Devil, staring down on his Matzah Ball like a harbinger of doom.

He shook the thought away. They still had plenty of time left to figure it out. Two days was more than enough time to set up a ballroom and fix a menorah.

"Watch out," a volunteer screamed from the center of the room. "Incoming!" One of the branches his team was working on collapsed into a pile of metal on the floor. Jacob bit back a grimace. "Sorry," the young man said.

"No problem," Jacob said. "Let's just keep working on it."

Jacob never let his team see him get flustered. He wished Shmuel was here. It would be helpful to have his colleague to rely on, but it was Shabbat, and Shmuel was observant. He wouldn't be returning to the Matzah Ball until after sundown.

Jacob had swung round to check on his alcohol delivery when his eyes caught sight of a most unexpected presence. Rachel was standing by the door. Wearing a formfitting pair of jeans, paired with a smart blue jacket and plaid scarf, she looked adorable. A winter fantasy. His heart melted at the sight.

Jacob forgot all about his to-do list.

"Hey!" He went over to greet her. "You're here!"

"I am."

"And…" Jacob hesitated. He didn't want to make decisions, for her or her body, but he cared about her. Rachel had a terrible tendency to put herself last. He wanted to be absolutely sure that she was not pushing herself because she thought she owed him something. "You're feeling better?" he asked cautiously.

"Yes," she said. "Martha has been incredibly helpful. I never realized how much effort it took to salt my own food."

Jacob laughed. "She can be a little over-the-top sometimes."

"Ya think?" Rachel said. "But seriously, Jacob, she gave me three days to just relax and completely focus on my health, which I don't think has *ever* happened in my life. So, thank you. It probably would have taken me a whole lot longer to recoup without her help."

"Good," Jacob said. "I'm glad she was helpful."

He stopped himself there. What he really wanted to say was, *You deserve it. You deserve to feel good, Rachel. You deserve to be pleasured.* He wanted to take care of her, send her people to do her laundry and buy her ball gowns for the rest of her natural life.

He also didn't want to freak her out.

Thankfully, her attitude had shifted. This was the woman who'd talked about brokenness over Shabbat. She was warm and genuine, with just a tiny drop of that quirky humor. He adored the way the red rose in her cheeks when she was blushing. He wanted to bring that red to her cheeks in other ways.

"So all that out of the way," Rachel said, getting down to business. "I'm here for a reason."

"Oh," Jacob dug his hands into his pockets. "Lay it on me."

"First off," she said, "I don't want your pity."

"I don't pity you—"

"Can you just let me talk?" she cut him off. "I realize that you're used to being in charge, but from this point on, I really need you to just be quiet and listen. The truth is… I don't trust you, Jacob. I want to trust you. I want to be wrong about you. But there's so much crap in our backstory. I can't make sense of it all."

"Rachel—"

"Let me finish, Jacob!" she said definitively.

He shut up.

"I'm here because we had a deal," she said firmly. "I promised to volunteer for your Matzah Ball in exchange for a ticket, and I keep my promises. Even though I'm sick—and sometimes have to bail on things last minute—I'm not flaky."

Jacob swallowed the instinct to correct her. Did she really not remember abandoning him on the dance floor at the Camp Ahava final dance?

He reminded himself of his grandmother's sage advice over rugalach and tea. *The trick is to know what's in the present...and what's in the past.* He was not going to let history impinge on his happiness anymore.

"Now," Rachel continued, "I may be sick, and I may not be able to do everything all the time, but I am very capable of doing a lot, more than most people, at least fifty percent of the time. If you can deal with those stats, here are my conditions. First off, no more costumes."

"There definitely won't be—"

"Stop talking, Jacob."

He shut up again.

"Secondly—" she took a deep breath "—I expect you to accommodate my disability over the next two days. I expect you to allow me time to rest, recoup and pace myself...and I want a chair."

"I have a chair with your name on it." He pointed to his bedazzled wheelchair, resting unused in a corner of the room.

"Jacob," Rachel said. "I'm still talking."

"Sorry."

"Finally," she said. "You need to call off Martha Poppins. She's been helpful and I am appreciative, but it's too much. I need my privacy. I need my space. Plus, the woman has started color coding my underwear. I can't emotionally deal with a person color coding my underwear."

He wanted to get it right this time, so he waited a moment. "Are you finished?"

"Yes."

He nodded. "Then I fully agree to all your terms."

"Good." Rachel sucked a huge breath of air. "Where do you want me to begin?"

Jacob led her to a long table covered in boxes. Before he began doling out instructions, he pulled out a chair for her. She sat down.

"Most of our suppliers are arriving today," he explained, grabbing a tablet. "Other volunteers will deal with unloading and organizing, but I could use someone to oversee them, especially with Shmuel off for Shabbat. Basically, all you need to do is sit here, and check that everything that has been ordered and paid for is delivered to our satisfaction."

"I can handle that," she said, taking the tablet.

"Good. Then I only have one more question..."

She eyed him suspiciously. "What?"

"You never told me your answer." He knelt down on one knee. It felt right, bending down before her, his heart thumping wildly in his chest. "Will you be my date for the Matzah Ball?"

"I don't know," she said.

His heart sank.

"But maybe, if you can refrain from acting like a total *shmuck* for the next two days, I might be willing to save you a dance."

Jacob beamed. Her upper lip ticked up into a tiny smile. The pair had formed a truce.

Rachel enjoyed her task for the day. It was so different from writing. She loved the chance to use her left brain, organizing and establishing systems, overseeing a staff. Plus, she was sitting down.

Periodically she would catch a glimpse of Jacob sprinting through the main ballroom. Sometimes, he would look over at her. Their eyes would meet. One of them would smile. But mainly he was so focused on whatever task was at hand that he did not have time to spend conversing with Rachel.

It reminded her of her father before the High Holidays. The way her *aba* would move from shul to office to home, checking on all the final details, making sure that everything was in order. It was hard to meet the needs of a congregation that boasted over one thousand families. She imagined that organizing a Matzah Ball had similar stressors.

It seemed impossible that this was the same man who put her in a matzah ball costume, but Jacob had layers. He was childish at times. Playful, with an almost boyish charm and innocent energy. In stark juxtaposition, there was the man. As CEO of Greenberg Entertainment, he was serious and responsible. A total leader.

She found the combination irresistible. He was the type of person you could stand around the stove with on Hanukkah, burning latkes together and laughing hysterically, but also rely on to clean up the dishes when you were done.

She wanted that in a marriage.

It also didn't hurt that she was wildly attracted to him. Her wandering eye kept falling on the man. She loved the way his arms looked, sleeves rolled up, muscles flexing. She adored the prominence of his nose. Rachel could never resist a good nose.

"This is the last load," a volunteer said, arriving with a dolly filled with boxes.

Rachel snapped back to reality. "These are the dreidels?"

"Yeah," the volunteer said. "Three boxes in total."

Rachel pointed with her pen toward a back wall. "Just put the boxes over there."

The volunteer obeyed and quickly marched on to the next task. Rachel jumped up from her seat and made her way over to the boxes. Grabbing a utility knife she wore on her belt like a pistol, she cut the boxes open. She wondered what high-end design these dreidels would hold.

Wading her fingers through crumpled-up packing paper and bubble wrapping, she pulled one out. It was not what she was expecting. The three-inch-tall dreidel was plastic, bright blue and, frankly, smelled a bit like cheese.

Rachel put the dreidel down and checked the order slip against her clipboard again. *Nope. They were the right dreidels.* She shrugged away any concern.

She finished unloading the dreidels and glanced down at her watch. It was getting late in the afternoon. The main room grew quiet as the majority of the staff finished their last tasks and took off for the night. She thought about bailing with them but didn't want to leave without saying goodbye to Jacob.

Rachel scanned the room, searching for him. In the process, she found herself secretly judging the aesthetic design of the Matzah Ball.

The small centerpieces decorating the tables were just *meh*. The chocolate gelt, which looked like it had been purchased in bulk from Discount Judaica, was unimpressive. The dreidels were one step up from the choking hazards handed out during Hanukkah Hebrew School parties. Plus, the well-meaning volunteers attempting to put the ten-foot floating menorah together in the center of the room had no idea what they were doing.

This was not the high-end party Rachel expected from the mastermind behind such events as Launchella and Sunburn.

But what did Rachel know about party planning? She was a Christmas romance novelist, after all.

She returned to her task as Jacob had directed. She left her dreidel and judgments behind. She enjoyed being helpful. She enjoyed being part of the real world, having a job where she could interact with other people. It was a privilege to be able to leave your house, and your bed. Rachel would never take it for granted.

With evening now firmly settled in New York City, the ballroom, which had been a hotbed of activity hours before, quieted completely. Rachel found herself alone. Standing up, she left her tablet and tasks behind, searching for Jacob.

She found him, along with Shmuel, in the kitchen. Their voices were raised, the tones high-pitched and nervous. She knew something was wrong as she approached.

"We can fix this, Jacob," Shmuel was saying, pulling out his cell phone. "Just let me call—"

"No," Jacob barked. "It's too late, we need to cancel."

"Are you out of your mind?" Shmuel shot back. "Morty will have our heads!"

"He'll have our heads anyway," Jacob said. "At least this way, we can avoid becoming a story in the *New York Daily News*."

Rachel hesitated. Through a crack in the swinging door, she could make out Shmuel, pacing back and forth. But it was Jacob that shocked her. Head in his hands, legs splayed open, he was full on losing his merde.

On instinct, she touched her heart. She was surprised by his outpouring of emotion. Totally caught off guard by the sight of him freaking out. Jacob was always the epitome of cool-as-a-cucumber dimples and charm. She was certain he could make steel melt simply by walking into a room. She didn't like seeing him upset.

Rachel pushed open the swinging door. "Everything okay in here?" she asked.

"Rachel-la," Shmuel said, waving her over. "Tell him. Tell him it's not that bad."

"Not that bad!" Jacob returned to life. "The centerpieces are made of tinsel! The dreidels are plastic! The *gelt* looks like something they handed out at my Hebrew school…twenty years ago!"

"That's what they had!" Shmuel argued. "You told me to order the best of the best... Well, this is the best of the best. What do you want from me, huh? I'm a party planner, okay? Not a manufacturer. You want nicer dreidels, go buy a factory and make them yourself!"

"You should have warned me. You should have given me a heads-up."

"I'm supposed to know you'd be unhappy with plastic dreidels?"

Jacob turned bright red. "Yes!"

Rachel bit her lower lip. Shmuel had a point. Then again, so did Jacob.

"We still have the food," Shmuel said, attempting to dissuade Jacob from canceling. "All Jews care about is the food, anyway. Once they're eating, they won't even notice the crappy decor."

"Potato latkes and boring old jelly doughnuts?" Jacob pushed a pink box of sufganiyot toward Shmuel. "Something you could get at any old Hanukkah Party? Does this seem high-end to you, Shmuel? Does this seem like something people would pay a premium for *and* post about on social media?"

"Well, what about the menorah?" Shmuel defended.

"The menorah?" Jacob scoffed. "Have you seen our ten-foot floating menorah that we had specifically designed and crafted for our event? The menorah is scrap metal! It's lying in a pile of—"

"The menorah can be fixed," Rachel interjected.

"What?" both men said at the same time.

"I took a peek at it during lunch," she explained calmly. "There are a few bent brackets and you need a replacement holder, but two hours and a trip to the hardware store—you should be fine."

Jacob stammered. "How do you know that?"

"Because," she said, since he was obviously an idiot, "every synagogue in America has a giant menorah on the grass for Hanukkah. Yours is bigger and has a fancy acrylic base, but it's basically the same design. It's not that complicated to put together. Especially if you've done it a zillion times since you were a baby. Menorahs are easy. Sukkahs are complicated."

Jacob's eyes drifted to Shmuel. "That only takes care of the menorah."

"But once the menorah is fixed," Shmuel shot back, "the rest will fall into place! Honestly, Jacob, it's not that bad. The dreidels, the centerpieces, the food. With the lighting, and the menorah, no one will even notice how cheap and terrible everything really is."

Jacob directed his gaze at Rachel. "And what do you think?"

Rachel hesitated. "You want my honest opinion?"

"Always."

"I've been to classier bar mitzvahs..." she admitted, "at the shul."

"Oh, God." Jacob collapsed his head into his hands again. "I'm gonna be the next Billy McFarland!"

Rachel refused to descend into panic alongside Jacob. She was a survivor, after all. All she knew about problems—everything she had learned from chronic illness and publisher ultimatums—was that *tzuris* needed to be dealt with head-on.

Rachel thought back to the main ballroom. It wasn't that their decor was bad, per se. Shmuel had done his job, seeking out the best of what was available. The party would have all the traditional accoutrements of Hanukkah: the latkes, the tiny dreidels, the kosher food. They had done everything technically right.

The problem with their final vision was that it was so traditional. It had all been done in the same exact way ten thousand times before. It had none of the *ruach*, or spirit, of her beloved Christmas romances. It did not inspire feelings of magic. And that was exactly what the Matzah Ball Max needed. *Ruach. Spirit. Vision.* It needed someone who was capable of thinking outside the Hanukkah box.

"I may be able to help you," Rachel said.

"How?" Jacob said, looking up at her. "You got ten million dollars lying around that I don't know about?"

"Not quite," Rachel said. "But we don't need that."

Both men perked up, curious. Rachel took a deep breath, gathering her courage.

"You've done everything right," she said thoughtfully. "You've checked all the boxes. But you've forgotten the magic. What we need to do is infuse this party with passion, with magic... with love."

"Love," Shmuel scoffed. "Jews don't do love!"

"Why not?" Rachel snapped back. "Why can't Hanukkah be just as magical as—"

"As Christmas?" Jacob interjected.

"Yeah," Rachel said carefully. "Except Hanukkah isn't Christmas, is it?"

A silence fell over the room. They were all thinking about the question.

"I mean," Rachel said, "I get that it's a minor holiday that nobody cares about and all, but that doesn't mean it can't offer something special. And isn't that the point, anyway? We're not the norm. We're not typical. We're Jews! So let's put Judaism on fleek! Let's celebrate—in the most outrageous and fabulous way possible—what makes us different."

There was a metaphor in there somewhere. Of that, Rachel was certain. And for the first time since being asked to write a Hanukkah romance novel, she could see herself in the pages.

"Okay," Jacob said, rubbing his forehead. "And let's just say, for purely hypothetical purposes, that any of this were possible. How would we manage to change everything now? We're completely out of money."

"And in forty-eight hours," Shmuel interjected.

"Well," Rachel said, picking up a potato, "maybe we don't

need to change everything. Maybe we just have to take what we have, and find the magic in it."

She could see Jacob considering it, thinking it over.

"And if you're wrong?" Jacob asked.

"Then I'm wrong." She shrugged, tossing the potato in Jacob's direction. "At this point, what do you have to lose?"

Jacob could feel his heart pounding. Rachel stood before him, fierce and ferocious, awaiting an answer. His first instinct was to refuse. Handle things, like always, alone. But this was the present. And in his present, Jacob desperately needed help.

"Okay," Jacob said. "We'll try it your way."

"Baruch Hashem," Shmuel sighed.

Rachel took a deep breath. "Great," she said, turning toward the door. "Then I'm off!"

"Wait," Jacob called out to her, completely confused. "Where are you going?"

"Oh," she said, returning to explain. "To make some phone calls. Actually, lots and lots of phone calls."

Jacob looked at Shmuel before glancing back at Rachel. "Well, do you need our help?"

"No." She turned again to leave, then stopped. "Actually," she said, squinting in his direction, "could you run down to Starbucks and get me some coffee?"

"Yeah." He shrugged. "No problem."

"The biggest one they have."

"Got it."

"Two, actually. Plus, a sugar-free Red Bull. And if you maybe want to pick me up something for dinner, like a falafel maybe, that would be really great. French fries *inside* the falafel. Very important."

He pulled out his phone, tapping her order like a secretary. "Falafel. French fries inside. Anything else?"

"Yeah." She grinned, playfully squeezing his arm. "After you buy me dinner, go home and get some sleep. You're gonna need it for tomorrow."

With that, she was off. He watched her disappear out the door and turned to Shmuel.

"What just happened?" Jacob asked.

"That," Shmuel said, wagging one finger at the sky, "is what we in the Jewish world call…a miracle."

Jacob moved to put his coat on. "Very funny, Shmuel."

"Like two swords," Shmuel mumbled, teasing him. "Each blade sharpening the other."

"I heard you." Jacob waved him off. "Thank you!"

Jacob emerged onto the street to find another snowy evening in Manhattan. Outside the Four Seasons, taxicabs flew by in a frenzy. Delivery trucks unloaded boxes while eager tourists in winter coats and scarves took in the sights. Jacob stared down at his tablet, then made his way to the Starbucks down the road to collect Rachel's order.

Yes, Rachel Rubenstein-Goldblatt—his first love, the girl who broke his heart—challenged him. She forced him out of his comfort zone, leaving him questioning all his fiercely held beliefs. He loved that about her. And now, for the first time since that fateful summer at Camp Ahava, he was relying on her.

Jacob offered up a silent prayer to the heavens and hoped she wouldn't let him down.

From: Lisa Brown <l.brown@cachingliteraryagency.com>
To: Rachel Rubenstein-Goldblatt <margotcross@northpole.com>

Sent: Sun, 19 December
Subject: RE: CONTRACT COMING!!!

Hey, Rachel!

Just got off the phone with Chandra! (Again!) Any ETA on when you can sign that contract for *The Hanukkah Grinch*?!?

Chandra is just super eager to get this on the production schedule…and we're all kind of curious what the holdup is.

Lisa

PS: You're not hesitating, are you?

29

Jacob was a man who prided himself on being reliable, and in his mind there were things that reliable people did. They took care of themselves and the people around them. They were always on time, if not early, to work and meetings.

But the following morning, on what would be night seven of Hanukkah, Jacob found himself dallying. Instead of rushing down to the Four Seasons and dealing with his quickly devolving professional life, he meandered. He ate six of his grandmother's rugalach for breakfast. He lingered over coffee. He walked the twentysomething blocks down to the Four Seasons.

The whole time, he thought about failure. He wasn't afraid for himself of his Matzah Ball not crossing over and recouping its investment. He worried for all the people who relied on him. His staff and investors. Shmuel and his family. It was the holiday season, after all, and everyone deserved to feel secure.

Around midmorning, Jacob finally arrived at the venue. With his hands dug deep into his pockets, he approached the stately hotel. He had no idea what Rachel was up to, but his phone had been oddly quiet all morning. Taking a centering breath, he made his way inside.

He pushed through the lobby and the maze of hallways, before coming to a full stop. The sight before him was so shocking he blinked to make sure he wasn't dreaming.

The three sets of double doors that led to the main entrance of the Matzah Ball had been decorated to look like tents. Large swaths of blue chiffon fabric cascaded down the walls, tied up together in a silver brocade rope. Projected onto the ceiling, lights in the shape of stars rotated, giving the appearance of a starry night. It was like something out of a Hanukkah-inspired biblical fantasy. Beautiful and magical. It had to be, considering the decor had managed to appear by itself overnight.

Swept up in disbelief, he entered the ballroom. Every corner of the place swelled with people and activity. Jacob didn't recognize most of the faces rushing past him. With hammers, fabric and fairy lights in hand, everyone was in the process of tearing something down or putting something up.

Finally he found Rachel. She was sitting in the bedazzled wheelchair, in the center of the room, surrounded by strangers. Holding a clipboard and with a Bluetooth device in her ear, she was barking out orders. "All right, I need at least two of you overseeing the new electric design. Avi and Ari, can you work with the technical department to make sure everything gets set up this morning?"

"Not a problem," the two men said eagerly.

"And Shana—" Rachel turned to a woman holding a baby. Jacob recognized her from Shabbat dinner. "How are those costumes coming along?"

"Great!" she said, bouncing the baby against her chest. "I only have one more to make, and then I'll move on to gift bags."

"Awesome," Rachel said, and made a note on her list. "How about we meet back here in an hour and regroup?"

The crowd dispersed. Jacob, still unsteady, took the opportunity to approach her. "Rachel," he said, and stumbled over the words. "Y-you're here."

"Jacob." She smiled. "You're late."

He was stunned into silence. It wasn't just that she was here, lovely as always. It was that Rachel Rubenstein-Goldblatt had shown up for him...and brought friends.

"What is all this?" he asked.

"This," she said proudly, "is your new and improved Matzah Ball Max."

"How did you manage this?"

"I didn't do it by myself. Mickey is helping. And half the people here are from Camp Ahava. You don't remember them?"

"Not really."

"Well, they remember you...and after I called Mickey, he called Kevin, Ari and Avi. Then I called Aviva, Shira and Dara. From there, it was just a giant game of Camp Ahava telephone, and six degrees of Jewish separation, which everyone from Jewish summer camp knows, is our very most favorite game in the world. When everyone heard about your problem, they wanted to help out."

"That's incredible, Rachel."

"Not really," she said. "We do it all the time. When someone's parent dies and you need to make a shiva call. Or if someone is visiting a strange city and needs a place for Shabbat. There are a lot of downsides to growing up as Rabbi Goldblatt's daughter...but there are some definite upsides, too."

Jacob leaned into her. "How are you feeling?"

"I'm okay," she said gently. "I'm making it a point to rest and not push myself too hard. Also, this chair is fabulous! I don't know what took me so long to get myself a bedazzled wheelchair."

He so badly wanted to kiss her. "I really appreciate you being here."

"Honestly, this has been a lot of fun for me, too. I never realized how much I enjoyed bossing people around. Plus, if anyone gives me trouble—" she yanked at the brake of her wheelchair "—I can just roll right over their foot. I don't know, Jacob. You may have created a monster here."

He laughed, falling into her smile. She was so joyful. Whatever magic resided in the room was nothing compared to the woman who had created it.

"You know," Jacob said curiously, "you never actually told me what disease you have."

"I have ME."

"ME?"

"Myalgic encephalomyelitis. It's sometimes referred to as chronic fatigue syndrome," she said. "Don't say it's not a real disease."

Jacob blinked. "I would never say that."

Her eyes softened. "People think it's just about being tired, but it's not. It's all encompassing. It steals *everything*. You can't imagine what it's like to have a disease that steals everything and yet has the stupidest name in the world."

"Is that why you keep it a secret?"

"Names are important."

Jacob didn't care. He heard the words, and the diagnosis. He knew the ups and downs of life with chronic illness. He'd lived with them before, wouldn't wish them on anyone. But when he looked into those beautiful brown eyes, he couldn't imagine a future with anyone else.

"And you're all right," Jacob asked, wanting to make sure, "using a wheelchair in front of everybody?"

"Because your mom didn't like them?"

"Yeah."

"I need this chair," she said. "I need this chair to help save your Matzah Ball, and keep myself healthy in the process. Anyone who doesn't understand, anyone who thinks they deserve some explanation of my life, my body, or my disability…" She met his eyes directly. "Screw 'em."

Jacob smiled. "I like that attitude."

"I bet you do."

"Rachel," someone called out to her.

They both turned. Mickey was standing behind them. An awkward moment passed between the two men. The last time Jacob had met Mickey, the dude wanted to kill him.

"You remember Mickey?" Rachel asked.

"Of course," Jacob said, forcing a smile, and the men shook hands.

Damn. He was tall.

It took everything Jacob had to swallow the little bubble of jealousy brewing in his chest. It was obvious that Mickey loved Rachel. He had even mentioned they were best friends. Then a terrible thought landed like a sledgehammer in the center of his belly. Had they ever been something more?

He didn't like the thought. Another man appeared at Mickey's side. He was considerably shorter than Mickey, with blond hair and a swath of freckles across a small upturned nose.

"This is Stefan," Mickey said.

Stefan looked up at the ceiling. "It could work."

"You think?" Rachel asked.

"With the right setup." He pulled out his phone and dialed.

"How long do you think it will take?"

"Maybe ten hours," Stefan said, glancing up at the ceiling again.

Rachel beamed. "Can you do it in five?"

"We can try."

"Thank you." She hugged the man. "I mean it—you and your friends are total lifesavers!"

Mickey and Stefan took off, leaving Jacob alone with Rachel once more.

"I'm sorry," Jacob said, slightly confused. "Who was that?"

"Stefan," Rachel said, making another note on her clipboard. "He's our dreidel."

"Our *dreidel*?"

"Well, technically, he's an acrobat, but for the purposes of our Matzah Ball, he is the *shin* on our dreidel."

"I don't understand."

"You need a dreidel that wows, right? Well, Stefan and his three very talented friends have agreed to be your dreidel." Rachel pointed up to the ceiling. "They'll do tricks, spin, float down on silks—you know, acrobatic stuff—wearing fabulous blue-and-white leotards with the Hebrew letters of the dreidel."

Jacob was gobsmacked. "That's...brilliant."

"I know." She smiled before wheeling off to the next station.

Jacob chased after her again. "But what about the costumes?"

"Well, they had the leotards," Rachel explained succinctly. "And Shana over there... Do you remember Shana from Camp Ahava?"

"No."

"Well, she taught sewing for six summers straight." Rachel stopped, sighing heavily. "You learn many useless skills at summer camp—how to wire a lamp, how to make *shakshuka*, how to sew a pillow—but sometimes, those useless skills actually come in handy."

Jacob was speechless. Rachel was remarkable. *Remarkable Rachel.* He wanted to knight her with the moniker forever, but she was already rolling her way to the kitchen. Jacob broke into a sprint to follow.

Pushing through the swinging doors, she raced past waiters and catering staff, stopping when she came to Shmuel bent over a counter.

"Shmuel, you need to stop eating all the hors d'oeuvres!"

"I'm just making sure they're up to par," he said, turning around.

He was licking his lips, a tiny fried latke decked out with tuna tartare held tightly between his stubby fingers. On the counter behind him, three silver trays were filled with the most impressive-looking appetizers he had ever seen. Jacob bent over the trays, attempting to analyze them.

The simple potatoes, once doomed to be boring old latkes, had been revamped completely. Eight potato pancakes now became the setting for a bevy of delicious additions, including tuna tartare, quail egg and smoked salmon.

"I present to you—" Rachel beamed proudly "—Latke Eight Ways."

Jacob's mouth began to water. No wonder Shmuel couldn't control himself. The food looked and smelled amazing.

"These—" Shmuel said, picking one up, "these are just truly delicious."

"I appreciate the five-star review," Rachel said, taking the item out of his hand and putting it back on the tray. "But like I already told you, these are samples for the caterers to follow tomorrow. If you eat all the samples, where does that leave us?"

"You're right. But did you have to make them so delicious?"

"I promise you can eat all the hors d'oeuvres you want at the Matzah Ball."

Shmuel beamed before turning to Jacob. "This is a good woman, Jacob. A smart woman. We could use a woman like her on our team."

"I don't deny that," Jacob said.

He swore he saw her blush. Perhaps Shmuel did, too, because he suddenly forgot about stuffing his belly. "Well," Shmuel said, wiping his hands against his shirt. "I should probably go check on those final food deliveries. You two behave yourselves, now. Hanukkah is when all sorts of magic can happen, you know?"

Shmuel took off, leaving Jacob and Rachel behind in the kitchen. A stillness fell over them. Even though caterers and staff were rushing back and forth, it felt like they were the only two people on the planet.

"Listen, Rachel—"

She interrupted him. "I know that I went a little overboard with everything. I tend to do that with holidays...but I hope you like it."

How could she ever think otherwise? "I love it," he said truthfully.

"Really?" she asked, surprised. "Because, you know, I had to make do with what we had. Some of the stuff, I know it could be higher-end, but I wanted to give the feeling of being—"

He was the one interrupting her now. "You've outdone yourself. Seriously. It's amazing. *You're amazing.* I don't know how you did all this, but... I'm grateful you're here."

A thoughtful smile swept across her face. She blinked, looking away, searching for words. The room quieted into silence once again. Jacob focused on her. She was beautiful. She was everything he wanted. Could she feel it, his heart racing, his breath quickening, as if he had only just discovered what it meant to be alive?

"Come on," she said, taking his hand. "Wheel me over to the bar. I want to show you one more thing."

Jacob did as commanded, taking her to one of the many bars being set up in the main ballroom. On the counter he observed a row of martini glasses. Beside them sat an opened box of sufganiyot. Powdered sugar lay piled up high on a plate while the rest of the jelly doughnuts sat next to it.

"What's all this?" he asked.

"This—" she stood up, stepping behind the bar and turning herself into a makeshift bartender "—is the Matzah Ball's signature drink."

Rachel got to work. Jacob watched as she dipped a martini glass into the powdered sugar, then set it aside to carefully select bottles from the row of alcoholic beverages showcased above her. She combined a mixture of creme de cacao and strawberry-flavored vodka with ginger beer before pouring the bright red concoction into the sugar-decorated glass. Lastly, she poked a toothpick through two small jelly doughnuts and added it as a garnish. She presented the glass to Jacob.

"Voilà! Spiced Sufganiyot Martini."

He pulled the drink to him and took a sip. "Wow," he said, shaking his head, the taste of strawberry and powdered sugar assaulting him. "That is dangerous."

She blushed. "Holiday martinis are kind of my specialty."

Jacob could feel his heart racing again. Maybe it was the drink, roaring to his head and causing him to lose all inhibitions. Or maybe he was still reeling from the way he felt when she had taken his hand. Rachel leaned over the counter once again. Her soft lips, edging into a smile, looked so inviting. The music in his mind returned.

"If we have time," she said, fondling the toothpick, "we'll drizzle some white chocolate over the doughnuts and let it harden before the party. My hunch is it will bring out the creme de cacao flavor perfectly, but I want to do some taste testing first."

Jacob swallowed. "You are a woman of many talents."

She leaned over the counter, taking a sip of his martini. "It seems really clever, but it's just a play on a Christmas martini I made last year."

"You made a Christmas martini?"

"Oh," she said, eyes wide. "No, I mean... I made it for Rosh Hashanah. Pomegranate seeds look a lot like cranberries. I just adapted a Christmas recipe for Hanukkah."

He corrected her. "You mean...for Rosh Hashanah?"

"Right," she said, shoulders tensing. "For Rosh Hashanah."

Jacob could feel her rigidity rising up between them once again. The easygoing girl was gone. He wasn't sure what had shut her down, but he fiddled with his drink and tried to bring her back.

"What can I do to help?" he asked.

JEAN MELTZER

"Well," she said, returning to plop down in her chair. "How are you with upper-level management?"

"I am an expert at telling other people what to do."

"Good." She took his hand one more time. "Because I need you to help oversee the setup of about a gazillion fairy lights."

30

Seven hours later, the Matzah Ball Max had finally come together. Rachel watched, along with her friends from Camp Ahava, as a team positioned the completed menorah center stage. A round of applause erupted from everyone in the room.

"Amazing," Jacob said, clapping the hardest for Rachel.

"A miracle worker," Shmuel agreed.

There was only one thing left to do. Affix the final bracket to the largest candle, thereby completing the menorah with the addition of the *shamash*.

"Well," Shmuel said, picking up the bracket, "I can only think of one person who should do us the honors."

"Rachel?" Jacob asked. "Are you up for it?"

She glanced at the small crane and ladder stretching toward the ceiling. "I think I can handle that." She rose from her wheelchair. After taking the bracket from Shmuel, she approached the ladder. It was a bit more wobbly than she expected.

"Jacob," Mickey suddenly called out, "why don't you help her out?"

Jacob turned bright red in the cheeks as he raced over to oblige. Stepping behind her, he followed her halfway up the ladder before placing his hands firmly around her waist.

"It's okay," he said. "I won't let you fall."

"I know."

Rachel reached up on tiptoe to screw in the final bracket. The room burst into applause at the shining example of their hard work.

Rachel took a look around the room of the Matzah Ball. The space had been transformed. Large swaths of blue-and-silver fabric draped every square inch of wall and ceiling. The gazillion fairy lights, which Jacob had hammered throughout the room, felt reminiscent of snowflakes, or stars. On the main stage, where the musical acts would perform, was the magnificent ten-foot menorah that Jacob and Rachel had built together.

It was dreamlike. Tomorrow, the final pieces would come together. There would be Hanukkah-inspired food, drinks and entertainment. Rachel was certain that Jacob's Matzah Ball could rival any party she dreamed up in one of her Christmas romances. She wanted to tell him that.

Instead, she glanced back at him, his strong arms steadying her despite the instability of the ladder, and felt the magic.

Suddenly the room was plunged into darkness. A quick gasp escaped Rachel's mouth as she realized she could fall. Jacob responded to her fear with his gentle strength. He grabbed her tighter and held her close. "It's okay," he whispered through the darkness. "I got you."

She believed him. She didn't know what the heck was wrong with the lights at the Four Seasons, and she waited for them to turn back on. Instead, she heard whistling. It grew and got louder, a familiar Jewish tune. Rachel groaned aloud. She had heard that Jewish song a million times before.

"What's going on?" Jacob asked.

"They're pranking us."

"Who?"

"Everyone from Camp Ahava," she said. "Just give them a minute."

The whistling turned into full-on singing and clapping. Rachel could make out a dozen small cell phone flashlights, feet shuffling and people grabbing bags, before the sound of the doors swinging behind her friends faded into silence. The electricity in the ballroom returned. When the lights came back on, Rachel and Jacob were alone. Just him and her. Their bodies pressed up against each other.

"I'm sorry," Jacob said, and squinted. "What just happened?"

"They were teasing us," Rachel explained as they began their descent back down the ladder. "They were whistling, and then singing *Od Yeshama*."

"I don't know what that is."

Rachel landed firmly back on the dance floor. She couldn't help but sigh over the stupidity of the joke. No doubt, her best friend since forever put everyone up to it. "*Od Yeshama* is played at Jewish weddings, or when couples announce engagements at Shabbat dinner, or during shul. They were teasing us, implying we were…"

Jacob smiled. "Heading toward marriage?"

Rachel smirked. "You barely know me, Jacob Greenberg."

"I know you. You're a miracle worker." When she laughed, he added, "And an expert menorah technician."

"Hmm." She nodded, allowing him to flirt with her. "This is true."

"Unfortunately," he said, taking her hand and twirling her on the ballroom floor before pulling her close and placing one hand on the divot in her waist, "I'm afraid I'm going to have to agree with your friends. We are, most definitely, heading for marriage."

"Are we now?"

"You should just come to accept it, Rachel. We'll plan it for Hanukkah of next year. It will be very romantic."

"And if I refuse?"

"I will wear you down," he said. "Just like I did at Camp Ahava."

"Careful," she warned him. "That's how you wind up with toothpaste in your sneakers."

He laughed. Their lips were nearly touching. She wanted him to kiss her. She wanted to spend the rest of her life in this fantasy with Jacob Greenberg.

"Do you like rugalach?" Jacob asked.

"I love rugalach," she whispered.

"Well," he said, his cheeks dimpling, "I know a place where we can get the best chocolate rugalach in town. If you're hungry, and if you're feeling up for it. I'd love the chance to thank you, personally, for everything you've done. Seriously, Rachel, you've saved my Matzah Ball. I owe you something."

Rachel couldn't resist the offer. "Okay."

"Great," Jacob said, pulling out his phone. "Let me just text the chef and let her know we're coming."

There were no cabs available that evening. The cold winter weather, coupled with the last of holiday shopping, meant that every vehicle, from the yellow taxicabs to the unmarked livery vans, was taken up with riders. With flurries falling down around them, and slushy mud piling up around their boots, they settled on taking the subway. They were lucky enough to catch the 5 train just as it rumbled to a stop in the underground station.

Jacob allowed Rachel to enter first, holding the doors for her. She fell, breathless and happy, into a set of seats.

"How are you feeling?" he asked, sliding down beside her.

"Good." He gave her energy.

Their thighs touched. A zap of electricity sprang through her entire body at the feeling of his thick and muscular quad brushing against her own leg. She wasn't sure what to do with the feeling so she clutched her purse tighter against her chest. In the process, she caught sight of two large banner ads directly across from them.

The first was for the latest release by Jason Peterson, a well-known crime writer of more than thirty books. Beside it, with just as many bestseller accolades, was an ad for *Christmas in the Caribbean* by Margot Cross.

Rachel felt her stomach dip and her mouth go dry. She was used to seeing ads for her books during the holiday season. That wasn't what bothered her. What troubled Rachel were the images used to represent both world-famous authors.

In the first, a large picture of Jason Peterson, smiling widely and wearing a collared shirt, accompanied the cover of his book. For Margot Cross, beside the dreamy cover of her newest Christmas romance was an image of a ribbon.

A stupid freaking red-and-green ribbon.

Rachel was annoyed. It seemed impossible, really. Unfair. To work so hard for something, to bring to life stories and characters that felt as real as any children, and then have that work be represented by a ribbon. Rachel Rubenstein-Goldblatt was more than just a piece of tartan fabric tied up in a bow.

"You a Peterson fan?" Jacob asked.

"Hmm?" she asked, snapping her head in his direction.

"You seem awfully interested in his new book."

"Oh," she said, forcing the words through her teeth. "Yeah. How did you know?"

"Well, I certainly didn't think you'd be reading Margot Cross."

Rachel could feel her chest sink. Jacob didn't mean it to come off as hurtful or offensive, but it stung anyway.

And yet this was her chance. Her opportunity. She could easily admit the truth, point out the fallacy in thinking that a nice Jewish girl and daughter of a rabbi couldn't engage in a little Christmas envy. But what would happen if Jacob didn't understand? Or worse, what would happen if her parents and people from their community found out the truth?

"This is our stop," Jacob said, rising from his seat and offering her his hand.

She took it, grateful for the opportunity to be removed from her own intrusive thoughts. Soon, they came to a modest midrise on the Upper East Side. It was not what she was expecting.

"I thought you said you were taking me out for the very best rugalach in the city?"

"I am." He held the main entrance door open for her.

She followed him onto an elevator. It was an old-world-style New York apartment. Unlike her fancy apartment on the Upper West Side, it had none of the newer and more modern amenities. Still, it was charming if not altogether terrifying. Rachel found herself offering up a silent prayer as the elevator creaked and groaned to the fourteenth floor.

Coming to a bumpy stop, she followed Jacob down a dim hallway to an apartment, a dusty mezuzah affixed to the doorpost. He rang the doorbell. Moments later, a tiny gray-haired woman wearing a flowered blue-and-white kimono threw open the door. Rachel recognized her immediately. This was no stranger. This was Toby, the elderly angel who had offered her spring rolls and sufganiyot on her very first day volunteering for the Matzah Ball.

"Rachel," Jacob said, pointing toward the old woman, "this is my bubbe, Toby."

"This…this is your grandmother?" Panic raced through Rachel's chest as she met Toby's gaze. She wondered how much Toby had told Jacob about her, whether she had revealed the terrible things that she had said about him. She wouldn't blame Toby for calling her out, or giving her a tongue-lashing. Instead, Toby raced forward, offering Rachel the warmest of hugs. The act was so kind and genuine that Rachel couldn't help remembering the love of her own grandmother, long since passed.

"Rachel-la!" Toby squealed, delighted. "What a *bracha* to see you again."

"You, too," Rachel said nervously. "I didn't realize Jacob was your grandson."

"I'm sorry," Jacob said, glancing between the two women. "Do you two know each other?"

Toby grinned. "We met the day I brought you lunch at the Four Seasons."

"We shared some spring rolls," Rachel added.

"And conversation." Toby winked in her direction before wisely changing the topic. "Come now, you must be starving. Jacob told me how you single-handedly saved the Matzah Ball with your brilliant and creative spin on Hanukkah. You'll have to tell me all about it over some rugalach." She took Rachel by the elbow, leading her inside.

It was a sizable New York apartment, large and stuffed to the brim with books and papers. The vestiges of Jewish life were evident. Rachel's eyes settled on the vast collection of *chanukiyot* displayed across the living room. There must have been a hundred of them. Her eyes fell on the silver menorah sitting on the windowsill, lit for the seventh night of Hanukkah.

"Come," Toby said, pulling out a chair in the kitchen. "Sit! Sit!"

Rachel sat down at the small circular table. Toby headed to the oven, putting on protective mitts and pulling out a baking tray filled with oozing chocolate pastries. Jacob busied himself making a pot of tea. Rachel felt like an honored guest.

"Let me help," she said, rising to her feet.

"Absolutely not!" Toby said, threatening to smack her hand. "You sit back down right now."

Jacob, however, was gentler in his execution. "Please," he said, pulling out her chair. "You're our guest. Let me treat you, the way you deserve."

She nodded absentmindedly, falling back into her seat. It was

JEAN MELTZER

all so perfect. His grandmother. The rugalach. The handsome millionaire serving her chocolate in his kitchen. She felt like a character from one of her Christmas romances. She couldn't suppress a laugh.

Jacob glanced back at her. "Something funny?"

"No," she said, waving away the question. "I'm just happy."

"Good," Jacob said, loading up a platter. "Then I'm finally doing something right."

He poured three cups of piping hot chamomile tea. Moments later, he and Toby were pulling up seats beside her and handing out plates. Rachel's mouth watered at the sight of cream cheese and chocolate layered inside flaky dough.

"Well," Jacob said, "let us know what you think."

Rachel picked up a tiny pastry. It was still warm as she placed it in her mouth, the sensation of sugar and butter sending shock waves of delight across her tongue. "Oh, my Gawd," she said, covering her chewing to be polite. "You weren't lying. These are amazing!"

Toby and Jacob laughed before beginning to pile up their own plates. But Rachel was not merely being polite. They were the best rugalach she had ever tasted. On par only with those rugalach she had experienced in Jerusalem during summer vacations and gap years with friends.

"They're a secret family recipe," Jacob said, taking a bite of his own pastry.

"Not so secret," Toby offered up, and smiled in Rachel's direction. "I'd be willing to share it, of course, pass it down for future generations, to the right person. If only my handsome grandson would find the right person."

Jacob put his puff pastry down, getting serious. "Bubbe..."

Toby turned to Rachel. "Jacob never makes time for dating. He's going to let me die old and alone, having never even held my first great-grandbaby."

"First off," Jacob defended himself, "I will have you know

284

that I already told Rachel we were getting married next Hanukkah—"

Toby beamed between them. "Oh, really?"

"And she flat out refused me."

Rachel exploded with laughter. "Way to put me on blast,
Jacob!"

"I'm a desperate man," he said. "Willing to pull out any future bubbe-in-law as necessary."

Rachel sighed. "Then I am truly doomed."

The teasing continued through another round of warm pastries. It was clear that Toby and Jacob had a close relationship.
Rachel liked seeing this side of him. He was a person who valued family. He also enjoyed eating. Food was just as important
to Rachel as all the rest. Reaching across the table, she grabbed
another chocolate rugalach and popped it into her mouth.

Jacob smiled at the sight of her enjoyment. "You have some
chocolate on your face."

Rachel tried to wipe it off with her hand. "Here?"

"No," Jacob said, before picking up a napkin. "Do you mind?"

Rachel shook her head and Jacob leaned forward, using the
napkin to wipe the chocolate from her face. His touch was soft.
Gentle. She could smell his breath, sweet and aromatic, as he
lingered mere centimeters from her lips. She couldn't help but
think about kissing him. He had been her first, all those years
ago, at Camp Ahava. The moment had given her butterflies.
Would it be the same now?

"Well," Toby sighed loudly, gathering up a plate of cookies
and her cup of tea. "I think I've had enough sweet treats for
one night. I'll be heading to bed now. You two…you take your
time, enjoy yourselves, eat as many rugalach as you like. *Yankele*,
dear, I'll see you in the morning. And, Rachel, I truly hope I
get the chance to see you again."

Jacob and Rachel said their good-nights, thanking Toby for

the rugalach. Left alone, Rachel took one last opportunity to continue teasing him.

She grinned in his direction. *"Yankele."*

"I knew that was coming, *Rachel-la.*"

They both blushed. The diminutive addition of *la* to a name, meaning *little*, was commonly used by Jewish grandparents and parents for their children. When that suffix stretched into adulthood, it was generally used as a term of endearment.

It was nice hearing him speak so sweetly to her; it was also getting late. Rachel didn't want to leave, but they had both had a long day. It would be unfair to take up any more of his time, especially considering he had a Matzah Ball Max to throw tomorrow.

"I should probably be getting home," she said softly.

Jacob perked up in his chair. "Let me come with you."

"I live on the Upper West Side," Rachel reminded him. "That's practically a long-distance relationship in Manhattan terms."

"Please." His eyes were serious. "I wouldn't feel right letting you head home alone."

Rachel hesitated. It had been a long time since she had let a man escort her home. There were good and valid reasons to say no, but she gave in to the bubbles pressing against her chest.

"Okay." She leaned into him. "But first, I want another rugalach."

31

Most people would consider it a trek to get to the Upper West Side, but Jacob liked the long walk to the subway, the carefree conversation and childish banter he and Rachel engaged in while they waited for the train to come roaring to the platform. He wanted to spend as much time with her as possible.

"Ugh," she said, swinging back and forth, holding on to a bar above her head as the subway rolled crosstown. "I'm so full."

"Me, too."

The subway lurched and jutted. "How would you feel about getting off early and walking?" she asked.

"You sure you're up for that?"

"Up for it?" She smirked. "I'm more worried you won't be able to keep up with me."

At the next stop, Rachel exploded from the train car and up the steps. Jacob raced to keep up with her, before landing somewhere near Central Park West.

It was quiet in this part of Manhattan. Without the hustle of shops, the only thing to keep them company were the overarching branches of the trees in Central Park, the snowflakes starting to float down from the sky and occasional locals out for a stroll with their miniature white dogs.

It seemed to Jacob that all cities were the same in this way. They had a hum and buzz that kept them moving. Like the lights above them, bright and twinkling, from the menagerie of apartments overhead. But not every city had Rachel.

"Woo-hoo," Rachel said, clutching her chest. "I feel like I could a run a marathon all of a sudden!"

She was high on sugar. Jacob had first noticed the signs of rugalach intoxication on the subway. "That's the second wave," he informed her. "Those rugalach have a kick that comes about forty-five minutes after."

"What the heck does she put in those things?"

"Sugar. Lots and lots of sugar."

"Jewish cooking at its best." She threw her head back and screamed up to the heavens. "I want all the sugar!"

She stretched her arms straight out at her sides and, making noises like an airplane, began zigzagging up the sidewalk. Jacob chased after her.

He couldn't help but laugh at her sheer delight. He liked seeing her this way. Happy. Free from the bonds of being the rabbi's daughter. Her joy was contagious; even the doormen and dog walkers smiled warmly as she zipped past.

She was also surprisingly fast. Even pretending to be an airplane, Jacob had to break into a sprint to keep up. He caught up with her on the corner, where a large menorah was displayed.

"It's pretty, isn't it?" she asked, staring up. "I always think of Christmas as having all the magic, but there's something really special about Hanukkah when you stop and pay attention to it."

"It's beautiful," he said, though he wasn't talking about the holiday decor. He desperately wanted to kiss her. He was wondering if she was feeling the same way, when her phone vibrated for attention inside her pocketbook.

"Sorry," Rachel said, reaching into her purse.

"Everything okay?"

"Yeah," Rachel said, putting her phone away. "It's just Mickey. He wanted to let me know that Stefan and his friends will arrive at noon tomorrow to set up."

"You and Mickey." Jacob could feel jealousy rising to the center of his chest. "You two seem really friendly."

"I should hope so. We've known each other since we were eight. We've done pretty much everything together. He was there for me, too, when I first got sick."

"Did you and him...ever date?"

"Oh, my Gawd!" Rachel burst out laughing. "No. I'm not Mickey's type."

"That's hard to believe."

Rachel laid one sympathetic hand on his shoulder. "Mickey is my best friend, and a fabulous human being. I would be lucky to spend the rest of my life with him...but unfortunately, I have boobs."

"Oh," Jacob finally put it together. "Ohhh."

"You really didn't know?"

"I've been out of the Camp Ahava loop for a while now."

She nodded. A quiet came over her. "I remember when you left." She turned to him, stone-cold serious. "I need to ask you a question. It might seem a little strange, but it's something I've been wondering about."

"Okay."

"The other day when you came to my apartment...you said you needed me. You needed a goodbye. What did you mean by that?"

He pursed his lips together. "So we're going there, huh?"

She shrugged. Jacob sighed. It was hard for him to talk about the bad in his life, about the childhood that had shaped him. There was always this fear lingering deep inside. He didn't want to be left behind on a dance floor again.

But looking into her big, brown eyes, he remembered the lesson of his grandmother. This was the present. Rachel had proved herself to be reliable. Even when he did his damnedest to push her away, she had shown up for him. It was time for Jacob to show up for her. A gentle flurry began to form in the sky.

"So I mentioned my mom was sick," he said carefully.

"MS."

"Well, what most people don't know, is that while my mom was sick my dad sort of stopped coming home."

She squinted. "I don't understand."

He smiled softly in her direction. Sweet Rachel, with her loving family. The idea of parental abandonment was so far from the reality of her everyday life she couldn't even imagine it. He tried to be clear in his explanation.

"I suppose the official word is *abandonment*."

She stopped walking, taking his hand. "I had no idea."

"At first it was just working a lot. Late hours. Missing dinner. Then it was business trips. After that, the phone calls got less frequent. The visits, too. Then we moved to France…and the phone calls and visits were pretty much nonexistent."

"That's…awful."

He nodded. What else was there to say, really? But he could see that writer in her again, that thoughtfulness. She was painting a picture in her mind, drawing up the story of his life. She swallowed. "Your mom…" she said. "You mentioned she passed away?"

"Two years ago."

"Was it the MS that—"

"No," he said quickly. "Actually, by the end of her life, she had the MS pretty well managed. It was cancer. Breast cancer. Stage 4. It was quick, though. Six months…and then it was over."

"I'm so sorry, Jacob."

"Anyway," he said somewhat sheepishly, "that's actually why I do a lot of this. The big events. The massive music festivals. It seems over-the-top, but I funnel a large part of the profits from Greenberg Entertainment into MS research and causes. I figured it's the best way to honor her memory."

Rachel's entire face edged into a frown. He didn't like seeing her that way. He moved, like always, to rectify the situation, flashing her a wide smile. "Well, now that you know my sob story—"

"Don't do that," she said, cutting him off. "Don't downplay your loss to make me more comfortable. It's not fair to you. Or necessary."

Jacob nodded. Chronic illness formed a band of secret sufferers. He was grateful that for once he didn't have to explain this part of his life to someone. "She was a good mother," he said. "The best, actually. She couldn't always be there for me—she missed soccer games and school field trips to the Louvre—but she was there for me in all the ways that mattered. I think she was always worried about disappointing me."

"I worry about the same thing."

"What?"

"Disappointing people."

"You haven't disappointed me."

"Yeah, but—"

"Rachel—" he lowered his voice in disbelief "—you do realize...you're incredible, right?"

She shrank a little at his assessment. "You don't know me, Jacob."

He cupped his hand around the base of her neck. "Then let me get to know you." He moved to kiss her. The music in his mind was rising again at the thought of touching her lips with his own, when all of a sudden she stepped back.

"No!" she said, hands in the air, eyes shut. "I need to tell you something first."

"Okay..."

"You're going to think it's a ridiculous story," she said, snowflakes falling down around her. "But just hear me out, okay? Listen to the end…and try not to completely hate me."

He raised his hands in the air, letting her speak.

In an absolute tizzy she returned to that summer. She began with the basics. Him pushing her into the lake. Her retaliating by leaving toothpaste in his sneakers. The way the stakes got upped and twisted before, finally, it was a whole elaborate game they played, pretending to be summer-camp archenemies. She remembered everything. Every detail of that summer. Every purposeful and heartfelt prank.

Then she described heading down to the lake. Their amazing first kiss, her certainty that they would be together forever, before seeing the boys of bunk 7B standing there with flashlights and cameras.

She confessed running back to her bunk, humiliated and heartbroken, calling her father to pick her up the next day. The swirl of confusion—followed by mono—that occurred in the weeks after she left. The never-ending spinning of Camp Ahava gossip. And Mickey, of course, her best friend since third grade, who loved her more than anything in the world.

"When you asked me to meet you at the lake," she said, "and all those boys were there… I thought you had set me up. I thought it was just another one of your stupid pranks. Like pushing me into the lake or leaving dead bugs in my siddur. But I know now that's not true. It wasn't you. And I'm sorry."

"So you did stand me up at the dance?"

"Yes."

"Because you thought I didn't care about you?"

"I was angry." She shrugged. "And hurt. And sick with mono. Plus my mom was doing all these puppet shows."

"Puppet shows?" He raised an eyebrow in her direction.

"It was awful," Rachel said, shaking her head. "My mom seems really sweet and innocent on the surface…but she is the queen of puppet TMI."

Jacob bit back a small laugh that Rachel didn't seem to notice. She was far too nervous, talking with her hands, trying to make everything right now between them. He let her keep rambling, mainly because she was just so cute when she told him the truth. Despite the fact that the snow was now falling with abandon, he felt warm.

"Anyway," Rachel said. "I'm sorry, Jacob. I didn't mean to hurt you. If I had known everything you were going through—"

"The matzah ball costume," he said, suddenly understanding.

She stopped rambling. "What?"

"That's why it didn't work." He closed his eyes, both thrilled and excited by this new revelation. "I thought we were playing a game..."

Rachel finished his thought. "And I thought you were still messing with me."

They both folded into quiet. Truth be told—and thinking about it from the perspective of an adult—it was all positively ridiculous. A whirlwind of unnecessary drama and tween hysterics. Something that could only happen to a couple of seventh graders in Jewish summer camp. It was a mistake Jacob was ready to put firmly in the past.

"Well, Rachel," he said, taking her hands inside his own, "let me alleviate any concerns you have about that summer. I liked you. I liked you...a lot. It's a shame you stood me up at the final dance, because had you shown up, I would have been waiting for you with a bouquet of wildflowers. I would have asked you to be my *permanent* and *full-time* girlfriend."

"Really?"

"Really *really*. But now, and given everything that happened between us, I'm afraid we'll just have to jump right into marriage. There's no other option. I'll speak with your parents tomorrow. Unfortunately, I don't trust you not to disappear on me again."

She laughed a little. "Jacob Greenberg...you are *so* weird."

"True. But we'll have the rest of our life to work out our version of normal."

She smiled, soft and thoughtful in his direction. "I like that."

"Me, too." He would have stayed with her outside all night, holding her hands and talking through secrets, but the snow was falling heavily. "So, now that we have all that out of the way, I need to know. Will you be my date for the Matzah Ball Max?"

She laughed. "Yes."

"Really?" He beamed back. "You won't stand me up this time?"

"I promise." Rachel met his eyes directly. "I will be there with my blue dress on."

It was all that he hoped to hear.

Jacob thought about kissing her, but the snow was beginning to blind them. "I should probably get you back home," he suggested, wrapping one arm around her in a protective manner. She allowed him to draw her close.

When they arrived at her building, he glanced up to the apartments lit up within her high-rise. In a few of the windows, he could still make out the flickering flames of the menorah. "You know," Jacob said, "I'm actually grateful to Mickey."

"Really?" Rachel, clearly, didn't believe him.

"Yeah," he explained. "I was a mess as a kid. Even worse as a teenager. Remember when I told you I went to Catholic school?"

She nodded.

"Well, what I conveniently left out is that I wound up in Catholic school...because I got kicked out of four schools before that."

"Oh, wow. You *were* bad."

He nodded. "As much as I want to tell myself that things would have been different had we stayed in contact, I probably would have just screwed up our friendship. I wasn't ready, Rachel. I needed to grow up. I needed to learn some things about myself, too. So I'm grateful to Mickey and the time he provided for that. I don't know...you'll probably think I'm some sort of heathen for saying it...but it kind of reminds me of something Father Sebastian, one of the priests at my Catholic school, used to say."

Rachel cocked her head sideways. "What did he say?"

"'Everything in life is designed to lead us to our higher purpose.'"

She paused, thoughtful and contemplative. "That's beautiful."

"I realize it's not Midrash, or Talmud, or—"

She shook her head. "I love that. Seriously. One of my new favorite quotes."

"I'm glad." Jacob blushed, rubbing the back of his neck. It was getting late. He knew that he had to let her go. "Well, I guess this is probably where I say—"

She kissed him. No explanation. No warning. She leaned into him, grabbing him by the neck, pulling him forward. He nearly doubled over in shock at the feeling of their lips finally meeting. And then he melted. His body warmed with her touch. She felt like coming home, like finding your place again and being wrapped up in a blanket after spending all day in the cold.

Rachel pulled away. "Oh, shucks," she said, glancing up toward her apartment. "We've been so busy with the Matzah Ball, I haven't even had a chance to light Hanukkah candles. Did you light for seventh night yet?"

"Um..." Jacob wasn't sure where she was heading with the question. "No."

She shifted in her spot nervously. "You could come upstairs to my apartment and light them."

Jacob felt his heart skip. "Are you sure?"

"Yeah."

"You're not too tired for...guests?"

"Nope."

"Because I don't want to push you—"

"Jacob…" Rachel smiled mischievously before leaning into whisper, "Don't make me leave toothpaste in your loafers."

Rachel hung up her coat while Jacob got acquainted with the now pristine space. There was a white couch with warm-toned throw pillows and a large painting on the wall above it. A small kitchen sat to the side of the main entryway, before two hallways branched off into separately defined areas. One of the doors was closed. The other—Jacob snuck a peek down the hallway—led to a bedroom.

"It's nice," he said.

"Thanks. Are you thirsty or anything? I have hot chocolate, tea…wine?"

"Wine sounds great."

He followed Rachel into her kitchen. Grabbing an already opened bottle of red, she poured two glasses, handing him one. He watched her take a small sip before placing it down on the counter at his side. "If you don't mind," she said, "I'd like to get changed. I feel all sorts of dusty from today."

"Do whatever you need," he said, then nodded at a *chanuki-yah* and box of candles sitting on the windowsill. "I'll get the menorah set up while you change."

She walked down the hallway and into her bedroom, closing the door behind her. Jacob opened the small blue box, pulled out eight of the multicolored candles and grabbed a lighter sitting on the side.

It was always a pain to get the tiny candles into their metal holders, and to keep them in place and not create a fire hazard, Jacob had to melt the bottom of each candle. Then, while still hot, he had to press it down into the metal holder, creating a seal. It was easy enough to do with steady hands for one or two candles. Eight candles was always a challenge.

On the sixth candle, he burned his fingers.

Shaking off the pain, he gazed out the window. It was late.

Most of the *chanukiyot* had already gone out. But there were still two menorahs flickering in a nearby window. The Jewish people were nothing if not resilient.

Jacob picked up the last candle and focused on setting it up safely. It was amazing that half of New York didn't burn down every holiday season. For all the ingenuity of the Jewish people, it seemed a failure of design. In over five thousand years, they had not come up with a better solution for lighting Hanukkah candles.

"Ouch!" he said when he burned his fingers again, sticking his pointer finger in his mouth.

The action did little to cool the stinging at the tip of his thumb. Still, victory was nigh. Grabbing a white candle to use as the *shamash*, he moved to place it into its rightful position, higher than the rest. Suddenly he heard a sound.

It was a strange sound. A whistle, followed by an electronic *chug-chug-squeal*.

He would have assumed it to be a mouse or some interference from the street down below, but the sound kept coming. Jacob moved closer, listening. Was he hallucinating? Was the combination of nerves and rugalach intoxication finally getting to him?

He was just about to leave the door alone when he heard that sound once again. The whistle, followed by the *chug-chug-squeal*, followed by a whirring. But this time—though he couldn't quite understand how—he was certain he heard Christmas music. Putting the *shamash* back down, he threw open the door.

Jacob's life had been full of shocking moments. There was his parents' divorce. His move to Paris. His father's abandonment. But it would have been unfair to place this moment alongside the rest. For this moment, standing in the doorway to what looked to be an office, superseded them all.

Christmas had thrown up all over the room. Jacob tried not to choke on his tongue as he surveyed the red-and-green scene before him. Garlands draped from every nook and cranny. A four-foot Christmas tree stood watch from the corner. Hundreds of tiny smiling Santas, an army of Christmas cheer, greeted him in various states of play.

The Santas were creepy, honestly, but they were nothing compared to the homage to Margot Cross displayed throughout the room.

Jacob stepped closer, attempting to inspect the space further. Leaning down to a bookcase, he ran his fingers across the spine of nearly three dozen books. Rachel must have owned every book Margot Cross had ever written, including some translations. Same with the posters to TV movies based on the stories. There were at least four of them plastered over the walls. Clearly, Rachel was a fan. Hopefully, she didn't have Margot Cross tied down to a bed somewhere.

His eyes landed on a series of gold statues laid out across the window. Jacob reached over her desk and picked one up. It was an award for writing romance. Once again, it belonged to Margot Cross. Jacob put it down, pursing his lips. The books made sense for a fan. The posters, okay. But why would Rachel have Margot Cross's writing awards?

Then he put it together. The awkward responses when he asked Rachel about her career. Her really nice apartment on the Upper West Side. The holiday cheer, which she so easily pulled from deep within, saving the Matzah Ball. Rachel Rubenstein-Goldblatt *was* Margot Cross.

Jacob laughed, falling into her chair.

She could have just told him. It wasn't as if she was selling drugs, or betraying high-level government secrets. She made people happy. She brought them romance and magic. In a world that was dark, Rachel Rubenstein-Goldblatt was the true *shamash*.

Jacob pulled out his phone and jotted himself a note: *Read all the Margot Cross books.* Then again, Jacob thought to himself, why wait till tomorrow?

Jacob caught sight of a manuscript sitting on her desk. Putting away his phone, he reached forward, reading the title. *The Hanukkah Grinch by Rachel Rubenstein-Goldblatt.* Curiosity overtook him as he realized she was writing a Hanukkah romance. Was this the real reason she had wanted a ticket to his Matzah Ball? Flipping to the first page, he began reading.

There are men who walk, and men who strut. Jason Goldstein strutted. But the glamour of his exterior appearance was only a front. For behind his dimpled cheeks and outward charm was a miser. An evil prankster, dreamed up by rabbis in a shtetl long ago. For Jason Goldstein, party planner and multimillionaire, was the world's most despicable man.

32

Rachel stood in her bedroom, her back pressed up against the door, breathing heavily. Her heart was racing. Her palms were sweaty. She needed a minute.

Jacob Greenberg liked her.

Pulling out her phone, she texted Mickey:

> You'll never believe it.

What?

> Jacob Greenberg is at my apartment.

BARUCH HASHEM!

> He likes me. We kissed.

And?!?

> I like him, too.

The final text came a minute later: **What are you texting me for, then?!? Go get it, girl!**

Rachel smiled, putting her phone on Silent and placing it on her dresser. In the process, she caught her reflection in the mirror. Taking a minute, she analyzed her current state. It had been a long day volunteering for the Matzah Ball. She smelled like hard work comingling with a Jewish bakery. But Jacob liked her.

It was something else, really. To like someone as spectacular as Jacob and have them like you back. It made the whole world feel magical. Like the skies were shining bright and all the sunbeams in heaven were directed down on you.

Rachel changed out of her clothing and into a smart loungewear set. She fixed her hair. Brushed her teeth. She debated spraying on perfume, but the chemical scent always made her feel woozy so she settled on pulling down the shoulder of her top. Her bra strap was showing, along with her collarbone. It was totally eighties and completely fabulous.

Taking a deep breath, she gathered her courage. Gathered her energy. Then, when she was certain that the racing in her heart would not be contained by anything other than *more* Jacob Greenberg, she threw open her bedroom door. There was a smile on her face as she made her way back to the living room, a skip in her step as she drew closer to Jacob.

And then…panic. Unadulterated and all-encompassing fear.

The door to her office was open.

Her feet moved in slow motion. Her pounding heart stopped beating inside her chest. *This was not happening. This could not be happening.* But there was no doubt. As if in a dream, Rachel pressed forward. When she came to the doorway, it was even worse than she thought. Jacob was sitting at her desk, reading her manuscript for *The Hanukkah Grinch.*

"I can explain," she said.

"Explain?" Jacob rose from his seat. *"You're writing a book about me."* He was hurt. Angry. His face turned red and his forehead was creased in outright disbelief. "So that's the real reason you wanted a ticket, right?"

"No…" she stammered. "I mean…yes, but—"

"You were looking for material? Fodder for your new book?"

"Jacob, please, it's not that simple!"

But it was that simple, wasn't it? She had used Jacob. She had lied to him repeatedly. She had written all sorts of terrible things about him in her manuscript. But she never expected to fall in love.

"You have a Christmas tree," Jacob said, point-blank.

"It's…a friend's."

"There is a picture of *you* sitting on Santa's lap!"

"It's cheaper than therapy."

"And the train?" He pressed her further. "And the garlands, and the music, and the creepy little Santas—"

"*Hey.*" Rachel stopped him right there. "Those Santas are not creepy."

Jacob tossed the manuscript to the side, breathing through his nostrils as he obviously tried to calm himself down. "And this Margot Cross person?" he said, confronting her directly. "Who is she?"

Rachel felt her mouth go dry. "She's no one."

"You're lying! You've been lying from the beginning. About your career, and why you wanted a ticket…and me. Were you lying when you kissed me, too?"

"No," she blurted. "Of course not."

"But that didn't stop you from writing awful things about me in your book."

"Jacob…"

He pushed past her into the living room and grabbed his coat. Rachel followed after him. She wanted to say something. Defend herself. But the conversation had moved beyond her ability to reason.

"Please," she said, reaching for him. "Don't go."

"You want me to stay?"

"Yes."

"Then tell me the truth," he said, stepping up to her. "Who is Margot Cross?"

The world stopped spinning. All she could see in that moment was Jacob, standing at her door, his eyes red with hurt. She was going to lose him.

Honesty. The word was so simple for other people. But Jacob had never been a rabbi's daughter. He had never experienced the ups and downs of a religious communal life. The way congregants gossiped, tallying up a scorecard of Shabbat dinners and sermons before negotiating your father's contract. The way women peered into your mother's shopping cart at the grocery store, checking on the *hechsher* of her items. There were rules to being a rabbinic family. There were expectations. Rachel had not met any of them.

She wanted to be courageous. Speak the words that for too long had been sitting upon her heart. But Rachel loved her parents. She loved her sometimes dysfunctional but always openhearted Jewish community. What Jacob didn't understand—because he relied on no one and therefore had no one to answer to—was that truth had consequences. Even for love, Rachel wasn't prepared to face them.

Eventually Rachel spoke. "I'm just a fan of her books."

Jacob did not hesitate. "Goodbye, Rachel."

The door shut behind him. She stood in her entryway, shellshocked, unsure how their kiss had turned into a catastrophe. She was not a crier, but tears welled up in her eyes. She had lost Jacob. She had ruined everything. All because of that horrible moniker Margot Cross.

Returning to her office, she picked up her Margaritaville Santa and threw it across the room.

From: Rachel Rubenstein-Goldblatt <margotcross@northpole.com>
To: Lisa Brown <l.brown@cachingliteraryagency.com>

Sent: Mon, 20 December
Subject: Bad News

Lisa,

I've had a change of heart. After much thought and consideration, I've decided to pull *The Hanukkah Grinch* from submission. It's a long story...but I can't sign a contract with Romance House. Not for this book.

Please tell Chandra, and everybody else, that I'm sorry for wasting their time.

Onwards,
Rachel

33

It was the morning of the Matzah Ball, and there was no time for heartbreak. Jacob stood in the main ballroom of the Four Seasons and took a careful accounting of the space laid out before him.

Drapes of silver and navy, decorated by fairy lights, stretched across the ceilings. Tables adorned with lush displays of flowers and candles sparkled with encrusted white gems. But the most resplendent part of the room was the ten-foot floating menorah. It peered over the main stage like a Goliath, an impressive symbol of Hanukkah.

"Let's test it one more time," he said, nodding to his stagehand.

The young man obeyed and tapped some notes into a tablet. Jacob watched a floating staircase move across his stage.

"Perfect," Jacob said. "Let's get it into position for tonight. When Rabbi Goldblatt and Dr. Rubenstein arrive, make sure there are plenty of appetizers and drinks for them in the greenroom. We'll bring them out to the main stage right before candle lighting."

"Yes, sir," the young man said, scribbling down notes. "Anything else?"

"No," Jacob said, turning his attention to his tablet. "You can head to the front lobby and finish checking in the talent."

After the young man left, Jacob let his thoughts drift away from the Rubenstein-Goldblatt family. He was grateful to have the Matzah Ball. Grateful for work, which always kept him busy. He didn't want to think about Rachel.

"There you are," Shmuel shouted, appearing from the kitchen. He was in a good mood. After shoving one last fried latke loaded with tuna tartare into his mouth, he wiped his hands against his shirt and met Jacob in the center of the ballroom. "It looks good. Better than I could have ever imagined it."

"It does," Jacob agreed. He didn't feel like smiling.

"So—" Shmuel grinned, leaning into him "—where is our little miracle maker today?"

Jacob feigned ignorance. "Who?"

"Who!" Shmuel was incredulous. "Rachel! The matzah ball! Come on, you know who I'm talking about."

Jacob felt his stomach turn. He did not want to think about Rachel. Or *Margot*. Whoever she was. He settled on filling in the blanks with an excuse. "It's not going to work out," he said, and headed away to check on one of the many sound systems.

"Hold on," Shmuel said, chasing after him. "What do you mean, *not going to work out*?"

Jacob bent down to a speaker and pretended to check the wires. Turning the power on and off, on and off, he was hoping that Shmuel would take the hint and leave him alone. Instead, the hamster only ran faster on the wheel.

"You and this girl," Shmuel said, leaning over the speaker, "you like each other, no?"

"Of course we liked each other."

"And you're both Jewish?"

"Obviously."

"Correct me if I'm wrong here, but yesterday, everything between you two was going great. You were building a menorah together. She was saving our Matzah Ball. And today, you can't even talk about—"

"We're not compatible, okay?"

Shmuel pressed his lips together. "Jacob—"

"We're done, Shmuel."

Jacob huffed a long breath of disappointment from his chest. He didn't want to talk about Rachel. She had confirmed for him the very worst of his beliefs in others. People could not be trusted. He could only rely on himself. But Jacob was a grown-up now. He wasn't going to stand on the dance floor with a bouquet of wildflowers and his heart in his hands, waiting for her to show up. He had learned his lesson well.

"Where are we on food?" he said, changing the topic.

"All ready to go," Shmuel informed him.

"And talent?"

"Everyone has arrived and been checked into their rooms at the Four Seasons. The only group going to be late is 8Nights. One of them has a sick kid. You have time for a quick meet and greet?"

He really didn't, but Jacob preferred to be overwhelmed with activity this morning. It seemed a better option than sitting in quiet solitude thinking about Rachel. "Plan it for four," he said, "and send the limo for Rabbi Goldblatt and Dr. Rubenstein right after."

"And the daughter?" Shmuel asked cautiously.

"What about her?"

"Should I have her wait with her parents?"

Jacob kept it professional. "She's not coming."

He continued talking shop, making notes and finalizing details until a commotion by the main entrance drew their attention away. Morty Schweitzer, dressed to the nines in a blue-and-white-plaid suit with red bow tie, came bursting through the doors. Morty was always one for an entrance, and today he came surrounded by a bevy of eager beauties and three underlings from his staff.

"Gorgeous!" Morty shouted aloud, throwing his hands in the air. "Just stunning! Now this...this is what I think of when I think of Greenberg Entertainment! This is the type of Matzah Ball that only Jacob Greenberg—my brilliant party moneymaker—could throw!"

Jacob greeted Morty with a firm shake of the hand. "I'm glad you approve."

"I do," Morty said, nodding happily. "Truly. There's only one problem..." Morty pulled out his phone, and Jacob tensed. "It's the day of the event, and I don't see it trending on Twitter. I don't see people posting stories about it on Instagram. Where is my hashtag, Jacob? Where is my social media firestorm that's going to pay me back with royalties?"

"Wait till tonight," Jacob said, voice booming, full of confidence. "I promise you, when it all comes together, when you see everything we have planned...people will be talking about it on social media. People will be talking about this Matzah Ball for years to come."

"They better," Morty said gravely. "Because I expect a return on my investment, Jacob. I expect to make a mint! Even if it means taking apart Greenberg Entertainment and selling it for scraps."

With the threat floating in the air between the three men, Morty took off. Shmuel waited for the man and his entourage to leave before turning back to Jacob.

"Was any of that true?" Shmuel asked seriously.

Jacob sighed. "I don't know."

"Well, then," Shmuel said, laying one hand on Jacob's shoulder. "Guess there's nothing left to do but pray for a miracle."

Jacob nodded. "I'll see you at four, then?"

"Sounds good," Shmuel said, and left to check on another team. "And, Jacob, whatever happens, I've enjoyed working with you all these years."

In the quiet of the main ballroom, Jacob took stock of his life. Was he at the end of something grand, or stepping into some new beginning? The only thing he knew for certain was that he didn't feel ready for either.

34

Rachel dug her fist into a tissue box, searching for relief. It was no use. The box was empty.

Her eyes were red and puffy. She had been crying all night.

Tossing the box aside, she leaned against the wall of her office and sucked back a ball of snot. She was all out of tears, fortunately, but that didn't stop the feelings from coming. Indeed, every time she glanced up at the half-empty shelves now lining her office, the reality of her life settled in like a sledgehammer to the belly. Christmas cheer would continue on for the vast majority of the world. But for Rachel Rubenstein-Goldblatt, the holiday season was officially over.

"Girl," Mickey said, appearing in her office, "where do you want me to put the tree?"

Mickey was holding the artificial Christmas tree that used to reside in the corner of her office. Now it was devoid of ornaments, ready to be stored.

"Just box it up with the garlands," Rachel said. "I'll work on the ornaments when I'm done with the Santas."

Mickey hesitated. "You sure you want to do this?" He had asked her that question at least a dozen times this morning.

"I have to do this," she said definitively.

Mickey shrugged sympathetically, then headed off to the living room to find the box.

Rachel returned to her task. Running her fingers over the row of tiny Santa figurines at her feet, she picked up another favorite. She had found Dog Walker Santa at a flea market down in Chelsea, negotiating the original price down to a cool eight-dollar steal.

It wasn't the most valuable of her Holiday Dreams Collection, but she loved the way Santa was pulled at by a dozen different golden retriever puppies. That figure had inspired another holiday bestseller, *Twelve Tails for Christmas*, about a couple brought together by a litter of abandoned puppies they rescued. That one became a children's movie.

Rachel smiled at the memory before grabbing a section of bubble wrapping and encasing Dog Walker Santa safely inside. Then, as she had done fifty-four times before, she laid it in a box alongside the rest of her collection.

"Only one hundred and eighty-one more to go," she informed the tiny smiling Santas.

They stared back enthusiastically but otherwise offered no words of encouragement. Rachel needed a break. She was talking to inanimate objects, after all.

Leaving her half-packed-up office, she headed into the living room to find Mickey. She caught him just in time. With one knee wedged against the box and a hand on the neck of the Christmas tree, he was attempting to shove the four-foot tree, still fully expanded, into the three-foot box.

"Here," Rachel said, coming over to show him. "Let me help."

Taking the tree from Mickey, she folded up its branches and

brackets, handing it back to him when it was a manageable two-foot rectangle of fake fir.

"So that's how you do it," Mickey said, surprised.

"Haven't you ever put away a Christmas tree before?" Rachel asked.

"Hell no," Mickey said. "We always leave Aunt Vivian's house straight after dinner."

Rachel finished putting the tree away and sat down on the couch. Mickey plopped down beside her. Her apartment was a mess. Boxes of half-packed Christmas items littered nearly every square inch. But after three straight hours of work, they were making progress.

"What are you going to do with all this stuff, anyway?" Mickey asked.

"Probably donate it," she said. What she really wanted to do was give it a Viking funeral. Send it floating down the Hudson, fully ablaze, to the curious amusement of the entire Upper West Side. "Or sell it on eBay. I might need the money when all is said and done."

"You could always just store it," he said, trying to be helpful. "I mean…what if in a few years, you decide you want to go back to writing Christmas romance?"

She considered the question. "I'm done writing holiday romances."

Her phone buzzed. She glanced down at the number, hoping it was Jacob. Instead, her heart sank. It was Lisa. Rachel knew exactly what this phone call would be about and that it wouldn't be pleasant.

"It's my agent," Rachel said, rising from the couch and pointing to her office. "Do you mind if I take this in the other room?"

"Do whatever you need to," Mickey said, grabbing the remote and putting his feet up on the couch. "I'll just sit here and watch TV while you blow up your life."

Rachel huffed. "Thanks."

He waved her off, and she went to her office. After closing the door behind her, she stepped over the box filled with the porcelain Santas and headed to the window. Gazing outside, she took a moment to appreciate the beauty of her view. Broadway was alive with the lunchtime crowd. Even the delivery men, who double-parked on the street while they unloaded, seemed to skip while they walked. Everyone was in a good mood with the holidays coming.

She put the phone up to her ear. "Hey, Lisa."

"Rachel!" Lisa was frantic, clearly walking. Her voice cut in and out as she struggled to catch her breath and be heard behind the buzz of background traffic. "I got your email. What do you mean you're pulling *The Hanukkah Grinch*?"

"I don't want it published."

"But it's your best work!"

It wasn't her best work. Lisa just wanted to get Chandra Brouchard some form of Hanukkah romance in order to salvage her contract. "Lisa, listen to me," Rachel said firmly. "I'm not the right person to write a Hanukkah romance."

"What are you talking about? Obviously you're the right person to write a Hanukkah romance. You're Jewish! Your dad's a rabbi! You know all about this stuff. Plus, you have all that experience writing Christmas romances. Who better than you to write a Hanukkah romance? You're the perfect person for this!"

Rachel sighed. How could she explain it to Lisa?

She could write Christmas romances because they were never her world. When Rachel closed her eyes and dreamed of snowflakes floating down on a small New Hampshire town, it wasn't her life. When she wrote about a sheriff finding a litter of puppies to foster while mourning the death of his first wife, it was all make-believe. Rachel had no experience with law enforcement. Or marriage. Heck, she didn't even own a plant.

Hanukkah challenged her to be real. She wasn't capable of it. She wasn't ready for it. More important, she wasn't going to build her new career on the back of Jacob. She had already hurt him enough. Whatever it cost, whatever it meant, she still needed to be able to look at herself in the mirror each morning.

"I'm sorry," she said once again. "But I've made up my mind. Pull the submission. If you want to talk about it later this week, we can meet for lunch. But right now—" she stepped over another box, picking up a photograph of her parents "—I need to figure things out."

Lisa was still talking when Rachel hung up the phone. Gazing back down at the photograph, she knew she had made the right call.

Rachel returned to the living room and slumped down on the couch beside Mickey. He was watching reruns of *The Golden Girls*. Blanche and Rose were arguing in the kitchen over cheesecake.

"All done?" he asked.

Rachel nodded.

He squeezed her hand. "So what happens next?"

"I don't know." She shrugged. "Maybe go to rabbinical school?"

Mickey grimaced. "Let's not do that to the Jewish people, okay?"

Rachel laughed before settling into a quiet smile. Her whole world had come crashing down around her like a kitten playing near a Christmas tree. Or in her case, a candle falling off a lit menorah. They were always designed so poorly.

"And the Matzah Ball?" Mickey asked.

"I can't go to the Matzah Ball."

"Why not?" he pressed. "You worked hard for that ticket, and you already have the dress."

"I can't do that to Jacob," Rachel said. "You take the ticket."

"What?" Mickey scoffed. "I can't take your coveted silver ticket."

Rachel had made up her mind. She raced to her bedroom,

threw open the nightstand and found the white envelope containing the precious last ticket for entry to the Matzah Ball Max.

"Here," she said, returning to the living room and holding it out for him to take.

"No!"

"Mickey," she said resolutely, "it's done. I'm not writing a Hanukkah romance. There's no reason for me to go to the Matzah Ball now. Take the ticket. You worked just as hard for it as I did, organizing Stefan's act and calling every single person we knew from Camp Ahava. Besides, you're single now. What better place to meet a nice Jewish boy than the Matzah Ball?"

Mickey furrowed his brow and considered her argument.

"Well," he said, snapping the ticket from her fingers. "I'm certainly not going to let an opportunity to meet my *bashert* go to waste."

"I'm glad." She smiled, plopping down on the couch beside him. "More important, what are you going to wear?"

"I don't know," he said, thinking about it. "I guess I should wear a tux?"

"Do you have one?"

"No," he said. "I mean, not one that's glamorous enough. I'll need something really special for tonight."

She pulled out her phone. "There's a shop on 58th where you could probably rent one last minute, but you better hurry. The Matzah Ball starts at six."

Mickey did not want to leave her. "Are you sure?" he asked, concerned. "I don't want to go if you're gonna start mass murdering tiny Santas."

She squeezed his arm. "I'll be fine."

He sighed. Rachel was stubborn. When she settled her mind on something, there was no point in arguing. Rising from his seat, he went to the coatrack and pulled on his jacket.

"And if Jacob asks about you?" Mickey inquired, tying his scarf around his neck.

"Tell him—" she swallowed hard "—goodbye."

With one last hug shared between them, Mickey took off. Rachel closed the door behind him. Leaning against it, she took in the silence of the room, the boxes of Christmas decor, half-packed, invading every square inch of her life. Then she headed to her kitchen, pulled out a bottle of red wine and cracked it open.

35

The Matzah Ball was in full swing. On the blue carpet outside the Four Seasons, in front of the banner for Greenberg Entertainment, eager paparazzi snapped photos of celebrities and dignitaries as they arrived via limo. Jacob watched from the sidelines, periodically glancing at his phone and attempting to appear casual. It seemed that everyone with a ticket had shown up.

Well, everyone except Rachel.

Jacob couldn't help but keep an eye out for her. He knew the chances of her attending tonight were nil. Their fight had solidified that they were completely wrong for each other. Still, he harbored a secret desire deep within his heart. He wanted her to show up. He wanted her to prove that she was reliable and that he was someone worth fighting for, after all. But that wasn't Rachel.

"Sir." Johnson, the six-foot-tall head of his security team, appeared. "We've done a perimeter scan. Everything is secure."

Johnson was a beast of a man, all skin and muscle. Even without the Taser strapped to his belt, he was terrifying. And his team of specially trained guards, all hulking ex-military, were the best New York City security had to offer.

Jacob watched a state senator emerge from a limo. "Good," he said, knowing Johnson would never let him down. "It's important that only people with a ticket get in tonight."

Jacob scanned the long line of hopeful attendees waiting behind a blue velvet rope. These were people without tickets who had come early, hoping to land an open spot. In truth, it would take a miracle for any of them to get in tonight. It wasn't just a numbers issue. Security had to be extra tight at an event like the Matzah Ball, where any psycho with a 4chan account and a penchant for anti-Semitism might show up.

"As for the line," Jacob said, tapping Johnson on the back, "remember what we talked about. Keep them under control, but don't send anybody home. The crowd is good for our image."

"Yes, sir."

With security handled outside, Jacob headed indoors. From the looks of the smiles stretched out across attendees' faces, things were going well. Spiced Sufganiyot Martinis were being passed out. Stefan and his team of acrobats spun from the ceiling as blue and white lights circled the room. On the main stage, in front of the ten-foot menorah still waiting to be lit, the first act had begun. Jewish pop music blared across the room.

It was an epic party filled with holiday magic.

And it was missing Rachel.

Jacob shook the thought away. No, that wasn't it. It wasn't that he was missing her, obviously. It was simply that there were signs of her everywhere. The drinks. The decor. The food being passed out on delicate silver trays. It was totally normal that his thoughts would keep veering toward her. She had left her mark indelibly.

It also didn't help that her parents were going to be here tonight.

Jacob scanned the crowd and found Shmuel planted by the

kitchen door. He was taste testing the food items as they appeared. Jacob was not surprised. Rachel's creative spin on latkes was clearly all the rage among the kosher crowd.

"Good news," Shmuel said, waving Jacob over. "I just heard from the driver. Rabbi Goldblatt and Dr. Rubenstein should be here in the next hour."

"The next hour!" Jacob glanced down at his watch. "They're already running an hour behind schedule."

"I know, I know," Shmuel said, waving away his concern. "They hit a little traffic on the expressway. But don't worry, Jacob. We're talking Hanukkah candles here. They can be lit anytime. An hour later, nobody's gonna notice or care." Shmuel pulled another latke off a tray, popping it into his mouth. "Especially not with all this delectable food to keep our bellies happy."

"First off, stop eating all the food." Jacob sometimes felt like he was dealing with a child instead of a colleague. "Secondly, if Rabbi Goldblatt is going to be late, we need to move the music acts around. Where are we with 8Nights?"

"They're in the greenroom," Shmuel said. "Eating all the food."

"Switch them up with Esther Shapiro," Jacob said, scrolling through his phone and making a note on the schedule. "We'll end with NezGadol and J-Pop instead."

Shmuel propelled himself off the wall and prepared to make the changes. "Anything else, your majesty?"

"Yeah," Jacob said. "Let me know the minute Rabbi Goldblatt and Dr. Rubenstein arrive. I want to make sure everything is perfect for them."

Shmuel offered a mock salute and took off. Jacob glanced back at the entrance of the main ballroom. Oh, how he wished Rachel would come storming through those doors.

Instead, he found Morty Schweitzer. The man was leaning against a bar, watching the spectacle unfold before him. He looked happy. Almost like he was having a good time. But good times were not enough to bring a return on their investment.

Jacob pulled out his phone. He didn't want to keep scrolling through social media, but seeing Morty standing there was irresistible. Usually, by the start of one of his events—sometimes even days before—he would see signs of trending. With Launchella and Sunburn, for example, people spent half the event with their phones in the air, snapping pictures and recording video.

But when Jacob scanned the room, checked the numbers of hits and SEO keywords for his Matzah Ball Max, nobody was sharing their experience.

His stomach turned. It was not good.

Jacob forced himself to think positively. It was still early in the evening, after all. They hadn't even lit the candles. There was still plenty of time—at least six more hours—to get this party going and save Greenberg Entertainment.

He put his phone away as a surprising sight caught his eye. Mickey was also near the bar, sipping a martini. He was impossible to miss, really. Mickey had paired a baby blue tux trimmed by black lapels with a stylish dreidel-themed bowtie.

Jacob recognized the young man he was talking to as Brandon, one of his investors' assistants. Mickey and Jacob made eye contact across the room. Mickey excused himself, coming over.

Jacob offered him his hand. "What are you doing here?"

"Rachel gave me her ticket."

"Ah," Jacob said, pursing his lips together. "I suppose that makes sense." He didn't want to show the disappointment he felt. Quickly he changed the topic. "You look great."

"You think?" Mickey ran his hands down the front of his tuxedo. "I had to rent it, last minute. This being the holiday season and all, it was all they had. But throw it together with some Hanukkah-themed accessories, and voilà... I am a Jewish fashion icon."

"You most certainly are."

Awkward silence stretched between them. Jacob wanted to ask about Rachel. He wanted to interrogate Mickey, pry every detail of her personal life from his unwilling lips, but he also knew that Rachel's best friend since forever would never betray her secrets. There was no point in asking because she was gone. She had made her choice.

"Look, Jacob," Mickey said, breaking the quiet. "I just wanted to say that… I know we got off on the wrong foot. But despite everything that happened between us, including you nearly killing my best friend with a stupid matzah ball costume, I don't think you're a bad guy."

"Thanks, Mickey."

"And I hope… I really do hope you and Rachel work it out."

Jacob swallowed the twinge of regret sitting inside his throat. He wanted to work it out with Rachel, too. But he couldn't be with someone who wasn't honest. He would not spend the rest of his life waiting for someone who would never show up.

"It's been really good to reconnect," Jacob said. "If you're ever in Paris, feel free to look me up."

They shook hands, saying goodbye. When they parted, Jacob knew it would be the last time he would ever see Mickey. After the Matzah Ball, he would return to Paris. He would leave New York forever, boarding a plane to escape the painful memories of his past. At least, this time, there was no reason to come back.

36

"Maoz tzurrrrrrr ye'shuati," Rachel slurred.

She was all alone in her apartment on the last night of Ha-nukkah, but that wasn't going to stop her from having a good time. Engaging in a rousing rendition of wine-bottle karaoke, Rachel lifted the half-drunk bottle to her mouth and sang to her make-believe audience of boxes.

"L'cha neah le'shabeach," she bellowed, and somebody on the street shouted at her to shut up. She stuck her head out the window. "Hey!" she yelled back. "Do you mind? I'm having a pity party for one up here, and you're interrupting!"

It took a full ten seconds for the critic to respond. "You suck!"

"Well, Happy Hanukkah to you, too," she said, before slam-ming the window shut. Rachel did not need that type of nega-tivity in her life.

Besides, she wasn't even that drunk. She could totally lead a Torah service right now, or even command a dance. Rachel sashayed through the living room, feeling like a graceful balle-rina, before tripping over a box. She fell headfirst into a stockpile of garlands. "Great," she moaned, pulling tinsel out of her hair. "Just freaking great! Can anything go right for me today?"

The universe did not respond.

Rachel lifted herself from the ground. Okay, maybe she was a little drunk. She didn't exactly have the best tolerance. It was a factoid made worse by the fact that she hadn't eaten or really slept in the last twenty-four hours. She had wanted to, but she had been too upset about Jacob.

She didn't want to think about it. She also needed to stop drinking. Putting the bottle of wine down, she headed for the refrigerator. It was pretty empty. There were some pickles. Some cream cheese, probably expired. She gave up on finding food in her kitchen and stumbled into the bedroom.

Somewhere, buried beneath a pile of clothes in her closet, she still had a *mishloach manot* gift basket left over from Purim. Falling to her knees, she rifled through a pile of summer clothes and found it. Nonalcoholic peach wine and two stale *hamentashen*, little triangular cookies filled with jelly, stared back at her.

Desperate for sustenance, she pulled out a cookie. It was no use. The dry and flavorless thing felt like cardboard in her mouth. She spit it out. Food. Sleep. Joy. Losing Jacob had affected her in ways she had never imagined. Sitting down on the bed, she caught sight of the blue-and-silver ball gown hanging on her mirror. It was so beautiful, and yet she hadn't even bothered to try it on.

What would be the harm now?

Slipping out of her pj's, she pulled on the dress. It really didn't match the grandma bra she was wearing. Or her unkempt frizzy hair, which stuck out in a thousand different directions. But it was beautiful. Perfect. Made for her. She wondered how one person could have pegged her so completely. Though she had made the right choice—protecting her parents and all that—she couldn't help feeling she had lost something important.

The buzzer on her front door rang. Rachel spun around,

squinting in the direction of the sound. She had no idea who it could be. Everyone she knew was at the Matzah Ball.

Of course, she hoped it was Jacob.

She peeked through the peephole. Toby was waiting outside. Rachel's stomach dropped. She was wearing a ball gown and was slightly inebriated. She was in no position to be entertaining bubbes.

Chewing nervously on one fingernail, she considered her options. The smartest thing to do was pretend she wasn't home. But she couldn't just ignore the poor woman. Not when Toby had been so incredibly kind to her over the last week. Despite her embarrassment, she opened the door.

"Rachel-la!" Toby said, joy oozing through every word, "I'm so glad I caught you."

Rachel stammered. "Ca-caught me?"

"It's the last night of Hanukkah." Toby held up a small blue bag. "I brought you a gift."

Rachel hesitated. It was kind of Toby to hike all the way to the Upper West Side. It was also unnecessary. Her relationship with Jacob was over. She didn't feel deserving of presents delivered by hand from his lovely grandmother.

"I also brought you some more rugalach. I know how much you enjoyed them the other day. Do you like apricot?"

"I love apricot," Rachel admitted. Plus, she was starving.

"A girl after my own heart!"

Toby entered Rachel's apartment. She raised a concerned eyebrow at the multitude of boxes laid out across the living room. But otherwise, she was kind enough not to mention the ball gown paired with fuzzy pink socks, or the half-drunk bottle of wine sitting open on the kitchen counter.

"Are you moving?" Toby asked.

"I'm just changing some things around."

"Change is good," Toby said. "Mind if I sit down?"

Rachel threw boxes and pillows out of the way. "Please. Make yourself comfortable."

She was grateful that Toby was here. Something about bubbes, with their sweet smiles and never-ending supply of baked goods, always made Rachel feel better.

Toby sat down on the couch, exhaling in loud relief. "My feet," she said, lifting her toes up into the air. "I try not to think about my age, but sometimes it creeps up on me when I least expect it."

Rachel nodded. "I understand." In the kitchen, she pulled out two small plates and napkins, and she set up the coffee table for snacks. "Would you like something to drink?"

"Water is fine."

Rachel poured two glasses, placing them on the coffee table before taking a seat beside Toby. The old woman opened the white bag and began pulling out rugalach, piling at least half a dozen on Rachel's plate.

"Please," Rachel said, trying to stop her. "I can't eat that much."

"Nonsense!" Toby added two more cookies to her pile. "Plus, they're so tiny. And you're so skinny. Come now, have some more. My mother always said, 'eat sweet things, and you'll have a sweet life.' There's mazel in eating cookies."

Rachel sighed, obliging the old woman. She could certainly use some luck in her life right now. She popped a cookie in her mouth and moaned. They were indescribably delicious.

"Jacob likes apricot the best, too."

Rachel's heart broke once again. She put her rugalach down, feeling guilty.

"You look beautiful, by the way," Toby said.

"Oh?" Rachel laughed. "I had forgotten I was wearing it."

"Well, go on…" Toby teased her, pointing to a space on the living room floor. "Model for me. I want to see you in all your glory."

Rachel didn't feel glorious. In truth, she felt like an extra from the cast of *Grey Gardens*. Her hair was a mess. She hadn't bothered to put on makeup. Plus, she was still wearing a pair of fuzzy pink socks. She had not brought the gown any justice, but Toby kept insisting.

"Go on, humor an old woman!"

Standing up, Rachel moved to the center of the room. Taking a deep breath, she did as Toby demanded, twirling several times before landing in a low curtsy. Toby broke into applause. "Stunning," she said happily. "Just stunning. There's only one problem." Toby reached for the blue bag. "It's missing something."

Rachel returned to the seat beside Toby. Taking the blue gift bag on her lap, she dug her fingers through tissue paper, pulling out a small box. She opened it, gasping at the sight. Inside was a pair of sapphire earrings encrusted in diamonds. She could tell by the design, the careful swirls in craftsmanship, that they were an antique.

Toby leaned over Rachel's shoulder. "I want you to wear them to the Matzah Ball."

"I can't accept these," Rachel said.

"Why ever not?"

"They're too expensive!"

"Nonsense," Toby said, waving away her concern. "The stones are glass."

"It's not real?"

"No." Toby explained, "My husband had them filled in with colored glass as a wedding present. We didn't have much money back then, and glass was all he could afford. Still, I think the glass makes them all the more precious, since the original stones saved my life."

"I don't understand."

"I was born in Germany," Toby said. "I'm a survivor."

"I didn't know," Rachel said. "I'm so sorry."

Rachel was not surprised. She had grown up with Holocaust

survivors and their stories. She recalled how they would sit at her dining room table over holidays, sharing their truth with tears and anger and then rolling up their sleeves to display the number tattooed on their skin.

Indeed, she had known about the Holocaust her entire life. It had always existed there beside her, a warning and a burden, the murder of six million Jews a story intimately tied up with her own.

"I was only eight years old when my mother sewed these earrings into the hem of my skirt, and placed me on a train from Germany to France."

"You must have been so scared."

"Terrified," Toby admitted. "I was a child, all alone and in the middle of a war, but I did have some things in my favor. I was female, which meant the Nazis couldn't check to see if I was circumcised. I had blond hair and blue eyes, which helped me pass as a French child instead of a Jewish one. And I had those earrings sewn into the hem of my skirt."

"You could use the stones as payment?"

Toby nodded. "Whenever I would come across some threat—a soldier that needed to be bribed, or some farmer to reimburse for food and shelter—I would unstitch those earrings, pull out a stone and pay them. It was a dangerous task, making my way through Europe alone. Eventually, I was able to make it to the south of France. With the help of the Resistance, I worked as a farmhand using falsified papers. I changed my name to Marie and lived like that for the next two years, never telling anyone the truth of who I was."

"That must have been so hard."

"It was," she said sadly. "Perhaps I would have forgotten who I was entirely, but I had my mother's earrings. I had her strength sewn into the hem of my skirt, carrying me forward."

Rachel ran her fingers over the glass stones. It was incredible to think of the journey those earrings had taken.

"When the war ended," Toby said, "I was twelve years old. I spent several years in a displaced persons camp, hoping to hear that someone from my family survived…but nobody did. Each of them deported and murdered in places like Sobibor, Treblinka and Auschwitz. I knew that I couldn't stay in Europe. Not after everything that happened. Eventually, a Jewish aid society arranged for me to come live with a foster family in America."

Rachel nodded. In the aftermath of the Holocaust, countless Jewish children found themselves orphaned. In response, Jewish detective agencies were set up all around Europe to identify these children and find surviving family. When a child was proved to be "100 percent orphan" they were relocated to new homes and families, often outside of Europe.

"It was the first night of Hanukkah when I boarded a ship for New York. I wasn't sure what my future would hold, but I knew…whatever happened, I was free. I took the remaining stone from those earrings, the smallest little chip of a diamond, and I bought some candles and a block of wood. I stood on the hull of that ship with other survivors and lit the candles on my makeshift menorah. And do you know what we said to each other, after those candles were lit and the blessings were done?"

Rachel shook her head. "No."

"'A great miracle happened here.'"

They were the same words inscribed as an acronym on the dreidel.

"You were so brave." Rachel choked on the words. "I don't think I could ever be that brave."

"Not brave," Toby corrected her. "I was scared, nearly every single second of every day during the war. I was scared after the war, too. But I was done hiding. I was done pretending to be somebody I wasn't. I was ready to be free, tell my story, and in doing so…brighten the light of someone else."

Toby took the earrings from Rachel and affixed them to her ears. Digging into her purse, she pulled out a small compact mirror, holding it up for Rachel to see.

"You are the perfect person to wear these earrings," Toby said. "Don't you see?"

Rachel analyzed her reflection in the mirror. The earrings swung down to her chin, truly stunning. Swirls of color, blue and white, highlighted the pinks and yellows in her cheeks. It didn't matter that they were glass. It didn't matter that they had no real economic value. It was their story that made them precious.

Tears fell from Rachel's eyes. She understood the lesson in the gift.

Truth could be scary. Darkness might always endeavor to snuff out the light, but the strength of those who truly loved us would always push us forward. This was how we brightened an otherwise dark world. We filled it with truth, and love, and light.

Toby put down the mirror and, taking Rachel's face gently between her hands, wiped away the wet spots with her thumbs.

"Do you love my grandson?" Toby asked.

Rachel blinked back more tears. "What?"

"Do you love him?" she asked, shaking her gently. "Does he give you sparks? Does he make you bubble?"

"Yes. I think so."

"Then fight for him." Toby smiled emphatically. "Fight for him, Rachel-la! So many people think Hanukkah is about miracles. But Hanukkah is really about fighting for the things you believe in. Everybody focuses on the oil, but there would have been no oil, no lamp and no miracle had the Maccabees not taken up arms and stormed that darn temple. That's the thing people forget about Hanukkah. We make our own miracles, Rachel-la. We're in charge of creating our own happy endings."

Rachel swallowed her sadness. Courage trickled through her like osmosis. She found her own strength in the earrings and their story. "Thank you," she said, kissing Toby on the cheek. "For everything."

Without wasting a single second more, Rachel jumped from the couch, pulled on her sneakers and bolted for the door.

37

It was the last night of Hanukkah in Manhattan, and the city was humming. Christmas trees and menorahs shone down from windows on the Upper West Side. Families and couples, their arms loaded down with shopping bags and baked goods, headed happily to holiday parties. The whole world drifted along like the snow falling over Broadway, gentle and content.

Rachel exploded onto the street. With only one thought on her mind, she rushed past her doorman. She needed to get to the Matzah Ball. She needed to speak with Jacob.

"Ma'am," the doorman said, chasing after her. "Can I help you?"

Rachel turned, frantic. "I need a cab!"

"Right away," the doorman said, glancing down at her evening gown precipitously paired with pink fuzzy socks and three-year-old sneakers. "Would you like to wait inside?"

"What?" Rachel said, before realizing she had not grabbed a coat. "Oh, no…"

In her rush to action, she had forgotten her purse. Oddly, she was not cold, but she could not take a cab or the subway without money or her MetroCard. Perhaps it was the wine, or the sheer adrenaline rushing through her body, but the last thing she wanted to do was go back upstairs to her apartment. She did not want to risk losing her courage.

She decided to make a run for it. If she bolted for the Four Seasons, if she used all the power in her thighs to sprint the entire way there, she could likely make it to the Matzah Ball before any subway or cab.

"Don't worry about it," she said, waving the doorman away. "Happy Holidays!"

Rachel took off. She wasn't much of an athlete after twelve years of deconditioning due to CFS, but she was still a woman. The adrenaline that coursed through her veins superseded any fatigue. If she crashed tomorrow…oh, well. At least, she would crash for a good reason. For now, she was going to use every bit of battery left in her body.

Sprinting down busy city streets, and despite nearly being hit by a cab, she made her way to the bustle of midtown. She had no idea what she was going to say to Jacob. She just knew that she loved him. It was a force strong enough to make her risk everything.

Rachel arrived at the Four Seasons out of breath and soaking wet. She couldn't tell whether the damp that soaked her hair was from sweat or snow, but she had other, more pressing concerns than the state of her appearance. The venue was packed. Limos stretched down the street. Men in black spoke into buds positioned inside their ears. Heading for the blue carpet, she found a long line of guests.

Rachel rushed past the revelers and up the stairs. She was just about to make her way inside when her attempt to enter the Matzah Ball was dashed. A man the size of Goliath, all head and no neck, glared down at her. Rachel's jaw dropped.

"Ticket?" he said.

Rachel realized her fatal mistake. She had given Mickey her coveted Matzah Ball ticket. Without a ticket, there was no viable way to garner entry. Her heart sank at the realization. Still, Goliath had to be reasonable. She had served as a Matzah Ball volunteer, after all. *She had kissed Jacob Greenberg.* Perhaps he would see the desire in her heart and be persuaded to help out.

"Please," she said, out of breath. "I need to get inside."

"Nobody gets in without a ticket."

"But I know Jacob," she persisted. "I was a volunteer for this Matzah Ball!"

"No ticket, no entry."

"But—"

"You can get in line and wait with the rest of the folks."

Rachel huffed, frustrated. It was no use. Clearly Goliath did not believe in happy endings. She debated bum-rushing him, and then a sight at the end of the street caught her eye. Her parents were exiting a limo.

"Ema!" she shouted. "Over here!"

She waved her arms like a madwoman, jumped up and down. It was all for naught. Her parents could not hear her over the crowd of people waiting for entry into the Matzah Ball. Frantic, she settled on the next best option. She would push her way through the crowd.

Ducking underneath elbows and pushing past paparazzi, she kept an eye on her parents. From her vantage point, she could make out Shmuel welcoming them. She watched as they shook hands and exchanged greetings, completely unaware that their daughter was having a panic attack just feet away.

"Shmuel!" she shouted, trying to grab their attention. "Ema!"

Her hand inadvertently smacked a reporter, sending his glasses crashing to the ground.

"Hey," he shouted. "Watch where you're going!"

"Sorry," she said, dropping to the ground to help him. "I'm so sorry! Are you okay?"

"I'm fine," he said, putting his glasses back on his face.

Rachel apologized again, taking off. By then, it was too late. She reached the door just as her parents slipped inside.

"No!" she shouted, banging her fists against the door.

Despite her efforts, no one heard her cries or opened the door. Defeat settled over her. It was no use. She had given up her ticket. She had left her cell phone and wallet at home. Plus, she looked all types of a mess. Perhaps the universe was telling her to give up.

Rachel slumped against the door. Folding her head into her hands, she breathed a heavy sigh of resignation. In the process, her earrings brushed against her thumbs. The feeling of the glass, the memory of their journey, solidified her resolve. Rachel didn't believe in miracles. But she did believe in happy endings.

Rising from her place, she balled up her fists at her sides. Screw the universe and its constant never-ending bag of mixed messages. She would be like the Maccabees on Hanukkah...and storm that damn temple.

Fortunately for Rachel, she already knew her way around the Four Seasons. Trying to act cool, she bypassed Goliath at the front entrance and slunk down an alleyway. She knew of a side entrance there, often used by staff for cigarette breaks. When she checked the lock, her heart sank. Normally the staff would use a wedge of cardboard to keep the door open. But with the party in full swing and security on max alert, the door was barred shut.

Defeat stretched through her body. There had to be some other way inside. Glancing up to the heavens, she offered a silent prayer to the Matzah Ball gods. And that's when she saw it, right above her head—the bottom of the metal ladder of a fire escape.

It was insane. Obviously, one of the worst ideas she had ever entertained. But bad ideas had never been reason enough to stop Rachel.

Hoisting up her dress, she made a jump for it. Her hands

skimmed the wet metal before she promptly fell to the ground in one slushy mess.

The noise of her crashing caused a few onlookers to glance in her direction. Quickly she hid behind a trash can, pushing her back firmly against the wall. Then, when she was certain the onlookers had moved on to other things, she stepped out of the shadows and tried again. She jumped. Once. Twice. Three times...before finally catching hold of the metal staircase and bringing it down in one crashing swoop.

"Victory," she whispered.

She glanced down the alley. No one was watching. Good. Hoisting up the bottom of her ball gown, she began to climb. The ladder was dangerous. Slippery and wet. Rachel nearly fell on several occasions, but she refused to be intimidated. Mustering her courage, she made her way up to the fourth floor. A window was open.

It would have to do.

Stepping off the fire escape and onto a ledge, she began the dangerous horizontal climb toward Jacob. She needed something to calm her nerves. She decided to hum Christmas music. But when she nearly slipped and almost went crashing four stories to her death, she switched over to Hanukkah tunes.

Finally she made it to a window. Using the tip of her sneaker, she pried it open wider. Relief spilled over her. She was just about to enter when a voice called out to her. Goliath was standing at the end of the alleyway. He had one hand on a radio device situated in his ear and the other precipitously guarding a Taser attached to his belt.

"Hey!" Goliath called out to her. "You there—stop what you're doing!"

Rachel hesitated. She had never been Tasered before, and Goliath was seriously scary. But whatever fear lingered in her heart lasted for no more than a heartbeat. She loved Jacob Greenberg. She was going to fight for him.

Without apology, she knelt down to the window and threw herself inside. The last thing she heard as she went tumbling onto the carpet was Goliath speaking into his radio.

"Security," he said, his voice echoing over static. "We have a break-in on the fourth floor. Be on the lookout for a female. Blue ball gown. Pink socks. Disheveled. Send all security immediately. I repeat, all security to the fourth floor. Now."

38

Jacob Greenberg was not a happy camper.

Standing in the main event room, he tried to place the source of his tension. Heart-pounding music, the epic rap beats of Ne-zGadol, blasted from the stage. Special effects, coupled with strobe lights, swiped across the smiling faces of his Matzah Ball attendees.

Almost everything was going according to plan and on schedule.

Still, he couldn't enjoy himself. Something was missing. Or rather, someone.

His eyes darted over the dance floor. He didn't want to keep looking for Rachel, but he couldn't help himself. It happened every time he saw a woman in a blue dress or caught the eye of a curvaceous brunette. He would smile. Move closer. Attempt to talk to her. Only to realize quite abruptly that the woman standing before him was not Rachel. Rather, an imposter sent to torment his aching heart.

The only thought that gave him any comfort was that tomorrow he would be returning to France. In the meantime, he tried to distract himself with the young woman with blond hair and blue eyes who had been chatting with him for the last fifteen minutes. Once she had learned he was Jacob Greenberg, CEO of Greenberg Entertainment, she had not left his side.

"This music is amazing!"

"I'm glad you appreciate it," he said. "Are you Jewish?"

"Oh, no," she said, slightly slurring her words. "But I love Jewish men."

"Ah."

"I'm on J-Mate," she offered up. "Jewish men make the best husbands."

Jacob smiled. He knew from his father that wasn't always true.

Still, she was pretty. Blond hair. Smoking body. She laughed at everything he said, uncomplicated and pleasing.

But she wasn't Rachel.

His heart waged a war with his head. He couldn't help himself. He missed Rachel's complications. He missed the way she rolled her eyes, offering up some snide remark, fearless about putting him in his place. She had a strange sense of humor. She said things that were quirky and altogether ridiculous. The irony sliced him. For all her lies, she was often quite real. Brutally honest, in fact. Unlike the woman standing before him, false smiles and platitudes.

"Jacob?" A staff member tapped him on the shoulder. "Rabbi Goldblatt and Dr. Rubenstein have arrived."

"Have they been set up?"

"They're waiting in the greenroom."

Jacob was relieved. He was looking for an excuse to exit. Turning back to the blonde woman, he kissed her hand and said au revoir.

He walked to the greenroom at a brisk pace, feeling uneasy as he followed his assistant toward the back area. He dreaded seeing Rabbi Goldblatt and Dr. Rubenstein. He knew that they would remind him of Rachel.

"Rabbi Goldblatt," Jacob said, putting his phone on Mute. "Dr. Rubenstein."

He was pleased to see that his guests had been properly situated. Rabbi Goldblatt sat upon one of the couches, filling up on Latke Eight Ways. Dr. Rubenstein, always a social butterfly, held court with some of his staff in the corner.

Upon seeing Jacob, both stopped what they were doing. Rabbi Goldblatt set his plate on the coffee table. Dr. Rubenstein excused herself, greeting Jacob with the warmest of hugs. Feeling her arms around him was wonderful. Oh, how he missed his mother. He missed the comfort of family on hard days.

Jacob pulled away. "I trust everything went well with you getting here?"

"We hit a bit of traffic," Rabbi Goldblatt said.

"But nothing that shouldn't be expected during the holiday," Dr. Rubenstein interjected.

"I hope the limo kept you comfortable then?" Jacob said.

"More than comfortable," Dr. Rubenstein swooned. "But really, Jacob. The limo was too much! We're New Yorkers, after all. We would have been happy to take the train."

"Nonsense," Jacob said. "You're honored guests of the Matzah Ball. It's my job to make sure you're safe and taken care of."

They moved back to the couch. It was important to Jacob to go over the particulars so that nothing about being onstage would catch the Goldblatt-Rubenstein family off guard. Dr. Rubenstein settled into her seat, palms folded on her lap. Rabbi Goldblatt picked his plate back up, listening intently between bites of food.

"Once Esther Shapiro is finished her set, we're going to lower the lights," Jacob explained. "There will be a bit of a show, some visual displays, fire and music, which will draw the attention of the attendees up to the main stage. After that, I'll bring you out.

There will be some introductions, applause, a few nice words… Then the curtains behind the stage will part, and the audience will see our ten-foot menorah."

"Ten feet!" Dr. Rubenstein gasped. "This sounds very elaborate, Jacob."

"Everything I do is elaborate. Now, this is the part you need to worry about. Once the menorah is showcased, I'm going to lead you to a staircase. Everything is mechanized. So, once you're at the top, light the *shamash*, and after you say the blessings, it will move on its own, slowly and under the direction of the stage crew. You're not afraid of heights, are you?"

"Not at all," Rabbi Goldblatt said proudly. "In fact, I climbed the snake path on Masada several times."

"Good," Jacob said. "Because it's high. You light all eight candles before placing the *shamash* back into its final position. At which point, there will be some more pyrotechnic displays and the music will begin again. Once that happens, you are free to descend the staircase."

Shmuel entered, untangling two mics in his hand. He was just the man Jacob wanted to see.

"I trust you've met Shmuel Applebaum," Jacob said as they all rose to their feet. "My business partner."

"Yes, he's been very helpful," Rabbi Goldblatt said.

"The pleasure is all mine." Shmuel smiled warmly. "It's nice to finally meet the *mishpacha* of our little matzah ball. She's been a real miracle worker. Completely saved our *tuches*, if you know what I mean."

"Excuse me," Rabbi Goldblatt said. "I'm not quite understanding."

Jacob swallowed hard. He had promised Rachel not to tell her parents, but he decided they were long past the point of keeping secrets now. Plus, he wasn't Rachel. He didn't like lying to Dr. Rubenstein and Rabbi Goldblatt. Especially since they had gone out of their way to be so kind to him.

"I'm sorry," Jacob said, apologizing for them both. "Rachel didn't want me to tell you."

"Tell us what?" Dr. Rubenstein cocked her head sideways.

"She has been helping us out with the Matzah Ball."

"Really?" Sheer delight stretched across Dr. Rubenstein's face. "How wonderful! No, she didn't tell us. But I'm incredibly happy to hear you two have been spending so much time with each other. Is she here tonight?"

"No. Unfortunately, Rachel and I... We had a bit of a falling-out."

Dr. Rubenstein frowned. "Oh, dear. Well, I'm sorry to hear that."

"Me, too," Shmuel said.

Jacob hid his discomfort behind a frozen smile. It was clear that the entire Jewish world was rooting for this *shidduch*. The pressure was real.

Still, none of them had seen that Christmas office. None of them had read that manuscript, *The Hanukkah Grinch*. But beyond all these things, Rachel wasn't here. She'd had a ticket and chosen not to attend. He couldn't love someone who wasn't reliable.

"Rachel's help has been invaluable," Jacob said honestly. "I'll always be grateful. Now, if you don't mind—" he pointed back to the couch, leading them and the conversation away from the topic of his love life "—I'd like to go over the last few details."

Dr. Rubenstein smiled. "Of course."

Everyone sat back down. Jacob took the mics from Shmuel. "Now in terms of sound," Jacob said, displaying the two mics. "You should know that the stage is already fully wired up. Anything you say up there can and will be broadcast to the audience."

Dr. Rubenstein chuckled at the thought. "That could be dangerous."

"These mics are just an added precaution. Should there be a

problem with our primary sound system, we'll switch you over to these backups. But the point is, again…be careful what you say up there. Assume everyone can hear everything."

"Good to know," Rabbi Goldblatt said.

He raised a mischievous eyebrow at his wife. She smiled, tapping his knee, and they both blushed. It was clear they were sharing some inside joke.

Jacob's heart ached at the sight. Their love was so evident, their marriage so strong even after countless years. How was it possible that Rachel had come from such a union? Then again, her issue was never loyalty. She was completely dependable when it came to her family. She just wasn't honest with them.

"There will also be 4K ultra-high-definition video," he continued. "So in addition to being careful what you say, try to remember that everything you're doing while onstage is being recorded and broadcast on monitors throughout the Four Seasons. It's also likely that the footage will then be repurposed to support future events for Greenberg Entertainment. So again, best foot forward and all that."

"Sounds like every Saturday," Dr. Rubenstein answered for her husband. "Hanukkah is about publicizing the miracle, after all. I'm glad we could help."

Jacob nodded. They were such good people. Thoughtful and giving, without ever asking for anything in return. He wondered if that's where Rachel got some of her fight. She had been so willing to come to his aid when the Matzah Ball was falling apart. The thought only made him miss her more.

"That's basically it," he said, waving a few of his sound crew over. "Mike and Tina here will help get you both set up. If you don't mind, I need to check on a few things. But I'll be back at half past to bring you onto the stage. Otherwise, if you need anything, you can ask anyone on my team. They'll be happy to get it for you."

Jacob took his leave. In truth, there was really nothing left for him to check on. He just needed air. Seeing the love between Rabbi Goldblatt and Dr. Rubenstein had left him feeling empty. Leaving them all behind, he headed for the service elevator.

He emerged onto the fifty-second-floor rooftop, the city shining bright before him. It was a beautiful evening in Manhattan. Snowflakes fell down around the city. Christmas trees and menorahs filled apartment and office windows with holiday cheer.

Somewhere, among those myriad tiny lights, was Rachel.

The door swung open behind him. Shmuel appeared, his cell phone pressed up against his ear. He waved briefly at Jacob, then returned to whatever pressing matter was occurring on his phone. Jacob could tell from the way Shmuel swung between Yiddish to English, and the soft coo of words that fell from his lips, that he was talking to his wife, Chava. He must have come to the roof to get some quiet.

Shmuel finished his call, hanging up the phone.

"How's Chava?" Jacob asked.

"She's good." Shmuel beamed proudly. "Can't sleep, but good."

"But everything else with the pregnancy is going okay?"

"Baruch Hashem." His smile was all teeth. "Another month and we'll have a baby."

Jacob was happy for his friend. "Well, please tell Chava not to worry. I'll have you back home in France in no time."

"I'm not worried," Shmuel said, digging his thumbs into his pockets. "Not about Chava, anyway. So nu? What are you doing on the roof all alone?"

"I just needed some quiet."

"Quiet?" Shmuel raised one eyebrow. "How very unlike the Jacob Greenberg I know. Why are you *really* on the roof, huh? It couldn't be because you're thinking about our little matzah ball?"

"I'm not thinking about—"

"Jacob," Shmuel interrupted him. "Lie to yourself all you want. But do me a favor, okay? As your friend and business partner of over a decade who's risked everything with you on this Matzah Ball...don't lie to me."

It was a fair statement. Jacob breathed deeply, feeling the cold winter air fill up his lungs. Shmuel and he were close to the same age, yet Shmuel had a wisdom to him that came from life experience. From being married, and raising children, and being committed to something other than himself. Jacob wanted to understand him.

"How did you know Chava was the one?" Jacob asked.

"Chava-la?" Shmuel said, thinking back on the question. "We were a *shidduch*. Her mama talked to my mama, who talked to the matchmaker. Eventually, we agreed to meet for coffee."

"But you must have had a dozen matches," Jacob pressed him. "How did you know Chava was the one? Beyond the first date?"

Shmuel played with the bottom of his chin. "She yelled at me."

"She yelled at you?"

"On our first date." Shmuel beamed at the memory. "Told me I was being rude to the waitress. Threatened to leave me right then and there. I knew, at that very moment, we were perfect for each other."

"That, seriously...makes no sense."

Shmuel shrugged. "You know what *bashert* is?"

"It's like a soul mate."

"How very modern of you," Shmuel teased. "*Bashert* literally means *destiny*."

"Isn't that the same thing?"

"Not exactly. Soul mate...it's a movie concept. It's the idea that you fall in love with someone, and off you go, living happily ever after. But in Judaism, that's not the point of finding your *bashert*."

"So what is the point?"

"Your other half exists to make you better. She exists to complete something you lack, and vice versa. You challenge each other, like *chavruta*, two blades which sharpen each other. But that's different than love, Jacob. In some ways, it's more powerful. Because only your *bashert*, your other half, can fill up what you lack…and help you fulfill your destiny."

"So what you're trying to say is that Chava yelling at you was something you needed?"

Shmuel sighed. "I'm not the most thoughtful man, Jacob. I get focused on something, and I forget everything else going on around me. But Chava-la, she makes me thoughtful. She makes me aware of the waitress in the restaurant, even when all I want to do is get the check and go home. She doesn't let me get away with anything. Because of her, I'm a better man."

Jacob didn't know Shmuel before he was married, but he had seen for himself how he had softened over the years. The way he rushed home for his children, or spoke softly to Chava over the phone, promising her the world. Shmuel could be a *nudge*, pushy and grating, but he was also a bona fide *mensch*.

"Rachel is good for you," Shmuel said definitively. "She's right for you."

"She's not who you think, Shmuel."

"And you? You're such a prize, Mr. Perfect?"

"I'm not perfect."

"But you don't need anybody, right?"

Jacob retreated into silence. He had learned early on people were unreliable. Loving someone would only lead to heartbreak. It was a belief cemented throughout the course of his life.

"Jacob," Shmuel said quietly. "When your mother died, you didn't even tell me."

Jacob defended himself. "You barely even knew my mother."

"I knew *you*," Shmuel said, refusing to back down. "What did you think, huh? You think I wouldn't care that your mother had passed? You think I wouldn't have bothered to come to the funeral, or to sit with you during shiva? At the very least, you could have given Chava-la the opportunity to make you a kugel. But you never want to give anybody the chance to even remotely let you down! You can't live that way, Jacob. You certainly can't have a marriage like that, either."

Jacob felt the words pressing against his chest. "She's not honest, Shmuel. I can't have a relationship with somebody incapable of telling me the truth."

"Maybe not," he said, seriously considering the question. "But she was the first person I ever saw you truly rely on, Jacob. You handed over the reins of your Matzah Ball to her completely. You gave up control, trusting someone else to help you with the problems in your life. That's not like you, Jacob. But when Rachel is around, you're different. She changes you. She makes you better. That has to mean something."

Jacob nodded reluctantly. His friend was right.

"Listen," Shmuel said, glancing down at his watch. "We still have fifteen minutes before candle lighting. I'm gonna go downstairs. Check that Morty Schweitzer isn't dismantling our event for parts. But think about what I said, okay? We don't always get a second chance—or a third chance, or a fourth chance—to fulfill our destiny."

Shmuel departed. Jacob stood on the roof alone, staring over the expanse of Manhattan. His heart ached. His soul longed for something, someone, tangible and real. A person to call his own and struggle through this broken world with.

And yet, when he thought of that person, when he envisioned himself standing at the end of an aisle, a *huppah* over his head, waiting for his *bashert* to walk down the aisle, he only saw Rachel. Rachel, his other half, his destiny. She was the *shamash*, the spark of light that set him ablaze and made him better.

What a shame that for all the times fate threw them together, they could never make their relationship work.

39

Rachel tumbled onto the carpet. Spinning from her fall, she pushed a tangle of bangs out of her eyes and shook herself to her senses.

She had made it inside the Four Seasons. Now she just needed to find Jacob.

Adrenaline coursed through her veins. Rising from the floor, she made her way toward the elevators. A young mother and her daughter were waiting nearby. Rachel approached, and the mother's mouth gaped open in horror. It was not every day a woman in a ball gown entered a hotel through a window.

"Excuse me," the woman stammered, pulling her daughter closer. "Are you okay?"

"I'm great!" Rachel said, truly meaning it. "I'm in love!"

"Oh…" The woman smiled politely. "Well, that's nice."

Rachel took off. Pushing her way past the elevators, she found an internal staircase often used by hotel staff to move between floors. Rachel reasoned rather quickly that it would be safer than the elevators, which the guests were using. She pushed open the door and flew down the first flight.

Her heart floated along with her toes as they *snap-snap-snapped* down the steps. There was so much hope in her heart. And then, tragedy. Goliath and his men were at the bottom of the staircase. Rachel ducked behind a banister.

"Hey," Goliath said, speaking into his radio. "Any sign of her?"

"No, boss," a voice boomed back.

"You take the front entrance. I'll head up the stairs."

Rachel bit her lower lip, her heart sinking. She needed to think fast. Quietly she pushed open the door leading to the second floor and found herself in a familiar location. Conference rooms with stunning glass doors stretched down the hall and overlooked the busy front lobby.

Rachel had just enough time to peek over the side without being noticed. Her stomach turned at the sight. It was like something out of one of Mickey's video games. Goliath had spawned, and a million tiny henchmen were swarming the location, seeking her doom. She was just about to give up when another sight caught her eye, causing her heart to skip a beat.

Jacob was exiting from the elevator.

"Jacob!" Rachel shouted, waving from her vantage point. "Over here!"

It was no use. He was too busy looking at his phone. His mind clearly on other things, he had missed her completely. Still, her outburst had drawn attention. A few of Goliath's henchmen looked up. Rachel ducked down.

Perched on her heels, she waited, listening for the footsteps of guards to come racing up the stairs. She was relieved when that didn't happen. None of them seemed to have heard her. Still, she needed to get downstairs without being noticed.

Crawling on her knees, the sequins on her dress scraping against the carpet, she made her way down the row of conference rooms on the second floor. She had no idea how she was going to get downstairs into the Matzah Ball, and to Jacob. She just knew she needed to keep moving. And then, victory. Sitting in the last conference room, propped up on a chair like it was waiting for her, was the matzah ball costume.

Rachel beamed. Rising to her feet, she entered the conference room and took a careful accounting of the costume. It did not look good. Then again, she had gone full whack-a-mole on the thing. It wore the evidence of its abuse. Its once rotund body was misshapen and deflated. Its mouth had morphed into nothing but a small red line, which paired disturbingly well with a cyclops-like eye. It also smelled terrible. The costume was a disaster by any stretch of the imagination, but Rachel wasn't planning on wearing it.

"I'm sorry," she said, grabbing it by the belly. "But you owe me one."

Gathering her courage, she returned to the half wall that overlooked the first-floor lobby. She took a deep breath and thought back to Toby, to all the Christmas characters Rachel had ever written, fighting so bravely for their happy endings. And then Rachel hurled the costume straight over the ledge of the second floor.

It floated down to the first-floor lobby with all the grace of a brick. In the process, it tangled with the Christmas tree, hovering there on the branches of the evergreen before taking half the silver and blue Christmas ornaments down to the ground with it. With a splatter of matzah and glitter, it landed in the center of the lobby.

The crowd gasped and turned. Rachel cringed. She had not wanted to destroy a Christmas tree, but simply create a distraction. Still, the Matzah Ball costume had served its purpose. With all eyes on the deflated costume, she bolted down the stairs. She had just enough time to make it past the tree when she heard Goliath's voice booming once again.

"Hey, you!" he shouted. "You in the blue ball gown! Stop right there!"

Rachel squealed but did not stop. Darting through the maze of hallways and back rooms, she attempted to lose him. It was no use. Every time she turned, another one of his henchmen appeared. She twisted right, moved left, sprinted down halls and ducked into closets. Eventually she made her way to the kitchen.

The coast was clear. Rachel grabbed a white apron, throwing it on. The disguise did little to hide the mermaid gown sashaying around her pink fuzzy socks, but she was determined. The main event room lay just beyond the kitchen. Grabbing a tray of latkes, she pretended to blend in with the waitstaff as she approached the door.

She was close now. So close she could hear music. Hebrew mixed with techno blasted through the air. Her heart raced. She stepped into the main event room.

Blue and white lights circled as special effects designed to look like flames crawled up the walls and formed explosions of light. It was epic. Spectacular. But she didn't have time to gawk. Rachel was on a mission. And guards were everywhere.

Tearing off her apron, she put the tray down and began hunting through the ballroom. The place was packed. She knew that somewhere among all the special effects, acrobats and fancy dresses was Mickey. And her parents. She just didn't know where they were. Still, if she found any one of them, her chances of getting arrested tonight would decrease substantially.

"Excuse me," she said, ducking underneath shoulders. "I just need to get through."

Thankfully, nobody noticed her. The entire audience was too busy, eyes focused on the stage, to pay attention to some Matzah Ball fugitive. Rachel kept moving, careful not to get elbowed in the face or draw the attention of the guards. When the light show finally dimmed and a moment of blackness fell over the crowd, she used the opportunity to slip up a ramp and make her way backstage.

She just needed to find Jacob. She just needed to explain… well, everything. Her eyes darted across the backstage area, packed with musicians chatting quietly, waiting for their set. And then Rachel's heart spun wildly. In the distance, on the other side of the stage, stood Jacob and her parents. She could just make them out beyond the curtains.

Rachel rose up on tiptoe, waving wildly, trying to grab their attention. Suddenly she realized she was cornered. Goliath and his men stood behind her, Tasers outstretched. None of them looked remotely amused.

"I can explain," Rachel said, attempting to appeal to their belief in love. "You see, Jacob and I, we have this sort of strange summer camp history and—"

"You can explain it to the police," Goliath interrupted her. "Now, you need to come with me."

Rachel stepped back. The music began to crescendo. The back curtains on the stage flew open, and the ten-foot menorah that Jacob and Rachel had so painstakingly constructed together came into view. A round of applause erupted into the air. Jacob and her parents stepped onto the main stage.

There was nowhere left to hide.

"Please don't let them Taser me!" Rachel screamed as she exploded onto the main stage. With Goliath hot on her trail and nowhere else to turn, she found herself falling into Jacob's arms.

Baruch Hashem. He felt good.

Not only was he preventing her from taking one thousand volts of electricity through her sequined back, he looked amazing. Jacob was born to wear a tux.

"Sir," Goliath and his men were shouting. "Step away from the girl!"

"What's going on?" Jacob asked.

"We caught her breaking into the Matzah Ball."

Jacob glanced curiously between Rachel and his security team. The poor man obviously had no idea what was going on.

"Please," Rachel begged, her mouth going dry. "Tell them I belong here."

"It's okay," Jacob said. "I know her."

Goliath sighed, waving his men back. With the threat of being violently apprehended fading into the background, Rachel stepped away from Jacob. It was then that she saw the full horror of the scene laid out before her. From her vantage point on the stage, she could see into the audience. Every single person had their phone out and was recording her.

She saw her parents standing on the floating staircase, midway to the *shamash*. Meeting their eyes, she felt the weight of her love for them. She did not want to disappoint them. But she also couldn't imagine losing Jacob.

And then a word drifted up from deep within her chest. *Bashert*. He was her other half.

Jacob leaned into her, whispering. "What the hell are you doing here?"

"I need to talk to you."

"Now?" he asked, looking around.

Rachel stammered. "I was afraid I wouldn't get a chance before you returned to France."

Jacob pursed his lips and said nothing. It was clear that he was still angry. It suddenly struck Rachel that she should leave. Turn right around and go into some sort of Matzah Ball Protection Program. She was just about to do it, too, when a familiar voice broke through the silence of the room.

"Excuse me," Mickey yelled, pushing his way through the crowd. "Coming through."

Mickey landed with a ferocious huff at the front of the stage. Meeting his eyes gave Rachel courage. He didn't have to say a single word. She knew she was supported. Whatever happened next was her choice.

She was ready.

Standing before the mic, Rachel began slowly. "You...you all know me as Rachel Rubenstein-Goldblatt. You look at me, and you see this nice Jewish girl...the daughter of a world-famous rabbi, and product of a Jewish school education...and all of that is true. I am that person. I am totally, one-hundred-and-ten percent invested in my Jewish community and faith. But I also love… Christmas."

A gasp went up from the crowd. She knew she was rambling, yet the words, which had once felt hard, started to come easily.

"I love the lights," she continued, admitting everything. "I love the trees, and the music. I love Santa. I love the escape of Christmas movies, and the scent of gingerbread cookies baking in the oven. And for my whole life, Christmas was this magic place…this secret world that I got to go off to…and no one expected me to be Rachel Rubenstein-Goldblatt. Because the rest of the world actually knows me as… Margot Cross."

A full-out uproar exploded from the crowd. She heard somebody curse. Felt the snap of a thousand flashbulbs from various reporters and guests. It was official. Her lifetime of living in the Christmas closet was over.

"I'm the bestselling author of over twenty Christmas romance novels and four made-for-TV movies. And, for a long time, I was okay with being a ribbon. I was okay with hiding all these important and essential parts of myself, like my career, and my chronic illness, and all the things I loved and cared about…" She looked at Jacob. "Until I met you."

Jacob finally spoke. "Me?"

"You make me want to be honest."

The uproar from the crowd turned into a gentle sigh. Rachel could feel the tide turning.

"When I first saw you again," she continued, "I thought you were still that horrible little boy I met at Camp Ahava. I thought you just wanted to torture me, and embarrass me, making me wear that stupid matzah ball costume all around your event. And yes, I only wanted a ticket because I needed to write a book about Hanukkah. But then I started to get to know you. I started to learn about you, and your mom, and your bubbe, and why Hanukkah was such an important holiday to you. And I began to see you for who you are, Jacob. You're not a horrible person. You're not the Hanukkah Grinch. You're kind. And philanthropic. You go out of your way for people. For me. And you deserve better than someone who lies to you."

"What is the point of this, Rachel?"

"The point is," she said, stomping her foot. "I love you."

She waited for him to say something.

He fixed a steely-eyed gaze upon her. She had no idea what he was thinking. She couldn't read beyond his pursed lips and thoughtfully furrowed eyebrows. If he hated her, she wouldn't blame him. She had just ruined his Matzah Ball.

"I'm sorry," she whispered, embarrassed. "I thought maybe… you felt the same."

She excused herself. Stepping down from the stage, she passed Mickey, rushing to escape. All eyes were upon her as she slunk toward the door. She needed to get out of here. Leave this venue, burn her dress and repress the memory of Jacob Greenberg forever. Otherwise, her heart would never recover.

"Not so fast," Jacob called out. "You just stop right there, Rachel Rubenstein-Goldblatt!"

Rachel twisted around slowly. "Wh-what?"

Jacob jumped off the stage, meeting her halfway across the dance floor. "What do you think you're doing, huh? You think you can just come here, make a huge scene, and then walk out on me?"

"No, I—"

"Because you stood me up at the Camp Ahava dance eighteen years ago…and I'd be a damn fool to ever let you walk out on me again."

Rachel blinked, trying to wrap her head around his words. And then, he kissed her. *Jacob kissed her.*

Grabbing her by the waist, he pulled her into him, planting those two perfect lips straight upon her own. She melted into his arms, strong yet gentle. They fit together. Like two puzzle pieces. Complicated edges. Rough angles and strange colors.

But when they came together, they created a picture that was just right.

The crowd broke into cheers and applause. The negative nellies, all the darkness of their naysayers, disappeared in an outright explosion of love. Rachel pulled away from Jacob, waving off their goodwill.

Mickey appeared, throwing his arms around her. "I'm so proud of you!" he said, tears in his eyes, before turning to Jacob. "You take good care of my girl, okay?"

"I promise."

"And you," Mickey whispered in her ear. "I better be your damn maid of honor!"

Rachel nodded. Mickey released her, and she leaned into Jacob. He put one arm around her, pulling her close. She felt safe in her honesty with Jacob. Somewhere between a matzah ball costume, a bedazzled wheelchair and a pair of earrings, she had found the space to be herself. Glancing over to Goliath, she saw him wipe away a tear.

"What happened?" Rabbi Goldblatt's voice came over the sound system. "I thought we were lighting Hanukkah candles?" It was clear he was talking to his wife, oblivious to what was happening down on the dance floor below.

Dr. Rubenstein responded, "Our daughter is a world-famous Christmas romance novelist."

"Ah," Rabbi Goldblatt said. "I thought we knew that."

"Of course we knew that! But now, she has finally found the courage to tell us."

Bittersweet tears filled Rachel's eyes. She could not believe what she was hearing. All this time, her mother and father had known the truth. How had she not seen it?

Glancing up at her parents, pride beaming from their faces, she understood. She had been too wrapped up in her own lies, too bound up by the *meshugas* of the unreliable narrator living inside her head to see what was always standing before her. Rachel was loved. She was loved unconditionally. For all her bad days, disappointments and disasters...she had never been invalid.

"So what do you say?" Jacob spoke to the crowd. "Should we light candles?"

The audience responded with a unanimous "Yes!"

Mickey, Jacob and Rachel returned to the stage. Rabbi Goldblatt said the prayers—plus a *shehecheyanu*, which seemed particularly fitting on this night of unusual firsts—and proceeded to light the last candles of Hanukkah.

The flames illuminated the room as the music began again, lifting into a swirl of eighties pop remixed with Sephardi rap. Surrounded by people she cared about—her world and her community—Rachel's authentic self shone as bright as the eight flames dancing upon the menorah.

From: Dr. Rubenstein <drrubenstein@rgfertility.com>
To: Rachel Rubenstein-Goldblatt <rache1RG2345@gmail.com>

Sent: Tue, 21 December
Subject: FROM MOM AND DAD

Rachel,

Daddy and I just wanted to let you know that we are very proud of you. Don't worry about anything at the shul. We love you, and believe it or not, several congregants are fans of your books!

We never wanted to put pressure on you. Only to see you happy.

Love,
Ema and Aba

PS: Will you be spending more time with Jacob this week? It might be nice of you to show him around town…you know, a woman can have excellent egg quality up until the age of 35.

Jacob Greenberg was going to miss his flight. And he was completely fine with that.

Standing three deep in line at Rachel's favorite coffee spot on the Upper West Side, he glanced at his watch. It was eight fifteen on Tuesday morning, and his phone was going nuts. "Two venti coffees. Black," Jacob said, reaching into his pocket as he glanced at a plate full of sufganiyot. "And three of those jelly doughnuts."

The woman at the counter set about filling his order, and Jacob picked up his ringing phone.

"Jacob!" Shmuel said on the other end of the line. "*Baruch Hashem!* What a beautiful morning!"

"It is," Jacob said, grabbing the coffees and bag full of goodies and then walking toward the door.

"The phones will not stop ringing off the hook!" Shmuel said, partly in disbelief. "Have you seen the news?"

"I just woke up, Shmuel."

"Everyone is talking about our Matzah Ball, and the world-famous rabbi's daughter turned bestselling Christmas novelist! Did you know she was Margot Cross, and so famous?"

Jacob smiled. "I had an inkling."

"Well, she saved our Matzah Ball. Her, and you, and that ooh-la-la kiss! People can't get enough of it. Profits are through the roof! We'll have more than enough to pay back our investors. Morty is thrilled, of course, and everyone wants to know what your next big idea is."

"My next big idea?" Jacob thought about it as he sprinted up Broadway, getting closer to Rachel's apartment. "I think I'm going to take some time off."

Shmuel laughed. "That sounds very unlike the Jacob Greenberg I know. Then again, I'm sitting in an airport lounge alone. By the way, thanks for the extra bag."

"I never gave you that bag, Shmuel."

"You didn't?"

"You know what?" Jacob said, laughing to himself. "Keep the bag."

"Really?"

"Yeah." Jacob pushed through the swinging doors of the highrise on the Upper West Side. After nodding to the doorman, he walked in and entered the elevator. "Use it in good health. Fill it with all the kosher baked goods you want. Consider it a small token of my appreciation for all your help with the Matzah Ball...and in life."

"You're a real *mensch*, Jacob Greenberg."

"One other thing," Jacob said, landing on the fourth floor. "This year, I want to do fifty-fifty on the proceeds to charity. Half to MS research and causes, and half to ME/CFS charities."

"Sounds like a good use of money."

"I agree."

Jacob came to Rachel's apartment. The door was unlocked. The lights were on in the kitchen and living room.

"Hey, Shmuel," Jacob said. "Let me call you back, okay?"

Jacob ended the call and began searching for Rachel. Checking the bedroom first, he was surprised to find it empty. The bed was unmade, but Rachel was nowhere to be found. After the night they'd had, he had expected her to be resting.

Jacob found Rachel in her office. Still in her pajamas, her hair an adorable struggle of wayward curls, she was bent over her computer, obsessively reading.

"Look at this comment on the article in *Holiday Romance World*!" Rachel said, pointing at the computer. "'I used to like Margot Cross's books...until I found out that she was Jewish. Now I realize there was always a certain magic missing from her stories. Can you believe this woman...trying to steal Christmas?'"

"Turn off the computer, Rachel."

Rachel twisted around in her seat. "I'm trending on Twitter, Jacob. There are videos of me exploding onto the stage and confessing everything all over the internet. There are memes of us kissing!"

"Well—" he laid the coffee down on the desk beside her "—it was quite the spectacle."

She fixed him with a frown. "I'm glad you think it's funny, considering that thanks to me and my massive confession in front of the entire world...your Matzah Ball is a huge and smashing success."

"It's true," he admitted. "I was thinking of selling my apartment."

"I hate you."

"What?" he teased her. "I'll need something bigger."

"Right."

"Something more appropriate for a wife, three or four children, a full-time nanny, and a cat named Paree."

Rachel feigned sadness. "I should probably tell you the truth then, Jacob."

"Oh, boy."

"I'm a dog person."

"And a dog," he said, and smiled back, unfazed. "Drink your coffee."

Rachel let her fingers graze the top of the cup before lifting it up to take a quick drink.

God, she was beautiful. The sun streaming through the windows, highlighting the hints of red in her messy hair. The cute way one of the buttons on her pink pajamas had popped open. She was completely herself. Honest. He was so very grateful that everything in his life had brought him to this moment.

"Oh, my Gawd!" Rachel suddenly screamed after turning back to her computer. "Look at what this person is saying about me on Twitter!"

"Okay," Jacob said, standing up to find the power cord. "Enough."

"No! Seriously! They're calling me a *mamzer*."

"I don't even know what that means."

"It's horrible," she said, shaking her head. "It's a horrible thing to call a Jewish person."

Jacob was tired of watching her get tortured by strangers on the internet. He pulled out the power cord. The entire computer shut down.

"What did you just do?" Rachel asked, twisting in her seat.

"I turned it off."

"Jacob!" she said, red with anger. "How could you do that?"

"Because it doesn't matter."

"But—"

He pulled his chair closer to her. "Look at me."

She met his eyes. He knew she was nervous. It was scary, facing the world as yourself. Especially when you were such a thoughtful and sensitive person. But he loved her. He loved everything about her. And she, quite remarkably, loved him. He would always take care of her.

"They hate me," she said sadly. "I'll never publish again."

"You will," he said, taking her hands. "Because you are a great writer, and a born storyteller. But right now, I think you should rest."

"Rest?"

"Vacation." He smiled. "With me."

She scoffed, shaking her head. "I can't take a vacation now. They're saying I've started a war on Christmas! They're saying—"

"Rachel," he said again, "it doesn't matter."

"But—"

"I love you."

She sighed. Glanced at her computer, and then back to Jacob. He ran his fingers across her knuckles. The tiny frown on her face was replaced by a soft smile. Jacob couldn't resist the temptation of her lips any longer. Leaning in, he kissed her again. A soft moan escaped her at his touch. Her neck arched upward, and she angled her entire body toward him.

It was him. And her. And nothing else mattered.

Rachel pulled back from their kiss, offering up a mischievous smile in his direction.

"Screw 'em," she said.

"Screw 'em," he agreed, before lifting her from the chair and taking her back to bed.

From: Rachel Rubenstein-Goldblatt <justrachel@rrgbooks.com>
To: Lisa Brown <l.brown@cachingliteraryagency.com>

Sent: Wed, 17 March
Subject: New Book

Lisa,

How the heck are you doing?!?

I realize I've been MIA for a while. (Paris with the man you love will do that to you, you know?) But we're back in New York, and I've written something new. Believe it or not, it's a Hanukkah romance. It's called *The Matzah Ball*.

Manuscript is attached. Would love to hear what you think.

Rachel

Epilogue

One Year Later

"Get away from those rugalach, Jacob Greenberg!"

Rachel slapped Jacob's hand away from the tray fresh out of the oven. It was the first night of Hanukkah, and if Jacob had his way, there wouldn't be any rugalach left for noshing on that evening.

"I'm sorry," Jacob said, raising his hands up in open surrender. "I couldn't help myself."

"You can help yourself," Rachel said, pulling the oozing cookie from his lips.

Laying them on a plate, she counted out three different types of homemade cookies. Toby would be arriving from China tonight. Rachel had been telling her soon-to-be bubbe for weeks, via Zoom calls, how she had been working on a special twist to her top-secret rugalach recipe.

"Go on." Jacob grinned in her direction. "I know you're dying to ask."

She bit her lower lip. "Are they as good as I think?"

He reached for another rugalach. "Let me just try one more—"

She slapped his hand again.

"All right," he laughed. "They're perfect."

"Really?" She squealed in delight. "I've finally perfected my bagel-lach recipe?"

"More than perfected it," Jacob admitted. "How did you ever think to add chives to the cream cheese? It's like…the perfect mixture of savory and sweet."

"Wait till you try my pastrami egg-roll-lachs."

Jacob sighed. "You had me at pastrami."

Yes, there was something different about Rachel's rugalach recipe. Just like there was something different about her apartment. Because now, instead of looking like she had robbed a Christmas store, Rachel had decked out her two-bedroom apartment on the Upper West Side in Hanukkah decor.

Menorahs of all different shapes and sizes decorated the countertops and tables. Silver-and-blue garland hung from the ceiling. But most impressive of all was the Hanukkah bush, covered in tiny Stars of David ornaments, which sat perched in the corner. Not that any of it was exactly kosher. But it was Rachel's choice, totally and completely.

Rachel laid her hands flat against the flour-covered apron Jacob was wearing. "And I really appreciate your help with the cooking, too."

He smiled. "I enjoy taking care of you."

"And I," she said, leaning into him, "enjoy taking care of you."

Rachel folded in for another kiss. They had been going long distance for the last twelve months, with Jacob splitting his time between New York and Paris. Though Rachel still wasn't ready to upgrade to a larger apartment, she had begun thinking seriously about the possibility of children.

Everything felt easier with Jacob's love and support. Also, his money. Greenberg Entertainment was a raging success, now firmly established on two continents, with Shmuel, his fifty-fifty partner, running the French side of things. After the wedding, Jacob would be moving permanently to New York.

"Okay," Mickey said, appearing from her office. "Let's save the kissing for the *yichud* room." He held up another menorah. "Where do you want me to put this?"

"That's my bubbe's," Jacob explained. "It was a wedding present. She wanted us to have it."

Rachel took it from Mickey. "Then I think it's the perfect *chanukiyah* to use for our first night. Let's light it when everybody gets here."

"I love that idea," Jacob agreed.

"Agreed!" Mickey said, before turning to the Alexa in the kitchen, ordering it to play some Hanukkah music. "Now, let's get this wedding weekend started!"

The sounds of NezGadol floated through the apartment. Jacob held out his hand to Rachel, and the two began to dance, periodically interrupting their private choreography to sashay across the room with Mickey.

It was an amazing thing, really. To be accepted, completely, for who you were. To find your friends…and your *bashert*. For all their flaws, mistakes and oddities, they were people who made the world a better and brighter place to live in. They lit up the room with love and support for each other.

"You're not nervous, are you?" Rachel asked, gazing into Jacob's dark eyes.

"Why would I be nervous?"

"Oh, I don't know. Maybe because we're getting married?"

"I've waited nineteen long years to marry you, Rachel."

"How very biblical."

"Now, now," Mickey corrected them both, referring to the well-known love story from Genesis. "The original Jacob only waited fourteen years to marry Rachel. So, frankly, our Jacob gets the prize for patience."

"You know what they say—" Jacob dipped her again. "Good things come to those who wait."

"And wait," Mickey teased. "And wait, and wait..."

"But everybody gets their blessing in the end," Rachel said, spinning around, "because everybody deserves a happy ending."

"Amen," Jacob said.

"And *Selah*!" Mickey added.

There was a knock at the front door. Rachel turned toward the entryway, her heart still swinging wildly in time with the music. Jacob took Mickey's hand and continued their dance around the room. Rachel opened the door to see her mother holding a large white garment bag up in the air. For once, the woman was expected.

"Ema!" Rachel beamed. "Is that it?"

"All ready for Sunday," her mother said, before gasping at the sight of Jacob. "*Chas v'chalilah!* What are you doing? Jacob can't see the dress before the big day."

"He can't see the dress," Rachel reminded her. "It's covered in plastic."

Dr. Rubenstein shot Jacob a mock scowl. "No peeking."

"I wouldn't dare."

Dr. Rubenstein entered the apartment. Handing the wedding dress off to Mickey, she raised one curious eyebrow at the state of her apartment. The Hanukkah garland trailing from the ceiling. The Hanukkah bush, loaded down with ornaments. NezGadol playing in the background.

She moved to Rachel's coffee table. On it sat a box of books. Her eyes widened as she lifted one up from the pile, reading the words splattered across the hardcover in flashy blue-and-white print.

"'*The Matzah Ball*,'" Dr. Rubenstein read aloud. "'By Rachel Rubenstein-Goldblatt.'"

Jacob radiated pride. "They think it's going to be a bestseller."

"It doesn't matter whether it is or not," Rachel said firmly. "Because it's my story."

Her mother cupped her cheek. Tears welled up in Rachel's eyes. She had fought hard for this happy ending.

Rachel had lived a decade of her life in secret, certain that her entire world would come crashing down if anybody found out the truth about her disease or her career. Instead—the irony struck her—it was the exact opposite. Everything good in her life had grown out of being honest.

She didn't quite understand it. But glancing back at Jacob, she wondered if the journey was always meant to lead her here.

"Enough of this," Rachel said, sucking back any trace of sadness. "It's our wedding this weekend, and I demand happiness. Come on!" She raced to her Alexa, blasting her Hanukkah tunes even louder. "Let's dance."

Jacob grabbed Rachel, taking her for another spin. Mickey and Dr. Rubenstein joined in, laughter and joy filling the room. The scent of rugalach filled the apartment. And in her office, across the desk and displayed on every windowsill, sat Rachel's new collection of menorahs.

From: Rachel Rubenstein-Goldblatt <justrachel@rrgbooks.com>
To: Dr. Rubenstein <drrubenstein@rgfertility.com>

Sent: Sun, 9 June
Subject: Doctor?

Ema,

I was wondering if you could recommend a good obstetrician in the city?

Love,
Rachel

PS: We don't need any more food.

Acknowledgments

It's hard to believe that less than a decade ago, I was lying in my bed thinking, "I will never spend two hours walking around a museum again." But here we are! A happy ending...or beginning, depending on how you want to look at things.

To my brilliant editor, Emily Ohanjanians, at Mira. Thank you for answering questions, calming my anxiety, letting me ramble on about Judaism, and pulling out all the depth in my fun little story. Lots of editors can make a better book, but you've made a better book *and* a better writer.

Thank you to all the hardworking folks at Mira and Harlequin and HarperCollins who made space on the shelves for a Hanukkah romance. To all my foreign publishers, you took what was already a dream come true and launched it into the stratosphere.

Carolyn Forde and Marilyn Biderman, I don't know how two people can work so hard, and still keep things feeling fun and easy. I appreciate the quick responses, revision notes, publishing guidance and random photos of babka. Thank you for making all my dreams come true and not shirking, at all, over the thought of representing a disabled rabbinical-school dropout.

To Addison Duffy and Jasmine Lake, my film agents at UTA, thank you for falling in love with this story.

Thank you to all the people who have supported my writerly pursuits over forty years of my life. Mrs. Lokuta, my sixth-grade English teacher. You began this journey, and I am thrilled to be able to mention your name in the pages of my book. Lena Flaum, for reading countless pages and offering up your brilliant editorial skills. Jules Hucke, you are one of the most talented writers I know. I am so happy that we get to be debut buddies! Donna Everhart, for trading pages back in the day. Eileen Di-Giacomo, for providing help with social media.

My gratitude also goes out to the folks over at the Write for Harlequin Community, including Danica Favorite and everyone involved in #romanceincludesyou, for answering questions and cheering me on. To all the Jewish and chronically ill romance writers who came before me, thank you for paving the way for this book to exist. Also, to Laura Hillenbrand—because of you I believed I could write a book.

Thank you to ME Action, who have offered support during the publication process.

To our hardworking booksellers, librarians, bloggers, and bookstagrammers—you change the world by sharing these stories! Thank you to everyone reading this book, talking about this book, or sharing this book.

So much of what made The Matzah Ball possible had very little to do with writing. Instead, it was the people whose love pushed me forward during the darkest days of my life with ME/CFS.

Thank you to Rabbi Aaron Weininger and Rabbi Aviva Fellman, two of the best darn people I know. Aaron, you never once flinched at using the word *disabled*. Through your courage and example, I learned to use the word for myself. Aviva, I am so grateful you were the only other female to latch on to in Mechina Bible over a decade ago. Thank you for answering any questions I had during the writing of this book, and for show-ing up through all the good and bad of my life.

Also, to Rabbi Josh Sherwin, who spent ten years asking about my writing and so lovingly offered to read any darn thing I wrote, including romance. Your support over a decade—when I'm pretty sure most everyone had given up on me ever publishing—meant everything.

Thank you to my friends in the ME/CFS community, those I met online and those I met through advocacy efforts. It takes courage to stand up and tell your story, but you made me feel less alone in the world. My hope is that this book pays it forward.

To all my friends, online and in person, thank you for your encouragement and support over the years.

To my family, who I love more than anything. To my big sister, Evelyn Meltzer, who told me that a book deal was only a question of *when*. You never once doubted me. To my little sister, Dr. Danielle Meltzer Chesney, for holding my hope on some of the very worst days of my life. To my parents, Drs. Jeffrey and Leslie Meltzer. Thank you for never doubting that I was sick, for supporting me in any passion I pursued and for giving me a strong Jewish foundation.

To my extended family, the whole Maskuli-Sanchez clan, and all the *machatunim* that comes with marrying a Meltzer girl. Thank you to Karen Maskuli for being the most supportive mother-in-law in the world. Also, to the Chesney and Cohen families. Paul, we all miss you terribly, but I know you were partly responsible for getting this book published. To Phillip Stashin, my beloved uncle with cerebral palsy. Thank you for letting me use a little bit of your story to create Paul. I know you are up in heaven, lifting a finger.

There is no person on this list that deserves more appreciation than my husband, Xhevair Maskuli, who served as my primary caregiver during the two years I was homebound/bedbound.

Xhev, you are my *bashert* in every sense of the word. Thank you for teaching me the true meaning of unconditional love. Thank you for fighting for me, and believing in me, even on those days when I couldn't fight for myself.

Most people never saw those bad days, but I want to acknowledge them here. The way you would set up a hospital tray by my bed before leaving for work, my laptop and cup of coffee lovingly laid out. How you would wash my hair in the bathtub when I was too tired to do it myself. That you bought a wheelchair for me and rolled me all around the Renaissance Faire, so that I could finally leave the house. Through ten years of marriage, you never once blamed me. You never once got angry at me. You whispered in my ear that you needed me and loved me, and to hold on. You are the light that kept mine burning.

This book would not exist without you.

Finally, my gratitude to Hashem. You and I have wrestled much over the last fortysomething years. For a long time, I didn't understand what you wanted from me. I also told folks I was gonna kick you in the kneecaps when I got to heaven.

But when I look at the above acknowledgments—when I hold up all I have against all that I have lost—I can see how blessed I truly am. I am grateful for this journey. I am grateful for where it has led me. But nu? Maybe go a little easier on me in the future?

Author Note

Ten years ago, I made the difficult decision to drop out of rabbinical school. My ME/CFS had progressed to the point where even a part-time schedule was impossible, and in order to keep up the facade of normal, I was living on a cocktail of Red Bulls, coffee and prescription stimulants. I knew that if I continued pushing my body past what it was capable of, I would die.

I called my parents in a blubbering mess, my life fully falling apart, certain that they would be disappointed. Instead, my loving *ema* pointed out that I had never really been well enough to work as a rabbi full-time. My father followed up to my mother with this sage wisdom: "You should write a book—just not a Jewish one because no one reads those."

If you want to understand one of the connections between me and Rachel Rubenstein-Goldblatt, that's a good place to start. I have been sick for a very long time. I have been Jewish even longer. Somewhere in between both those events, I began writing. *The Matzah Ball* is a work of fiction. Its characters and scenarios are created fully from my imagination—but it is also my story.

And yet, at every stage of writing this book, I have been aware that there will be Jewish people and people with ME/

CFS whose experiences are different from my own. I want to acknowledge that here.

To the Jewish community, please know that this book was written from a place of love. It was written from all my best memories of Shabbat dinners, and Kiddush luncheons, and ridiculous Jewish singles events. It was written out of a true fondness for the variety of faces and personalities I have met along my path, and I did my best to reflect the diversity of our Jewish community in a joyous and loving way.

That being said, this story takes place in an Ashkenazi community. It is based on my experiences growing up as an Ashkenazi Jew in the Northeastern United States. It does not represent the wide and varied spectrum of Jewish experience, nor should any one book ever speak for all members of its community.

For *The Matzah Ball*, I was primarily interested in exploring the experience of Jacob, from a (shoddy) Hebrew school background, in contrast to Rachel, who went to Jewish day school. The reason for this is twofold. First and foremost, it reflects my experience with Judaism. Before I entered rabbinical school, I could *barely* read Hebrew.

Secondly, their stories allowed me to create a space on the page where both secular and observant Jews could find their footing.

This is why I believed the addition of extra Christmas material was important. It was not simply that I have always had a (not so secret!) love for the magic of the winter season; it is that many Jews do, in fact, celebrate Christmas. Like Mickey (and me!) they have non-Jewish parents, partners and relatives, and the reality is that there will be many Jews reading *The Matzah Ball* who feel more comfortable with Christmas than Jewish traditions.

For my more observant Jewish readers, I tried very hard to be as halachically accurate in my descriptions as possible. I also purposely included jokes that someone from a more religious background may recognize. I hope you enjoy these, and if I got something wrong—either because I had to omit something for time or, more likely, because I am a rabbinical school dropout—I hope you'll forgive me.

To the ME/CFS community...

Let me begin by saying, I see you. I know how much you have lost. I know how much you suffer. We still have a long way to go in terms of recognition and treatment, but I hope this book helps make your daily struggles, often hidden from the world, visible.

Rachel is a character based around my personal experience with ME/CFS. I have tried to be as truthful to my experience as possible, while at the same time crafting a hopeful and entertaining narrative tale.

However, and I feel it is important to reiterate this point, ME/CFS is a spectrum disease. There are people with ME/CFS that are much sicker than Rachel, and there are people with ME/CFS that have much milder cases than Rachel. This book is not representative of all patients; nor should it be held up as an example of what patients should be able to achieve.

ME/CFS causes significant functional impairment and a lower quality of life. It can strike anyone at any time. It affects men, women and children, and it is estimated that up to thirty million people worldwide have the disease. Twenty-five percent of patients are severe. Seventy-five percent of patients will not be able to work full-time. Yet, despite these staggering statistics, it is a disease that has been mischaracterized and stigmatized for decades.

It is this mischaracterization that leads directly to medical neglect. In the United States, less than one-third of medical schools teach about ME/CFS. Across the globe, in places like the UK and Sweden, ME/CFS patients are *still* being institutionalized, forcibly removed from their homes, their physical symptoms attributed to psychosomatic conditions. There is a crisis in clinical care and research funding, and patients are being abandoned.

I spent a long time debating using the name chronic fatigue syndrome in this book. Like many patients, I prefer the more medical sounding name, myalgic encephalomyelitis.

My decision became resolute when I developed a co-morbid condition during the writing of this book. For the first time in twenty years, I was once again maneuvering the medical system, searching for treatment, and at every medical appointment the same thing would happen. I would write ME/CFS on the intake form, and the doctor would point to the abbreviation and ask, "What's this?"

Inevitably, I would have to explain chronic fatigue syndrome.

Aside from a cure, I would like nothing more than the name of our disease to be changed, but until that day arrives, I will settle for people understanding what CFS is.

Finally, I would be remiss to end this note without talking about hope. Chronic illness brings you to your very lowest places. It robs you of choice. But just because your life is different doesn't mean it's bad. It doesn't mean it's over, either.

What is normal? I'm about to turn forty-two years old. I have been sick since I was a freshman in college. I know there was a time in my life when I woke up feeling well, when I woke up feeling rested, but I don't remember what that feels like anymore. You could look at my story and see all sorts of sadness. I've spent years homebound. I won't have children. I write through brain fog and pain, and will never finish rabbinical school. But I'm happy.

My life got smaller with chronic illness, but it was in those dark spaces, without the costumes and facades, that I learned to hold on to the most important things. The people who love me and who I love in return. Taking a walk on a perfect spring day, my puppy dog panting happily at my side. *Joy.* Whether this book sells a zillion copies or none doesn't matter. My life has worth. Yours does, too. *Do not give up.*

I hope you enjoyed my super-Jewy, chronically fabulous Hanukkah romance. To all my readers—thank you for spending your time with me. Thank you for giving me the chance to share this story.

My heart is full.

Resources

To learn more about ME/CFS, or to involve yourself in research and advocacy efforts, please see the following links:

SOLVE ME/CFS INITIATIVE
https://solvecfs.org/

ME ACTION
https://www.meaction.net/

The
Matzah
Ball

Jean Meltzer

Reader's Guide

mira

Questions for Discussion

1. Though they were both raised in the Jewish faith, Rachel and Jacob had very different upbringings. How do you think their childhoods influenced their characters as adults?

2. Rachel's family is Jewish, but she loves Christmas. Have you ever had an affinity for a holiday or event that your family didn't celebrate?

3. What did you think of Rachel's decision to hide her career from her family for most of her adult life? Would you hide something of importance from your family if you felt they wouldn't understand it?

4. Rachel and Mickey are best friends since forever. How did you feel about the way their friendship was depicted in the story? Do you have a friend you're as close with as they are with one another? What has that friendship meant to you in your life?

5. Living with chronic illness has affected Rachel's life in almost every way imaginable. What, if anything, did you

learn about myalgic encephalomyelitis, aka chronic fatigue syndrome?

6. Rachel feels frustrated that the more commonly known term for her illness, chronic fatigue syndrome, comes with a certain amount of stigma, and people don't take it seriously. Can you think of any other conditions that are treated similarly by the general public?

7. Both Rachel's mother and Jacob's bubbe tend to feed (or overfeed!) their loved ones. This is considered a common way to show affection in many cultures, including the Jewish culture. What are some traditions in your culture, and how are they expressed in your family?

8. Though Rachel and Jacob did not personally experience it, they are both influenced by the Holocaust in subtle ways. What are some ways in which that influence manifests itself? Are there any events in your family history that continue to influence you today, even though you did not directly experience them?

9. Rachel quotes Midrash, saying, "God only works through broken vessels." What do you think Rachel means when she says this? How do Rachel and Jacob both come to accept, and create meaning out of, their brokenness?

10. On Hanukkah, Jews use a *shamash*, one flame that lights all the candles on the *chanukiyah*. What are some of the ways that the characters in *The Matzah Ball* act like a *shamash*, spreading light to others?

11. What are some Jewish traditions and rituals you recognized while reading *The Matzah Ball*? Was there anything that surprised you? Are there any traditions you would like to learn more about or incorporate into your own life?

12. Who was your favorite character and why?

13. If you could cast the movie version of *The Matzah Ball*, who would you cast as the leads? How about the secondary characters?

If you enjoyed The Matzah Ball,
stay tuned for Jean Meltzer's
next irresistible romcom,

Mr. Perfect on Paper
coming in 2022!

When third-generation matchmaker
Dara Rabinowitz finds her search for love thrust into the spotlight
after her grandmother outs her list for
"The Perfect Jewish Husband" on live television,
a nationwide hunt ensues. But finding Mr. Perfect on Paper may
mean giving up on the charming—and totally not Jewish—reporter
following her story…

Turn the page for a sneak peek.

Dara Rabinowitz was certain that her Bubbe Miriam had finally lost it. They were on live television, after all. Smack-dab in the middle of an interview with the deliciously handsome head anchor of *Good News New York*, Christopher Steadfast. It was not the time to be pulling out drawings from one of her many nieces and nephews.

It was only when Dara looked past the poorly rendered images of kitty cats and flowers that her heart stopped. She knew exactly what her grandmother was holding. It was a list created drunkenly with her older sister Shana on the evening of her thirty-fourth birthday. It was also a list that was never supposed to see the light of day.

Dara's heart stopped at the realization. Time slowed as the heat of the cameras bared down on her, beads of sweat gathering at the nape of her neck. A cameraman stepped into frame as her grandmother held the crinkled paper high in the air for everyone in the studio and watching at home to see for themselves.

THE PERFECT JEWISH HUSBAND

Christopher Steadfast returned to his seat behind the interview desk. "So, Miriam…what do you have there?"

Miriam smiled wide. "My beautiful and extremely wealthy granddaughter has created a list of everything she would like in a future Jewish husband. I was wondering if anybody would be interested in hearing it?"

Dara decided to stop this fiasco. "I don't think anybody is really interested in hearing—"

Chris interrupted her. "I'm interested."

Dara swallowed hard. Even though she had just met Christopher Steadfast three hours ago in the greenroom, she had been watching him for years on *Good News New York*. His outright unwillingness to put an end to this *balagan* felt like a personal betrayal.

Dara quickly considered alternative options. She could snap the piece of paper from the old woman's hands and tackle her to the ground, before tearing up that stupid piece of paper. On second thought, she decided against it.

Miriam Rabinowitz was not just her beloved grandmother, she was one of the most respected *schadchanit*, or matchmakers, in their Jewish community, personally responsible for the creation of over three hundred Jewish marriages. Besides, how would it look for Dara—her granddaughter and creator of the world's most successful Jewish dating app, J-Mate—to be violently attacking her eighty-nine-year-old grandmother on national television?

There was no other option. Dara would simply have to power through this nightmare of a scenario. She glanced beyond the cameras to find a clock located on the anterior wall. Situated just beneath the control room, it counted down the time left in their segment with blinking red numbers. *Two minutes left.* How much damage could her bubbe really do in 120 seconds?

"Please." Chris smiled, resting his chiseled chin on one perfectly situated fist. "I'm dying to know what the very single creator of J-Mate is looking for in a future spouse."

With permission granted, Bubbe Miriam returned her attention to the crumpled piece of paper in her hands. Putting on the reading glasses dangling around her neck, her hands may have been shaky but her voice never wavered once.

"Well, obviously—" Miriam fixed an accusatory eyebrow in the direction of Christopher Steadfast "—he needs to be Jewish."

Chris smiled, unaffected. "Obviously."

Miriam continued onward. "'He should be a lawyer or a doctor. Preferably a doctor, though, because it's always good to have someone in the family who can write prescriptions.'"

Chris squinted, amused. "Does it actually say that?"

"Of course."

Bubbe Miriam held up the list to prove she wasn't lying. Chris considered the words scribbled beside item number two and added his own thoughtful take on the situation. "So a Jewish doctor or lawyer? That shouldn't be too hard to find in Manhattan. Maybe we can help Dara—"

Miriam interrupted him. "There's more."

Dara folded her head into her hands.

It was only going to get worse from here.

"'In addition to only being a doctor or lawyer,'" Miriam said, "'he should have the soul of an artist. He spends his Sundays painting bowls of fruit or writing poetry. Either one is acceptable. He has also taught himself a second language, just for fun. Bonus points if he uses that second language to engage more fully with the world, such as volunteering for Doctors Without Borders or lending his legal expertise to Amnesty International.'"

"It was a joke," Dara spit out the words. "All of it! I don't actually expect—"

Her grandmother ignored her. "'He has a swimmer's body, but hates watching sports. He *loves* going shopping, holding her purse, and giving back rubs. He orders appetizers on a date, but not appetizers *and* dessert, because he's fiscally responsible. Unless it's a special occasion, of course…then he orders both.'"

"Of course." Chris beamed.

"He prefers the pool to a beach, but would never be caught dead swimming in a lake. He is close with his family and he calls his mother twice a week. However, he doesn't have any baggage. No previous marriages. No previous children. Also, he needs to be taller than Dara when she is wearing heels, though not above six feet. She doesn't want to have to stand on tiptoe when kissing somebody."

"Guess I'm out of the running," Chris jested.

"Finally," Miriam exhaled. "He should have a big apartment—with the word *apartment* in quotes. Actually, I don't know why the word *apartment* is in quotes. Oh wait, there's something else on the bottom here…by the corresponding asterisk. It says—" Miriam brought the paper close to her face "—'but not too big. I'm not a vending machine, you know?'" Miriam put the list down. "I still don't understand what that one means, honestly."

Dara peeked through her fingers to see Christopher Steadfast biting back a small smile.

"Well, Dara," Chris asked, knowing full well what she had meant by the euphemism, "would you like to explain that one to your grandmother? How big should Mr. Perfect's apartment be?"

The whole world was awaiting her answer. Dara choked out a response. "Between six hundred and eight hundred square feet?"

"Dara!" Bubbe Miriam shook her head, disappointed. "That's a very small apartment."

A strange moment of silence settled over the studio. It lingered, terrible and pressing, an awful indication that she had just been humiliated by her very own grandmother on national television. And then, all at once and without any warning, Christopher Steadfast exploded into laughter.

It was a rare sight. Strange enough that even some of the crew, cameramen and producers began laughing with him. Dara had been watching the show for years. She had never once seen the seasoned professional lose his composure. But in the wake of her final shameful confession, he turned bright red, unable to speak through his own hysterics, banging his hand against his desk repeatedly.

"I'm sorry," he said, over and over.

Dara crossed her arms against her chest. She was glad someone thought it was funny. She glanced back up at the countdown clock, ticking off the seconds in neon red numbers. *Fifteen seconds left.* She only had fifteen seconds until this nightmare of an interview was over.

Chris did his best in those final heartbeats of television. Looking directly into the camera, he ended the episode, forcing out the words of his signature closing line. "I'm Chris Steadfast," he said, sucking back air in gulps and gasps. "Till next time, America… I'll be waiting for you."